A Thin Gold Thread

A Thin Gold Thread

LISA ROSEN

Chapter 1

Impulse was Addy's weakness. It had gotten her in trouble before, and there was a better than even chance it would trip her up again. She couldn't help it.

Heads turned as she strode through the warren of cubicles in the Humanities Department on the third floor of the university. The low heels of her new spectator pumps tapped briskly. They were a spring splurge, and perfect with her lavender dropped-waist dress, but now she wished she was wearing something a little more severe. The plain black suit she saved for funerals would have been more appropriate for stomping off to argue with her department head. *Or maybe something more masculine,* she thought, *like pinstripes and a tie.*

As she turned out of the stairwell on the second floor and yanked the door open, she nearly barreled into a tall woman, all flowing khaki topped with tidy white hair.

Dr. Diane McGregor, the eminent American Studies scholar who had been Addy's mentor for the last five years and her dissertation director for three, neatly stepped out of the way. Addy grabbed at the door handle to keep from toppling over.

"Dr. McGregor. Did you get a copy of this?" Addy waved the letter that had sent her on a reckless quest for vindication.

"I did. I was just on my way to head you off at the pass."

"What? *Why?* You can't be on his side; he's just picking on me because—"

Dr. McGregor gave a quick, sharp shake of her head. "Not in the hall, Addy. Let's go sit in my office to talk about it."

Addy followed the older woman into her office, barely getting the door closed behind her before blurting out the rest of what had boiled up in the hall. "He's just picking on me because I'm a woman, and you know it!"

Dr. McGregor settled into her deluxe ergonomic chair and turned to stare out the window, as she often did. Her ability to sit and think deeply had always impressed Addy, and when she was being totally honest, also made her a little nervous. She shook the letter again, bolstering her indignation.

Dr. Torrisi, the head of the History Department and director of the American Studies program, had rejected Addy's request for a leave of absence from her doctorate degree. She wanted to stop the clock, take a break before she buckled down to work on her dissertation. The dissertation was the last step—one culminating intellectual exercise, one measly little book. It was all that was standing between her and her PhD. She was so close she could taste it, having worked toward this degree since her undergraduate days. This was the fun part, everyone said. She could really dig in now, plumb the depths of the questions that she'd always wanted to explore, they all said.

But she wasn't ready to write it, and Dr. Torrisi knew it. He had rejected her request because she was a woman, plain and simple. He'd been department head for a year, and life for the female graduate students, especially the ones who had been around longest, like Addy, had gotten increasingly difficult. Addy had secretly been concerned when she applied to teach summer school that she wouldn't get a full load of classes. But apparently her male peers had all gotten research fellowships, so the summer sections had been fobbed off on the female TAs like an unpleasant chore.

For a moment, it seemed as if Dr. McGregor hadn't heard Addy's outburst, but when she swung her chair around, her face was resigned.

"I was afraid this might happen. The writing was on the wall." Dr. McGregor waved her hand in Addy's direction, inviting her to sit.

Addy felt a ripple of unease. She needed Dr. McGregor to back her up and call Dr. Torrisi out for his blatant discrimination. She sank onto the edge of the chair at the far side of the wide desk, as far away from the seat of power as she could be. She felt a sudden pang of sympathy for the student who had come to see her this morning, picking at his cuticles, sullenly unsure how his essay had gone wrong. Here she was in the student chair, dreading the verdict she suspected was coming, and having watched him struggle with a similar anxiety not ten minutes ago, the irony was not lost on her. Though, obviously, his issue was not as dramatic, not as threatening, not as unfair.

Wherever you are, Jackson, please don't stress. I'll give you an extension, I promise. You can rewrite the paper—take all the time you need.

"He can't do this. I need to stop the clock, just for the summer."

"Unfortunately, he can do this."

"But why? He's favoring the guys—all of them." Addy waved a wide, angry arm, encompassing the whole department. "Can't you tell him I need this extra time? I can wait while you call, or I can come back in a bit…"

Dr. McGregor sighed, and something in her posture softened and wilted, almost imperceptibly. She was an old-school feminist who had worked hard to get where she was and made a point of nurturing and mentoring female students. She had always been willing to go to bat for Addy—for any of her advisees—and the defeated look on her face now was even more alarming than the blunt rejection from Dr. Torrisi.

She spoke slowly, choosing her words carefully. "I'm afraid we don't really have much of a leg to stand on, Addy."

"What do you mean?"

"Well, he's right. You've used up all your leaves of absence. You don't have any left." Dr. McGregor looked out the window again; she had a tendency to wait silently for the other person to speak.

Addy reflected on Jackson's troubled posture and vowed to say something—anything—encouraging next time she saw him.

"That's never mattered before."

"No, but…" She looked directly at Addy. "I will deny I ever said this, but we both know he's on a mission to get students finishing faster. He wants to prove himself."

Addy's stomach sank. Nothing had felt right in the department since Dr. Torrisi took the helm last year, but she'd always been able to count on Dr. McGregor. "Are you sure you can't do anything at all?"

"No. Like I said, technically, he's right. That's the situation we're facing. You'll just have to get the dissertation done, that's all."

"Dr. McGregor, I'm not ready. I don't have a topic. I'm this close! I swear I am. I read something the other day about the history of Sephardic Jews in Charleston, South Carolina, and I think there might be something there. I'm working on it."

Dr. McGregor sighed again. "You've been ABD for three years, Addy, and that really is two years too long. You're not the first student to take several years—believe me, I know that—but Dr. Torrisi is within his rights to insist that you make documentable progress at this point."

Addy heard a subtle criticism in the academic slang—short for All But Dissertation. The dissertation was the most significant part of the degree; it was her chance to prove she had both the skill and the stamina to make an original contribution to her chosen field of study. So many people never managed to finish. The structure of classes and the rigor of exams could only get you so far; that last independent piece of work was the real test. It felt more like a free fall.

Her eyes skimmed over the books on Dr. McGregor's shelves as if an idea might be hiding there, waiting for her to pluck it from between the pages of some century-old tome and spin it into a worthy exegesis that would gain her admittance into the proverbial ivory tower. That was all she needed—one measly little idea. Damn Dr. Torrisi and his efficiency study. Addy wasn't interested in tedious details like retention and attrition rates. Graduate students were meant to have nobler goals than all that.

"Just for the summer semester," Addy said. "That's all I need. I'll have a prospectus ready in the fall. I promise. We can go ahead and schedule it now, as a matter of fact." She dug her phone out of her pocket. "How about sometime in October? Maybe right after break?"

"No. I'm sorry, Addy. There's nothing I can do. You're out of time. Your credits are going to start expiring. And to be perfectly honest, you don't have any political capital to spare." Dr. McGregor leaned forward on her desk, her calm hands folded together.

Addy felt like a butterfly pinned under her gaze.

"But in all my years, I've never yet advised a PhD student who didn't manage to graduate. I'm only two years from retiring; you're not going to ruin my record at this point. I'm not going to let you fail, Addy. To that end—" Dr. McGregor pulled out a familiar manila envelope and carefully poured a small stack of papers onto the desk. "You loaned me these papers a couple of months ago, remember?"

The sudden segue threw Addy off balance. "Oh, I thought you might find them interesting, that's all. I found them in some of my grandmother's papers after she died last year. Letters and stuff I just grabbed for something to remember her by. Then I found them later in my apartment and realized it was stupid to hang on to them. I was getting ready to toss the whole pile, but I thought you might want to see them first." She stopped, regretting that she'd babbled on.

Dr. McGregor specialized in letters. Specifically, she had built a career on compiling and editing collections of wartime letters from the home front to soldiers abroad. Other people have studied letters from soldiers, but no one had ever looked at the big picture of what loved ones tended to communicate to their fighting boys. She'd gone as far back as the American Revolution, and published one book that was dedicated solely to letters from mothers and another heartbreaking collection of letters from girlfriends. That was the one that had catapulted her work into the realm of public popularity, an enviable rarity in academic circles. Addy knew she'd been extraordinarily lucky when Dr. McGregor agreed to be her advisor.

"It's not much, but it's something, I think." She plucked a yellowed envelope out of the pile and handed it across the table.

Addy gingerly opened the letter, so long folded now that the creases seemed embedded on a cellular level. She scanned the crabbed handwriting and realized what she was looking at. It was a letter from one R. M. Britton, Sr, informing Martha Cameron that her services at the Biltmore Company were no longer required. It was dated January 1, 1925. There was something particularly harsh about the notion of losing one's job on New Year's Day. When she'd first found it in the box of old letters, it rang with a note of pathos she thought would appeal to Dr. McGregor's fascination with the depressing ordinariness of everyday life.

"Addy? What do you think?"

"I think my mother's head would explode if I tried to write a book about my great-aunt getting fired on New Year's Day. Or maybe my great-great-aunt. I think she was my grandmother's sister, or maybe…" She narrowed her eyes at Dr. McGregor. This was not the conversation she'd been planning to have.

Dr. McGregor shook her head, a quick twitch, as if to shake off an annoying buzz. "You're not thinking. Look at the bigger picture—the pattern. It's not about your great-aunt. It's about women in the workplace, about gender discrimination, and a rural economy and socio-economic upheaval. Here's your title—Patriarchal Repression of Working Women in Rural Appalachia. Now go write the book to go with it."

Addy stared at Dr. McGregor and chewed on her lower lip, trying to ignore the idea that had just been born in her mind. "I don't know. That's not what I was thinking about at all. I really liked this idea about the role Jews played in Charleston politics—they've been there since before the Revolution, you know." Addy shuffled the letters that had spilled out of the envelope. The little snips of her grandmother's handwriting looked out of place, exposed on Dr. McGregor's desk.

"But you don't have an angle. This is perfect; the letter gives you a way into the topic, a personal stake. It's always better if you have a deep investment in the material. That's how I got interested in letters, you know. My uncle kept all the letters he received when he was in Vietnam, and because I knew the personalities of the writers, I was able to interpret them and then apply my conclusions to a broader field. You can do that too. Find out about Great-Aunt Martha, or whoever she was, and then figure out what was typical about her experience." She handed Addy the manila envelope and sat back, arms folded.

"I'm not actually kidding. My mother's head will explode. She is the most private person you've ever met. We're talking pathologically private. Besides, I don't know anything about this Martha person—I'm not even sure when she died—I never knew her or anything." Addy knew she was fighting a losing battle.

"That's what research means. Find out who Martha was, shake the family tree a little. And then take a look at the broader context of the time and place in which she lived. It's not as if the dissertation will actually be about her—her story is just a way to personalize the topic, make it more poignant for readers."

Addy sat silently for a moment, mentally comparing her bank statement and her credit card bill. She couldn't afford three months without a paycheck. Damn that Dr. Torrisi for putting her in this position. She'd show him.

"I could go spend the summer at my parents' house." Addy could feel her ears turning red like they always did when adrenalin surged through her. "That way I could survive without the summer teaching money. I'd have three whole months to totally immerse myself and crank out the whole paper. I can't believe I'm even thinking this, but it might work." She jumped up, ready to turn on a beautifully sculpted heel and start packing.

"Wait, not so fast. I didn't mean for you to leave town entirely. Won't that make it harder for you to balance whatever the issues are with your mother?"

Addy took a deep breath and held it for a second before she forced herself to speak calmly, focusing on the words, looking straight ahead as if she were wearing blinders. This was not an idea that would bear close examination, but it was a solution, and any solution was better than none, especially if it would show Dr. Torrisi that he had underestimated her. "It'll be fine. My parents desperately want me to finish the degree anyway; point of pride and all. Besides, realistically, I can't afford to stay in town if I'm not teaching. And I can't teach full time and write. So it'll have to be fine." She sank back down on the edge of the chair. "Although I am contracted for the classes."

"I can smooth that over at least. I'm sure some first or second-year will be thrilled to take them."

"Is there any chance I could get some research money? That would help a lot."

"I can ask. It's late, but given all the other funding that students have gotten this summer, it's worth a try. You're sure about this?"

"Absolutely," Addy said, putting on her most confident smile.

"Well then, problem solved."

Addy nodded, trying to ignore the objections bubbling up in her brain. This was totally out of hand. The whole conversation was absurd. She couldn't just pluck a topic out of the clear blue sky and crank it out in three months. She couldn't disrupt her whole life on Dr. Torrisi's whim—she had a roommate, and bills to pay, and plans for the summer. She didn't want to give up those classes—teaching was leaps and bounds more fun than research. Could she really write a whole dissertation about dull patriarchal whatever in rural Appalachia? More to the point, could she spend a whole summer with her parents? She smiled again and tamped down the doubt, then picked up the manila envelope and the letter to Martha Cameron.

"Thank you, Dr. McGregor. I won't let you down. I'll be totally focused. I'll have a prospectus for you by the first of September."

"Unfortunately, the schedule's a little tighter than that." Dr. McGregor looked uncomfortable. "I'm going to have to give Dr. Torrisi some evidence that you're making consistent progress."

Addy swallowed a protest. Clearly she and Dr. McGregor had been backed into this corner together. She nodded. "All right, then. I'd better get a move on."

Chapter 2

After an evening of self-doubt bordering on panic, Addy set about convincing herself that her plan was actually a stroke of genius. If she was entirely honest with herself, she had been kind of hiding from the kind of work that would have to go into her dissertation. It seemed overwhelming, but her friends had all written theirs and survived, so she just needed to break it into chunks and not dwell too much on the enormity of the whole. But she had shoved those thoughts aside, packed a summer's worth of clothes into the back of her elderly Honda, and told her roommate to sublet her room just for the summer—she'd be back before the fall semester started.

Forty-eight hours later, Addy thought about what lay ahead and behind while she drove back into the Blue Ridge Mountains for the first time since her grandmother's funeral nearly a year ago. Perhaps she could think of the time in Asheville as an extended retreat—she'd been away from her hometown for so long there would be no distractions, no social life, nothing to do except crank out the work. She could spend some quality time with her younger sister, Lacey, who was about to graduate from high school. She wouldn't even be leaving a boyfriend behind in D.C.; she hadn't been on a date since—she thought backwards, horrified—*New Year's?* How depressing. It compounded her feeling of slipping inexorably backward through time.

The idea of writing about employment statistics gave her a bit of a headache, but she was trying to look on the bright side. If she could suffer through a few months of tedium, she'd be done. Maybe she could even defend her dissertation in time to graduate in the December ceremony. She didn't dare fantasize about that for fear of jinxing it. *Dr. McGregor had a point*, she thought as she exited the interstate near Asheville. If she was really committed to the academic life, it was time to prove it to herself and to her colleagues. Besides, her parents had been pleased—as far as she could tell—when she called to warn them she was coming.

She hadn't mentioned Aunt Martha's letter. Her mother was going to have a fit. In her high school creative writing class, Addy had written a series of poems about her grandmother—her skin, her thinning hair, her habit of sniffing the lotion on her hands—and when Eleanor saw them, she made Addy throw them away and start over. "Private family business is not appropriate for public consumption," she said. Addy had been furious, and kept the poems on the hard drive of her computer. She still had them—as poetry goes, they were dreadful, but Addy had reread them right after Grandmama Nellie's death and found they evoked much of what she had loved about her grandmother. Eleanor's irrational obsession with privacy was a thing she had worked around all her life; the dissertation would be no different.

Addy pulled into the gated community she grew up in and slowed down as she drove along the familiar streets. Beautiful old houses sprawled on expansive green lawns. The neighborhood was tucked up next to the Biltmore Estate, and its proximity to the rambling property gave it a rarified air. A moment later, Addy put her car in park on her parents' perfect flagstone driveway. As she wrestled a suitcase from the trunk, she glanced toward the wide front porch of the house she grew up in. Lush green ferns spilled out of an even row of hanging baskets. Paddle fans turned slowly over the white wicker chairs on both sides of the front door. She knew they'd all be sitting there in a couple of hours, holding sweaty glasses of iced tea and watching the evening creep across the lawn and darken the mountaintops. It was a ritual, an indispensable part of her mother's seasonal ceremonies.

As she dragged the second bag out, her father materialized next to her.

"Daddy!" She dropped the heavy bag onto the driveway and threw her arms around his neck to give him a stiff hug. Eleanor and Mason were not huggers, a fact that Addy and her sister had determinedly ignored their entire lives to no avail. It was like hugging a wall. Inhaling the smell of him—shaving cream and starch and the Windex he used on his glasses every morning—she was surprised to realize she'd missed those smells.

"Welcome home, Addison." Mason reached around her for the handle of the bag.

"Where's Mother?"

"She's inside, wondering what took you so long." He gave her an inscrutable look. "She's been running around like a chicken with its head cut off getting your room ready."

"She didn't need to do that," Addy protested, even though anything less from Eleanor would have surprised her. She pushed through the wide front doors into the cool house. She closed her eyes, inhaling; the faint scent of bergamot dragging her right back to childhood more effectively than any photo album or scrapbook could.

"It smells exactly like home."

"Well, I should hope so." Eleanor appeared in the kitchen doorway and stood ramrod straight and still.

Addy shimmied reflexively, throwing up jazz hands as if to herald her own arrival. Sometimes her body had a flair for the dramatic that couldn't be contained. She could feel her mother's cool blue eyes scrutinizing even as she wrapped her arms around Eleanor's stiff, bony shoulders. Eleanor's cheek was cool and dry against her flushed face.

"We were beginning to wonder if you were ever going to get here."

"I wondered myself. Road construction was awful."

Addy was suddenly aware of how rumpled and sweaty she felt next to her mother, who never looked anything less than fresh and delicate.

"Why don't you go tidy up? I'll get you a glass of tea; you look exhausted."

Addy twirled on her toes. "I know it's wrinkled, but don't you love my dress? It's vintage."

Eleanor arched one eyebrow. "I can tell," she said in a dry voice. "Go on, scoot upstairs. I'm getting dinner ready. Lacey will be home from rehearsal any minute now."

Ignoring her mother's command, Addy went back out to the porch in time to see Lacey pull up in the Honda Mason had bought for her graduation present.

"Better take care of that car. I'm still driving mine," Addy said, laughing as Lacey flung the car door open and lunged around it to crush her in a hug.

"I can't believe you're here for the whole summer," Lacey said, as they each stepped back to look the other up and down.

"Neither can I," Addy said. "This is the best part."

Addy felt, as she had since Lacey was born, that she was looking at the reverse image of herself. They had always been a matched pair even with the ten-year age difference, Addy's riotous chestnut hair the contrasting negative to Lacey's golden curls. The most significant distinction was the plain practicality of Lacey's wardrobe juxtaposed against Addy's passion for girly, vintage pieces. Lacey's typical warm-weather uniform was a boxy t-shirt and baggy jean shorts that were replaced with baggy jeans and a boxy button-down in winter. No one would ever accuse either of the Quick girls of choosing clothes at random. Nor would their mother ever stop lamenting the inappropriateness of their choices.

She'd never felt the years between them so acutely before. The weight of the work she needed to do this summer multiplied her twenty-eight years, while Lacey had no idea that she was in the last long stretch of freedom before the reality of college set in.

Lacey slipped an arm around Addy's waist, and they stepped up onto the porch in tandem. "It'll be fun. You can meet my girlfriend; we can do stuff together. You'll love Asia."

Addy nodded, wishing the unbridled nature of Lacey's excitement was contagious. "I can't wait. How is that going, by the way? With Mother, I mean."

Lacey rolled her eyes. "She's still pretending I never came out. Refuses to use the word girlfriend. It's not bad—not like some parents of gay kids. She just ignores it. They both do."

"She's good at denial," Addy said, disentangling herself and holding the screen door open for her younger sister. "In the meantime, I guess we ought to help with dinner."

But Eleanor ejected them both from the kitchen, insisting that she'd rather do it herself. Lacey wandered out to the dining room, unperturbed, but Addy felt a little guilty; it had been a long time since she'd been in the habit of letting herself be mothered.

While they were settling at the table, everyone in the seats they'd sat in her whole life, Addy filled her family in on most—but not all—of the details about the abrupt change in her summer plans.

"I don't understand, Addison," Eleanor said, "why you didn't give us a little more notice that you were coming. We could've had a little get-together."

"Oh, I'm so glad you didn't, Mother. Please don't. The last thing I want or need is anyone making a big deal out of my being in town. I don't even have time."

"But when did you decide?" Mason asked. "When I was working on my dissertation, I spent months narrowing my topic down to a very specific niche."

Addy focused on cutting her trout very carefully as she spoke. She'd been hearing all her life about her father's exacting process. His commitment to his family's textile business had kept it afloat when so many failed, but that kind of finicky patience was one trait Addy had not inherited. "On Tuesday," she said, putting down her knife and smiling brightly.

"This past Tuesday?" Eleanor sounded shocked.

"Yes. But it'll be fine. I can access most things I need—the stuff that's not physically here in Asheville—online. Dr. McGregor thinks I'll probably get a publishable article out of it, and maybe I can even present at a conference or two."

"Tell us again exactly what you're writing about?" Mason said.

There was a photograph in the living room of her father in full academic regalia, holding her in his arms, her roving toddler hands trying to pull on his strange puffy hat while he looked directly at the camera with proud gravitas. Dr. Mason Quick had put his PhD in chemical engineering to lucrative use in the textile company his great-grandfather had started, but the image of the gentleman scholar had been a constant in Addy's life for longer than she could remember. Somehow, it had grown to encompass her over the years and become a point of pride for her mother particularly. Sometimes Addy thought she had been pushing against her parents' expectations her whole life.

She faced her father, now ready after all these years to show off her expertise.

"Well, it's about that letter I found in Grandmama Nellie's things. You remember, I told you that it was from Judge Britton, the manager of the Biltmore Estate? It was to Martha Cameron—she was our great-aunt, right, Mother?"

Eleanor frowned a little. "Great-great-aunt. She was my grandmother's—your Granny Isabella's—sister. She died quite young, if I recall correctly. I never knew her."

"Anyway, apparently she used to work at Biltmore. I'm not sure what she did exactly, but he fired her. Told her that her services were no longer required. On New Year's Day, no less."

Eleanor put her fork down and stiffened slightly in her chair. "I don't see what that has to do with your dissertation."

This was the wall Addy knew she would come up against; the only surprise was that it had taken half an hour to hit it. "Dr. McGregor thinks it'll make a great personal introduction to a paper on how difficult it was for women to find and hang on to work outside the home in the early 1920s, especially in a rural area like this."

Lacey giggled. "Asheville isn't exactly the backwoods."

"It was much smaller back then," Mason said. "So your advisor is on board with this, is she?"

"Of course. It was—" Addy hesitated, unsure how much of her own culpability for the situation she wanted to reveal. "It was a joint effort. But it's a great idea," she rushed to add. "It's going to be great."

"Let me get this straight," her mother said, frowning. "You're going to write your dissertation, and maybe an article or something, about how my great-aunt Martha was fired from her job at Biltmore? Am I understanding that correctly?"

"It'll be a lot more than that because I'm going to use her as an example to explain larger socio-economic patterns in the region. But, yes, in a nutshell."

"Well, I must say, Addison, I think it's a terrible idea."

Addy held her face as carefully neutral as she knew how, and made a modestly sympathetic but noncommittal noise.

Eleanor was undaunted. "You're going to pull all our family skeletons out of the closet for anyone to read about. I'm not comfortable with that, not at all. I can't believe you'd allow such a thing, Mason," Eleanor said, turning on her husband.

Mason shook his head. "Pass the asparagus, would you please, Lacey?"

Eleanor pressed her lips together tightly and looked back down at her plate.

"Besides, how can this be a skeleton in the closet, if we didn't even know about it?" Lacey asked.

Addy shot her a look of gratitude. Sometimes she was surprisingly astute for a teenager.

"It'll be fine, Mother, you'll see. I won't write anything embarrassing. I promise," Addy said soothingly.

Eleanor continued to push food around on her plate.

Addy scrambled for something to distract her. "So, catch me up on all the news," she said, attempting to placate her mother. If there was one thing she could count on, it was her mother's determination not to dwell on anything she found embarrassing or unpleasant. Addy had little-to-no interest in the gossip of her parents' country club community, but Eleanor was all too ready to change the subject.

"Well, do you remember that Oliver boy you went to school with? What was his name? His sister was a couple of years behind you, I think."

"Catherine," Lacey volunteered.

"Okay, I have a vague memory. What about him?"

"He's running for mayor."

Addy forced a smile. "That's great. Tell him I said congratulations."

"You can tell him yourself. I'm sure you'll see him around the neighborhood. Oh, and you'll want to congratulate Genevieve Ingram too. She's getting married."

"Finally," she murmured. Genevieve Ingram had been angling for a husband since their junior year of high school.

"Addison," Mason warned.

"That's wonderful," Addy said, more properly now. "I'm sure she's thrilled."

"Her mother is too," Eleanor said. "She's just swamped with the wedding plans."

An awkward silence settled over the dining room. *The more things change, the more they stay the same*, Addy thought, looking around the room. The same ivory brocade drapes still framed the wide windows overlooking the front lawn, and Eleanor's good china still gleamed in the china cabinet. Addy's fingers pleated the edge of her linen napkin. She felt as if she were floating in time, unsure which shore, which decade, she was going to pitch up on.

Lacey dragged her back to the present. "Anyway. I'm going to have a huge graduation party, Addy. I'm glad you're here; you can help us plan it," she said.

Eleanor made a pfft sound. "Yes, well, she'll have plenty of other things to work on as well. Speaking of, we have an appointment with the lawyer on Monday, Addison. Since you're going to be here for a while, I thought we should take advantage of the time to work through the details of your grandmother's estate. No, Lacey"—she raised one hand to preempt her younger daughter's protestation—"you'll be in school. We'll fill you in on what he says. But since Mother saw fit to include you girls in her will, we might as well deal with it while Addison is in town."

"Of course. Whatever you want," Addy said in a conciliatory tone.

"And I have another project for you while you're here," Eleanor continued.

Addy groaned inwardly. She'd known there would be strings attached to staying here. There were always strings where Eleanor was concerned.

"I would like to get a historical marker made for Mother's house, and I'd like you to write the text for it. It's an excellent example of an Arts-and-Crafts-style bungalow, and that whole era is getting a lot of attention right now. I thought it would be appropriate, given how long it's been in our family. Mother inherited it from her mother, you know."

"Oh." Addy stared at her mother. Suddenly the whole long day caught up with her, and her throat tightened. She reached for her glass of tea, trying to loosen the knot that had caught her voice. "I think that's a wonderful idea," she said after sipping her tea. "I'd be honored."

"Well, it shouldn't be too difficult," Eleanor said brusquely, "relative to a dissertation. I just thought it would be nice to honor Granny Isabella's side of the family since I had to use your great-grandfather's side for my DAR membership."

"You should have been here, Addy," Lacey said. "It was…a production."

Addy nodded.

Eleanor had wanted to be a member of the Daughters of the American Revolution for as long as she'd wanted Addy to go to graduate school; she always seemed to feel that it was the one social door in Asheville that she couldn't get through. A distant cousin in Virginia had finally turned up evidence of a Revolution-era ancestor, which was the admission ticket Eleanor needed. According to Mason and Lacey, she'd treated the ceremony with as much pomp and circumstance as a wedding, or maybe even a coronation.

Addy had heard all about it, of course, complete with droll commentary in her sister's texts and calls. The induction ceremony was during exams, and while she certainly wouldn't say so to Eleanor's face, she'd never been so relieved to have an excuse not to come home.

Addy knew her absence had been a rebuff, and felt guilty ever since. She also knew, on some level, that this request for a historical marker was Eleanor's way of extracting something like an apology. It would be a painless, possibly even interesting hoop to jump through as long as it didn't take too long.

"Of course. I'll work on it."

Addy caught the look that passed between her parents.

"What? I will."

"There's a deadline," Eleanor said.

"For a historical marker? That's excellent," Lacey said. "We were talking about irony in my English class. I'm going to use that as an example."

"Don't be facetious, Lacey. It's my deadline. I want it done by the end of the summer," Eleanor said.

"Why?" Addy asked.

"Because I do, that's all. I just don't want it to drag on forever."

Addy glanced at her father for confirmation that this was absurd, but that look passed between her parents again, and she understood. They doubted whether she'd get it done. Suddenly she was a teenager again, studiously ignoring the small lines of disapproval etched around her mother's mouth the night Mason brought Addy home from the police station. She hadn't done anything terribly wrong; rules against dancing in fountains were silly. It wasn't her fault the officer had no sense of humor. She'd only splashed him a little.

"I said I'll work on it."

"You needn't take that tone."

Addy bit back a retort. *I am an adult*, she reminded herself, and took a calming breath. "I'd love to work on a historical marker, Mother. It's Grandmama Nellie's house—it'll be fun."

After a second, the room seemed to breathe again.

She stood up and reached for her father's plate, but Eleanor swatted at her hands. "I'll clear. You all go on out to the porch. I'll bring the cobbler out there."

Addy followed her father and sister out of the dining room, not sure how she'd been made to feel like a puppy with its tail between its legs.

"I'm stuffed," Lacey declared a little while later, setting her dessert bowl on the railing next to the porch swing.

Addy leaned back against a white column at the top of the porch steps where she sat and draped her skirt over the top step. It was early still; the sun had only begun to sink toward the tops of the Smokies, but fatigue and home-cooking were pulling her toward sleep. She wanted very much to be content. She sat in the deep shade of the porch, listening to the creak of the swing as Lacey pushed it back and forth with one toe.

"I'm going to have to turn in soon. I'm exhausted."

"Of course you are," said Eleanor, who, in her usual mercurial fashion, seemed to have forgotten her earlier distress. "You had such a long drive. Your room is ready. We can catch up more in the morning."

Mason cleared his throat. "You know, Addison, I'm thinking about your dissertation. When I was working on mine, I had to spend about twelve hours a day in the library. Do you need me to call someone at the university and see if they'll let you have a desk of your own for the summer?"

Addy shook her head, trying to hide her smile. "No thanks, Daddy. I've got it under control. I have privileges as a visiting researcher, but I can probably do most of my digging right here from the house, online." It was sweet, and she knew he was just trying to help, but it was funny how much her parents still thought of her as a teenager. Maybe they'd give it up when she started putting "Doctor" in front of her name. She closed her eyes, still smiling, but too tired to talk about it anymore.

Evening birds swooped and dove in the spring sky, and the spicy smell of boxwood wafted up from the wide slope of the front yard. Addy sat still. She needed to head up to bed, where she could be alone with the welter of feelings that had been piling up all day. Part of her—a large part—wanted to get in her Honda and head right back to Washington D.C., her tiny little apartment, and her even-tinier office, where her life clicked along predictably, her students respected her, and colleagues accepted her as an equal. She wondered if other people found it this disconcerting to visit their childhood homes, and if so, why no one ever talked about it. She shook her head. This broody train of thought would get her nowhere, and she ought to haul herself up to bed before her energy ran out entirely, but it was so peaceful on the porch.

About that time, a battered Volkswagen pulled into the driveway and stopped behind Lacey's Honda. The rhythm of Eleanor's rocking chair came to an abrupt halt.

"It's Asia," Lacey said, bouncing out of the swing.

Recognition clicked in Addy's head and she turned to glance at her mother. This was the girlfriend Lacey had been talking about for several months. From what she'd gathered in Lacey's hurried phone call earlier in the week, the Quicks had gotten a call from the headmaster about the girls' "inappropriate public display of affection" at the prom, and Eleanor had been none too pleased. Asheville, on the whole, might be a comfortable place to be openly gay, but Eleanor had been ignoring reality since Lacey came out the year before. Based on the expression on her mother's face as the car door creaked open, she still hadn't come to terms with it.

A thin young person wearing baggy overalls and a sleeveless undershirt got out of the car just as Lacey reached her. The only hint that she was a she was the pink bandana holding back her dirty blonde hair.

As the two teenagers loped toward the porch, arms entwined, Addy heard her mother mutter to Mason, "I thought we were having a quiet family evening."

"Asia, meet my sister, Addy."

Addy stood up, and the girl peered intensely at her, then pulled her into a ferocious hug. Addy stumbled against her, surprised by the strength in such a slim girl. "Addy. You're here."

"It's nice to meet you," Addy said, disentangling herself from the bare, wiry arms.

Asia bounded past her, up the porch steps, and bent to hug Eleanor and Mason. Addy stifled a grin. She could see good manners and total squeamishness doing battle right there on her mother's face.

"So, what are we doing on this fine family evening?" Asia asked as she settled onto the porch swing next to Lacey.

"Not much. I think Addy was about to head off to bed. Isn't that right?" Lacey winked.

"Maybe in a little while." Addy stifled a yawn. There was no way she was leaving now.

"Oh no! You can't do that. I just got here." Asia sprung up from the porch swing and peered into Lacey's empty bowl. "What are we having for dessert, Mrs. Q?"

Addy whipped her head around to catch her mother's expression, and couldn't hold back the smile this time. She didn't know much about Asia except that the outfit was unfortunate, but Lacey had gushed about her on the phone like the love-struck teenager she was, so Addy was predisposed to like her. Her gumption, though—that was impressive.

Eleanor pursed her mouth and gave her a stern look. "We had strawberry cobbler."

Asia didn't seem to notice the hesitation or disdainful look. "Don't get up, Mrs. Q. I'll get it myself. I'm totally used to waiting on myself at home. Anyone else want seconds?"

They all shook their heads, and the screen door slammed as Asia headed inside like she owned the place. Addy giggled and glanced up at Lacey, who had a small, secret smile on her face.

"She's adorable," she mouthed.

"I suppose you've heard about your sister's latest dubious acquaintance?" Eleanor looked as if she'd sucked on a lemon slice.

"Mother! Don't be rude," Lacey said. "She's my nearest and dearest, and you know it. And she can probably hear you through the screen."

Addy glanced at her father, but he was examining the flowers that decorated the rim of his bowl.

Eleanor peered over her shoulder into the dark interior of the house, then looked resolutely forward toward the darkening mountains. Addy felt a wave of sympathy for Lacey. Her mother had always been reserved when Addy had boyfriends over—even the ones she ostensibly approved of. Her definition of family was narrow, at best. Addy wondered idly whether it would be any easier when—if—she got married. Somehow, she couldn't imagine her mother ever really accepting anyone else into the family.

Asia stepped back out onto the porch carrying a bowl full of cobbler and plopped down next to Addy on the top step.

There was an awkward silence while Asia took a bite, then closed her eyes. The look on her face was pure bliss. "Mrs. Q, this is the best cobbler I've ever had. I mean, you're just an amazing cook. Not even a cook, really—a chef. The top is so flaky and perfect, and it's like it has spices and stuff, you know? And the strawberries taste like real strawberries, not that gooey stuff you get out of a can."

"Thank you," Eleanor said stiffly. "That's because they are real strawberries."

"I knew it!"

She looked so pleased with herself, Addy couldn't help but like her. "So, Asia, are you graduating next month with Lacey?"

"No, I'm only a junior. Lucky Lacey, getting out of here."

"You'll come visit," Lacey said, nudging Asia with her toe.

"Yeah. Maybe. Rhode Island is far."

"August is a long way off. You don't need to worry about that now," Eleanor said.

An uncomfortable silence fell over the porch, broken only by the rhythmic creak of Mason's rocker.

"Well, on that perky note, I'm off to bed. Sorry, Lacey. Nice to meet you, Asia." Addy patted Asia on the shoulder as she stood up. Even in the dim light, she could see the frown on Eleanor's face. She shook her head because it seemed some things would never change. "Don't anyone wake me up in the morning. I intend to sleep till forever."

"No, I don't think so. There's a homeowner's meeting at ten. I'll need you to help get things ready," Eleanor said.

"Here? Are you serious? Mother, I'm exhausted. Just pretend I'm not here yet. You don't really need me."

"Yes, I do. Many hands make light work. Besides, everyone will know you're here—your car is in the driveway. It would be rude not to make an appearance."

Addy was too drained to argue. Maybe things would look a little brighter in the morning. At the very least, she'd be well-rested enough to survive a command performance. She dragged herself up the stairs.

Chapter 3

"Get that, please, Addison," Eleanor said when the doorbell rang for the first time the next morning.

"Lacey, get that!" Addy called to her sister because she was technically closer to the door. Addy was in the odd little area that her mother called the butler's pantry, between the kitchen and dining room, arranging great puffy pink and blue snowball hydrangeas in a tall vase. It wasn't, strictly speaking, a butler's pantry because the whole notion of butlers was laughable in the twenty-first century, but Eleanor had always ignored her daughters' attempts to call it something reasonable like china cabinet or walk-through.

"Addison. I asked you to answer the door. Lacey, come get this carafe of coffee."

They gave each other a look, and Lacey folded the last of the linen napkins and grinned as she headed back toward the kitchen. "The show begins, and you're on. You're dressed better."

Addy rolled her eyes, but took off the apron she'd been wearing to protect her dress. The loose sheath was a tissue muslin sprigged with tiny pink flowers, and her ballet flats moved quietly as she went to open the front door. Lacey was right—Addy had played right into Eleanor's agenda with her carefully chosen outfit.

A steady stream of neighbors kept her running back and forth for a full twenty minutes, accepting hugs and welcomes and gossipy updates about the close-knit gated community she'd grown up in. When it seemed that everyone had arrived, filling Eleanor's formal living room to capacity, she slipped into the kitchen to escape the clamor. Mason, starting another pot of coffee, handed her a glass of water. When she had drained it, he turned her back toward the murmur of voices.

She pushed back against his hands on her shoulders, setting herself against him, against them all.

"Don't be rude, Addy."

"Five more minutes. I'm not sitting through the meeting. I shouldn't even be allowed to. I don't live here anymore, remember?"

Addy stepped reluctantly back into the living room just as a petite blonde stepped in from the front porch. She was the sartorial opposite of Addy's garden-party style in a slim black skirt, an immaculate white blouse, and an equally immaculate blonde chignon. Her heels clicked on Eleanor's polished oak floor, and her left ring finger flashed as she patted her hair.

"Hey!" the young woman trilled from across the room, dragging the word out into two syllables in the shrill drawl Addy remembered from high school.

The chattering group stilled, and Addy backed up a step as if a runaway train were headed right for her. Genevieve had that fresh-from-the-spa look.

"It is you. Oh, my God. Look at you…you haven't changed a bit!"

"Genevieve. What a surprise." Addy found herself in a limp hug, Genevieve leaning in toward her shoulder, but holding back from actual contact.

"Oh, my word. I didn't expect to see you here. How have you been? Where have you been? My goodness, I'm just in shock."

"I got in last night. I'm in town for a few months, working on my dissertation. I needed to do some local research, probably up at Biltmore." The words shored her up, grounding her identity, her real life. Out of the corner of her eye, she could see Eleanor threading her way toward them from the front of the room.

"Oh, you're still in school?" Genevieve patted her smooth hair again, waving her left hand around and obviously waiting for Addy to notice.

"Yes, well, graduate school, you know. It takes forever. But I'm on the last lap now. I'll finish up my dissertation this summer." It was the first time she'd said the words out loud, and she crossed her fingers behind her back hoping she hadn't jinxed herself. "So what are you doing these days?"

Genevieve giggled, flashing her left hand. "Planning a wedding! My goodness, it's practically a full-time job. Don't you remember Emory Pace? We're getting married! Can you believe it?" Her tan arm linked in Addy's elbow, pulling her over toward the row of chairs.

"My goodness, Mrs. Quick," she said as Eleanor joined them. "You didn't tell me Addison would be here." Her smooth forehead furrowed as she turned to Addy. "It is still Quick, isn't it?"

Eleanor gave them a stiff smile. "I didn't find out myself that she was coming until a couple of days ago. But we're thrilled that she's spending the summer at home."

"Only the summer? But you'll come back for my wedding, won't you? It's in October. My save-the-dates are going out next week. Oh dear, I'll need to have the calligrapher change the address on yours, since you're here."

"It's fine, Genevieve. You don't need to send me one. I hate to be rude, but there's no way I can make it. I teach full-time, and October is midterms. I couldn't possibly get away."

Eleanor took hold of Addy's elbow, gripping it a bit too tightly. "Of course, we'll check the calendar. I'm sure we can figure out a way to make it work. But it's 10:30, so we need to get on with our agenda now. Perhaps you two can get together for lunch one day and catch up."

Addy stared at her mother for a second, flabbergasted, then beat a hasty retreat from the crowded living room. Mason had taken up his assigned seat with the board members at the front of the room, so the kitchen was empty, but Addy didn't stop. She went straight up the back stairs, limp with relief to have the morning over with.

In her old bedroom, she changed into capris and a loose blouse, and settled in to finish the unpacking she'd been too tired and too emotional to do the night before. She had come up for bed to find her bedroom just as it had always been. When she was last here for her grandmother Nellie's funeral, she encouraged Eleanor to redecorate it, but nothing had changed. A feather boa was still draped across a lamp, cut-glass atomizers cluttered the dressing table, and the wardrobe was stuffed full of the various identities she'd tried out and discarded during high school. Even the pale pink bedspread, scattered with violets, that she'd longed for all through ninth grade was still on the bed, faded but freshly laundered. Memories clung to the hodge-podge of comfortable antiques that she'd grown up with.

She emptied a suitcase full of shoes onto the floor and started shoving them into the bottom of the wardrobe. When they wouldn't all fit, she dumped the rest on top and slammed the doors.

This wasn't going to work. When she went north for college, she'd sworn she would never come back to Asheville. The irony of her current situation struck her sharply. "You can't go home again," Thomas Wolfe had said when he left Asheville. Well, he was wrong. Sometimes you had no choice, and had to suck it up and cope.

She'd tried not to rock the boat, but couldn't help it. It was like she had some kind of perverse instinct that steered her in the wrong direction at every turn, and she could feel Eleanor's agitation building already. Her mother's peculiar social paranoia pushed all of Addy's buttons. She hadn't even been home twenty-four hours and was already struggling to remember how to behave like an adult. And her mother was already making noise about church on Sunday mornings. Addy hadn't been to church since she'd left for college, and had no desire to go back now and be trotted around like Eleanor's trick pony.

She unzipped another suitcase, this one full of underwear and lingerie. While folding silky nightgowns, slips, and stockings, she thought through her options. She couldn't turn tail and go back to Washington D.C. Dr. McGregor would think she'd lost her mind. So would her mother and father—she'd told them she was coming for the summer, and could already imagine the ruckus it would cause if she changed her mind and left. In one fell swoop, she'd managed to make a total hash of her life.

On the other hand, when else would she have such a substantial chunk of time to take care of business here? Her grandmother's estate had been a nagging obligation hanging over her for almost a year. It wasn't a huge inheritance or anything, but Grandmama Nellie had left it to be divided evenly between her only daughter and her two granddaughters. When Addy brought it up the day after the funeral, trying to be helpful, Eleanor had locked herself in her bedroom and didn't speak to Addy for almost a month. There wasn't much cash—she had checked, discreetly—but if they could sell the house, Addy might clear enough to pay off all of her credit cards. The problem with being a TA was the pay—it wasn't nearly enough to live on. Mason and Eleanor paid her tuition, but unbeknownst to them, she'd been relying on credit cards to cover the gaps for too long now. This was her chance to get that under control before she went out on the gloomy job market.

Dr. Torrisi had done her a favor, her inner optimist reiterated. This summer interlude was a blessing in disguise, and she would find a way to make it work. She had to.

There was a vase of peonies in every shade of pink imaginable on the dresser—the thought that had gone into that gesture touched her. She bent to smell them. Peonies had always been her favorite, and no one in the world knew that except her family. Even Josh, the tweedy linguist from the State Department, hadn't bothered to figure that out, defaulting to roses after they broke up. Too little, too late.

Chapter 4

Monday morning, Addy was up before her alarm. She dressed carefully in a long navy-blue skirt with deep knife pleats and a white middy blouse. Punctuality and crisp linen bolstered her confidence and she squared her shoulders.

Eleanor didn't protest when Addy volunteered to drive separately to the lawyer's office in Biltmore Village. Addy made a mental note: *perhaps independent transportation is a good way to give us both a little space.*

They sat in careful silence in the lawyer's tiny waiting area, Eleanor fidgeting with the leather-bound notepad in her lap. The maroon loveseat and wingback chairs were a little worn around the edges, and in a different environment would look terribly dated, but somehow it worked in the Village. The Arts-and-Crafts buildings had been constructed in the early 1900s, an early version of planned urban development. Looking around, Addy concluded that both the wide plank floors and the windows were original. The Village had originally been constructed as a community for estate workers, but the well-preserved buildings had been converted to pricey boutiques and cafes. A few small, discreet businesses still hung on to their offices, most of which had been in the Village through several cycles of growth and contraction.

She looked around, not even sure what the name of this firm was. She hadn't been paying attention when she held the door open for Eleanor, and in the waiting area, there was no indication of whose office it was. Probably some old crony of her parents, she concluded, just as the inner office door opened.

Addy's eyes widened, and she stood up quickly. Micah Britton stared back at her, looking as surprised as she felt. They hadn't spoken since her junior year of high school when she transferred, at the headmaster's "suggestion," to the public school out in the county. She squared her shoulders, trying to exude professionalism.

"Addison Quick. I heard you were back in town." He stepped forward, one hand extended. Ten years had tempered his mischievous surfer-boy looks, and he looked more textured, somehow, than Addy remembered. His voice was deeper too, rougher. Addy shook the proffered hand.

"Micah. I didn't realize…" She shrugged, wracking her brain for some memory of how he had come to be back in Asheville. "I thought you were out west somewhere, being a big shot lawyer to the stars or something."

"Addison," Eleanor said, a warning note in her voice.

"It's fine, Mrs. Quick. I was," Micah said, ushering them into his small office. "But my dad is sick. I came back about a year ago to help him shut down his practice, and now I can't seem to extricate myself."

"I'm sorry to hear that," Addy said, wondering if she'd known this and forgotten.

"Don't be. It's been a good thing, mostly. Aside from the Alzheimer's, of course. And now you're back, too."

"Only for the summer. I'm finishing up my dissertation, and need to do some research here in Asheville."

"She's almost finished with her PhD," Eleanor interjected, a familiar note of determined satisfaction in her voice.

"What are you writing about?"

"Early twentieth century repression of working women in rural Appalachia."

Micah blinked at her. "That's very…specific."

Flustered, Addy let the comment hang in the air. For a brief moment, the silence was suffocating. She rummaged in her purse for her phone and opened the note-taking app.

"Anyway. Since I'm here, I wanted to help Mother tidy up my grandmother's estate. I gather you're the person in charge of that?"

"My father was the executor, in his capacity as Mrs. Sumner's lawyer. So, since I'm handling his files now, yes. I'll be happy to handle probate for you."

Eleanor fidgeted with the notepad in her lap, but didn't write anything down. Addy's thumbs flew over the tiny screen on her phone.

"What have we accomplished thus far?" she asked without looking up.

"Well, to tell you the truth, nothing. Your grandmother set up her savings account so that the taxes would be paid automatically, and so when no one wanted to move on it last year after the funeral, my dad seems to have set the file aside. There was no rush, so I've only just looked at it this morning."

"Well, I'm only in town for the summer. So I guess the most pressing thing is selling the house, right?"

"Well, that's not as straightforward as you might think, actually."

"I bet not. It's been sitting empty for a year." Addy could feel Eleanor next to her, drawing into herself, almost visibly shrinking in the small wooden chair. She hesitated, then reached over to put a hand on her mother's forearm.

Eleanor stilled.

"Mother," she said softly. "We're going to have to do it eventually."

Her mother uncrossed and recrossed her legs. She fanned herself with the blank notepad. "Yes, well. It's a bit soon, I think. Besides, there's so much work that needs to be done over there. I've been terribly busy."

"Which is exactly why we need to get on with it while I'm in town."

"Well, that's a conversation for later. I'm sure Micah doesn't want to hear about our cleaning project."

"It's not a problem, Mrs. Quick. These are the decisions we all face eventually, one way or another. I just want to do whatever I can to make the process easier for you." He glanced down at the file on his desk, then looked back up at them. "And you're right, Addy, that the house is really the only big thing to deal with. But there's a complication with the house."

"What do you mean?" Eleanor asked.

"There's something on the house called a perpetuity. It's sort of like a lien.

I haven't figured out the details yet—the note is a little cryptic, actually—but it seems to be attached to the deed. I'm going to have to do a little more research. I'm sorry, I only just found it this morning and it's a sort of complicated area of the law."

"I don't understand any of what you just said," Addy said.

Micah sighed. "I'm sorry. It's all that legalese. Okay, I think there is some sort of condition attached to any potential sale of Nellie's house."

"What kind of condition?" Addy asked. She glanced over at her mother, who looked mildly shell-shocked.

"It looks like—and as I said, I really have to do more research. I wish my grandfather was still alive since he drew it up. Anyway, if I understand it correctly, you can only sell the house if the terms of the original gift have been met."

"What gift?"

"Yes. That's the slightly confusing part. It seems the house was the original gift. Do you know anything about that?"

Addy stared at her mother, who shrugged.

"A gift? No. I grew up in that house. I think my mother grew up there too, but honestly, I'm not sure," Eleanor said.

"Well, from what I can tell, Nellie inherited the house from her mother, Isabella. Does that sound right?"

"Granny Isabella," Addy repeated. "Yes."

"Well, somewhere along the line, the house appears to have been a gift."

"From whom?"

Micah looked down at the papers on his desk. "I'm not sure. I mean, my grandfather signed the perpetuity, but I haven't found the deed yet. To be honest, I'm finding a lot of odd things like that." He looked past them as if searching for words. "I think things were different then. My grandfather was, frankly, pretty powerful around here, before the Depression anyway, and as a judge, he would've been able to play a little fast and loose with the rules."

Addy stared at him. "So what are we supposed to do?"

"Well, I think you should move forward with your plans. Get the house ready to go on the market, if that's what you want to do."

"That's it? Just ignore this condition, whatever it is?"

"Perpetuity. Yes. I mean, the chances that it'll prevent the sale are slim. Plus, like I said, I'll do some more research and let you know what I find out. It should be simple enough to run a title search. I just have to get over to the Register of Deeds office to track down the paperwork."

"Isn't that stuff all online nowadays?" Addy asked.

"They're working on it, but this will go pretty far back, I suspect."

"And we're supposed to just trust you, that it'll be fine?"

"Addison!" Eleanor said.

"Well, what am I supposed to say?" Addy looked from her mother back to Micah. "I mean, really. I remember what happened last time I trusted you."

There. She'd said the thing that had been bothering her since Micah invited them into his office. He'd betrayed her in high school—thrown her under the bus to save his own skin. Admittedly, she'd been happy to transfer to the public high school, but the fact that Micah had given up her name and walked away unsullied had irritated her ever since.

He closed his eyes for a second. When he opened them, a shadow lingered around the corners of his eyes. "Did I ever apologize?"

"No, actually. But you did turn my life upside down, so there's that."

"Addison Quick," Eleanor said, her voice strained. "That is all water that passed under the bridge a very long time ago."

"Fine." Addy looked directly at her mother. "Shall we go ahead and make a plan to sell Grandmama's things? Maybe an estate sale? Or how about an auction? How about if Micah gets the ball rolling on that? Isn't that what estate lawyers do, Micah?"

Addy was pleased by the look of chagrin on his face, but then she turned. Her mother looked as if she might breathe fire.

"Are you suggesting we drag my mother's possessions out on the lawn for all her neighbors to just paw through? Lay her life bare for all the world to see? All those gossipy women who live over there will have a field day."

Micah jumped in before Addy could snap back at her mother. "It wouldn't have to be like that, Mrs. Quick. An estate sale is not quite as…public as a yard sale. And if you held an auction, you'd have a great deal of control. It could be as discreet as you choose. Of course, you could always just donate the entire contents of the house to a worthy organization. You have choices."

Addy wasn't quite prepared to be grateful to him, but she knew he had just defused a difficult moment. She bit back the urge to snipe at him again, and awkwardly patted Eleanor on the arm. Perhaps they needed to finish up and leave before things deteriorated any further.

"I'm sorry, Mother." Addy wasn't sure what she was apologizing for, but saying she was sorry had always been the quickest way to soothe Eleanor, especially in public. She patted her arm again. "We can go slowly. Maybe I should start by going over there and assessing what needs to be done?"

Eleanor looked at Micah; Addy repressed a flicker of irritation.

He nodded. "That sounds like a plan. You work on a list of tasks, and I'll do some more research into the perpetuity and gather some information on what you'd have to do to hold an auction. Just information, no commitment."

"And my own work, of course. I am here for a reason, after all." She couldn't help throwing that in. She didn't want him thinking she had nothing to do except cater to her mother.

"Of course," Micah said, standing up. "Let me know when you're ready to move forward. And I'll let you know when I have more information for you."

Addy shaded her eyes as she followed her mother out onto the sidewalk.

"You could've mentioned that it was Micah, don't you think?" The words exploded out of her. "Seriously, Mother?"

"Who exactly did you think it would be?"

"How would I know? You hang on to every detail like you're hiding state secrets! How in the world can I help you get this work done if you don't tell me anything at all?"

"As you keep pointing out, you've moved on. You don't live here anymore. I don't see why it matters to you that the Brittons are handling Mother's estate. They've handled it for years."

A thought clicked in Addy's mind. "You didn't even think to mention it at dinner the other night, when I was going on about Martha being fired? By his grandfather?"

"That has absolutely nothing to do with selling Mother's house. And as I believe I mentioned, our private family history is not appropriate material for a dissertation, anyway."

Addy threw up her hands. "Normal conversation, Mother. When I mentioned Judge Britton, you could've given me a heads-up, something like 'Oh, by the way, we have an appointment with your old boyfriend on Monday.' It would've been nice."

Eleanor stood rigid on the uneven brick sidewalk, her lips pressed in a taut, pale line. "People are staring."

Addy flung her arms wide, for all the world to see. "Who is staring? No one cares, Mother! No one's watching! Look around. No one's paying a bit of attention to us."

Eleanor turned on her heel. "You're making a scene."

"Never mind, then. If you don't want my help, I can't force it on you. I'm going over to Grandmama's now. To work on my project."

Eleanor rounded on Addy. "Don't you dare throw anything away. Not a scrap, do you hear me?"

Addy's toes wiggled in her sling-backs as if they were counting to ten, reminding her to rise above. "Of course not," she finally said, trying to bring her voice back to neutral.

"And another thing, young lady: there is no way I'm going to stand by and let strangers paw through my mother's things. We are not those people." Eleanor got in her car and slammed the door, leaving Addy standing on the sidewalk, squinting against the optimistic sunshine and shaking her head.

Addy parked her car on the street in front of Nellie Sumner's tiny bungalow and sat still for a moment, looking around at the familiar neighborhood. It was only a fifteen-minute drive from her parents' house, but it felt like a world away with its smaller lots and more modest homes. She'd loved it here as a child—she'd always felt freer in Nellie's working-class neighborhood.

She'd been a wreck last time she was here, in a hurry to run back to D.C., away from her sadness. It hadn't worked, she realized now. That was the day she had blindly opened Grandmama's closet to bury her face in the dresses lined up on their hangers, and plucked the manila envelope full of papers off a shelf. It was funny how that moment had dragged her back almost a year later.

She shook herself, determined not to let the melancholy take hold, grabbed a box of garbage bags from the back seat, and stepped out into the grass. Eleanor might feel compelled to hang on to every scrap of paper, but she wouldn't miss the real junk that Addy knew was still there. The lawn was freshly mowed; grudgingly, Addy realized that her mother must have hired someone to do basic yard work. The house had been standing empty for almost a year, but from the curb, it didn't look as neglected as Addy had worried it would.

Family had always used the kitchen door at the side of the house, under the carport, but Addy couldn't see that it mattered at this point. She made her way up the walk and onto the front porch. The small wooden porch seemed bare without her grandmother's pots full of petunias and geraniums. She unlocked the door and stepped into the front room.

Addy and Lacey had always been amused by their grandmother's insistence that her tiny, stuffy, velvet-draped living room was a parlor. Addy closed the front door behind her, and twilight settled again over the room. She pulled back the sheers; light from the windows just made everything look dustier. She surveyed the velvet chairs, now faded to a color somewhere between rose and drab, and the coffee table she had scratched with a toothpick when she was small. While the outside of the house had been maintained just enough to not be an embarrassment, the inside had clearly been sitting undisturbed since Grandmama Nellie's death.

Addy's frustration with her mother flared up again. The clock was ticking on her time in Asheville, and she couldn't afford to spend the summer waiting for Eleanor to stop grieving.

Addy made her way to the kitchen, the center of her grandmother's life, flipping on lights as she went. Thank goodness Eleanor had kept the power on. In the kitchen, she opened the door and a couple of windows to let some fresh air in. She stood, gathering her thoughts. Her mother's adamant refusal to consider an estate sale or auction was going to make the disposal of all this household detritus very difficult. She opened a drawer, just out of curiosity. Wooden spoons, spatulas, a manual can-opener—all were jumbled together just like they had been for as long as Addy could remember. She pushed the drawer closed, its finish a little sticky with age and damp, and opened another.

This one was crammed full of used plastic bags—grocery bags, freezer bags, the filmy bags from the produce department. Addy slammed it shut.

Grandmama Nellie's entire life was reduced to crumpled plastic bags and scorched wooden spoons. Addy blinked back tears. She hadn't expected the air of loss that hung over the rooms like a pall, and it made her mother's words sting even more. Eleanor wasn't the only one who missed Nellie.

Addy shook herself. This was no time to get maudlin, alone in this creaky little house that smelled so much like Grandmama. She went into the spare bedroom that she had slept in so many times as a child and opened the closet door. The high shelf was stacked with shoe boxes and hat boxes, the tidy archive of her grandmother's life.

Addy pulled down a box and looked around for a place to put it. The only available surface was the twin beds she and Lacey had slept on when they stayed over. Hesitating, she touched one of the quilts. It would be a shame to damage it, but it was probably too late for that anyway. These quilts had been well-used and loved. Grandmama had always said her mother made the quilts for her trousseau. Addy remembered Granny Isabella, if only from pictures, as a hunched, gnarled figure with long gray hair that she wore in an old-fashioned bun. Addy looked at the quilt more closely. She didn't recognize the pattern, but she'd never really studied quilts. Maybe there'd be time when her dissertation was done. The thought was encouraging. She spun out a fantasy of endless free time and exploring rabbit holes of esoteric research as she dropped the shoebox on the worn quilt and reached for another.

When she had all the boxes spread on the bed, she began systematically opening them to assess the contents. There was no way she could dig through all these bundles and files of paper in one day, or even a week, most likely, but perhaps she could get a sense of how they'd been organized.

One box was filled with remnants of her own childhood—childish drawings, random school worksheets, and even a large envelope full of her grandmama's handwritten copies of every report card Addy had ever received. Addy sank down on the corner of the bed, oblivious to the dust that rose into the air around her like a cloud of memories.

In another box were the same records of Lacey's childhood, a thinner pile, given Lacey's age, but evidence nonetheless of Grandmama Nellie's role as keeper of the family mythology, right up until the very end of her life.

In yet another box—a pink hatbox tied with a gold cord—Addy uncovered yet another childhood recorded: Eleanor's. Her hand hovered over the bundles of report cards and newspaper clippings. It was like a time capsule of her mother's life, and she'd never seen any of it before. The temptation was terribly strong, but she knew once she started flipping backwards through her mother's history, she'd be distracted for hours. With an effort of will, she put the lid back on the box and put it on the shelf in the closet. It would still be there when she had more time to sift through the contents. Hers and Lacey's boxes went back in the closet as well, leaving four boxes on the bed.

One box proved to be letters from Grandmama's friend Geraldine, who had apparently gone into the AWACs during World War II. Addy had already seen some like this in the envelope she'd loaned to Dr. McGregor. She skimmed quickly through the return addresses; it didn't look as if Geraldine had ever gone overseas. Addy remembered her as a thin, tidy woman who grew zucchinis the size of rolling pins. Military service must have been unusual for a woman from the mountains back then, and Addy made a mental note to pass the letters along to Dr. McGregor. They looked fairly mundane, but she might find them interesting.

Another box contained a seemingly random assortment of memorabilia from her grandmother's life with her husband, whom Addy had never known. She put it aside and reached for the last box. If there wasn't anything in here about Great-Aunt Martha, she didn't know where she'd look next.

When she lifted the faded lid, she found more newspaper clippings and a handful of what looked like very old student essays. None of the handwriting was familiar, but when she flipped through the stack, she realized that these were old student papers. The yellowed newspaper clippings must all be about the exploits and triumphs of former students. Grandmama Nellie had retired from teaching when Addy was born, but throughout her childhood, Addy had heard the refrain all over town: "Your grandmama was my fourth-grade teacher. She was fair, but boy was she tough." Addy put the papers back in the box. It would be nice if she could track some of the students down and tell them Nellie had watched from afar as they grew up and moved on in life, but that, like the box full of her mother's memorabilia, would have to wait until she'd made some research progress.

She put the last boxes back on the shelf and poked around in the bottom of the closet, looking for any stray bundles of papers and trying not to think about her mother's fear of brown recluse spiders. But there was nothing else in the closet except clothes and shoes and the faint smell of cedar. A tiny black moth fluttered past, confirming her belief that while cedar might be natural, it couldn't compete with mothballs. She pulled out one of Grandmama's favorite dresses, plain brown with a khaki collar, in a style Addy thought of as "classic old-lady," and held the fabric up to the light. Sure enough, it was riddled with moth holes. Another wave of sadness washed over her. Grandmama Nellie would be so disappointed to know that her things had been allowed to molder like this; she'd always prided herself on taking care of her little house and its tidy garden.

Addy put the dress back and closed the closet, not sure where else to look. Her grandmother's desk was in the kitchen, but as far as Addy knew, she'd only ever used it for paying bills and storing art supplies for the girls to play with. They'd had free run of the drawers, so she would remember if there were old papers of any kind. Just to be sure, she went into the kitchen and did a quick inventory of the desk's contents. Legal pads, construction paper, telephone books, felt tip pens, and a dried out box of watercolors were all she found. The tray on top that she had used to sort her correspondence was empty; Eleanor must've done at least a little bookkeeping and bill-paying, given that the electricity was still on.

Her stomach was starting to growl, so Addy decided to finish up and come back another day. She sat down at the desk and pulled out a legal pad to make a few quick notes.

She started by making a list of materials she needed for her dissertation research, moved on to an order of operations she and her mother and sister would need to follow to get the house ready for sale, and finally jotted down some cursory notes about the historical marker Eleanor had asked her to work on. When she got to the bottom of the sixth page, she looked up, her fingers stiff from gripping the pen. Half an hour had slipped by, and her head was beginning to hurt. At the top of the first page, she wrote SNACKS in block letters. She needed to put something in her purse to keep from getting so famished; her mood was starting to jump around, making it difficult to concentrate.

Addy wandered through the bungalow, making sure the windows were all closed and locked, even though it felt a little silly. Maybe if they left it wide open, someone would break in and clear it out. Then she could just put all her energy into the other insurmountable task: the dissertation. Her emotions were an uncomfortable jumble. She closed her eyes for a moment and conjured up an image of her office back at the university. As tiny as it was, it was hers, and gave her a sense of self-sufficiency that she'd been missing since she drove into town a few days ago. She stood up straight, trying to draw on that feeling of competence, and stepped out into the sunlight. Breathing in the fresh air, she closed the front door on the work she wasn't ready to face.

Chapter 5

After a good night's sleep, and fortified with toast and two of the tubs of yogurt Eleanor seemed to subsist on, Addy was ready to tackle the research again, this time with a plan.

She felt a bit like she was retracing her steps from the day before, though, as she pulled her car into the very same parking spot in Biltmore Village. The state archives were two doors down from Micah's office. She looked around, wondering where he was, and hoped the sense of déjà vu wasn't a portent of how the day was going to go.

Several hours later and, despite being armed with a list and a rough idea of where to begin, she had accomplished nothing beyond a minimal understanding of North Carolina's income tax history. Her eyes were bleary from staring at microfilm. The 1920 and 1930 census records were incomplete and would have to be ordered. Income tax was only instituted in North Carolina in the early 1920s, so those records were useless for a broader historical perspective. This branch of the state archives, tucked away in the mountains hundreds of miles from the main office in the capital, was mostly a repository for large private collections of documents from local individuals, with a few institutions like small colleges thrown in for good measure.

Finding any broader employment patterns in those records would take years of close reading and number-crunching, or an army of assistants, neither of which Addy had.

She rubbed her stiff neck, then flipped the top page of her notepad. The next destination on her list was the Biltmore archives.

At the turn of the 19th century, the Biltmore Estate was the biggest employer in the mountains. Addy hoped their records would tell her what she needed to know about who was working there in the 1920s, and what kind of work they were doing. She also hoped those records would include, or at least point her toward, the kind of primary documents that would give her dissertation heft and respectability. Original source material was the key to being taken seriously.

She signed out at the front desk and headed to her car. The Biltmore archives were housed in the corporate offices downtown. Addy rolled her windows down to feel the late-spring breeze, and noted all the restaurants, bars, and coffee shops that had sprouted up or closed since last time she drove this way. Asheville's reputation as a vacation spot guaranteed a certain amount of turnover. She was momentarily cheered by the prospect of checking out all the new places while she was in town, but the thought of her credit card bill squelched that curiosity.

At Biltmore's records office, her mission came to a grinding halt. The records weren't open to the public. She'd need to submit a visiting researcher application online, which would take at least two weeks to process.

Trudging back out to the parking deck, Addy calculated that she had exactly seventy-eight days left before the beginning of fall classes. Was it possible to actually feel her blood pressure rising? Two days in and she needed help already. She needed access to the estate archives. She also needed a quick way to pluck out what she required from the quantity of information hiding in plain sight at the state archives. She had no experience with statistics. This was not the dissertation she had expected to write, she thought for the hundredth time. It galled her to have to ask for help, but seventy-eight days didn't leave a lot of room for aimless wandering.

The line to get out of the parking deck looked interminable, so Addy pulled out her phone and plugged in the earbuds.

Swallowing her pride, she dialed her advisor's number while she waited for the idling cars to move.

As usual, Dr. McGregor sounded unsurprised.

For once, Addy found it easy to match the older woman's composure. Apparently, despair was the key to muting her usual ebullience.

"I need some help, and you have so much experience with this kind of research. I need to tap into your wisdom, if you have a minute."

"What can I do for you?"

Addy's thoughts crystallized as she stumbled through recounting her frustrations of the last couple of days, and she tried to strike a careful balance between her own competence and the obstacles she was encountering. The line of cars inched toward the exit booth.

"So how can I help?" Dr. McGregor asked when Addy finally finished.

"Two things, I think. First, I need to get research privileges at the Biltmore archives. And second…" Addy hesitated, hating the way she felt.

"Spit it out."

"I hate to ask, but remember you mentioned finding some funds for an assistant? I think if I could hire someone here, maybe a student from the university, just to do an initial pass through the census data, separate the wheat from the chaff, so to speak, I think that would free me up to focus on interpreting the information and finding more primary material."

"Biltmore's not a problem. I probably know someone who knows someone," Dr. McGregor said. "But the funding is more of a challenge. I asked last week and didn't get an answer. You really should have applied in January."

"I know. I'm kicking myself now." She ran a finger around the edge of the radio's digital display, looking for non-existent dust. "What if I call Dr. Torrisi directly? Do you think that would be a mistake?"

The pause dragged on so long Addy wondered if the call had failed, but she waited, holding the phone with her shoulder while she dug her wallet out of her purse.

"I don't think it'll get you funding, but taking personal responsibility for your predicament might earn you some political capital. Which is a good thing."

"Of course. You're right, that's great advice." Addy wondered if she was laying it on too thick, but Dr. McGregor didn't seem offended. She plunged ahead. "Oh, I found something else I thought you might like. A stack of letters from my grandmama's best friend. I didn't read them—I've been so busy with the research—but it looks like she was an AWAC. Would you like me to bring them when I come back to D.C.?"

Addy could almost hear Dr. McGregor's sharp curiosity biting into the idea.

"That's intriguing. Do you suppose the author is still alive?"

Addy mentally scrolled backward through her grandmother's narrow social world. "I'm not sure. Why?"

"Interviews are the best kind of primary source material."

"Hold on." She handed the parking attendant a five-dollar-bill and pulled out onto the street and turned right, not thinking about where she was going. Her memories of Grandmama's friend Geraldine were hazy at best. Was Dr. McGregor planning to come all the way down here to talk to some little old lady she'd never heard of? And did she expect Addy to do the legwork to make that happen? Then the penny dropped.

"Oh, you mean for me to interview her."

"Of course."

"Well. An AWAC really kind of takes it out of the realm of rural Appalachia, doesn't it? I mean, that was a military operation. Besides, that whole phase of the women's movement has been so well documented. I don't know that there's really much left to be said about it."

"You may be right. Well, it was a thought. Keep kicking those ideas around. And yes, I'd love to see the letters, if you're sure you can't use them. Or maybe I'll have another idea about how you can. And, Addy…you aren't doing this in an isolation chamber, you know."

Addy frowned. "No. Of course not." A car honked behind her; the light had turned green. She pulled into a church parking lot. This conversation was taking longer than she'd expected.

"You're on the right track, and I'm confident you'll get it done. This is exactly the kind of focus I like to see in my students. But you tend to want to go your own way, without collaborating. The network is everything, Addy. Be politically smart is all I'm saying."

Relief washed over Addy. It wasn't the criticism she'd assumed.

"You're right, of course. I'll work on it. In the meantime, you'll make some calls about getting me access to the Biltmore archives?"

"Right away. And I've drawn up a list of interim deadlines for you, just to keep you on track. Every day matters, at this point. I'll send them along in an email, shall I?"

Addy could hear faint clicking.

"There. It's on the way, but the key bit that you need to focus on right now is the prospectus. I calculated that you really need to send that to me in two weeks. That's the only way you're going to be able to stay on track to graduate in December."

"Two weeks? That's awfully soon. I'm not so sure…don't you think I need to sort of weight the time toward the front end? Spend a little longer planning, and then really crank through the writing?"

"I don't. If you'd started a year ago, or even six months, maybe. But you have to defend by the end of October. That means I need a draft on my desk by September thirtieth at the very latest. But the fifteenth would be better."

"Yes, of course. I've done the math."

She hadn't done the math, of course, not really, and she couldn't stop to do it now. After they hung up, she edged the car into the shade of an oak tree and called her department head before she lost her nerve.

Dr. Torrisi sounded distracted and harried. "Those funds were all disbursed months ago. I'm sorry, Addy, but I can't just conjure up money out of thin air."

Dr. McGregor's words echoed in Addy's mind: personal responsibility. "You're right, Dr. Torrisi. I really screwed this up by waiting so long, but I'm fully committed now. I just need a little bit of research money." Groveling made her feel ill.

"I can give you six hundred dollars. That's it. Use it wisely—it's a one-time deal."

"Thank you so much," Addy said, then hung up, exhausted.

The two conversations together had left her feeling a little hemmed in. She needed to shake them off. Driving always helped her focus, and she had a full tank of gas, so she headed toward the Blue Ridge Parkway. She turned onto the scenic mountain road and took the first hairpin turn a little faster than she'd meant to. It had been years since she'd driven out in this direction, but perhaps it would still be the same balm it had been for her in high school. Her muscle memory quickly settled into the familiar rhythm of mountain driving, but her subconscious was not so easily fooled.

Steering hard to the right around the edge of a deep green ravine, she saw a hawk, wings outstretched, at the same altitude as the road she was on. She slowed, watching the bird ride an updraft. Behind her, a car honked. She sighed. It wasn't working. This winding road had sheltered her from the problems of her teenage years, but not even the hazy green beauty of the Smoky Mountains could soothe her now. She pulled onto the shoulder to let the car pass before she turned around to head back into town.

By the time Addy pulled up in her parents' driveway, she had worked herself into a state of minor panic. The number—seventy-eight days—had gone around in her head, becoming a rhythm that she couldn't drown out. She thought about all the office hours she'd spent helping students with their essays, their research, their lives, and understood why her graduate peers had given short shrift to their teaching work in favor of weekends in the library and summers doing field work. She'd been a soft touch, and was beginning to regret it. Now she needed to make up for lost time.

Eleanor called out to her through the screen door. She must've been listening for the car.

Addy sighed and headed for the kitchen to wash her hands and do her mother's bidding.

"Put out the silverware, if you would, dear, and come back for the plates. I'll dish up in here."

"Don't go to that trouble, Mother. Let's just put the pots on the table. It's easier."

"But it's so much nicer this way. I don't mind."

Lacey passed through the kitchen. "Don't forget Asia's coming," she said, in the loud flat voice of a person wearing headphones.

Addy glanced at her mother and found the thin line of Eleanor's lips confirmation enough, so she counted out five sets of silverware and pushed through the swinging door to the dining room.

When Addy was small, none of her friends' families ever ate in their dining rooms, but her family did, every night. The kitchen table was strictly for breakfast and dinner was always an event in the Quick household, and it was reserved for family. The rules must have loosened in her absence, given how casually Lacey announced Asia was joining them for this sacred family ritual. She made a mental note to consider how she felt about that at some point, and contemplated the table, which, without being extended, held eight people. Normally, they all clustered at one end, Mason at the head, Eleanor on his right, and the girls together on his left. She wondered where to put Asia. It seemed unfair to put her next to Eleanor and awkward to put her at the far end, so she decided to seat herself next to her mother and let Lacey and Asia sit together opposite them.

Had it really just taken her that much thought to set the table? She shook her head. She could hear Asia clattering in through the kitchen door as if she belonged there. Addy's dark mood began to lift a little, and she smiled. *Asia certainly makes things more interesting*, she thought as she stepped back into the kitchen.

Eleanor was standing at the stove, her back turned resolutely to the room. Asia, dressed again in overalls and her pink bandana, was sitting on the bench by the door, untying her shoes while Lacey sat next to her with one arm draped over her back, whispering in her ear. Addy looked between them and Eleanor, then scooped up two plates and scurried back into the dining room.

Lacey and Asia came in with the rest of the plates as Mason ambled in from the living room. They all sat down and waited for Eleanor. When she finally joined them, Addy noticed she had taken off her apron, put on fresh lipstick, and even brushed her hair. Her mother's insistence on proper appearances, even for an ordinary weeknight family dinner, was an old bone of contention between them. Addy glanced down at the apricot-colored muslin dress she'd put on that morning, and was glad it had held up after all her running around.

It turned out, though, that Addy was not the focus of Eleanor's agita that evening. Lacey and Asia seemed to be carrying on some private conversation of their own, all whispers and elbows and significant looks. Eleanor's posture radiated tension; Addy felt like she was sitting next to a marble pillar, perfectly straight and constitutionally frozen.

"Dinner is delicious, Mother," Addy said, trying to set a less awkward tone.

Eleanor poked at the thin slice of lamb on her plate and set her fork down delicately on the edge of her plate.

"It's undercooked," she said, and gave Addy an acerbic look.

Addy tried to kick Lacey under the table to tell her to behave and help her bail them all out of the miserable tension, but she couldn't quite reach. She turned instead to her father.

"Moving right along, then. Daddy, how was your day?"

"Fine. And yours?"

It was an opening, so Addy jumped in. "You know, it was a mixed bag. Harder than I thought. I went down to the state archives first, which was moderately useful, so I'll go back. But I think the Biltmore archives are going to be more useful. I don't know for sure, though, because they wouldn't let me in. It's such a nuisance."

"Why in the world not?" Eleanor asked.

Addy was surprised to feel gratified by the tone of indignation in her mother's voice. "Apparently they're not open to the general public."

"Well, I never," Eleanor said. "General public, indeed." She pushed back from the table.

"Wait, Mother. It's not a crisis—it's just another little roadblock to work around, that's all. Most private archives are, well, obviously, private."

Eleanor still looked as if she were going to bolt up out of her chair at any second.

"I think Mrs. Q is right," Asia said. "That seems kind of elitist to me."

She sounded and looked like some kind of New Age hippie to Addy, who struggled to keep her face neutral. Poor Asia—her willingness to agree with Eleanor was cute, but did she really not understand what was bothering Eleanor? It wasn't the elitism that was the problem—it was the fact that Addy wouldn't automatically be allowed into that elite circle.

"It's not that unusual. It takes a lot of money and equipment and staff to make a paper archive safely accessible. Very few small private operations have the resources to do that. It's not really a museum or anything; that's what Biltmore House is for."

"Well, it's not exactly like the house has an egalitarian history, anyway," Lacey said. "Asia, have I told you my great-grandmother was a maid at Biltmore?"

Eleanor looked pained. "That was a very long time ago, Lacey. Nearly a century."

"Wow. Wouldn't it be interesting to know what that was like? I went there on a field trip in the sixth grade, and we saw the tiny little rooms where the servants slept. I bet they worked her hard," Asia said.

"She only worked there briefly before she was married," Eleanor said. "I can't really imagine that it was at all interesting. Like I said, it was a very long time ago and not really worth dwelling on."

"Oh, but don't you like to imagine what it was like?" Asia said. "All those glamorous parties, and the fancy food, and the rich people swanning around." She fluttered her eyelashes and waved her hand like a fan.

Lacey grinned and imitated her until they both giggled.

"And the clothes," Addy said. "I fantasize about the clothes."

"Oh, when I went with my class, we saw the most beautiful black lace dress on a mannequin. It was amazing! It had a long train spread out behind it, all lace, with a matching lace parasol…but that's exactly what I mean about it being hard. I bet the servants were worked half to death taking care of all those clothes, and those rich people who didn't know squat about how to take care of themselves. Rich people…humph." Asia said.

An uncomfortable silence settled over the dining room. Evening sun slanting in through the window burnished the wide oak floor planks. Light bounced off Eleanor's Waterford glasses, refracting into a scattering of rainbows across the linen tablecloth. Addy pushed her glass with one finger, watching the tiny rainbow waver and disappear. Asia made a little face at Lacey, who winked back at her. Addy could see the movement of Lacey's arm and realized she must be reaching for Asia's hand, to reassure her.

"Anyway," Addy said, "I'll just have to get permission, that's all." She sipped her iced tea. "As a matter of fact, I had a thought about that. Remember the other day, Daddy, when you said you could call someone at the university to get me a research card there? I don't need that, but I was wondering if you could help me out with the Biltmore Estate. I thought maybe you could call

Mimi Cecil, and see if she'd be willing to write me a letter of recommendation or something, so I can get into their archive?"

Mason's eyes flickered to Eleanor so quickly that Addy barely caught the look. He cleared his throat. "I don't see why not. I'll give her a call tomorrow."

Eleanor really did push back from the table then, and this time she picked up her full plate and marched into the kitchen, leaving the rest of them in silence.

Asia leaned over to Lacey and whispered, *sotto voce*, "I guess that means there's no cobbler tonight."

Chapter 6

Lacey met Addy at the coffee shop in Biltmore Village since she'd gotten out of school early and was waiting for Asia to catch a ride over from the public high school out on the edge of town. Addy was sitting with her laptop, making yet another list. She moved things from one list to another and reprioritized each, but not marking anything off made her feel as if she was running into brick walls at every turn. She'd spent the last two days at the university library, photocopying articles from old journals. One of the many challenges of historical research was that the really old stuff couldn't be found more quickly and easily online. Addy found it incredibly tedious, but not as bad as actually reading the articles, which she knew she was avoiding. As soon as she hired an assistant, she'd have to get to the hard part.

By the time Lacey showed up, Addy had set the pile of photocopies on the table, dug out and arranged a selection of multi-colored highlighters and pens, and opened the file on her computer optimistically entitled "nationwide wage patterns for women 1910-1930." If she was going to argue that the Appalachian states were in any way different from the rest of the country, she would need to determine what the pay range was in the rest of the country first.

She banged her head against the table as Lacey sat down with three cappuccinos.

"At least you don't have AP exams next week. I have three. Woe is me," Lacey said. She didn't seem terribly anxious.

"Poor you. But you can't even imagine how hard this is."

Asia tiptoed up behind Lacey and nuzzled her cheek. Lacey's face lit up, and she turned to pull Asia down next to her in the booth. Their bodies seemed to instinctively prop each other up, as if they fit together like jigsaw pieces. Asia's plain pink t-shirt hung loosely over a pair of khaki Bermuda shorts, and her hair was pulled back in a plain ponytail.

Addy stared at her wondering where all her personality had gone.

"You look perturbed," Asia said.

Addy realized she'd been staring and looked down at her cappuccino, rubbing between her eyebrows. "I am. Perturbed and…" She groped for a word that could match the character of her frustration, but her brain was empty. "Bored. I'm just bored. I hate this topic."

"I'm sorry," Asia said. "It's no good to spend your time on things that make you miserable." Her face went still, as if all the light had gone out of her, and for a split second, she looked much older than sixteen.

Addy wondered what her story was, but Lacey covered Asia's hand with her own and the smile came back, albeit smaller.

"Why do you hate it? You haven't mentioned that before," Lacey said.

"I'm trying to convince myself it's going to work out. It's just that I don't have a lot of time left and this whole women's work thing was really Dr. McGregor's idea, and I kind of hate it, so whatever you do, don't get a PhD." She bit her lip.

"I had no idea," Lacey said.

Addy sighed. "I didn't mean it like that. I don't really hate it. I'm lucky to have the whole summer to focus on my research. It feels scary and hard, but I know it's a luxury. Don't worry about me." She tried to inject some enthusiasm into her voice. "How was school?"

"Senioritis. Spring fever. Pointless." Lacey looked at Asia. "How was your day, babe?"

Asia shrugged one shoulder. "Fine." She took a sip of her cappuccino.

"Where's your bandana?" Addy asked, half-joking in an effort to jolly them out of their ennui.

Asia put one hand up to touch her thin, stern ponytail. "It's gone," she said.

The few seconds of silence told Addy she'd touched on a sore subject, but she couldn't imagine why.

Seeing the look that passed between Asia and Lacey a moment later, Addy had an unexpected flash of emotion. She'd always thought of Asheville as a tolerant, liberal kind of town where it was easy to live as an openly gay person, but when she looked more closely at Lacey and Asia, they both seemed curiously guarded. She had a sudden urge to gather them up in a giant hug.

"What's wrong?" she asked.

Lacey gave her a wry smile, and the wariness was gone. Her sister was back. "Just the usual," she said. "You know what it's like at the end of the school year. Everybody's got too much to do. Teachers are sick of us. Parents are a pain in the ass. Nothing new."

"I remember," Addy said. "Not much you can do except hang on and get through it. It's not that different from college, actually." She paused, not wanting to leave Asia out of the conversation. "What are you going to do this summer, Asia?"

"Work, I suppose. I need to make some money."

"Where do you work?"

"I work on an organic farm now. They'll probably let me work more over the summer. Hopefully. And it's next door to where I live, so I can ride my bike."

"Do you not live in town?"

"No. Out in Madison County."

"It's a nuisance," Lacey said. "It's like a forty-five minute drive."

Now the girl's intermittent appearances made more sense. "Is there even a proper town in Madison County? What do your parents do out there?" Addy asked.

Asia's face went carefully blank, giving her a shuttered look. Her hand crept up to touch the ponytail again. "I live with my aunt and uncle, actually. He works over the mountain, in Tennessee. She stays home with their three little kids."

"He drives to Tennessee every day for work? That's quite a commute."

"You'd be surprised. Tennessee is not as far away as you might think." Asia shrugged. "But I'd rather get some kind of job in town."

Lacey touched Asia's elbow with her own. Asia's return smile looked a little halfhearted.

Addy opened her mouth to say something motivational, but right at that moment, her phone alerted her to a text message.

"Oh, Daddy came through," she said with relief. "Mimi says I can get into the archives any time, and I can go do some digging up at Biltmore House. Wow, I didn't expect that."

Lacey and Asia looked politely interested, but neither said anything, so Addy went outside to call Dr. McGregor and update her.

"That's excellent," the professor said after Addy explained. "Well done. Now you don't need any help from me. I'm glad you figured that out. Now you can really buckle down."

"That's what I'm planning to do. Maybe I'll go up to the house tomorrow, and get the lay of the land."

"You need to go up there with a plan, a goal. That way you won't waste time wandering aimlessly. Speaking of wasting time, I was looking at the calendar and did a little back-step planning for you. Hold on, I'll email it." Addy could hear faint clicking. "There. It's on the way, but here's what I wanted to say about it: write your prospectus with an eye toward the outline. Always be thinking ahead to the next step. I calculated that you really need to have the outline done in about four weeks, so you need to keep moving."

Addy thanked Dr. McGregor and hung up, the number four bouncing around in her head. She rejoined the girls at the table, but they quickly picked up on her distraction.

"We're out of here," Lacey said.

"Sorry," Addy said, mustering a smile.

"No worries. We've got stuff to do anyway."

Addy watched as they made their way toward the door, their pinky fingers linked together. After Lacey and Asia left her sitting alone at the coffee shop, she switched to decaf and opened the calendar on her laptop, plugging in the dates from Dr. McGregor's email. There was really no leeway. Seeing it there in black and white, each day an impossibly tiny square, wiped away any last illusion she'd been harboring that the summer was stretching out in front of her in a vague expanse of time with no fixed endpoint.

Basically, she needed to have an outline of an entire book in less than a month. Even with the jump-start Dr. McGregor had given her on the idea, it didn't feel like she had a solid sense of what the topic was, never mind any original, constructive thoughts about it. Was this going to be the moment when the rest of the world decided she didn't have what it took, after all?

Chapter 7

"So you can use this desk, if you want. I'm sorry it's such a small space; we're pretty cramped up here, I'm afraid." The head of the museum department at Biltmore House was a tall, lanky man with thinning gray hair and sharp cheekbones. Though professional, he seemed so distracted that Addy felt as if she'd been imposed upon him. They were standing in a small room tucked up under the roof of a side wing of Biltmore House.

The desk was indeed small, and it was in a cubicle, not an office. It opened onto one of several other cubicles where a middle-aged woman was rummaging in a cavernous purse while listening to something in her earbuds.

Dr. Gruber cleared his throat. When the woman didn't turn around, he coughed loudly, then finally put a hand on her shoulder.

She yelped, then whipped around, yanking the earbuds from her ears.

"Richard. You scared me half to death, sneaking up like that."

He cleared his throat again. "Susan Blake, this is Addison Quick. She's the researcher I told you about. You'll get her settled in, right?"

"Of course." Susan turned to Addy with a warm, friendly smile as Richard beat a hasty retreat, clearing his throat again.

Addy watched him go, trying not to panic at being called a "researcher"—

she didn't feel nearly that official—then turned back to her new cubicle neighbor, who was shoving a smartphone into the front pocket of her khakis.

"Welcome. I was totally expecting you, I promise. I just didn't realize you'd be here so early."

"I was anxious to get started. I'm writing my dissertation, and to tell you the truth, I've kind of dawdled around longer than I should have. Unfortunately, that means now I'm on a brutal deadline."

"Then I'll go ahead and show you around a little so you don't get lost, and you can get on with it."

"Excellent. I have a list. I thought I'd start with an inventory of the employment records, if they're up here, and then maybe move on to examining some more personal documents." She pulled out her notepad, but decided to slow down because of the look on Susan's face. "But, you know, I don't want to get in anyone's way…"

"Oh no. It's fine. Richard had me pull together some material for you, so I put that file on your desk. You'll probably want to start there. But I didn't know what you would need, so it may be useless."

Addy glanced at the very thin manila folder. She reached for it, anxious to see what she'd be starting with, but Susan turned and headed out of the small room. She had to move quickly to keep up.

For the next half hour, Addy tried to form a mental map as she followed Susan through a series of work rooms and dusty storage areas. The museum staff were headquartered in an upstairs wing that had originally been used to sequester unmarried male guests from the rest of the house, and so named as the bachelors' quarters. After George Vanderbilt's death, when his widow began implementing cost-cutting measures in earnest, it was converted to an apartment. Edith had closed up the rest of the rooms, let go of most of the staff, and limited her household to the more manageable space. It was cramped, but a frisson of excitement went through Addy at the realization that she was going to have such behind-the-scenes access. Deadline pressure notwithstanding, this was a childhood fantasy come true. Once, when she was small and her mother had dragged them all up to the house for some event, she'd been overcome with curiosity about what was in Mrs. Vanderbilt's closet, and when people started yelling at her as she tried to pull the heavy door open, she had scooted under the big bed to escape the noise. Looking back on her childhood curiosity now, she felt a little as if she'd been handed the keys to the museum.

She had no idea how she was going to find her way around; it was like a rabbit warren. She met another curator, Beverly, and a conservator, Casey, both huddled over a brocade settee in a bright, airy workroom, but otherwise, the entire museum operation appeared to take place in twisting, cramped corridors. Ancient wooden file cabinets lined most of the walls. In one room, barely bigger than a closet, old wooden crates were piled haphazardly. Addy sneezed, and Susan shot her a look of alarm.

"You might want to stock up on antihistamines. It's pretty dusty everywhere you go up here."

"I can see that. I guess I didn't expect it, given how immaculate everything is downstairs."

Susan sighed. "I know. It's a pretty stark contrast. We're doing our best to get it all organized and documented, but you know how hard that is. And in a house this old, of this size…well, we aren't a large staff, that's all. It's a work in progress."

A faint alarm went off in Addy's head. "Honestly, it looks a little overwhelming. Like I said, I can show you my list, if you think it might help…"

Susan waved her off, grinning. "You'll have your work cut out for you, I reckon. Let me know when you have questions."

"All right, then. Good thing I like a challenge," Addy said. She met Susan's grin, even though she felt more like running out to her car and racing back to her parents' house. "It'll be like a treasure hunt, right?"

The older woman laughed. "A filthy treasure hunt. You might want to dress down a little." She glanced down at her own knit shirt. "We aren't required to wear the uniform up here since we stay away from guest areas, but you sure don't want to wear nice things. I have three boys—did I mention that?—so I can barely keep up with the laundry at my house as it is. A dress like that would last about thirty seconds in my life."

Addy looked down at her dress. A floral slip lined a sheer lavender layer with a drop waist and a swishy full skirt. She found herself really liking this woman's frank practicality, and didn't want to look frivolous. But there was no way she was wearing an outfit like that—khaki pants and a knit shirt were only a step up from a fast-food uniform in Addy's mind.

"Oh, first day and all. I wasn't sure…" She did a quick mental scan of the clothes she'd unpacked over the weekend. Had she even brought any long pants?

"Don't worry about it—it's your dry-cleaning bill, not mine. Anyway. You've seen all there is to see here, and I've got piles of work to do. Anything else I can do for you right now?" She touched the pocket where her phone was stashed as if it were a talisman, and continued to lead Addy back to where they'd started in the cubicle room.

"Um, a map? Or maybe a tracking chip, in case I disappear entirely," Addy said, only half-joking.

Susan chuckled. "You'll find your way around in no time. It looks confusing up here, but it's really not that big." She opened the door and let Addy lead them back to their neighboring desks. "Besides, if you run into real problems, you can always ask Ford. He knows everything. Isn't that right, Ford?"

A wiry old man moving between the cubicles stopped and gave them his attention. Addy stepped forward to meet him, ready to be distracted from her anxiety. The bony hand that gripped hers was strong. He looked up at her, and she was surprised to see sharp, twinkling eyes in his deeply lined face, still bright green in spite of his apparent age. She wondered how old he was; his white hair was so thin she could almost make out the curves and bumps of his skull. That hair, so carefully combed into place, reminded her of the table of elderly gentlemen that her paternal grandfather had met for breakfast every Wednesday at the country club when she was small. He'd taken her with him in the summers, before he died. Were any of those old guys still living? Her father would know.

His voice brought her back to the cramped maze of cubicles. "I reckon I do. I've been here eighty-seven years. Seen it all."

"Eighty-seven years? Are you serious? Pardon me for asking, but how old are you?"

He broke into a dazzling grin. "Well, I'm eighty-seven. I've been right here since the day my mama brought me into the world."

"You were born here? How is that possible?" She turned to Susan, looking for an explanation.

Susan shrugged a shoulder toward Ford. "Don't ask me. Ford's your man." She pulled her phone from her pocket and sat down at her desk. "I'm here if you need me."

"I heard you were coming," Ford said, as if this explained everything.

"Please, have a seat," Addy said, putting a hand on his back to guide him toward the chair behind the desk, and pulled up a straight-backed wooden one for herself. He was a relic, and he was adorable. "How'd you hear I was coming?"

"From Missus Mimi."

"She was very kind to let me poke around like this. I'm working on my dissertation, and I hope I can find some of the old employment records from the early days of the estate."

He nodded. "She's a good person. She and Bill, they try to do right by Missus Edith. I appreciate that."

Addy nodded slowly, trying to do the math in her head, but she wasn't quick enough.

"I was born on the first of January, 1928, if that's what you're wondering."

"I was. That's fantastic. And you've always lived right here?"

"I have. Born and raised. My mama and daddy were too. Collinses been here a long time."

Addy was mesmerized by his cadence. It had been a long time since she'd just sat and listened to the rhythm of mountain speech. He sounded as if he came from another era, which she supposed he did.

"That's amazing. I didn't realize anyone stayed on like that, for so many years."

"Used to be right many of us, but I'm the only one left."

"I bet the changes have been unbelievable for you."

His gaze wandered over the room, then came back to her. "I get worn out trying to hang on to it all." He hesitated, as if he was sifting through the words. "I don't reckon I'll be able to for much longer. That worries me some. Nobody else 'round to remember it all." He seemed so forlorn.

Addy wanted to wrap him up in a hug, but then he seemed to shake off his melancholy.

He pointed at the folder on the desk. "You won't find much use in there. If you've got questions, you talk to me, you hear?"

"Absolutely. How about if I get your phone number, so I can call you if I need to?"

He made a face. "Shoot. You don't need to be calling on the telephone. I'm around." He reached for his cane, and Addy stood up to help him to his feet.

"Well, all right then. I'll keep an eye out for you."

His sharp eyes searched her face for a moment, then he turned his back to her and shuffled off.

Addy spun around to ask Susan what that had been all about, but her cubicle was empty. She shrugged and sat down.

Opening the folder, she glanced through a small pile of papers, all printouts or photocopies. There was a legal pad and a box of pens in a desk drawer. She rummaged in her purse for her list and began to copy the items over onto a fresh page. She felt a bit untethered, as if she was alone in a vast empty space, unsure where to begin.

By the time she got into her car to drive home, the doubts had mushroomed. A narrative was beginning to take shape in her mind, but the research seemed insurmountable and it was hard to even figure out where to begin. She grew tired just thinking about the scope of it all.

She rolled down all the windows in her car and cranked up the radio, trying to blow the cobwebs out of her brain, as she turned onto Approach Road. A storm had passed through while she was cloistered in the house, leaving a few misty tatters of steam in its wake. The breeze that lifted her hair and played over her arms was cool and smelled damp. Droplets glistened on the trees. It seemed as if the sunlight itself glowed green, shining down through new spring leaves. Addy took the curves faster than she should as the road wound down toward town.

She thought back to the small pile of documents she had gathered. There was a housekeeping ledger from 1918, a private journal that had been written by the first housekeeper, Mrs. King, and something called an accounts book that appeared to have been kept by Mrs. Vanderbilt in 1921. All would give texture to her great-aunt Martha's story, whatever it was, and other women like her in the 1920s, but she needed to look beyond Biltmore. Being behind the scenes, able to look at the minutiae of a long-gone lifestyle, was a thrill and a dream come true, but perhaps she'd been hasty to think it would be the resource she needed. The thought was uncomfortable—her parents had called in a favor for her. She didn't want to seem ungrateful, but she didn't have time to chase after old dreams right now.

The elderly gentleman, though—Ford. He seemed to want to tell his stories. She wasn't sure how she could work him into a narrative about patriarchal repression, but something about him made her smile. He carried himself with a dignity that centered Addy, made her feel less like she was trying to corral her thoughts and more like she could tune out the noise and hear the important bits. Perhaps someone in the folklore department could come out and record his memories; folklorists were always doing oral history projects like that. Or maybe there was even someone at the university here in town who might be interested. She made a mental note to make some calls, but that got her thinking, reluctantly, about her own to-do list again.

The state census records she had requested hadn't come in yet, but when they did, she would have to go through them with a fine-toothed comb. The prospect of such tedium filled her with dread. There had to be a quicker way.

Her phone rang. "What's up, Mother?" Sometimes she couldn't resist pushing Eleanor's buttons.

"Hello, Addison." Exasperation clipped her words even more sharply than usual. "I wanted to remind you that your father and I are leaving for the weekend."

"I remember."

Eleanor and Mason were leaving for a trip they'd planned months ago.

"You'll keep an eye on Lacey, make sure she spends some time studying? She tends to get so caught up in rehearsals. And the two of you should go to church Sunday morning."

Addy rolled her eyes. "We'll be fine, Mother. Lacey would be fine even if I weren't here, you know."

"But you are, so keep an eye on her. By the way, I ran into Genevieve this morning at a DAR meeting. She asked about you, and I'm sure she'd love to have lunch one day."

Addy grimaced. "It was nice of her to ask, but I can't imagine that she's really all that interested in me. It's been so long." The thought of ingratiating herself with Genevieve Ingram and her debutante friends made Addy cringe.

"Well, it would be the polite thing to do. You should call her. And the meeting reminded me: have you thought any about the marker for the bungalow? This weekend would be a good time to work on it. Things are going to get busy with Lacey's show and graduation coming up."

"Yes, Mother."

"And…I don't want that Asia at our house all the time," she said, the latter coming out in a rush. "Lacey seems to think she is immune to judgment, but she isn't."

"Nobody cares, Mother."

"People talk, Addy. They always do. One day when you're older, you'll understand that."

Addy rolled her eyes, but bit back a retort. Her mother's instructions had given her an idea.

"We'll be fine, Mother. Go. We'll see you Sunday."

When she stopped at the traffic light to exit the Biltmore Estate, she texted Lacey, telling her to invite Asia for dinner. The girl appeared to be at loose ends while Lacey was tied up with theatre and graduation. Maybe she'd be willing to help out with some research if Addy could give her a specific list of tasks. And even better, maybe she could help do some cleaning out over at Grandmama Nellie's house. Addy had been trying not to think about it all week, but she was going to have to deal with it before she went back to D.C. Dr. Torrisi's stipend wasn't much, but maybe it would be appealing to a high school student. Asia needed the money, and she needed the help.

She pulled into the grocery store parking lot thinking she'd pick up strawberries and some cream for dessert, and that might help her get Asia on board; she seemed to have an insatiable sweet tooth.

Her phone buzzed with a text, and she glanced down, thinking it was Lacey, but it was an unfamiliar number. The message was from Micah Britton.

"Got your number from your mom. Lunch next week? Would love to catch up now that you've had time to settle in."

She slowly typed "sure" but her fingers hovered over the screen for a second before she hit send. She was still feeling a little stunned that her summer had been turned so thoroughly upside down, seemingly overnight. She'd barely had time to unpack, much less unwind from the end of the semester.

Chapter 8

Addy woke up early Saturday morning to the patter of rain on her window. The house was otherwise silent; Lacey was in rehearsal all day. Addy rolled over, her hand coming to rest on the notes she'd scribbled as she was finally drifting off to sleep the night before, and sat up in bed. The notes were sloppy, but they made sense in the dim morning light, so she hopped out of bed. She'd had a glimmer of an idea about how to structure her prospectus, and was actually sort of excited about the project for the first time in days. Perhaps with some caffeine and a bit of luck, she could actually write a couple of pages.

Six hours later, still in her silk pajamas and a pair of embroidered slippers, she'd had three cups of coffee and hadn't eaten anything. She felt like she might be able to levitate soon, but had written ten pages. She couldn't believe it. Dr. McGregor was expecting a thirty-page prospectus by the end of next week—an outline, basically, in essay form. At the rate she was going, she was going to get it done with a few days to spare. Feeling quite pleased with herself and totally deserving of a break, she grabbed her phone, put in her earbuds, and pulled up the Andrews Sisters playlist she'd been perfecting for years. Slipping the phone into the breast pocket of her pajamas, she danced into the kitchen to find something to absorb the coffee.

After slamming cabinets and jitterbugging, she smeared peanut butter on the heel end of a crusty sesame loaf and drizzled it with honey. There wasn't any cream left from the day before yesterday—Asia had made quick work of it—but there were a few strawberries. She couldn't be bothered to do anything to them other than dropping the green caps into the sink as she popped the whole berries into her mouth.

Asia had been pleased enough with the research assistant idea, but Addy hadn't seen her since Lacey drove her home late Thursday evening.

The steady, light spring rain made her disinclined to venture out. Besides, her brain was still buzzing, words and images running on a loop. She switched her coffee mug for a teacup and sat back down at her laptop. Now that she was on a roll, she wanted to see how much she could crank out.

The afternoon slipped by as quickly as the morning had. When she heard Lacey clatter into the kitchen, Addy looked up from her computer, disoriented.

"Hey. Why are you sitting in the dark?" Lacey said as she walked into Mason's office and flipped on the desk lamp. "And why are you still in your pajamas?"

Addy rubbed her eyes. "I forgot to get dressed. But I've been writing!" She glanced down at the page total. "I can't believe it. I've got eighteen pages. I'm so exhausted." She slumped forward, face down on the desk.

"Me too. And hungry. What's for dinner?"

Addy rolled her forehead back and forth across the blotter, shaking her head no. "I have no idea. All circuits are on overload." She rolled to rest on her left cheek and peered up at her sister without lifting her head. The paper was scratchy against her face. Her body wanted to go to sleep, but her brain was still electrified. It was a discordant feeling.

"Fine. I'll order a pizza," Lacey said, rolling her eyes. "Some parent you're turning out to be."

They ate the pizza in the kitchen, standing at the counter and looking out the window at the back garden. The rain had stopped at some point, and the sky had begun to clear from the west as the sun sank toward the horizon. The clouds in the east looked as if they were lit up from the inside, lavender and gold and apricot. The last white blooms on the dogwood glowed in the rose-colored light.

"I'm going for a walk," Addy said.

"Not me," Lacey said. "I'm going to vegetate and watch junk television."

"Mother said to remind you to do your homework."

"Yeah, right. I'm practically finished with high school. Homework is the least of my concerns."

"Lacey," Addy said. "Seriously, don't blow it off now. Don't ruin your record."

"You sound like Mother."

Addy looked back out the window. "God forbid. Do whatever you want—you're on your own. I need to get some fresh air."

She threw on a pair of capris and a thin sweater, put her earbuds in, and went outside, leaving Lacey on the couch. The air was clean and soft, and smelled like green growing things. She headed down the street, picking her way around puddles and watching for twigs and slick pine needles that had blown down. As her muscles loosened up and the Charleston piped into her ears, her mind quieted, and she picked up the pace.

She walked for an hour, intentionally not thinking about the writing she'd done and instead focusing on the breeze that ruffled her curls and the occasional hiss of tires on wet pavement. The crape myrtles that lined the driveway by the golf course were fully leafed out, but it would be a few weeks yet before the full heat of summer coaxed them into bloom. The crinkly pink flowers would eventually litter the ground, then the leaves would burnish and fall. She'd been walking this neighborhood her whole life, but she'd never seen the crape myrtles so clearly.

She reached up to touch one of the lime green leaves, and a shower of droplets fell on her face. Addy wiped her cheeks, then went home and fell into bed. She slept fitfully, and woke up early Sunday morning, determined to push through to the end of the prospectus.

By lunchtime, when Lacey came downstairs, ready to head back to the theatre, Addy was proofreading the final pages. She had done it. She had constructed a proposal that seemed to make sense, and ahead of schedule. The accomplishment boosted her confidence—she composed a breezy email, attached the document, and hit send. Dr. McGregor would be impressed. That warranted an afternoon of shopping, she was certain.

Chapter 9

Monday morning, Addy parked in front of her grandmother's house. She hadn't yet heard anything from Dr. McGregor about the prospectus, of course, but the weekend's momentum was still energizing her. Even Eleanor's cleaning in the kitchen late the night before, ever trying to be the martyr, had failed to undermine her confidence. She had drawn up a list of things she wanted to know about the elusive Great-Aunt Martha, and was on a mission to find whatever evidence she could about the woman's life. There had to be more in Grandmama's house than she'd found on her first foray.

She threw open windows as she walked through the little bungalow, hoping the fresh air would blow out the dust and keep her on track. It felt strange to be touching things, invading her grandmother's space and belongings, even though she'd spent half her childhood here. It was Grandmama's absence, she supposed, that made the place seem remote and strange. She popped in her earbuds; perhaps she could convince her brain to ignore the lurking sense that she was ultimately going to be responsible for cleaning out the entire house. She pulled out the list; having it in front of her would help. Having Asia's promised help would be good too, but she still hadn't seen any sign of her since their conversation Thursday evening.

Teenagers, Addy thought.

Opening the old junk drawer that she'd loved playing in as a child, she rummaged for a roll of masking tape. It was full now of twist ties and canning jar lids—no tape. Her grandmother hadn't canned anything in years. Addy remembered watching her stir down blackberry jam in a wide pot, the sticky purple-red juice burbling and popping. It was hot, messy work, but Grandmama Nellie had made that jam for years, filling their pantry. Other kids had grape or apple jelly on their peanut butter sandwiches, oozing out in translucent blobs, but Addy and later Lacey always had that thick, sweet jam full of seeds, barely spreadable. It never oozed out of the sandwiches Eleanor made for them, cut into tidy squares.

Addy pushed the drawer shut. Why in the world had she saved all this junk? What was it about old people that made them all become hoarders? She'd seen enough estate collections and piles of "treasured family heirlooms" to know it wasn't just her grandmother; there seemed to be some universal compulsion to hang onto everything in the twilight years. Her mind was tipping over into maudlin now, she could feel it. This kitchen had been the heartbeat of Grandmama Nellie's home, maybe even of Addy's life. This was where she had finger-painted and eaten peanut butter out of the jar and washed her feet in the sink and made instant lemonade to sell on the corner. Life at home had been particular, careful, punctuated by her mother's fastidious sense of propriety.

Addy caught herself. *Focus!*

She rummaged around in a desk drawer until she found an old roll of Scotch tape, all sticky and warped with age. Trying to escape the pull of nostalgia, she headed into the back bedroom where she and Lacey had often slept, and put her list up on the wall so she could see it.

She had remembered the night before that the nightstand set between the twin iron bedsteads in this room was actually a cedar chest, covered with a lace-edged linen cloth. Somewhere in the deep recesses of her mind, she had a vague memory of Grandmama telling her it was covered up so the lid would stay closed.

Addy gently set the matching Victorian-style globe lamps with pink glass shades painted with gaudy flowers on the floor. They left blank circles on the yellowed linen cloth. She slid it off carefully, trying not to kick up a cloud of dust, and tucked it under the equally grimy dust ruffle of one of the beds. Lifting the lid of the chest, she saw that it was, like the rest of Grandmama Nellie's papers, tidily organized into bundles. One end was covered in tissue paper. She lifted a corner and saw a neat pile of fabric—laces and silks and wools. Her fingers itched to pull them all out, but she tucked the tissue back into place. With any luck, there were some bits she could wear, but vintage-clothes exploring would have to wait.

She carefully began excavating the papers. Each bundle was tied with a length of twine. She'd need scissors to cut it, but for now she could tell at a glance what each contained. The organization system was the same here as it was in her bedroom closet. Each packet was devoted to one family member—but these went further back.

Addy scanned through the piles, going backward in her family tree from Nellie to Granddaddy Sumner, back to Granny Isabella and her husband, whom Eleanor had always called Papa McLean even though Addy knew he'd died long before Eleanor was born. She wasn't sure if her grandmother had even remembered him, since, if she recalled correctly, he had died when Nellie was very young.

That was the bottom of the pile. Addy sat back against the bed, holding Granny Isabella's papers in her lap. Damn. She'd been hoping to find at least something left from Martha's life. She flipped through the tops of the pages without untying the bundle, trying to confirm the loose family tree she'd worked out in her head. Martha had been a Cameron, the sister (Younger? Older? She'd love to know, not that it mattered) of her great-grandmother, Isabella, who had married a McLean. She didn't know his first name and didn't know anything about their respective families. She did know that they'd had one child, her grandmother, who had married George Sumner. They'd also had one child, her mother. Two successive generations of only children was an odd pattern for the time period, she realized now, thinking about it. She felt a small swell of affection for Lacey. Eleanor was a burden best shared.

Toward the back of the pile, she found Isabella's marriage license, her name and that of Angus Norman McLean written out in old-fashioned calligraphy, the letters difficult to decipher. They'd married in 1921. She wished there was a photograph; she could only imagine that they'd come from the hardy, frugal Scots-Irish stock that had settled in Appalachia back when North Carolina was just a colony.

Next in the pile was a small, oddly-sized piece of paper covered in recipes, handwritten in pencil, for what appeared to be home remedies—a spring tonic, a milk soup "for convalescents," a calf broth that purported to "strengthen the blood," and a tea "to bring on the milk." Addy grimaced, and flipped the page over.

There was one last item in the bottom of the chest: a cigar box tied with more twine. It had a little heft in her hand. She settled the box on her lap and carefully slid off the string. Bits of the box's paper covering flaked off into her lap. Carefully, she lifted the lid, and was disappointed to see that there wasn't much inside, just a few papers, and under them, a bible.

But the papers, when she unfolded them, were pay dirt. On top was an obituary notice of the death of Martha Rose Cameron, of Madison County, in June of 1925. She'd died only six months after she was fired. There was no other information; it was no more than a blurb, succinct and impersonal. Addy held the crumbling scrap of newsprint between two fingers, shocked. Her first thought was suicide. Would that explain the lack of information in the obituary? Had the family tried to keep it quiet?

She looked around her grandmother's guest bedroom and reeled in her imagination. In 1925, it could've been anything. She'd seen enough about living conditions in the hollows and backwoods of the surrounding mountains during the Depression to know that life couldn't have been easy, even before the economy tanked. She wondered where in Madison County Martha had lived. It was odd to think this was her relative; she'd always felt, acutely, the socio-economic divide between Asheville and the surrounding countryside. Madison County was deeply rural, and always had been to her knowledge.

The next slip of paper was a tiny waxy envelope, smaller than a playing card. It was obviously a lock of hair, but she peeked inside anyway, curious. It was dark brown, tied with a thin gold thread. She touched one hand to her own curls of the same chestnut shade. The genetic connection—because it obviously had to be Martha's hair, hidden away in this old cigar box—struck her again. She put the little packet down.

Next up were several condolence letters, all addressed to Isabella. She skimmed them quickly. The first, in loose, shaky handwriting, was from Ephraim Cameron. It was addressed to "Daughter," and expressed condolences for the loss of her sister, but not much in the way of sympathy. At the end, he encouraged her to continue to read her bible. Addy quickly counted back the generations—this had to be her great-great-grandfather. He sounded like an uptight ass. She wondered if the bible in her lap was the one her great-grandmother had read. She'd saved these mementos of her sister's death—how had it affected her? Had it been a tragedy, or an embarrassment, or an expected end? That hadn't occurred to Addy before. Maybe Martha had been fired because of an illness. Tuberculosis still ran rampant in those days, or maybe it was some other lingering misery. Cancer or polio or even pellagra would've been disfiguring and debilitating. Addy flipped to the next slip of paper, shoving aside her emotional investment in the scenario that was playing out in her head. She needed more information.

The next letter was from someone named Lottie. It was sympathetic, but said nothing revealing. Addy wondered who Lottie was, and put it to the side. The last one was on monogrammed stationery. The signature was that of R. M. Britton. Addy stared at it, disoriented for a second, and again had to calculate the generations. This must be Micah's—her Micah's—grandfather. The man who had fired Martha had sent a sympathy letter to her sister six months later. How interesting. She reached up and put the letter on the bed, intending to show it to Micah next time she saw him.

She glanced at her watch and found she'd been sitting on the floor for an hour, and had made no real discoveries except the date of Martha's death. It might not be useful for her research, but it would make an interesting tidbit to share with Eleanor and Lacey.

She flipped open the bible, half wondering if there was a family tree or anything else written in the front where people often kept family records, but there was nothing. This was the size of a normal book, the leather binding terribly cracked. It looked well-read. As she gingerly flipped through the pages, bits and scraps fell out: a pressed pansy, a four-leaf clover, a ticket stub from a baseball game. It looked like the usual memorabilia of a young woman's life tucked away for safekeeping. Perhaps she hadn't been chronically ill after all.

Tucked inside the back cover was another envelope, stuffed full of more folded paper. Underneath it was a slim packet tightly wrapped in a single sheet of newspaper. Addy unfolded the crumbling newspaper to find a sturdy, yellowed envelope smaller than a manila envelope, but larger than a normal letter-size. In the upper left-hand corner were several notes in faded pencil: *RMB*, followed by the date, *June 23, 1924*, the word *burn*, in tiny block print, then the initials *MRC*. Martha, she assumed. She flipped it over, finding the back flap was monogrammed with a highly stylized, curlicue *ZSF*. She carefully withdrew a sheet of thin, old-fashioned onion skin paper. The handwriting was bold but inconsistent, with strong, looping strokes in the first half, while in the second half, sloppier cursive alternated with childish printed words. There were just enough similarities to suggest it was all one hand; it was as if the author had been interrupted, and returned in a completely different mood.

Sugar—

"If you forget me, think of our gifts to Aphrodite and all the loveliness that we shared." —Sappho

We are snug as bugs in a sweet little bungalow on the coast. Our village is not far from Nice, not far from the ceaseless activity of the port, the ships, the eternal striving of human industry. I know you're here, somewhere, sipping the sweet nectar of the honeyed moon, but when I look over the bay, toward the town, I can't imagine you there, outside of your celestial aerie.

Our neighbors are all wildly urbane and glamorous, and fond of a glittering soirée, but your particular variety of elegance—your calm grace, the ease born, not of noblesse oblige, but of a broader, more genuine humanity—is sadly lacking. The witty conversation goes on all night, but without that true meeting of the minds that so enraptures.

Here the handwriting made its sudden switch.

Scott does vex me so sometimes. He has taken up with a group of flyboys, all agog at their feats of derring-do. Really they're just barnstormers, at loose ends since the war ended. I fear he may try to join them, if his inspiration doesn't return soon. He claims the scirocco has driven it away, but I suspect the gin may be to blame. I cannot bring myself to expect a response to this missive any more than the previous three (my foolish heart can't help but keep a tally), as I know you are yet away with John, but I have enclosed a little tale. If it should offend, do credit it to the workings of a fevered brain. The heat here does beat all, as my mama would say.
Do love me, darling—love me do.
Z.

Addy was utterly befuddled. Was this a love letter to Martha? Who in the world was Z? She reread the letter, considering the Sappho quote. Maybe that was why Martha had been fired—she'd been in love with a woman who went by the initial Z. Something didn't fit, though. The letter-writer referred to the recipient being away with John. And the language was all wrong. Addy looked back at the condolence letter from Ephraim Cameron. It was difficult to reconcile such disparate writing styles being directed to one woman. Something didn't fit, but perhaps that was part of the explanation.

Glancing at the next thin sheet of onion skin, she could see it was the "little tale" the letter alluded to. Typewritten text covered three pages. At the top was the title "The Diamond in the Magnolia." Scrawled to one side was this penciled note:

The Murphys have a typewriter, of course they do. I roll my eyes at the notion of serious work under this azure sky. Nonetheless, I am burning through the ribbons, inspired, no doubt, by the flights of fancy woven by the pilots we've been entertaining. Scott seethes. This little bit of fluff is for you.

Addy skimmed the pages, mindful of the time, but intrigued. It was, as the headnote indicated, nothing but a little bit of fluff. Even Addy, with no real expertise in literary appraisal, could see that. It was a heavy-handed morality tale about the perils of missed opportunity, sort of "The Ant and the Grasshopper" turned upside down. When she got to the end, she turned the pages back over and began again.

She'd been hoping for something that would tell her about Martha's employment at Biltmore and why she'd been fired, but this was useless. She glanced again at her watch, and realized she'd frittered away the whole morning and gotten nowhere. Her eyes were grainy from the dust and poor light. She needed a break. She had seen an adorable pair of flowered linen pedal-pushers in the window of a boutique on Lexington. They had sort of a mid-sixties vibe, which wasn't usually her thing—she preferred more of a flapper look—but with a sweet blouse, they'd be perfect for lounging around, or even a casual date. A couple of hours of shopping would be just the thing.

Chapter 10

The next day, wearing her new outfit, Addy met Micah for lunch at a sandwich shop near his office. They stood in line to order, each looking around the room in different directions. It wasn't till they'd gotten their drinks and sat down that Addy was ready to deal with the unspoken tension.

"So. I never expected to be having lunch with you. Before your office last week, the last time I willingly spoke to you, you were busy getting me kicked out of school."

Micah grimaced. "I know. Like I said the other day, I'm really sorry."

"You didn't, actually."

He looked confused.

"You never said you were sorry. My mother changed the subject like she always does."

Micah blinked at her, and she noticed again that a shadow seemed to darken his eyes. They'd made her heart pound years ago, those eyes, until they made her want to spit with anger. It was confusing now, all the memories of breathless infatuation and heartbreak and self-righteous anger that had calcified over the intervening years.

"Well, I am. I'm very, very sorry. I have no excuse, except that I was young and stupid. Hopefully, I've grown up a little since then."

They had collaborated, when Addy was a junior and Micah a senior, on a letter to the editor of the local newspaper, accusing their exclusive private school of accepting funding from a tobacco company. The letter itself, which, at the last minute, Micah had chickened out of signing, was the final step in a campaign they'd waged anonymously over months, trying to pressure the school to stop accepting money from an industry that they nominally discouraged in the classroom. The paper in the capital, with a much larger readership, had picked up the story, and while the pressure had worked, it had also resulted in the headmaster declaring that Addy wasn't "Asheville School material." Eleanor had taken to her bed for a week, and barely spoken to Addy for another month after that. Even Grandmama Nellie, who was generally unflappable, seemed embarrassed. No one in Addy's family had mentioned it since.

Addy shook her head once, to clear it. She'd been nursing that hurt for a full decade, but the raw spot didn't seem to be where she thought it was. "Fine," she said, grudgingly. "Apology accepted. Even though you really were an ass."

"I know. That's all I can say. It's been bothering me for years. I was hoping maybe we could put it behind us since we're both back in town. Especially since we're going to have to communicate about your grandmother's estate."

"I know." Addy looked at him for a long moment. "If I'm totally honest, it wasn't the end of the world. I hated being in private school. You didn't exactly convince me to write that letter. I thought I'd rather sacrifice myself on the burning pyre of my ideals than suffer through another day of socio-economic elitism."

"Believe me, I remember the idealism. You were the righteous sword of justice. And was public school the egalitarian utopia you thought it would be?"

"It was a mosh pit. Just as cliquey, just as soul-killing. The grass is always greener, I guess. On the bright side, I think I'm a better teacher because of it. I saw a lot at Roberson that I never would have seen at the Asheville School. So, okay. You're forgiven."

"Excellent." He picked up the sandwich that had been delivered to the table and bit into it. "So tell me what you're working on. I've been buried in my dad's files for almost a year now, and I keep forgetting there's a world outside of Asheville."

"I'm not going to be very entertaining, then. I'm writing about"—she sat up tall and did her best droning professor imitation—"Patriarchal Repression of Working Women in Rural Appalachia. Strictly early twentieth-century, but that's too much of a mouthful. I think."

Micah grimaced. "Not exactly high excitement, then. Maybe I'll stick my head back in the wills and small claims."

"No, not high excitement at all. I'm kind of dreading the actual writing of the thing."

"Then why are you doing it?"

She put her sandwich down and looked at it. As so often happened, her blabby mouth had opened her up to a question she didn't want to think about. She pushed the scattered sesame seeds into a tiny pile. "My dissertation director got a bee in her bonnet about this letter I found from some old great-aunt that I never knew. Diane McGregor; you probably don't recognize her name, but she's kind of a big deal, academically. She specializes in letters. Anyway, I think she sees me kind of following in her footsteps. So it's probably the right thing to do—take her advice on the topic and crank it out over the summer. I don't want it to drag on forever like some people do, you know?" She reached up with her left hand to fluff her hair a bit, sensing her ears had gone dark red.

Micah looked suitably impressed. "So what will you do after you graduate? Will you come back here and teach at the university?"

She waved a hand. "Heavens, no. I have no idea, just depends on what kind of offers I get. Anyway, moving right along. Have you figured out anything else about my grandmother's house? You said there's some kind of condition on it?"

"Yes. I haven't quite figured it out yet, actually. I was trying to ask Dad if he knew anything about it, but he's had a couple of difficult days. Basically, there's a perpetuity that says if the conditions of the agreement are violated, the house will revert to its original ownership. It's the conditions that are still unclear."

"What do you mean, original ownership? Who else owned it?"

Micah cleared his throat. "Well, that's another tricky detail. The only other signature on the document besides Isabella McLean's—your great-grandmother, right?—is my grandfather's. Maybe he had power of attorney for someone else? I'll get to the bottom of it, I promise. It just might take me a couple more weeks."

Addy shrugged. "It's not as if my mother is going to have it cleaned out and ready to go on the market any time soon. I was hoping we could get it done while I'm in town—I assume I need to be involved in the sale?"

"Just signatures. That's easy enough to manage from anywhere. Assuming y'all are in agreement, that is."

"And therein lies the rub."

Micah nodded, and that shadow flickered around the corners of his eyes again. He seemed lost in thought.

"I'm sorry about your dad, by the way. I meant to tell you that the other day. I can't imagine how difficult it must be."

He nodded again.

"How's your mom doing?"

"She copes. We have a helper for Dad around the clock. I don't think she likes having someone in her space, but she can't do it herself, and she won't let him go to a nursing home."

"That part I can relate to. My mother ran herself ragged taking care of Grandmama there at the end. She said she didn't want people to think she couldn't take care of her own mother."

"That physical stuff isn't so taxing with the home health care person always there. The worst of it is shutting down the law practice. He inherited it from his dad, and there are still open files from before the Second World War. I have to go through every one, and make sure our responsibility has been fulfilled before I can dispose of the files. The sheer quantity of paper is unbelievable."

"Oh, I know. Grandmama's house is like that. I believe she saved bank statements from before my mother was born. I told Mother, 'If it's older than you are, and you've never seen it, we probably don't need to keep it.'"

"Are you going to be able to talk her into the auction?"

"I don't know. I'll keep working on it, but she's totally distracted and difficult right now. Lacey's about to graduate, and they both have high celebratory expectations, but they can't agree on what that will look like. Honestly, I think on some level Mother's still wigged out about Lacey being gay."

Micah frowned at her. "Come on, Addy. Your parents aren't like that. This is Asheville. It's 2015."

"I know it sounds ridiculous. Daddy doesn't seem to care at all—I think he kind of likes Asia, when he pays attention. But no, I think Mother is still kind of grappling with it. Maybe not the theory, but the reality. Specifically, the girlfriend."

"What do you mean?"

"Well, I think as long as Lacey wasn't in anyone's face about it, Mother could kind of ignore it. It's when the girlfriend is around that she gets really difficult."

"She didn't like me all that much either, if I recall correctly."

"She loved you. She just didn't love us making out on the front porch."

Micah gave her a wicked grin. "Good thing she didn't see what we did in the back seat of my car, then."

Addy chuckled. "Yeah, well, if she ever stumbles across Lacey and Asia *in flagrante*, which is entirely possible because they're totally lovey-dovey, I suspect she'll have a heart attack. Her histrionics are actually the only embarrassing part of it all. Poor Asia."

"Tell her she has my sympathy. I've been the outsider with your mother."

"I will. She's agreed to help me with some research. The census data from the time period I'm looking at isn't online, so I need to go through all these microfiches at the State Archive. It feels a little like busywork, but I've got a tiny stipend from my department, so I thought I'd hire her as a research assistant. She seems like she's kind of at loose ends, with Lacey in rehearsals all the time."

"That's handy. What do you need census data for?"

"Employment statistics."

Micah looked at a point somewhere over Addy's head, and his eyes darted back and forth, as if he was scanning a book. "I might be able to help. I've got a buddy from law school who's at the Labor Department now. Shall I see if he has access to anything useful?"

"Would you? That would be fantastic. I'm on a deadline, so I'm trying to get a lot of research done in a very short time."

"Sure. But why the deadline?"

She waved him off. "Just typical graduate school scheduling issues. And I need to be back in D.C. for the fall semester. It would be great if your friend had anything I could use." She pushed her chair back from the table. "This was nice, Micah. I'm glad we're on a clean page."

"Me too. Are you in a rush?"

"A bit. That whole deadline thing, you know?" She stood up.

"Of course. Shall we do this again, maybe next week?"

Addy looked at him. For a second, it felt like time had collapsed in on itself, and her heart thudded. The moment had gone before she could see it clearly. "I'll text you," she said, and walked away, not giving him a chance to argue.

Chapter 11

Addy drove slowly, thinking. It had been a frustrating afternoon. She'd gone to her grandmother's house looking for something—anything—she could use to link Martha's firing to the premise of her dissertation. She had plundered the desk in the kitchen, and Grandmama's nightstand, as well as the bookshelves in the den. She was looking for pay stubs, tax records, letters home from Martha's time on the estate—something to give texture to her story, which Addy planned to make the introduction to her paper. But she'd come up empty-handed, and was beginning to worry that she wouldn't be able to make the connection clear without more documentation.

The entire paper—how long? Would two hundred pages be enough? Three hundred? Her shoulders crept up toward her ears at the thought of composing all those sentences, stringing them together, one after another. The whole thing was going to have to be based on the statistics and writings of others, people who were more competent, more dedicated, more creative than she was.

There. She'd hit on the sensitive spot: this whole topic made her feel about as creative as an old boot. How had she gotten herself into this awful position, having to write about something that made her yawn? It was all so wearying and bitter.

Being in her grandmother's house didn't help. It reminded her of how much she missed her grandmama, and of the knowledge, finally sinking in, that it really was going to fall on her to get the house cleaned out and sold. She couldn't go there, couldn't let herself think about that project, or she'd lose the little bit of momentum she had on the dissertation. She shoved the worries about the house to the back of her mind.

She'd brought a few of the things she'd found with her, mostly in a futile attempt to feel productive. She had the sympathy note from Micah's grandfather to show him, and see if maybe there was some explanation in the law firm's files.

She'd hung onto the perplexing short story and accompanying note as well. She thought about the note, letting her mind drift out from under the gloomy weight of the dissertation. The more she thought about it, the more she wondered who Z was. The monogram on the back of the envelope stared up at her from where it lay on the passenger seat. Something about the letter was nudging at her brain. Pulling onto the shoulder of the road, she tipped the pages out of the envelope and skimmed the letter again. Perhaps it was just the change of perspective, being in the car, out of the maudlin atmosphere of the little bungalow, but the names began ringing bells—the Murphys, Scott. She pulled out her phone and began googling.

Several minutes later, Addy folded her hands together in the attitude of prayer to stop them from trembling. In her wildest dreams, she could not have hoped to find a letter from Zelda Fitzgerald, but all the pieces fit. She reread it, her certainty growing.

The timing worked. In June of 1924, the Vanderbilt's only daughter Cornelia had been on her three-month honeymoon—*the honeyed moon*—in Europe with John Cecil. Scott and Zelda Fitzgerald were on the French Riviera. So the text all seemed to make sense. Besides, the sentence about Scott and his "inspiration" sealed the deal: *I fear he may try to join them, if his inspiration doesn't return soon.*

Which meant…

She looked at the short story again, wondering if it had ever been published. In high school, Addy had idolized Zelda Fitzgerald, dressing in flapper clothes and styling herself a rebel against convention. Zelda's tragic death by fire, just a few miles away, had been easy enough to ignore. There was a certain disconnect between the charmed life of the Jazz Age darling and the broken, abandoned woman who had perished, locked in her room in a mental institute.

She knew, though, that she didn't have the academic expertise to understand whether these papers were really of any significance. She was no Fitzgerald scholar, just a fan. Idle speculation was just another way that her brain was trying to distract her. She folded the papers back into the envelope and dropped it back onto the passenger seat, covering it with her document list, as if removing it from her view would force it out of her thoughts.

She guided her car back into the flow of traffic, at the same time guiding her thoughts back into their familiar loop of worry and self-doubt.

Dinner that night was a strained affair. Lacey's show—her last with the high school drama department—was coming up in a few days, and the pressure of rehearsals, behind schedule because of a spring snowstorm, combined with the prospect of graduation three days after the show, made Lacey grumpy and a little demanding. Addy had no idea why Eleanor was tense, but it wasn't unusual enough to hold her attention for long. She found her mind wandering, withdrawing from Lacey's loud control of the conversation.

The letter from the mysterious Z was upstairs, on her desk. She kept telling herself it might have nothing to do with Zelda Fitzgerald, but on some level, she didn't believe that at all. It had to be from Zelda. She felt as if she were on a roller coaster, alternately flying to the top with excitement, then hurtling to the depth of stress. With her fork, she idly pushed a tiny new potato around on her plate, only half seeing the trail it made through the white wine sauce that had pooled next to her untouched piece of chicken.

She must have sighed out loud without realizing it.

"Addy? What's on your mind?"

She looked up at her father's voice and realized everyone at the table was watching her.

"Oh. Well, I'm not sure what it is. I found something at Grandmama's house. I think it's kind of a big deal. I mean, I don't want to make too big a fuss, but..."

"Tell us already," Lacey said. There was more than a touch of sarcasm in her voice.

Addy ignored it, making sure they were all three looking at her before she spoke. "It's a letter from someone who signed with the letter Z. And—get this—there was a short story with it."

They all waited, expectant. She hesitated, aware before she'd even said the words, how implausible they would sound.

"I think the Z might be Zelda Fitzgerald. I think I found a story by Zelda Fitzgerald in her own handwriting."

She looked around the table at them. Lacey had tipped back in her chair. Eleanor's face had the mouth-only smile that meant she was listening because it was the polite thing to do. Only Mason looked as if he understood the significance of what she'd just said. He put his knife and fork down and leaned forward, elbows on the table.

"What makes you think it's by Zelda Fitzgerald?" he prodded.

"I don't know exactly. It mentions Scott, and the Murphys, and Nice, and writing, I think. There's a monogram on the envelope—ZSF. Her maiden name was Sayre. It's just a hunch."

"You're talking about *the* Zelda Fitzgerald who died at Highland Hospital?" Eleanor asked. "That sounds awfully far-fetched to me. Why would my mother have had any correspondence with anyone from that place?"

"I don't think it had anything to do with Grandmama," Addy said. She'd been wondering something similar herself, but hadn't yet been able to make sense of it. "When was she born?"

Eleanor's lips were a thin line.

Addy knew she'd asked a touchy question; age, like money, cancer, politics, and about a hundred other topics, was taboo in Eleanor's mind. But she managed to answer, pushing the words out as if they tasted bad. "Sometime in the 1920s, I suppose."

"I still have the bulletin from the funeral. I could check," Lacey said.

"No, it's fine," Addy said. "The letter is dated in June of 1924. Clearly it had nothing to do with Grandmama. It was mixed in with a bunch of stuff that was Granny Isabella's, I think."

"Even so," Eleanor said, "I still fail to see why any relative of mine would've had anything to do with an inmate at Highland Hospital."

"They weren't inmates, Mother. They were patients," Addy said. "But you're not listening, this letter was written in 1924. Zelda Fitzgerald wasn't at Highland until later, I think."

"Wait, I'll tell you," Lacey said, typing into her phone.

"Not at the table, Lacey," Eleanor said. She seemed to be trying to respond to everyone at once, as if she could shepherd them all back onto more comfortable ground.

"1936," Lacey said.

"Where did you find it?" Mason asked.

"In the big cedar chest in the back bedroom."

"What cedar chest?" Lacey asked.

"Between the beds," Eleanor said, her face still tight. "What were you doing in that old thing, Addy?"

"Mother. We're going to have to go through all of it eventually. Sooner rather than later." All the air went out of her. "Not that it matters. The whole thing is an interesting tidbit, but I don't have time to screw around with it right now."

"Wait. If this is a story by Zelda Fitzgerald, wouldn't it be worth a lot of money?" Lacey asked.

"Maybe," Addy said. "If it really is what I think it is, and if it can be authenticated, and if—" She put both hands up, as if to stop Lacey from pursuing it. "I really can't afford to be distracted. Whatever it is, it'll still be there when I finish my dissertation. I'll think about it then."

"You didn't leave it over there at the bungalow, did you? I'd be worried about mildew," Mason said.

Eleanor glared at him.

"No, it's upstairs. I didn't want it to get misplaced in the shuffle over there."

"I don't think it matters anyway," Lacey said. "I mean, the more I'm thinking about it, what are the chances you've found an old Zelda Fitzgerald story? Even I know enough to know that doesn't just happen. You probably have a better chance of winning the lottery."

Addy looked down at her plate. She knew, of course, that Lacey was right. She was getting her hopes up over something that would turn out to be a ludicrous fantasy.

"Lacey's right," Eleanor said. "The whole notion that my mother was hanging on to a letter from some disreputable flapper who had to be locked up—it's all foolishness. No one in my family would have gotten involved with people like that."

Something galvanized in Addy. She gave her mother a long, hard look. "Well, don't let it worry you, Mother. I'll hang on to it. At least till I get through my research. Speaking of which"—she turned deliberately to Lacey—"have you heard anything from Asia?"

Lacey's face darkened. "No. She's not answering my texts or anything. Her fosters are psycho. I bet they're punishing her for something and took her phone."

"Fosters?" Addy said. "I thought she lived with her aunt and uncle."

"Same thing. Her parents died in a car accident when she was little, and her mother's sister and her husband agreed to foster her. It's not like they did it out of the kindness of their hearts or anything. They get a check from the government and a live-in babysitter. They get pissed whenever she doesn't fit in with their ideas about the perfect little family. They took her bandana last time, and threw it away. I bet they've taken her phone now. Assholes."

"Lacey," Eleanor said sharply. "Language."

"Whatever," Lacey said, pushing her chair back from the table with a scrape. "I'm done."

Chapter 12

Addy woke up the next morning out of sorts. She'd sat up late, plundering the internet for information about the Fitzgeralds and their connection to Asheville, which seemed to be neither well-documented nor a particular point of civic pride. Then her sleep had been broken by her least-favorite recurring nightmare, in which she walked into a classroom full of waiting students and realized they had all done the reading, but she hadn't. Knowing that it was a classic response to anxiety didn't make it any less troubling in the middle of the night.

It took her a while to get settled at her desk with a second cup of coffee. When she saw all the tabs still open on her computer from the night before, she closed them quickly before she could get distracted. Glancing at her email, she saw the one she'd been waiting for from Dr. McGregor.

```
Addy—the prospectus looks good. I've
approved it and sent it on to the rest of the
committee for their signatures, but that's
just a formality. Once all the signatures
have been collected, you should receive an
```

```
official notification from Dr. Torrisi that
your prospectus has been filed.

You're doing great—just stick to the schedule
we worked out, and you'll be fine.
```

So it was official. Now all she had to do was write the three hundred or so thoughtful, original, well-researched pages.

The thought left her cold.

She clicked over to Dr. McGregor's timeline (that 'we worked out'? That was the very definition of revisionist history) and calculated, again, how many days she had left. By finishing the prospectus a few days early, she'd bought herself a little bit of cushion, at least within the framework of Dr. McGregor's schedule. The fact that it was her own fault that she was, at this point, calculating her status in days rather than months—well, it was too late to be dwelling on that now. The three extra days would be her carrot, the treat she could use to motivate herself when the going got tough.

She opened a new document file, labeled it "Outline," and began to work.

An hour later, her coffee gone and her butt beginning to go numb in the uncomfortable desk chair she had used in high school, she sat back, ready for a break and a stretch. She scanned back over what she'd written, steeling her mind against the insidious tendrils of anxiety that kept trying to worm their way in. She stood up, intending to walk it off, but there on the nightstand where she'd left it the night before, was the envelope containing the letter and short story.

The house below was silent—no one was around to pass judgment on how she spent her time. She'd already put in a solid hour. She had an extra day in the schedule. And she wasn't going to be able to settle back down until she'd satisfied her curiosity, and put the notion of Zelda Fitzgerald out of her head.

Addy picked up the envelope and grabbed her purse. It was time for a break.

As she pulled out of her parents' neighborhood on a beeline for her grandmother's house, Addy drove right past Micah's office. When she spotted a parking space in the next block, she pulled into it on a whim. Walking down the uneven brick sidewalk, she pondered the fact that she had no particular reason to be dropping in on him, and slowed her steps. But by the time she pulled the office's front door open, she had devised a mission.

The dim waiting room was empty; beyond it, the door to Micah's office was open, but he wasn't at his desk. She stood still for a second, feeling foolish. She'd been impulsive, again—always a mistake.

About that time, Micah's blond head poked around the door.

"Hi." He looked confused. "We didn't have an appointment, did we?"

"No, sorry. I thought I'd check in and see if you have the authorization forms for the estate auction."

"Sure. Well, we can print them out from the website." He motioned her into his office. "I could've just sent you the link."

"I was driving by anyway."

"Not a problem. Let me get them for you." He sat down at his computer and started clicking.

Addy sat down on the edge of one of the client chairs.

"I'm surprised. I didn't think your mom would come around so quickly."

Addy waved a hand vaguely in the air. "She hasn't quite, but the clock is ticking. I will be in Washington D.C. for the start of the semester, come hell or high water. If she wants my help with settling all this, we need to get a move on."

The printer spat out several sheets of paper, which Micah tidied by tapping them against his desk. "You know she'll have to sign these, right?"

"It'll be fine. She's just having trouble adjusting, that's all." She held out a hand for the forms.

Micah tapped them on the desk again. "Are you sure you aren't rushing things a little?"

"I was at my grandmother's house yesterday, looking for some pay stubs or tax forms or something, and I found a letter from Zelda Fitzgerald to Cornelia Vanderbilt." Addy closed her mouth with a little snap. She hadn't been planning to say that. The words had popped out of their own accord, and now the echo of them hung in the quiet room, taking up all the oxygen.

"I'm sorry, you found what?"

"A short story too. By Zelda Fitzgerald." Now that she'd started, she might as well tell him the whole thing. Maybe he'd know what to do with it. So she did, sketching the broadest outlines of what the letter said, and the slightly immature, derivative quality of the story.

Micah listened, his full attention making her increasingly self-conscious. "And you're certain it's by Zelda Fitzgerald?"

"Not a hundred percent, no. It's only signed with a Z, but the monogram is right. I have a hunch, and it keeps getting stronger."

Micah tapped the auction forms on the desk again. "Okay. So, do you still want these?"

She snatched them from him. "Of course I do. Were you listening?"

"Yes, but I don't see the connection. Letter, story, auction…" He looked at her as if he expected her to spell it all out.

Addy threw her hands in the air. How could a reasonably intelligent person be so obtuse?

"We have to get on with cleaning out the house. There's no telling what's in there. What if there's another story? Or a story by someone else?"

"Addy, why would your grandmother have been hoarding letters and stories by famous writers? That doesn't make a single bit of sense, and you know it." Now when he looked at her, Addy saw something suspiciously like pity in his eyes. "Grief is difficult. I've dealt with quite a few estates since I came back to Asheville, and I've learned a lot about how people come to terms with the loss of a loved one. Maybe you need to take a break from your grandmother's house for a few days. It sounds to me like you've tried to do too much, too soon."

She bristled, glaring at him. "What are you, a funeral director? Stop trying to analyze me. I'm coping perfectly well, thank you. I'm just busy."

"Exactly. Like I said, give yourself a break. Don't worry about Nellie's house for a few days. The auction has waited this long—a few more days won't matter. Give your mom a little longer to get used to the idea."

Addy rolled her eyes. "Oh, for Pete's sake, Micah. You're missing the point. If this really is Zelda Fitzgerald, which I'm certain it is, I just won the lottery." As she said the words, something clicked in Addy's brain, as if a kaleidoscope had turned a single notch, and the entire pattern had changed. She could feel her ears beginning to turn red. "That's it," she whispered. "I just won the lottery."

She bounced up out of the chair. "Remember you said you would call your buddy and see if he could get me some old labor statistics? I don't think I need them after all. I'm really sorry; I hope it doesn't cause you a problem."

"No, it's fine, but Addy, you really ought to take a deep breath. Slow down and think about whatever you're doing."

"I can't slow down, Micah. That's the whole problem, but it's okay now. I just had the most brilliant idea ever; this is it. I have to go." Holding the authorization forms in front of her like a prize, she bolted out the door before he could talk her out of what she was about to do.

Addy practically ran back to the privacy of her car. As soon as she had shut herself in, she called Dr. McGregor.

When her advisor answered in her usual smooth voice, Addy took a deep breath, then jumped in with both feet. "Dr. McGregor. I know this is out of the blue, but—" she tried to corral her thoughts. "Let me back up. Yesterday I was at my grandmother's house…"

For the second time in ten minutes, the tale tumbled out of Addy's mouth. It had already taken on a life of its own, her certainty shading the inflection, the tone. Sentences had found a pattern; this was how myth was written, meaning accreting around a grain of fact like the growth of a pearl from an inconvenient speck of grit.

She crossed her fingers and clenched her eyes shut. "I guess what I'm saying is, I think there's something here that I need to pursue. I was wondering if you could put a stop on that prospectus."

In the silence that followed, she could almost see Dr. McGregor turn toward her window, lips pursed, thinking, waiting in her familiar stillness. But this time the silence stretched on longer than Addy could bear. She felt as if everything was hanging in the balance—her future, her career, the shape her life would take going forward from this moment.

"Dr. McGregor? Did you hear my question?"

"Of course I did. I also sent you an email just this morning, regarding my acceptance of your prospectus. I trust you have checked your email?"

Addy's heart sank at the acerbic tone. She had pushed too hard, but she couldn't stop now.

"Yes, of course. And thank you. But I think this is a big deal."

Dr. McGregor spoke slowly, choosing her words carefully. "I am concerned, Addy, that you are still allowing yourself to be distracted by mirages in the desert. Such illusions are just that—illusions. They can lead only to disappointment and failure."

"I promise, Dr. McGregor, this isn't an illusion. At least, I'm nearly positive. I feel it. I can't explain why, but I have this feeling. It's so strong I almost can't breathe. I need to look more closely at this."

"I'm not suggesting you toss it aside without another thought. But this is the very definition of wild goose chase, Addy, which is precisely why I tried to steer you toward a manageable topic and a clear schedule. Your susceptibility to distraction is the entire reason you are in this situation. Now is the time to develop a habit of self-discipline."

"But I can't just ignore it."

"Postpone it. There's a difference. Put this letter away, out of sight, where you know it'll be safe. Get your dissertation done. Then you have a new project ready to go as soon as you graduate."

A young mother walked by pushing a stroller, her features blurred by the haze of luminous pollen that had settled over the windshield. Addy watched her pass. The thought of hiding the story away in a bottom drawer or even a safe-deposit box made her itch. The questions had begun to drill into her brain; she didn't think she could stop thinking about them, even for two months. She had to take the risk.

"Where is my prospectus now?"

"Like I said, I emailed you this morning. I sent it out to the other members of your committee."

"So they have it? But Dr. Torrisi doesn't, not yet, right?"

"Addy, I couldn't object more strenuously to this line of questioning."

"But I'm right? He doesn't have it yet?"

There was another beat of silence. "No, no one else has seen it yet. The department still requires paper copies at this stage, so I gave it to Judy to copy and distribute."

"Please, Dr. McGregor. Pull it back. Give me a couple of weeks—if it proves to be nothing, then I'll just pick up right where I left off."

Dr. McGregor sighed. "I want you to know that I highly disapprove."

"But you will? Thank you. Thank you so, so much."

"One week, Addy. Just one. I'll hold the prospectus for one week; that way, when you go back to it—which you will, I am confident—you won't be irreparably off track."

"One week. I can do that." She scrunched up her face, anticipating Dr. McGregor's response to her next question. "I have one more tiny little favor to beg."

"I think you've used up all of my favors!"

"I know, and I'm deeply grateful, really, but you—" She searched for the exact right words to the fine line between flattery and brown-nosing. "You're so good at networking. I was wondering if you knew who is currently the best expert on Zelda, and how I might contact that person. If I only have a week, I need to get right on it."

"Fine. I'll have to email you the contact information." Her voice was abrupt, but she had agreed.

Addy let out a small sigh of relief. "Thank you so much. Really. I won't let you down."

"I certainly hope not. Good luck, Addy. You're going to need it."

Addy clicked off her phone and tossed it onto the passenger seat, her limbs suddenly gone wobbly. It was possible that she had just alienated the one faculty member who had always been on her side.

There was nothing to do now but keep moving forward. She put the car in drive and headed back to her grandmother's house. If she could find something—anything—to back up her hunch, then maybe Dr. McGregor would give her a little more leeway. Surely there were more clues there, tucked away in the boxes and bundles that represented several generations of memorabilia.

Chapter 13

Addy let herself in through the kitchen door, dropped her things directly on the table, and in what had become routine, went from room to room opening windows. Nellie had never installed air-conditioning; it would be hot as blazes in the bungalow in August, but in late May it was perfect with the breeze blowing through, carrying the faintest hint of lily-of-the-valley.

She began in the back bedroom, for lack of a better idea, heading straight for the cedar chest she'd left hanging open the day before. There were no more papers, though, just clothes. On top, a small white cotton dress with a hand-smocked yoke had the tiny stitches picked out in red, and a pair of matching red patent leather shoes. Under that, wrapped in tissue paper, was a somber gray suit, with Chanel-style piping in black velvet, and then another, less tailored suit, in a shade that her grandmother had always called "ashes of roses." It hadn't held up well, especially the tiny pillbox hat with its three-inch veil. It looked familiar. Holding it at arm's length, Addy squinted her eyes and studied it, finally realizing where she'd seen it—in pictures. It was Grandmama Nellie's wedding dress.

She worked her way down through the pile, finding increasingly older-looking pieces, all of which looked increasingly handmade the further down she burrowed. At the very bottom was a small, neatly folded scrap of muslin. Addy unwrapped it carefully and found a badly yellowed baby's dress—perhaps a christening gown, given the lace trim and collar. Looking more closely, she could see, in spite of the age, that it had once been a treasured piece. Tiny, delicate tucks, maybe a dozen, encircled the hem and sleeves, all sewn with a thin gold thread. It was stiff and fussy, and entirely inappropriate for a baby, she thought, trying to decide who might have been christened in it, and who might have spent hours laboring over the perfect stitches. She didn't know enough about styles of baby clothes to be able to judge the age, so she wrapped the scrap of muslin back around it, and put all the clothes back in the chest.

Not sure where to look next, she checked her phone, hoping Dr. McGregor had emailed a contact, but there was nothing. She went out in the hallway and looked around with a growing sense of urgency, trying to think of a closet or trunk that she might have missed, but it was a humble house, too small for hidden spaces. There was no attic or basement to stuff secrets into, and she'd plundered every drawer and cupboard she could think of. She was still standing there debating what she might have missed, when she heard a clatter in the kitchen.

"Addison? Are you here?" Eleanor called.

"In the hallway, Mother."

Eleanor didn't answer right away, so Addy stepped into the kitchen. Her mother was flipping through the auction forms that Addy had dropped onto the table when she came in.

"What exactly were you planning to do with these?" Eleanor looked as if she'd been punched.

"Nothing, Mother." Addy slid the papers out of her mother's hand and rolled them up, tucking them in her purse. "It was a mistake. I got them from Micah, but…nothing. We got our wires crossed, that's all."

"What did you tell him?" Suspicion gave her voice a sharp edge.

"I didn't tell him anything. Calm down. Trust me, we're not plotting behind your back. Look, I'll just throw them away." She pulled the offending pages back out of her purse and dropped them into the trash can under the sink.

"What were you doing at Micah's office?"

Addy thought for a second, trying to remember exactly why she'd veered over to the curb and hopped out of the car. "It was kind of an impulse, really. I just wanted to check in." She shrugged. "I don't really have a lot of friends left in Asheville, you know? I guess I felt like I needed a little social interaction."

Eleanor was still frowning, but her posture began to relax just a little, as if her hackles were slowly going down. "Is that wise? Micah is our lawyer at the moment. I don't know if you should be mixing your social life in with my legal affairs."

"It's fine, Mother. Don't worry about it."

"Stop telling me not to worry about it. You have a history with him, and I'd rather avoid a repeat of all that embarrassment. And while we're having this little chat, I'd like to know exactly what you're hoping to accomplish over here, going through Mother's things. Have you even started working on that historical marker yet, like I asked you to?"

Addy closed her eyes, breathing in through her nose. She was not going to get sucked into her mother's histrionics, not right now. She could print out more auction forms later, when Eleanor was less volatile, if that ever happened.

"Stop worrying. The forms are in the garbage. I'll get the marker done. And as for Grandmama's papers, we talked about that, Mother. It's my dissertation—" Addy's phone pinged, telling her she had an email from Dr. McGregor. She pulled it out immediately. "Speaking of which," she said, scanning the email. "Give me a minute."

```
Addy—

This is against my better judgment, but
if you insist on pursuing this distraction
right now, you should do so in the most
efficient way possible. Dr. Myrtle Cavendish
is the leading expert on Zelda Fitzgerald's
life; she wrote Biography of a Flapper.
Email her.
```

At the bottom was an email address. Addy sat down on the loveseat that took up one side of the kitchen, and began composing an email to Dr. Cavendish.

"I suppose you've finished speaking to me now?" Eleanor asked. The sharp tone penetrated Addy's distraction.

"Sorry, it's Dr. McGregor. Let me just send this email."

She'd been mentally planning how to approach this expert for the last hour, so it only took a minute. She gave a quick summary of the letter, the title of the story, and explained where she'd found them. What she needed was some advice on how to proceed, or whether this Dr. Cavendish even thought it was plausible that Zelda would have known Cornelia Vanderbilt. She hit send.

"Sorry. Dr. McGregor gave me the name of an expert on Zelda Fitzgerald, and I wanted to get in touch with her as quickly as I could."

Eleanor had turned to the counter and was inspecting the bits and pieces Addy had pulled out of a drawer the other day. After a moment, she swept it all back into the drawer, which she closed with a little thump. It was all Addy could do not to stomp her foot in frustration. She took a deep breath, and had an idea.

"Are you listening, Mother?"

Eleanor turned around, her mouth a thin line.

"That email I just sent—it was to an expert on Zelda Fitzgerald. Dr. McGregor gave me her name. I think—" She hesitated, choosing her words carefully. "We think there's something to that letter and story I found. I'm going to spend a few days looking into it, and see if maybe I can write about that instead of the whole employment history thing."

Eleanor's eyes roved about the room, not meeting Addy's. "What does this have to do with our family?"

"I have no idea. Maybe nothing. I mean, it's inexpressibly bizarre that these things would be buried in Grandmama's cedar chest, but if there's a connection beyond that, I haven't found it. But it doesn't matter. If I can prove they're by Zelda, maybe it won't be relevant why they're here. I'm betting I can write a perfectly acceptable dissertation without even mentioning the Sumners, or the McLeans, or the Camerons, or anyone else related to us."

"Well, that's better, I suppose. And what does Dr. McGregor say about it?"

"She thinks it's a great idea," Addy said quickly. "Like I said, she just sent me the name of an expert she wants me to talk to. It's going to be fine, Mother, really."

Eleanor dusted her hands off and looked around. "Now you've gotten me all worked up and I can't even remember what I came over here for."

"Sorry about that. I was wondering, isn't there any kind of attic space, up in the eaves?"

"No, why?"

"I have to be missing something," Addy said, opening and closing kitchen cabinets yet again, even though she knew her grandmother would never have been disorganized enough to squirrel papers away behind the dinner plates or coffee cups. She opened the drawer that her mother had just closed, and pulled all the little bits of detritus back out, dumping them on the counter again.

"Addison, stop that. You're making a mess."

Addy rolled her eyes. "We can do this all summer if you want, I take the junk out of the drawers, you put it back." She re-sorted her piles: canning lids, matchbooks, several of the old-fashioned church keys that Grandmama had favored for punching holes in cans. One had a plastic cover on the handle, with the word "Hawaii" stamped on it, the gold lettering flaking off. Grandmama had never been to Hawaii, to Addy's knowledge. She wondered fleetingly which of her friends had brought it to her, the last souvenir of someone else's dream vacation. "But eventually, one of us is going to have to throw it in the garbage."

"This conversation has worn me out. I'm going home."

She did suddenly look tired, Addy thought, looking at her. As if all the color and life had drained out of her, leaving shadows under her eyes. Addy nodded. The bungalow really wasn't big enough for both of them to be having emotional outbursts.

Eleanor picked up her purse. "What else do you think you're going to find, anyway?"

"Something that would tell me about Martha's time at Biltmore. A diary, or even an old calendar, or letters. Anything."

"So you *are* still digging around in my family."

Addy threw up her hands in exasperation. "No, I'm just trying to figure out who knew Zelda Fitzgerald, and why that envelope was tucked away in the cedar chest. Here, come back to the bedroom and take a look at some of the things I found."

Eleanor stopped by the door and turned around, hands on her hips. "You know what? Never mind about that historical marker. I'll do it myself. I don't think I can trust what you say on it, anyway. I can't understand why you don't just go back to D.C. and write about something that has nothing to do with us."

Addy's jaw dropped. She didn't know what to do with that; didn't even know where to begin. Had her mother just told her to leave? Her brain couldn't process that notion. She opened a cabinet and grabbed the first jar she saw, filled it with water, and drank it all down without stopping. Then she refilled it. "I have things to do," she said, and walked out of the kitchen. Without paying attention to where she was going, she walked into her grandmother's bathroom and closed the door.

Even after two years of disuse, the tiny room still smelled faintly of Cashmere Bouquet. She heard the screen door slap closed in the kitchen; Eleanor had gone. In the silence, her thoughts threatened to coalesce into words, or tears. She pulled out her phone and put on a playlist, first letting the music spill out into the room, then, when the phone's tiny speakers wouldn't go loud enough, she put in her earbuds and turned it right up, searching for more decibels. She needed to do some mindless busy work for a little while, to stop herself from dwelling on what Eleanor had said.

Addy took a deep breath, inhaling the scent of countless summer mornings, Grandmama Nellie helping her up onto the footstool so she could wash her hands for lunch. "Don't forget under your nails, Addison. You don't want dirt under your fingernails, or people will think you're dirty." Shrugging off the memory and blinking hard, she opened the medicine cabinet and began pulling out bottles of aspirin and iodine and witch hazel. She had loved Grandmama Nellie, loved damming up the creek behind her house in the summer and building snowmen in the winter and bombing squirrels with windfall apples. Her childhood had been that little bit freer here, at this slight remove from her mother's constant worry about what the neighbors thought. She'd been inside all the neighbors' houses—mostly little old ladies like Nellie, all busy thinking about their own screwed-up lives. They were no different from anyone else in the world, but she'd never been able to convince Eleanor of that.

Eleanor didn't mean what she said, Addy told herself. *She was just being paranoid, reacting without thinking. This summer, with me back in the house and Lacey graduating, is pushing everyone's buttons.*

She closed the empty medicine cabinet, and looked at her reflection in the silvered glass of the mirror. She was caught—trapped between her mother and Dr. McGregor. The whole situation was impossible.

The shelves at the end of the bathtub were next; she attacked them grimly, tossing bottles and pots and boxes wholesale into the garbage bag. Finally, she peeled the alarming shaggy throw rug off the tiles. Its vinyl backing had begun to rot, and she had to go find the broom and sweep up little putty-colored flecks from all over the floor. But then the bathroom was empty. Just like that, the bits of her grandmother's most intimate routines were bagged up and tossed, and her own agitation had begun to settle. By the time she gently pressed the light switch down, Addy felt nothing but a hollow pang inside. What had she been hoping for here? Some great vote of confidence from Eleanor? Or even more ludicrous—some kind of insight? She might as well ask for the moon. This little bungalow held no secrets. There was nothing except the shabby remains of one woman's ordinary life. Melancholy tugged at her, but she shrugged it off. She could do denial just as well as her mother could.

Addy closed up the bungalow before she left, but instead of getting straight into her car, she sat on the steps and pulled out her phone. The little old lady across the street straightened up from the peonies she was staking, and waved. Addy waved back, but wasn't about to cross the street and chat. She didn't have enough emotional energy to put on her charming face. Besides, she was curious about the name she had gotten from Dr. McGregor.

Myrtle Cavendish was seventy-five years old, had a history of eccentricity, and lived on a goat farm outside of a town in Alabama that Addy had never heard of. The map told her it was near Tuscaloosa, but that didn't help—Addy had no frame of reference for Alabama. Seventy-five years old and quirky, though—that was a concept she understood, and it did nothing to boost her confidence. She wondered for a moment if Dr. McGregor was sabotaging her. Even if it wasn't intended that way, recommending someone who was so obviously a bit flaky was less helpful than just not giving her a name.

She'd met plenty of elderly, eccentric professors who refused to adapt to computers. As a matter of fact, the professor appellation was not essential— even Eleanor, who wasn't close to elderly, still viewed the internet with suspicion, at best. "You might as well put your private business on a billboard," she'd huffed when Lacey tried to set up a Facebook page for her.

Addy deliberated, wondering how quickly she could get a copy of the woman's book. It was too hard to search the university's database on the tiny screen of her phone, and they'd be closed now, on a Friday night in summer term. She'd have to wait a few hours.

The next day, at the university library, she found the Cavendish biography of Zelda, plus two others, as well as biographies of Scott and their good friends the Murphys, who were referenced in the pencil note scrawled at the top of the short story. Sadly, it seemed no one had ever bothered to write a biography of Cornelia Vanderbilt. She wondered why. Lack of interest? Lack of material? She jotted a note to find out whether Cornelia had kept a diary or journal.

Addy checked out what she'd found, plus Zelda's own semi-autobiographical novel, *Save Me The Waltz*, then went to a tapas bar downtown. She wasn't ready to face her mother after that comment about going back to D.C. Besides, several weeks of eating her mother's light meals, usually consisting of leafy salads and delicate fish dishes, had left her craving something heartier. Mindful of her credit card bill, she settled at the bar and ordered just enough to feel indulgent—a glass of wine and a savory Spanish omelet of potatoes and onions—and cracked open Dr. Cavendish's exhaustive account of the life of Zelda Fitzgerald.

Two hours slipped by before Addy realized her back and tailbone ached from sitting on the hard barstool. She paid up and headed home, looking forward to a long soak in the tub, where she could think through a new approach to her prospectus. Maybe she could slip into the house without having to engage in a long conversation with anyone. The biography was completely absorbing; even now, driving along Biltmore Avenue, her brain was full of Dr. Cavendish's engaging language and the train wreck that was the Fitzgerald marriage. This, then, was what Dr. McGregor had meant for her to do. The advantage of being here, in Asheville, away from the commitments and distractions of her life in Washington D.C., was that she could lose herself completely in research. Sitting at a traffic light, she pulled out her phone and put on some music. Ella Fitzgerald's rich, yearning voice filled the car, and Addy drove on, feeling more content than she had in days.

The house was quiet when she slipped in through the kitchen, so she went straight upstairs and locked herself in the bathroom. She read in the tub until the rose-scented water went cold, then she ran in more hot and soaked for a while longer. She switched over to *Save Me The Waltz*, which she had read years earlier and forgotten, and was remembering just how deeply troubled and sad Zelda's later years had been. It was utterly depressing. She let the water out of the tub and reached for her pajamas, ready to crawl into bed and read until she fell asleep.

There was a knock on the bathroom door. "Addison?" It was Eleanor.

"Just a minute, Mother."

When she was dressed, she opened the door, letting a billow of steam out into the hall.

"How long have you been in there?"

"I don't know. A long while. I was reading." She moved toward her bedroom.

"Where were you all day?"

"Working. Research. The library."

"What library?"

"The university."

"Where's Lacey?"

"Not with me." She waved a hand back toward the empty bathroom, as if to say "See?"

Addy held up the book and stepped around her mother, hoping she wouldn't ask any more questions.

Eleanor's face was perfectly neutral, perfectly still, as if their argument the day before had never happened. She had never been prone to dramatic displays of emotion; she was too proper for that. As a result, she was sometimes—often—difficult to read, and Addy sometimes—often—wanted to shake her.

She didn't believe in stuffing down feelings. She wore hers like a badge of honor. She had tried, since she hit her twenties, to be more respectful to her parents than she had been as a teenager, but being back in the same house with them was difficult. It was too easy to slip back into the instinctive patterns that had been set a decade earlier. All of this played through her mind now, watching Eleanor's still face, and feeling vulnerable in her thin robe and damp hair.

"How is your research for that historical marker coming along?"

Addy pressed her lips together, not sure whether to laugh or bang her head on the wall. Did Eleanor really think this tactic would still work on her, pretending yesterday's outburst had never happened? She stared at her mother for a second, but finding herself helpless to step out of the well-worn path they were on, she took a breath and mirrored her mother's determined civility.

"I haven't forgotten. I'll get it done. But I'm a little busy for the next few days."

"For your grandmother's sake. Since you are apparently going to auction off all her things to the highest bidder."

Addy rolled her eyes. "Stop it, Mother. You're trying to make me feel bad. I said I would do the application for the marker, I want to. Stop harassing me about it."

"Your phone has been chirping for half an hour. It's giving me a headache." With that, Eleanor went into her own bedroom and closed the door, leaving Addy standing in the hall, the loose-limbed calm of her long bath replaced by the frustrating sense that somehow she had just missed an opportunity to stand up for herself.

She got dressed and checked her phone. There was a call from an unfamiliar number, as well as several emails. She listened to the voicemail, and was surprised to hear Genevieve's voice asking if they could have lunch one day soon. Addy groaned. The thought of a solid hour of Genevieve's perky wedding updates was more than she could bear. She sent a text to the number: *Sorry, swamped with work. Maybe another time.* And put the number in her contacts so she wouldn't accidentally answer any further calls.

There was no email from Dr. Cavendish, not that she'd expected one. Addy contemplated her options, and looked back at the email she'd sent earlier. It had been a day and a half. Perhaps she should find someone else to ask. On the other hand, it had only been a day and a half. Perhaps she should wait awhile longer. At least until Monday. Perhaps this Dr. Cavendish was the kind of person who didn't check email on the weekends. It was, of course, entirely possible that she didn't actually check email at all, but Addy was going to be optimistic.

She crawled into bed with her book, intending to read until she got sleepy, but it didn't work that way. She was well into the second half of the book now, and was seeing the early evidence of Zelda's mental illness, watching the not-really-disguised narrator lose her hold on reality.

She'd read the book once before, in an undergraduate class, but that had been an academic experience, parsing sentences, deconstructing the text, analyzing the narrative structure, and looking for theoretical meaning. This reading was something entirely different, with that peculiarly changeable handwriting tucked away in the drawer of her desk. There was something intensely personal about watching the woman unravel on the pages of a book.

Addy put the book down. She pulled out the letter and short story, and looked them over again. Opening up her laptop, she tried pulling out various phrases from the story and Googling them, but found nothing. As far as the internet was concerned, this story didn't exist.

Clearly, Zelda had been—and continued to be—an intriguing figure. Her life was picked apart and documented from every angle, as evidenced by the pile of books Addy brought home from the library. But she felt compelled to add her own homage to the pile. The letter and story she'd found were yet another glimpse into the real Zelda, the woman she'd been before the illness took over. That was the woman Addy wanted to memorialize. And any doubt she'd had that they were penned by Zelda had evaporated.

She opened a new file, titled it "Prospectus-take 2," and began jotting down her thoughts. A couple of pages later, she scanned back over what she'd written, and closed the word-processing program with a sigh. It was a mess of sloppy, disjointed rambling. She couldn't write anything useful in this mood.

Her fingers hovered over the keys while she did a mental scan, trying to decide what would dispel her funk. Almost against her own judgement, she typed in the words unpublished manuscript auction, and lost herself down the rabbit hole of speculation and fantasy.

She looked at websites for auction houses, lingering over sales figures and news releases for a recently discovered story by Arthur Conan Doyle and another by Edgar Allan Poe. Then she stumbled across a website for a magazine whose mission was publishing recently discovered works by deceased famous authors. On impulse, Addy clicked on the Contact link and dashed off a quick email, just a couple of sentences, describing what she'd found. She followed other links from the magazine's website, tracking down a couple of publishing houses that had put out books in the zone of what she was envisioning for her dissertation: one about Edith Wharton and another about Carl Sandburg. Those were both promising; she jotted down the contact information on a sticky note and put it on the wall above her desk. Maybe her prospectus could do double-duty as a book proposal.

Having sent that email, she figured she might as well put out a feeler in another direction as well. She found the email address of the academic publisher that put out Dr. McGregor's books, and sent a short query. She was careful to emphasize that the documents hadn't yet been authenticated, but also mentioned her close working relationship with one of their most commercially successful authors.

She went back to the auction websites and clicked around in catalogues and price lists. A letter from Gertrude Stein had sold for a couple of thousand dollars, while one to Jack Kerouac looked as if it would soon go for many times that, if the excitement surrounding it was any indication. The figures went high enough to make her a little breathless, and she closed the tabs, almost afraid of jinxing herself with her own excitement.

When she finally turned out the light, exhausted, her dreams were stalked by an auctioneer, who kept selling off her credit hours one at a time, in that rapid-fire, impenetrable language auctioneers use. When she ran out of credits, he started selling off her family, one member at a time.

Chapter 14

Addy woke up Monday morning still in a funk. The cryptic conversation with her mother, particularly, had irritated her, and the next morning they had argued about Addy's refusal to get up and play the role of dutiful daughter at church. She was determined to shake the weekend off. She stared at her research list, chewing the inside of her cheek. There had to be another place she could look, somewhere she might be able to find something that would tell her how Martha came to acquire the story and letter. But nothing came to her, except to go back to her grandmother's house and pry up the floorboards or burrow into the walls, not that she would've gone so far to hide things. Eleanor might, of course—everything was a secret with Eleanor. But was this even a secret? That was the problem—she was bumbling around in the dark, without even knowing what she was looking for.

She gathered up her things to head over to the bungalow, for lack of a better idea, when she remembered Micah's lunch invitation from a few days earlier. Maybe it would be good to take a little break and clear her head. She'd think more clearly afterward.

Micah said he'd meet her at a taco place in the old warehouse district. What had long been an industrial wasteland was gradually being turned into art galleries and coffee shops. Addy drove slowly, taking in the gentrification of a neighborhood she wouldn't have set foot in when she lived in Asheville. When she found the taco place, she had trouble parking, and the line to get in was wrapped halfway around the building.

Micah was already in line. Addy joined him, and found herself suddenly a little tongue-tied. They waited quietly for a few minutes. The weather had fully committed to summer, finally, and Addy's dress had short, loose petal sleeves that fluttered in the breeze. The sun was warm on her arms, and it lit up Micah's hair like a halo around his head.

"You don't look much like a lawyer, you know," she said.

"You don't look much like a professor."

Addy squinted up at him, thinking about that. "Yes, I do. At least, I look like all the professors I know. In that there isn't really one right way to look."

"Is there a right way for lawyers to look?"

"Of course. Business-like. Not like you're about to go hiking."

"Everyone around here looks like they're about to go hiking."

"Exactly my point. Not very lawyerly."

"What are you about to go do?"

"Research."

"Is that a research dress?"

"For me it is. That's half the reason I do what I do. So I can wear anything I want."

Micah gave her a skeptical look, but it was their turn at the counter, so he placed the order and went to get their drinks while Addy went outside to find a table.

When he joined her, she went back to the topic. "I don't mean I'm getting a PhD so I can wear anything I want."

"I wouldn't put it past you."

"Academia is kind of a world unto itself. There's room to be a little different, which is one of the things I love about it. I've been in the academic world for so long now, I'm not sure how I'd manage outside of it. I'm not a very good conformist."

Micah grinned. "No, you never were. How's the research coming? Any progress on your brilliant idea?"

She shrugged. "It's slow, but I'm increasingly convinced that I've found an unpublished story by Zelda Fitzgerald. I started putting out some feelers over the weekend; things like this can be worth a lot of money. In addition to being a brilliant dissertation topic."

Micah sighed. "I guess you'll need me to sort out the legal status?"

"I've been a little concerned about that—I don't know much about the legalities of copyright and public domain. Do you suppose the Fitzgerald estate will claim it? It was in my grandmother's house. Doesn't it belong to us?"

"Well, probably, but there are some weird copyright laws. I'll have to look it up. And I'm afraid I haven't figured out the perpetuity yet. Sorry."

"It's not as if Mother is in a big hurry to sell. Don't stress—research is a pain—I should know," Addy said, but then a thought occurred to her. "You know, your office is one place I haven't done any research."

Micah frowned at her. "Why would you?"

"Well, think about it. I'm trying to figure out why this short story and letter were in my grandmother's house. You're trying to figure out how she wound up with the house itself. Why don't I come over to your office and help you go through the files?"

"Why would there be a connection?"

"There might not be. But frankly, I don't know where else to look at the moment, and maybe I'll at least be helping with the probate, even if I don't find anything good for my dissertation. I'm mostly waiting for email replies at this point, anyway."

"It'll be all legal mumbo-jumbo. I haven't even been through it all. It's kind of a mess."

"Oh, come on. It'll be fun. Remember when we had biology lab together, when you were a junior and I was a sophomore?"

"Right. When you wanted me to wear a Kermit mask, in solidarity with the frog we were dissecting."

Addy beamed. "I had forgotten that! I was good, wasn't I?"

Micah gave her a look full of innuendo, and she blushed all the way to the tips of her ears.

"You know what I meant," she said.

"Of course. I just like embarrassing you. Come over later in the week, if you want. Just text first, so I'll be sure to be there. And remember, you'll owe me."

When Micah left for the courthouse to file an order, Addy sat for a while longer, contemplating their conversation. She didn't know what it meant, but she had a sneaking feeling it would lead to something delightful and messy and probably guilt-inducing.

Chapter 15

The conversation with Micah was still pulling at Addy the next day. High school seemed like a lifetime ago, but in some ways, when he teased, it seemed like yesterday. Had she really let go of being so angry about the way he'd bailed on her ten years earlier? She thought about it, like pulling at a scab to see if it would bleed, but it didn't. That had all been so long ago, and they'd been so young. It would be so easy now to slip right back into their old romance, but would it be smart? Would it be fair, knowing she was going back to her life in Washington D.C. as soon as possible? Maybe it was a complication she didn't need. On the other hand, she was starting to feel a little lonely, which wasn't helped by spending too much time with her parents and sister. Maybe she and Micah could just be friends. Maybe that's what they already were, and she was overthinking it.

Eleanor had said she was going over to Nellie's house in the afternoon, as she said, "to do a little work." Addy didn't have a lot of faith in a little work, but she thought it might be a good chance to make nice with her mother. The tension between them was wearing her out. Maybe they could get back on a better footing if she spent a couple of hours doing Eleanor's bidding.

She parked her car in front of her grandmother's house and got out, feeling turbulent and a little antsy. The air felt restive. A late-spring storm was brewing, heavy clouds blooming out from behind the Smokies like a bruise. Eleanor's car was in the driveway. Addy went around to the kitchen door because she knew Eleanor didn't want her trekking in and out of the front door "for all the neighbors to see all our business."

"Mother?" Addy called.

"I'm back here, in the bedroom."

Addy hovered at the threshold, trying to read Eleanor's mood from her posture, or the air in the room. All she could figure out was that her grandmother had owned at least six pairs of bedroom slippers—house shoes, she'd called them—which Eleanor was lining up in a tidy row at the foot of the bed.

She looked up. "I didn't realize you were coming over here today."

"I've been here a lot."

Eleanor glanced up at her, eyes roving over Addy's face, but her gaze didn't linger. She shrugged. "Well. Why don't you get started on the kitchen? I've barely even looked around in there. It's—" She looked down at the slippers, then squatted down and moved the powder-blue pair to the other end of the row, next to the white terry-cloth ones with the tiny pink roses embroidered across the toe. She tidied them carefully, aligning the heels perfectly.

Addy watched her mother, frowning. "Are you okay, Mother?"

Eleanor's back stiffened. "I'm perfectly fine. I just don't know what to do with all these shoes."

"Why don't we bag them up and take them to What Goes Around? I don't mind taking them. I'll get you a receipt for your taxes."

"They're still in perfectly good condition."

"That's great. Someone will be very grateful. I'll go get some bags." She turned toward the kitchen, but Eleanor's voice stopped her.

"You can take them back to D.C. when you go."

"What? Why would I do that?"

"I don't want to see my mother's things walking around town on other people."

"Mother, that's ridiculous. They're slippers. And even I know Asheville's not that small. Besides, who cares? Do you really have a lot of friends who get stuff from charity shops?"

Eleanor turned away, crawling into the back of the closet. Her voice, when it came, was muffled. "It's run by the Junior League."

"Nice," Addy mumbled to herself. It wasn't the charity recipients whose scrutiny Eleanor wanted to avoid, it was the volunteers who ran the shop. Addy was struck with the small sadness of her mother's worry: that people would pass judgment on her based on what her dead mother had left behind. Surely the women at the thrift shop had more interesting things to think about.

"Anne Ingram helps out, and so does Rebecca Lambert. That makes me uncomfortable, the thought of them going through all of Mother's old house shoes, judging what price to put on them. No, thank you." She backed out of the closet, pulling out three more dusty shoe boxes. "Speaking of Anne Ingram," Eleanor continued, brushing a wisp of wavy blonde hair out of her eyes. "I saw her this morning at the club. She said Genevieve wanted to have lunch with you. You should call her."

"Oh, that. I already told her no when she texted."

"Addison! Why would you do that?" Eleanor stood up and faced Addy, vigorously brushing the dust from her hands.

"Because I don't want to. I have nothing in common with Genevieve." She tried to put some regret and sympathy into her voice, as if she were breaking bad news. "We were never really friends, Mother. We were just children who grew up together."

"Well, Anne is my friend, and I would prefer that you be civil to her daughter."

Right then, a soft jingle came from Addy's pocket—the tone she had set for Dr. Cavendish's emails. Her heart leapt, overruling the exasperation that had been about to boil over.

"Wait, hold that thought, Mother. This is important." She opened the email and read it quickly.

```
Ms. Quick:

    Thank you for your inquiry. I am most intrigued
    by the letter and story you describe. The
```

sentences you transcribed from the letter
are tantalizing, indeed, and I would love
to be able to tell you definitively that
you have stumbled upon previously unknown
materials penned by Zelda Fitzgerald.

In order to do so, however, I would need to
look more closely at the full texts. I am,
sadly, unable to travel easily at this point
in my life, but I would be happy to meet
with you in Tuscaloosa. I still maintain an
office at the university, as I am a faculty
member Emeritus.

Shall we say next week? I can be available on
any day that is convenient for you. Barring
that, I would be happy to look at a scan
(600 dpi resolution or better, please). I
look forward to hearing from you by return.

Sincerely,
Dr. Myrtle Cavendish

Addy grinned. This Dr. Cavendish was a surprise. It was too bad they wouldn't get to meet. Now she just needed a scanner.

"Do you have any idea where I could find a really good flat-bed scanner?" She looked up at her mother, who looked as if ice wouldn't melt in her mouth.

"Those phones are the rudest things I've ever seen in my life."

"It's work! I have an intense deadline, Mother." She frowned, typing in a search for 'scanner Asheville.'

"And whose fault is that?"

"Thanks. That's really supportive." Her plan to make amends with her mother was not going well, but she was distracted now. The deadline clock wouldn't stop ticking just to humor Eleanor.

"I know. I bet Micah has one," she said, typing out a text message.

Her mother shook her arm. "Stop that."

"I'm texting Micah to see if he has a scanner. I just said that. Stop pulling on my arm."

"Put that phone down."

Addy finally looked directly at Eleanor. "No. It's the whole reason I'm in Asheville, remember? To write my dissertation. I need to get this done."

"What does that have to do with Micah?"

"Oh, for Pete's sake, Mother. Could we not have this argument, please? Let's rewind. Go back five minutes. We were talking about Grandmama's house shoes."

"Never mind the shoes. I told you, I don't want to run into strangers wearing my mother's shoes. I'll take care of them."

"How about if I take them over to Hendersonville, and drop them off at the Goodwill there?"

"No, thank you." She stepped around Addy to the door of the room.

"You don't trust me, do you?"

"Well, how am I supposed to? You've upset the Ingrams, which matters very much to me, and now you're texting Micah, for I don't know what. I don't think you're at all concerned about what people think!"

"Of course I'm not! Why would I be?"

"Because the rest of us live here, Addison. I deal with Anne Ingram every week, at DAR meetings. We're on committees together. Micah is my lawyer— he's helping me deal with my personal, private business—my mother's estate. You can't just waltz into town and start rocking the boat." Eleanor turned and walked toward the kitchen, her back to Addy.

Addy absorbed her mother's tirade, unsure which piece was most important. The lawyer bit had gotten her attention, though. She followed Eleanor. "Micah is a lot more than your lawyer, Mother. You do remember that we dated in high school, right?"

"Oh, I remember. All too well. That's precisely what I'm talking about. All the gossip—people talking about us, behind my back."

"Whoa, that was your imagination. No one cares about my love life. They didn't then, and they barely even remember me now."

"My friends were paying attention. Believe me." She pushed open the screen door.

"Wait, where are you going, and what business is Micah dealing with, besides Grandmama's house?"

Eleanor stepped back in, letting the door close.

Addy rolled her eyes.

"Keep your voice down, or the whole neighborhood will hear you. Mrs. Adcock is out there right now, puttering around in her yard, listening to us. She sees everything that goes on in this neighborhood, including this house. And that's what Micah is dealing with. Settling the estate."

"That's not exactly private, Mother."

"It is too." She turned to leave again. "I'm finished with this conversation. You may not care what people think, but I do. You need to have lunch with Genevieve Ingram, and leave Micah Britton alone to do his job."

A few seconds later, Addy heard Eleanor's car start. She scratched her head and looked around the little kitchen. Her attempt to make nice had been a train wreck. Conversations with Eleanor always were. The woman refused to listen to reason. Clearly, moving to D.C. was the smartest thing Addy had ever done.

She needed to get back there as soon as possible. Being in Asheville was killing her, in more ways than she had expected. She pulled out her phone at the insistent chirp of Micah's text reply. He—and his scanner—would be at the office for the rest of the afternoon.

Chapter 16

Still fuming from the argument with her mother, and annoyed with herself for having felt guilty enough to try making peace to begin with, Addy started to close the windows, then changed her mind. It wouldn't take her long to zip back to her parents' house, grab the documents, and take them to Micah's office to scan. The clouds were still clinging to the mountain tops; she'd be back before it rained.

Driving toward Biltmore Forest, she kept half an eye out for her mother's car. Hopefully, she could slip in and out of the house without having to continue their argument. It was just like the arguments they'd always had, with Eleanor ranting about what the neighbors thought and Addy trying to make her see that the neighbors were too busy with their own lives to be worried about anyone else. The main reason she'd gone to college in Washington D.C. was because she wanted—needed—to be in a bigger city than she'd grown up in. There was a tiny part of her brain that worried, usually in the wee hours when it was dark and all her embarrassments and mistakes loomed large, that her mother might be right. Maybe the neighbors, her teachers, her friends' parents, her father's golf partner were all secretly judging her. If they were, she knew, deep in those dark, silent moments, that she would come up lacking. In the grand scheme of things, what did she really have to offer the world?

What her mother didn't realize, Addy thought, pulling into the empty driveway, was that if people weren't judging you, they had probably forgotten you exist. And that might be the worst fate of all.

Breathless from running up and down the stairs, but glad her mother hadn't come straight home, Addy got back in her Honda. She didn't want to dawdle in the driveway, so she ignored the alert on her phone lying in the passenger seat until she pulled up in front of Micah's office.

It was another email, this time from the magazine editor she'd contacted over the weekend. Between lunching with Micah and arguing with her mother, she'd forgotten all about the message she had sent. He was offering to fly to Asheville and take a look at the documents. She looked again at the date he suggested, in three days. Her heart skipped a beat. All of a sudden it felt as if she had more plates in the air than she could manage without dropping one or two.

When she burst into Micah's office with the manuscript in one hand and cellphone in the other, he was standing behind his desk holding an ancient-looking legal file.

"Hey, I have something to show you," he said, looking up.

"Me first," she said, holding her phone out to him.

He took it and read the email. "Okay, who is this guy?"

"I don't know him, but I've heard of the magazine. I stumbled across the website this weekend, did a little background research, and this is his thing—publishing newly-discovered stuff written by deceased famous authors. Maybe artists, too. Anyway, I emailed him. Did you see? He's willing to fly down from New York this week!" She sounded giddy even to her own ears.

Micah nodded, handing the phone back to her. "Is he going to help you authenticate it?"

She looked back down at her phone, thinking. "Well, you read the email. He says he'd love to publish it, if it's what we think it is, so I'm not sure. I've never done this before. But I've got this professor in Alabama who's going to look at it right now."

"Right." Micah looked sober. "Don't you think you should slow down a little? Take it one step at a time, make sure you've got the authentication and provenance straight before you start bringing editors down from New York?"

She lifted her chin. "That's what I'm doing. Which is why I need to use your scanner." She held out the manila envelope.

He didn't take it, but picked up a similar envelope from his desk and held it toward her. "Trade," he said.

"What is that?"

"Open it."

Addy accepted the envelope, flipping it over in her hands for inspection, then opened and began tipping the pages out onto the desk.

"How much do you know about this guy? What are his credentials, and how much do you trust him? Have you looked into what this story might be worth?"

"Only a little," Addy said.

"Well, bear in mind that you, your mother, and Lacey own it jointly, since it was in your grandmother's papers. That's why I mentioned the value. Admittedly, cultural property is not my area of the law, but I could find you someone to talk to."

Addy chewed on the inside of her lip, trying to look as if she was thinking it over. She didn't want to get into all the gory details with Micah about her deadlines and credit cards and the predicament she'd gotten herself into between her mother and Dr. McGregor. "It'll be fine," she said brightly, and looked down at the papers she had tipped out of Micah's envelope.

In her hand was an official-looking document typed out on letterhead bearing the name of R. M. Britton, Sr. She looked more closely at the signature on the bottom—Martha Rose Cameron. *Great-Aunt Martha.* She went back to the beginning, trying to understand the dense legal language. It appeared to be a contract, but it didn't make sense to Addy.

"What does this mean?"

"I found it today. It's the source of the perpetuity on your grandmother's house. It's basically an old-fashioned version of what we'd call a non-disclosure agreement. It says that everything your great-aunt Martha learned working for the Biltmore Company was confidential and proprietary, and if she tells any of it, the ownership of her house will revert to my grandfather or his estate."

"Are you serious? Meaning you? My grandmother's house could go to you?"

"Well, not me—my dad is still living—but theoretically, yes. But it's ridiculous, don't worry about it. Obviously, she didn't tell anything, and it's not like anyone would care now if she had, right? And she's long gone, so as far as I'm concerned, it's all moot anyway."

Addy frowned, studying the document. There was something troubling about this scenario, but she couldn't think what it was. "What's this about ninety-nine years?"

"Oh, it just means the perpetuity is good for ninety-nine years. But like I keep saying, I think it's irrelevant because she never told any deep dark trade secrets or anything, right?"

"Beats me. I don't know the first thing about her. But the ninety-nine years…from when it was signed?" She scanned the page until she saw January 1, 1925. It only took her a second to do the math, but even so, she felt like she was missing something. "It's only been ninety years. So ownership could still revert?"

Micah's eyes roved around the room as if the answers might be hiding right in front of them. "Perpetuities are complicated, and I'd think after this long it would be hard to prove. Besides, like I said, I don't care, and I know for a fact my dad doesn't. He barely remembers where the bathroom is in our house, which he's lived in for thirty-five years."

"Oh, Micah. I'm sorry. I didn't mean to be insensitive."

"Don't worry about it," he said. "I'm getting used to it. All of this"—he waved his hand at the files piled everywhere—"keeps me pretty well tethered to reality."

Addy truly felt bad for what Micah must have been going through for some time now. She reached out to touch his arm, and he gave her a wry smile.

"Anyway, your other question at lunch the other day was about copyright, so I did a little research. Technically, a story written in 1924 by someone who died in 1948 is in the public domain. So if it is what you think it is, you're within your rights to publish it. Assuming your mother and sister agree. But—"

"There you go. My dissertation director recommended a Zelda expert in Alabama who should be able to verify it for me. I trust her. And she says she can work from scans, which, like I said, is why I'm here. It's kind of a miracle."

"Why?" Micah asked, carefully tipping the contents of Addy's envelope out onto his desk.

"She's been retired for a while. I just figured the technology would be beyond her, especially since she started by wanting me to drive to Alabama."

"That doesn't seem unreasonable to me, given that your New York guy says he'll fly down just to look at it. It sounds like this kind of thing is a pretty big deal in the academic world," Micah said.

Addy wondered if she heard a hint of reproof in his voice. "Well, yes. It was just the technology piece that surprised me. Given her age."

"My mother is teaching herself Italian using YouTube videos and an app on her phone. Age is sort of irrelevant when it comes to technology."

Addy flushed. She wasn't that person, passing judgment and stereotyping people, or at least she thought she'd always tried not to be. "Really? My mother won't even learn how to text. Anyway, there it is." She pointed at the story. "You can read it if you want."

He glanced at his watch and gathered up the pages. "I don't really have time right now, but I'd like to. Do you care if I send myself a copy of the scan?"

"Of course not." Addy flushed again. There was no mistaking the reproof in that comment. If he'd meant to throw her balance off, he'd succeeded. She followed him into a room with walls lined with boxes upon boxes of files. The centerpiece was the most complicated copy machine she'd ever seen. There were stacks of files on a work table next to it.

"Pardon the mess," Micah said, ignoring her discombobulation. "I'm working on getting all of this scanned, but it's slow going and unbelievably tedious. People keep quitting, and I can hardly blame them."

Addy looked around the room, relieved to move on to a topic other than her questionable judgment. "All this? You're trying to scan all of it?"

"No, I'm going through and purging as much as I can. Then I can get the necessary stuff scanned. But I haven't had time to go through the oldest stuff yet, and there's years' worth in storage too. If you still want to do some research, though, you're more than welcome."

"Why?"

"Why what?"

"Why are you doing all this? It looks like a nightmare. What about your own practice, in Los Angeles?"

Micah shrugged and looked away. "My mother needed help when it became clear my dad couldn't handle it."

His words hung in the quiet that followed.

Finally, Addy pointed at the papers in his hand. "You were in a hurry, right?"

"Yes, of course." He set about scanning the story and the letter while Addy watched.

"The highest resolution you can, if you don't mind," Addy said.

Micah gave her a look. "I figured. It should be in your email. By the way, you owe me even more now."

The change in tone was a relief, but it came too late. This new Micah, the grown-up who told her to be careful and gave up his whole life to take care of his parents had squelched her earlier good mood. She felt a little guilty for taking up his time when he so clearly had more than enough to do.

"Thank you. Send me a bill," she said, still thinking of his time and wondering what his hourly rate was in California. She shoved the thought of her credit card out of her mind.

He clutched at his chest as if he were wounded. "That was harsh. I was thinking about it after lunch, maybe you could go with me to Pritchard Park sometime. For old times' sake?"

Surprised, Addy couldn't think quickly enough to muster up a flirty response.

"Are you mad?" he said.

"No. Just stressed. Pritchard Park. Is that drum circle still there on Fridays?"

"It's huge now, especially at this time of year. Come on, it'll be fun."

"Sure." Addy took the original pages and a photocopy from him. "Maybe next weekend? Lacey's play opens tomorrow, but Friday is senior night, so I have to go to that, and then her graduation is Monday. I don't think I should take off another evening right now. But text me. We'll make a plan."

He nodded.

For a second, she wondered if the inscrutable look on his face was disappointment.

She held the pages awkwardly in front of her, like a flimsy wall between them. "Thank you for this, really. And for explaining the perpetuity, too. I appreciate it."

Addy sat in the car in front of Micah's office and emailed the scans to Dr. Cavendish. Then she stared at the email from the editor, torn. She didn't want to admit Micah was right about her acting too impulsively, so she forced herself to think rationally. What was the worst-case scenario, if she emailed him back and said she wasn't ready to commit at this point? She might not get another chance with that particular journal. Did that matter? He'd responded so quickly—surely that meant there'd be someone else who was interested. And it wasn't as if she was losing face. She'd only told Micah. Without giving herself time to second-guess, she replied to the editor's email, saying she appreciated his interest, but wasn't quite ready to move forward.

As she finished, a fat drop of rain landed on her windshield with a splat. The open windows at her grandmother's house flashed to the front of her mind, refocusing her on the here and now. She drove quickly, mulling over her conversation with Micah and her argument with her mother before that. Both had managed to get under her skin.

Eleanor hadn't changed one iota in Addy's years away. Addy ran backwards through her mother's rant trying to remember what had set her off. It didn't matter—her mind slipped easily into the comfortable rut of blame and righteous indignation. The only thing Eleanor ever cared about was putting on a perfect front for the world to see, and she had never understood that Addy just didn't care. When Addy was in high school, they had fought over all the normal stuff—clothes, hair, make-up, boys, grades—but always under the umbrella of Eleanor's primary complaint: What will people think?

The only boy they hadn't fought about was Micah. The more Addy thought about that now, the more irritated she got. Even when she was kicked out of private school, which she still laid at Micah's feet even if it had only taken her two seconds to forgive him the other day, her mother was more concerned about what Micah's parents thought than his betrayal of Addy. They'd written the letters together, collaborated on the entire plan to bring down the school's hypocritical investment program (Tobacco is bad, kids, but tobacco *money* is good—it can even build a new home for the headmaster!), but he had come out of the scandal unscathed, while she had been shamed and expelled. And now he had the gall to make her feel bad because she still didn't get along with her mother. Fine, they could have each other.

When she pulled up at the next traffic light, she got out her phone and checked the calendar, counting down the weeks before her deadline again, just to be sure. Less than seven. She just had to ignore all the drama for a little while longer.

She sighed. She had agreed to go with him to Pritchard Park, even if it was more than a week away. Was it a date? She thought about it for a second, trying to fit it into some other category of friends or work or nostalgia, but her own compulsive honesty wouldn't let her. It was a date, and she was looking forward to it, even if he had made her feel guilty. Maybe that was all in her head, anyway. Maybe something social—some dancing and harmless flirting—was exactly the distraction she needed to get out of her head a little. She hadn't really done anything fun since she'd returned.

She turned on the radio for distraction, trying to dispel the irritation that made her feel as if her skin didn't fit quite right. She had driven past the front edge of the storm, so she rolled down the window. The air was heavy on this side of town. The wind smelled like ozone and damp asphalt, blowing through her hair and rustling the papers on the passenger seat. She snatched at the loose pages before they scattered on the floor, and tucked them under the manila envelope that contained the copy of the perpetuity. She would need to consider it when she started putting together the materials for the historical marker—yet another thing hanging over her head. What was it that was bothering her about that document? Her mind had clutched at something earlier, a connection, but it had slipped away.

The rain seemed to be coming from behind her, so when she pulled up in her grandmother's driveway, the first drops were just spattering the pavement.

She glanced at the windows as she ran toward the kitchen door, and stopped short. The windows were closed. She thought back to her dash out of the house. Maybe she was misremembering and had closed them after all. Or had Eleanor come back? She reached out a tentative hand and pulled the screen door open. The door had been closed and locked. It must have been Eleanor.

Addy let herself into the kitchen. Her breath caught in her throat at the sight of Asia standing in the doorway between the kitchen and dining room. They stared at each other, startled, for a moment.

"I'm meeting Lacey after her dress rehearsal," Asia finally blurted. "She said this would be a good time for me to get started helping you clean up, and it was starting to rain, so I came in to close the windows. You weren't here."

"No, I had to run out. Where's Lacey?"

"She's not here yet. They're probably running late again."

Addy eyed her for a minute. Her eyes were red-rimmed and a little swollen. There was an air of defeat about her. "Is everything okay?" Addy asked.

Asia shrugged. "I'm just tired. End of the school year."

"Are you sure you want to work on this right now?"

"Sure. It'll help me find my Zen. Plus, like I said, I'm meeting Lacey."

Addy looked around the kitchen, trying to think about how best to use this unexpected labor. She wasn't really in the mood to work on the clean-up project right now, but maybe it was for the best since Eleanor wasn't around, and it might be awhile before she heard anything from Dr. Cavendish.

"Well, since you're here, we might as well get something done." She got out a box of garbage bags and handed it to Asia. "Go through the cabinets. Anything edible needs to be tossed if it's expired, or donated if it isn't."

"Okay." Asia began opening cabinets.

"I'll be in the bedroom if you need me. And why don't you call Lacey and see when she's going to get here."

"Oh…I forgot my phone."

Addy dug hers out and set it on the table, then headed toward her grandmother's bedroom to retrieve the shoe boxes Eleanor had pulled out of the closet that morning. They'd been hovering in the back of her mind ever since; she wanted to see what was in them. Squatting, she lifted the dusty lid from the first box. There was a stack of report cards on top. She wondered how one smallish family could accumulate so many report cards. These had Nellie's name on them, though, and she realized that these boxes must be the bits and pieces her great-grandmother Isabella had hung on to. Maybe this was where she would finally find out something about the elusive Martha. She dropped all the way to the floor and began flipping through the report cards.

Apparently Grandmama had been a model student.

A while later, Addy felt absentmindedly for her phone to check the time. She'd been so absorbed—charmed—by her grandmother's childhood that it took her a second to come back to reality. She rubbed at her temples where a headache was beginning, and stood up. The storm that chased her across town earlier had petered out, leaving the air heavy and unsettled. Dinner time had come and gone, and she needed to get outside and clear the cobwebs.

She scooped the three boxes up, oblivious to the dust, and headed for the kitchen, planning to put them in her car. Her phone was on the table, but Asia had left. There was no sign of Lacey.

She shook her head. There was only a year or two difference between her students—college freshmen—and her sister. They were all a little unpredictable. It must be the hormones.

Addy walked back through the bungalow, checking the windows, then pocketed her phone and headed out to her car, making doubly sure she locked the door on her way out.

Chapter 17

The rest of the week passed in a slow blur of waiting to hear back from Dr. Cavendish, writing and rewriting the beginnings of a new prospectus, and avoiding Eleanor. Addy had several moments of doubt when the words wouldn't come in the same great flood of the first version. The problem, she realized, was that she hadn't yet figured out whether the short story had any real academic value or not. Her brain looped back again and again over the same list of questions. Where did the story come from? How did Great-Aunt Martha come to have it? Why was there no record anywhere of Zelda and Cornelia knowing each other, when it was so patently obvious that they had? She avoided checking her email, hoping Dr. McGregor wouldn't call her to account for a few more days.

The evenings were punctuated by Lacey's play. Addy went to all three performances. She was happy to be in town supporting her sister, but she insisted on driving separately from her parents, not wanting to be trapped in an awkward jaunt down memory lane. There were limits to filial loyalty.

Guys and Dolls was a typical high school performance with plenty of missed cues and handmade props. Lacey, who couldn't sing to save her life, played a stern matron, proving to Addy that she really could act—the part couldn't have been further from her bubbly personality.

She had tried out for a male role, she'd told Addy when she called after the audition, but hadn't gotten it. Addy was consoling, but secretly, she thought it for the best. She wasn't sure Eleanor would've coped well with her daughter playing a gangster, no matter how dapper his suit.

When Friday night's performance ended and the cast had taken their bows, and final bows, and the seniors had come back out for yet another final bow, the audience lingered. Parents and students and teachers stayed on, waiting for the actors to change out of their costumes. Addy stood up and turned around to see Micah heading toward her, pushing against the flow of the outgoing crowd.

"I didn't expect to see you here," she said as he stepped into her row, nudging her over with a hand on the small of her back. Her eyes were directly level with his lips. She watched, rather than heard, his response.

"It seemed like a good opportunity to get Dad out for a little while, and give my mom a break."

His lips pursed a little on "opportunity," and when he stopped speaking, the left corner of his mouth lifted in a small smile that woke memories. She tore her eyes away and took a breath, trying to drag her mind back to the theatre and the present.

"I know they must be so glad to have you back in town, helping out," Eleanor said from behind Addy.

She had almost forgotten for a second that her parents were waiting to file out of their seats, making her even more aware that she was standing in the shelter of Micah's body. A giggle tried to break from her throat, and she half-coughed, half-choked on it.

"Sorry," she said. "You startled me."

"I can't stay. I just wanted to say hi." He leaned around her to shake Mason's outstretched hand.

He smelled exactly like he always had, a mix of pine and laundry soap.

"Plus I wanted to say hello," he whispered into her hair. "Since you wouldn't go downtown with me."

"Where's your father?" Eleanor asked.

"Sitting in the back." Micah turned to point, breaking the spell.

Addy let out a breath.

"I have to get back to him. Don't want him wandering into traffic."

He stood aside, letting them file past. Addy waited until her parents had moved past her, headed in the elder Mr. Britton's direction, and fell in beside Micah.

"Here," he said, reaching into his pocket. "I brought you a key to the office." He dropped it into her hand.

"You don't have to do that. I can just go sometime when you're there."

"That's fine too," he said. "But I thought you might want to get on with it, and this way you can go when it suits you. I pulled out the files I thought you might want, but I didn't have time to go through them. They're on the floor next to my desk. Help yourself."

"Thank you," Addy said. She touched his elbow, making him look at her. "Really, thank you."

His grin spread, slow and satisfied. "No problem."

Chapter 18

Addy got up early and walked to Micah's office before the Saturday morning shoppers descended on Biltmore Village, half hoping he'd be there, half hoping he wouldn't. Her conscience was still nudging her, reminding her that she wasn't staying, it wouldn't be fair, she didn't need the distraction.

Micah wasn't at his office yet, but the key worked just as he had promised, so she let herself in. It was quiet and still and smelled faintly of burnt coffee. The old, wide floorboards creaked as she made her way into the main office and looked around. Micah had left her a banker's box full of files. She took the lid off the box and peered in. She lugged it up onto the desk and started taking out files, reading labels, and triaging as she went. When they were divided into piles for all of her mother's relatives and ancestors that the firm had represented, plus one unlabeled manila envelope, she went into the tiny kitchen and made herself a cup of tea. Then she sat down at his desk and picked up the oldest file.

The first few pages were a random jumble: her grandmother's birth certificate (April 1925), a copy of the deed to the house that Micah had mentioned—which she put aside, knowing she'd need it later for the historical marker—and several letters from Granny Isabella, thanking Micah's grandfather for his help. Addy wondered if sending your lawyer a thank-you note used to really be a thing. It seemed overly proper.

She sipped at her tea and kept flipping pages.

About halfway through the pile, she found a small, old-fashioned receipt book, the kind with the perforated pages so that a stub remained in the book when the receipt was torn out. It was nothing but stubs; she flipped through and saw that they were almost identical. Each listed an amount of one hundred dollars, followed by the scrawled initials of *RMB, Sr,* and the date it was written. The only thing that changed from one to the next was the date. The book in her hand was for the year 1930; she shuffled the rest of the papers in the file, but there wasn't an explanation.

She surveyed the tidy stacks she'd made on the desk, and reached for the manila envelope. It was lumpy and slightly weighted. The ancient tape had lost its adhesive and come loose, so she tipped it over and sure enough, a pile of similar receipt books tumbled out.

Her tea got cold as she flipped through one after another. There was one for each year, from 1925 through 1946—twenty-one years. Looking more closely at the cover of the very first one, she saw the initials *ICM,* her great-grandmother. She sat looking at it in startled realization. It appeared she had stumbled across twenty-one years' worth of payments to her great-grandmother from the lawyer who had fired her great-great-aunt. Who also happened to be a judge, and the manager of Biltmore Estate. And Micah's grandfather.

She had no idea what to make of it.

Maybe Micah would know. She pulled out her phone and texted him, then stood up and paced the room, thinking, waiting for his response. Finally, she sat back down, put all the receipt books back in the envelope, and forced herself to look carefully at the last few items in the file bearing Granny Isabella's name.

It was mostly more of those odd thank-you notes in her grandmother's handwriting. She skimmed each and turned it facedown. The very last item in the file was her grandmother's birth certificate. Addy glanced at it, flipped it over, and then flipped it back. Something was odd. She skimmed the document, then searched back to the very first item she had looked at. Another copy of the birth certificate.

Now that she thought about it, why would Grandmama's birth certificate even be here in a lawyer's office, never mind two copies? Who even had multiple copies of a birth certificate in 1925?

She put them side by side, and the difference jumped out at her. She stared, uncomprehending. The first copy listed Isabella and Angus McLean as the parents, as expected. On the second birth certificate, the one tucked away at the back of the folder, the space for 'Mother' contained the name Martha Rose Cameron. The space for 'Father' was blank.

She jumped up from the desk and paced blindly out to the waiting room where she'd sat with her mother on that Monday morning just a few weeks earlier. She laughed out loud, a sharp, hollow sound in the quiet office.

The distance from the front door of Micah's office back to his desk was eighteen steps. Addy counted them, then counted them again, as she hurriedly paced. Her brain had come up against a wall that hadn't been there five minutes earlier, had never been there in her twenty-eight years, and she didn't know how to understand it. She felt like one of those kittens that had never been exposed to vertical lines and kept crashing into chair legs.

She circled the desk a couple of times, wary, as if the official-looking documents might reach out and grab her. Micah's office suddenly felt too small to contain her confusion. Impulsively, she shoved all the papers except the two birth certificates back into the folder and dropped it back into the box it had come from. She rummaged in Micah's desk for an empty folder—*how had he not found this?* She slid the birth certificates into an empty folder, unwilling even through the blur of confusion to risk damaging historical documents.

When she stepped outside and didn't see her car, it took her a second to remember that she had walked to the office. She sighed, and started toward home.

As she walked, the scholarly part of her brain took over, superseding her emotions. Rational analysis felt familiar and comfortable. This was a puzzle, a problem to solve. She patted the folder poking up out of her purse and thought about the implications.

Which certificate was the real one? Why had it been changed? Who knew about it?

The receipt books popped into her head—she'd forgotten about those. Was there a connection? It seemed too coincidental to ignore. She texted Micah again, and when he still didn't respond after a few minutes, she considered that maybe his father was having a bad morning.

No one was home when she got to her parents' house, so she texted Lacey. *Where are y'all?*

Lacey replied almost immediately. *Grandmama's. HELP. Mom hauled me out of bed to come over here & she's driving me crazy. HELP.*

Rolling her eyes, Addy replied, *On my way.*

Addy drove slowly, thinking. Every question she'd had, all the way back to that moment in Dr. McGregor's office last month, had revolved around the elusive Aunt Martha. She gripped the steering wheel in frustration, feeling she could kick herself for not asking Grandmama more questions when she had the chance.

She parked on the street in front of Nellie's bungalow and strode up the lawn, shoulders squared, determined to get some answers.

"Hey," Addy called as the screen door slapped behind her.

"We're in the den," Lacey called.

Addy crossed the kitchen to her grandmother's desk and found a legal pad. She took the folder from her purse, then pulled the phone from her pocket, turned off the ringer, and laid it on the table. There was no sense giving Eleanor anything extra to get agitated about.

In the small, dark-paneled den, Lacey was kneeling on the floor, pulling crumbling sheet music out of the piano bench while Eleanor stared out one of the windows, arms folded across her chest. The den had always felt dark and damp to Addy; awnings over the windows kept sunlight from penetrating, and the overhead light was too weak to dispel the darkness that shadowed the corners of the room.

"Have a bookshelf," Lacey said, pointing. "But be careful. I keep thinking silverfish are crawling up my arms."

"Never mind that. Come see what I found," Addy said. She plopped down on the couch, holding her breath against the cloud of dust that puffed up around her. "Gah! There's nowhere to sit in here."

"Good reason not to sit," Lacey retorted.

"Seriously. You both need to see this." She opened the folder across her lap.

Eleanor glanced over her shoulder, but made no move toward the couch.

Lacey shuffled over on her knees. "This is a nightmare," she muttered under her breath. "What do you want?"

Addy caught her gaze, and pointed at the two different mothers named for the same baby on the documents—Martha and Isabella.

"This is Grandmama's birth certificate," Addy said, quietly.

"Which one?"

"Both."

"What the hell?" Lacey said, a little louder this time.

"Right." Addy said. "Bizarre, isn't it?"

"I heard that, young lady," Eleanor said, still standing by the window.

"What does it mean?" Lacey asked. "Mom, come see this."

Eleanor glanced over her shoulder.

Addy could see curiosity warring with irritability in her face and posture.

She turned back to the window and asked with her best disinterested tone, "What is it?"

Addy stood up and held the two certificates between the window and Eleanor. Grasping them, she held them up to the light for inspection. Addy watched her back stiffen, then she finally turned around again.

"What in the world are these, and where did you get them?"

"I found them in the files at Micah's office. They're Grandmama's birth certificate. Certificates. Plural."

"I can see that," Eleanor snapped. "What am I supposed to do with them?"

"Wait, there's more. Receipt books. With all these payments made to Granny Isabella for a hundred dollars each. It's beyond bizarre."

"What do they mean?" Lacey asked.

"Good gracious, Lacey, I have no idea. I don't see why you feel compelled to dig up all this ancient history, Addison. Can't you just leave things well enough alone?"

"No, Mother. I can't. I have a dissertation to write." Addy reached for the certificates, but Eleanor held them out of reach.

"Not about this, you don't."

Addy pressed her hands on top of her head as if it might blow off. "What exactly is this, Mother?"

"I don't know. Probably just a clerical error. But it doesn't matter. Whatever it is, it happened a long time ago. It's not worth wasting your time on."

"A clerical error?" Lacey asked. "That seems like a pretty big mistake."

"What are you not telling me, Mother?" Addy asked.

"Nothing. I've never seen those before. And I can't fathom how they're even remotely relevant to your dissertation, so you ought to just give them back to Micah and not worry about it."

Addy reached again for the certificates, wrapping her fingers gently around Eleanor's wrist. It felt like she was holding a thin bird in her hand. She could even feel her mother's pulse, throbbing wildly. Carefully, she slid the pages from Eleanor's fingers. "Something is not adding up, Mother. Please help me think it through." She sat down on the couch again and picked up the notepad.

"Not if you're going to make a spectacle out of my family history."

Addy ignored her and began writing. "Let's make a list of questions. One: What was Martha's job at Biltmore, and why did she get fired? Admittedly, that's less relevant now that I've changed my topic, hopefully, but I'm still curious."

Lacey made a murmur of assent, then fell silent, listening as Addy thought out loud.

"Two: How did that short story get here, and why? Does it have anything to do with Martha? I have to think it does, since her initials are on it, but she clearly wasn't the intended recipient. Obviously, she came into possession of it as a result of her job, since Judge Britton's initials are on it too—see question one." She scribbled furiously, trying to corral her thoughts before they could scatter and disappear.

"Question three: Why are there two birth certificates for Grandmama? Again, Martha's name is on one of them, and Granny's is on the other, like it should be. So that's just super weird, and this is now a lot of coincidences revolving around this woman that we don't know anything about. Finally, what is the deal on the perpetuity, or whatever it is Micah said is on this house, and is it going to impact us selling it? Micah found the contract, but we're still not sure what it means."

Something tugged at her consciousness again—something about the perpetuity that had been bothering her for days.

Addy looked up for her audience's reaction. Lacey had sat back against the foot of the leather recliner and was frowning in concentration. Eleanor still leaned against the windowsill, but her frown looked much more dangerous.

"Thoughts?" Addy asked. The word sounded loud in the silence.

"Why is there no father on that one?" Lacey asked, pointing.

Addy made another note and looked at it for a second. "Maybe they got halfway through filling the first one out, then scrapped it and started over, and that's why all the blanks got filled in?"

"Ooh, maybe"—Lacey reached forward and peered at the names again—"Angus was having an affair with his wife's sister, and got her pregnant?"

Addy grinned at her. "It's beginning to sound like a soap opera."

"It seems like too much to be a coincidence, though, doesn't it?" Lacey asked.

"Don't be ridiculous. That's my grandfather you're talking about," Eleanor snapped. Her voice was thin and high. "You two are looking for a scandal that isn't there."

"Then why are you so wound up about it?" Addy asked. "Why do you care, if there's nothing to hide?"

"That's precisely why. Because there's nothing there. Nothing to tell. You're looking for a mystery or—" she pressed her hands against the sides of her head, looking as if she could barely contain her exasperation "—or a conspiracy. There just isn't one. This isn't real, whatever it is. There's a sensible explanation."

"I'm not making this up, Mother. These birth certificates are *real*. The perpetuity on the house *is* real. Even if I'm imagining the rest—and I don't think I am—those two things are tangible legal documents. And they don't make sense." She tapped her pen on the notepad, thinking.

"It doesn't matter, though. Family history is private."

"But it's not," Lacey said, jumping in. "You used family history for your DAR membership."

"You know what I think?" Addy said, jumping in to cut off Eleanor. "I think Martha had Nellie, and when she died—did I tell you I found her obituary? It's in the bedroom. Anyway, I think Isabella adopted Grandmama. I don't know why they changed the birth certificate, but other than that, the pieces fit."

"That's the most ridiculous thing I've ever heard of," Eleanor said, turning back to the window.

"You know, in 1924, being pregnant and unmarried was probably enough to get a woman fired," Addy mused.

"Maybe she died from childbirth," Lacey said. "I wonder if we could check that. Did they have death certificates back then?"

"Of course," Addy said, and jotted a note to remind herself.

"You realize this is my mother's birth you're talking about," Eleanor said in a strangled voice, still facing the window.

"But even if I'm right, it's not like it's Grandmama's fault. You can't help who you're born to."

"But what will people think? You can't just go around telling the world that my mother was an illegitimate child!"

"Whoa, hold on," Lacey said. "Slow down a minute. It's not like you're just going to make an announcement, right, Addy?"

Addy looked at her mother's rigid back and felt a twinge of guilt. "Of course not. We're just speculating, that's all. I need to talk to Micah about it and do some more research. But—"

Eleanor turned to face them, her face aghast. "You can't talk to Micah about this! Everyone in town will hear about it!"

Addy rolled her eyes. "Oh, for heaven's sake. I have to, Mother. The birth certificates were in his grandfather's files. If there are any answers, they might be there. He can help me figure it out. But it's okay, no one will care. Like you keep pointing out, it's ancient history anyway. It doesn't *matter* now—it's just interesting."

Addy and Lacey stood still for a minute, listening to their mother stomping down the carpeted hall and onto the kitchen linoleum. The screen door rattled, and a few seconds later a car door slammed and the engine started. They looked at each other.

Chapter 19

"Do you think she knows what it's about?" Lacey asked.

Addy shrugged. "Probably not. She would've started ranting before she even looked at them."

"What do you think they mean?"

Addy thought some more. "Well, I don't think it was an accident or a mistake—" She heard the screen door in the kitchen squeak and close again. "I'll tell you later. Mother's back."

"I don't think so," Lacey said, and darted past Addy into the hall.

Asia was in the kitchen with a backpack slung over one shoulder. Lacey hovered over her, patting and murmuring, checking her like a mother reunited with a child. Addy looked the other way. She remembered feeling as if a few days apart was the end of the world. For a second, she allowed herself to feel that thrill again, then shrugged it off.

"Hi, Asia," she said, reminding them that she was there. "What are you doing over here?"

Asia let her backpack drop to the floor. "Meeting Lacey," she said. "Hanging out in my new favorite house. Do you need me to do some more work around here?" She looked around hopefully. "I could clean out some more cabinets if you want."

Addy wondered what 'new favorite house' meant, but before she could ask, Lacey changed the subject. Something felt odd, but Addy couldn't put her finger on what it was.

"We're going to a party later," Lacey said, "but right now we need a snack. Aren't you hungry, Asia?" She began opening and closing cabinet doors.

"There's nothing there," Asia said. "I cleaned out the food. Except for the canned soup. There's enough canned soup to survive the apocalypse, I think."

Lacey looked dubious. "I could make some."

"No thanks," Asia made a face. "I'll survive." She sank back into the corner of the couch with a look that Addy could only interpret as contentment.

Lacey shrugged, still examining soup cans. "What are you going to do about the birth certificates?" she said to the kitchen at large.

"I don't know. Think about it, I guess. Think about everything. I don't know what else to do."

"What about birth certificates?" Asia asked.

"Oh, it's just some stuff I found doing research this morning. It turns out our grandmother had two birth certificates, and I can't figure out why. That's all."

"Can't you get multiple copies of a birth certificate? Why is that strange?" Addy waved the question away.

"They're different," Lacey said. "Two different mothers."

"Whoa. That's intriguing," Asia said. "What do you think it's about?"

Addy walked back to the den to retrieve the things she'd left. She tucked the certificates back into the envelope, along with her page of notes, and put them in her purse. When she got back to the kitchen, Lacey glared at her.

"Why are you being weird all of a sudden?"

"What did I do?"

"Why are you acting like we can't talk in front of Asia?"

Addy's jaw dropped open. "I didn't know I was. It's not a secret, in spite of what Mother thinks. Nothing is secret nowadays—that's what the internet is for. Tell Asia anything you want. I don't care."

"Are you mad that I'm here?" Asia asked.

"No, of course not. Why would I be?"

Asia shrugged and sank even farther into the couch, her eyes darting around the room. Addy looked at her more carefully. She looked even more rumpled than usual, with circles under her eyes and an air of vulnerability. Addy felt a pang of guilt; she hadn't meant to hurt either girl's feelings.

"I don't know how interesting it'll be, but here are my notes." She handed Asia the envelope and sat down to check her phone while the two teenagers emptied out the contents. She had missed a text from Micah.

Kind of tied up with my folks today. Will text when I can.

After they had looked through the notes, Asia looked up at Addy. "So what do you think happened?"

"I think—" Addy took the page of notes and glanced at them "—I think Martha got pregnant when she was working at Biltmore and got fired. And maybe she died having the baby? For whatever reason, it must have been easier to just make Isabella her real mother, rather than adopting. That's the only way I can make sense of it. The pregnancy was an embarrassment, so when she died, it was easier to just pretend it hadn't happened."

"The only thing is, I think the neighbors would have noticed if the pregnant woman disappeared and the non-pregnant one suddenly had a baby," Lacey said.

"Out in the backwoods, ninety years ago? People could get away with a lot out in the hills and hollows," Addy said.

"Even now, you go out there, down a couple of dirt roads, up the side of a mountain, and the number of people in any given household can change and no one bats an eyelash," Asia said.

After a few moments in silence, Addy could hear the staccato beat of a woodpecker drumming on a tree across the street. She looked at the pictures on the wall over the couch: a matched set of framed second-grade photos, one of her and one of Lacey, and above them, one of Eleanor. The scenario was becoming clearer in her mind. A humble little house in the woods, a shameful pregnancy, a sad, sudden death that made everything simpler. The receipt books exactly spanned Nellie's childhood. The deed to the house, the birth certificates, the receipts, the letter firing Martha—all were signed by the same man.

"What if Judge Britton was the father?" Addy was certain she was on to something now. "All the pieces fit."

"Would it explain the perpetuity?" Lacey asked.

"I have no idea. I still don't understand that entirely. I read it again last night, and basically it says Martha's work at Biltmore was confidential and if she broke that agreement, she'd lose the house."

"This house?" Asia asked. "What did Martha have to do with this house? And what is the perpetuity?"

"The house," Addy said slowly, as the thing that had been bothering her finally clicked. "The house was a gift to Martha. It must have been from the judge—a bribe, maybe?" She frowned, trying to remember if there was an address on the perpetuity.

She picked up her phone again, checking for a text despite its silence. "Micah said he'd text when he got free; I'll ask him," she said. An email alert that hadn't been there a few minutes earlier was from Dr. Cavendish, who had gotten the scans and concluded that the letter most certainly looked like Zelda's handwriting.

She sat for a second, grinning at her phone and absorbing this information.

"What is it?" Lacey prompted.

"That professor I told you about, the one who wrote the biography of Zelda Fitzgerald. She says the handwriting on the letter looks legitimate. Even the switch. Wow. I thought it was, but this is super-exciting." She stood up and paced across the kitchen, turning at the window and pacing back.

"What switch?" Asia asked. "What do you mean? I'm confused."

Addy pulled up the scan of the letter on her phone and handed it to Asia. "See how the handwriting changes in the middle? Dr. Cavendish says that began to happen more and more often throughout the 1920s as her mental state deteriorated."

"That's kind of sad."

"It is. You know she died in a mental hospital right here in town?"

Asia looked up from the tiny screen, frowning. "No, I don't know anything about her, except that she was married to the guy who wrote *The Great Gatsby*. What happened?"

"She was probably bipolar. She spent years at Highland Hospital, up on Zillicoa Street. She died in a fire—several women were locked in their rooms that night and couldn't escape. It was apparently horrific."

"That's sickening," Asia said, dropping the phone on the couch.

Addy nodded, picking up the phone and looking at the letter again. "Yeah. What a way to go."

"Do you think she was really bipolar?"

"Well, it's hard to know, isn't it? At the time, the diagnosis was schizophrenia, I think, but who knows? Dr. Cavendish's book speculates that it was bipolar disorder."

"Maybe it wasn't anything."

"Oh no, she was definitely ill. Look at that handwriting." She handed the phone back toward Asia, who tucked her hands under her legs, looking agitated.

"What's wrong, babe?" Lacey asked.

"Back then they used to lock people up for being gay," Asia said.

"Well, yes, and I can see why you'd say that, based just on that letter, but I don't really think that's enough evidence they were— Believe me, Zelda Fitzgerald was definitely mentally ill. There was a problem with her brain chemistry. It's sad, but it happens."

"I know it happens," Asia said, her voice strained. "But I also know that there have always been people who believed that homosexuality is a mental illness. Trust me, there are plenty of people who still believe that right here and now." She bolted up from the couch. "I can't sit here. I know y'all are busy, so I'll just get out of your hair." She grabbed her backpack and pushed through the screen door.

"Asia! Wait," Lacey called. She turned to Addy and said, "Really? I can't believe you just did that!"

"I didn't mean to— I'm sorry." She grabbed her phone and keys. "Come on. We'll catch her at the corner."

"No. You'll just make it worse. She's too upset. The mental illness stuff is a trigger—her asshole fosters keep telling her she's mentally ill."

"Oh dear. I had no idea. That's awful. What can I do?"

"Nothing. I'll handle it. I'll see you later."

Guilt settled in Addy's stomach like a rock. She started pacing, marching down the central hall of the bungalow and back, trying to outrun her regret. Should she go after them? She peered out the screen door, hoping Lacey had caught up to Asia. She hadn't meant to upset the teenager—damn her big mouth. But how was she supposed to know this would upset Asia? Too much was happening at once; she needed to find a quiet space in her brain to process it all.

The first order of business was to finish the new prospectus and send it to Dr. McGregor. That was a concrete, manageable step. It was already a day late; hopefully, the professor was enjoying a summer vacation somewhere and hadn't noticed. Addy went back into the kitchen and turned the notepad to a fresh page. It was time for a new list.

Standing at the kitchen counter, trying not to feel guilty for upsetting her sister's girlfriend, she focused on jotting down all the threads and worrisome questions that she could think of. She still hadn't found out whether Cornelia Vanderbilt kept a diary and now that had become a priority, but the Biltmore offices and archives were closed over the weekend; she'd have to go downtown on Monday. She needed to thank Dr. Cavendish. She needed to find out how the story and letter ended up at her grandmother's house. She needed to decide what to do with them—they couldn't just molder in her desk indefinitely. Behind all these thoughts, tugging at her, was the image of Asia, distraught, running out the door. Addy pressed her hands on top of her head, hoping Lacey had found her.

She paused her list-making for a moment, assessing her sisterly concerns. She was worried about both of them—Asia and Lacey. What were they encountering in the world? Was it crumpling their souls? Even Lacey, who was well accustomed to Eleanor's 'what will people think' refrain, was bound to be affected by her mother's discomfort. Addy started pacing again.

It was a difficult balance. She wanted to comfort them, to tell them the critics didn't matter, that they should just ignore Eleanor, but that felt wrong.

She knew from experience that hypocrisy would leave a sour taste in her mouth.

She sighed out loud. This was a problem that wouldn't be solved today. The most she could do was be supportive and get her dissertation done. The stories—all these troubled young women—Asia, Lacey, Zelda—were beginning to bleed into each other in her head. She looked down at the notepad again, and continued the list, trying not to think about the wounded look in Asia's eyes.

It was the question of why Zelda's odd, handwritten story was at Nellie's house that was tripping her up. She looked at the scans again, and then it hit her—they had to have come from Biltmore. Why hadn't she seen that sooner? She mashed her hands on top of her head again, trying to squeeze her brain. Obviously, Martha must have brought them from Biltmore for some reason. She sat with that thought for a moment, turning it over in her mind, looking for the chinks. Was there any evidence that Zelda and Cornelia had ever even met? She'd have to go back up to Biltmore and poke around some more. That sweet old gentleman, Ford, had said he'd look at the story and letter—maybe he'd be able to dredge up some memories that would shed light on what Cornelia was like.

She made a note on her list to seek out Ford when she went back up to the house to look for Cornelia's diary.

She went back to her grandmother's bedroom to dig out the obituary she'd seen in one of those boxes of papers. There were no clues there, though, and definitely no death certificate. She starred the note she'd already made, reminding herself to go back to the state archives and track down Martha's death certificate. With any luck, it would list a cause of death. Her hand hovered over the page for a second before she drew a thick blue line through the item she had just starred. Did it matter what Martha had died of, or what her death certificate said? She had died in the spring of 1925, that much was clear, and it was really the only relevant fact. Chasing down a death certificate would only take up a morning that Addy couldn't afford to waste—it wouldn't answer any of the real questions.

She put the lid back on the box and the box back in the top of the closet. This had been Eleanor's bedroom when she was growing up, and there was still one salmon-colored prom dress hanging in the back. Addy pulled the chiffon toward her and looked at it. The halter top and deep flounce at the bottom of the skirt screamed 1970. She shuddered and put the filmy fabric back into the musty-smelling depths of the closet. She didn't dare toss out something that had so obviously belonged to Eleanor, so she shut the closet door and began closing up the house to leave. It had been a long day.

Walking from room to room, pulling down the windows, Addy thought about Eleanor storming out earlier, and her determination to keep family history private. *This is going to be an uphill battle*, she thought grimly, tugging on a window stuck in its frame. If her dissertation was going to be about the short story, it would have to lead to Martha, which would lead to the peculiar birth certificates, which would lead directly to Eleanor forbidding her to air their laundry in public. There was no easy way around that particular obstacle.

All roads also seemed to be leading back to Micah's grandfather. Again, her impulse was to text Micah and ask if he had any ideas. The thought she'd had earlier, before Asia got upset, settled back in her brain. What if it really was Micah's grandfather who had gotten Martha pregnant?

The implications gave her pause. She dropped slowly onto the kitchen couch, flipped to a clean sheet of paper on her notepad, and sketched out a quick visual aid. Could she be related to Micah? Her face flamed red as she thought about it.

Did it matter? Would it matter to Micah? How much was she assuming, to even wonder what he might think? It wasn't as if they were teetering on the edge of a relationship or anything. They'd known each other their entire lives, had dated in high school, but now they were just good friends. Was that what she wanted? And back to that earlier question—did it matter? Her life was in Washington D.C. and she had a career to get on with.

She gazed at the list, thinking soberly about the conversation they needed to have as two sensible adults, being responsible.

Was that who she had become? An ordinary grown-up? Realization hit her that she was becoming her mother. Lacey had always teased that she would, but Addy had never taken it seriously. She couldn't—wouldn't—be that. *Forever stiff and careful, forever worried about outward appearances. Clutching her secrets tight to her chest like a miser, lonely in his hoard. Holding life and people at arm's length, unable to relax and embrace the juicy messes because "what will people think, Addison?"*

If Addy was right about the birth certificates and the receipts, Eleanor's head really was going to explode this time. For a brief second, she struggled with the image, then shoved it aside and stood up a little straighter.

She wasn't going to become her mother, protecting empty secrets. She was going to tell this story.

Chapter 20

There was little she could do on Sunday, however, beyond sitting at her computer, avoiding her mother who had, with a martyred air, stopped nagging Addy about church. Addy pretended not to think about the question of her grandmother's parentage. She couldn't imagine how Eleanor was going to react, and was in no hurry to find out. Several times she reached for her phone, thinking she'd text Micah and ask him about it, but each time she put the phone down. Some deep self-defense instinct told her she needed to process the whole scenario a little more before charging forward as she tended to do.

By the time she had wrestled a few paragraphs onto the screen, it was time to get dressed for Lacey's graduation. Lacey, of course, had been at the school all morning, rehearsing and carousing with her friends. There were only about seventy-five kids in her class, and most of them had grown up together through the most prominent private schools in town.

Addy had been part of that crowd a dozen years ago, until her abrupt transfer in junior year. She hadn't gone back for graduation and had cut her ties with those kids, never regretting it, not really. She was happy for Lacey today, but mindful of the grey cloud of remembered teenage angst hovering just at the edge of her consciousness.

Still processing mixed feelings, she dressed in the amazing dress she'd found at an estate sale in Virginia. It was an ivory chiffon sheath over a lavender silk slip, with a deep pleated insert in the back of the skirt that peeked out through a high slit in the chiffon. She'd paid a small fortune for it, but it was perfect. A tiny clutch dripping with silver bugle beads completed the look.

Eleanor and Mason, still dressed for church, were waiting at the bottom of the stairs. Addy stepped carefully in a pair of Louis heels. She could feel the silk pleats sliding across the backs of her calves like a whisper.

"Where in the world did you get that outfit?" Eleanor asked.

"Isn't it gorgeous?" she said, twirling to show off the back. "It's new. I got it at an estate sale a couple of months ago."

"And you're wearing it? You're wearing clothes from a yard sale?"

"Not a yard sale, Mother. An estate sale. You know full well there's a difference."

"You're wearing a dead person's clothes. Not exactly new," Mason said.

"Oh, Addison," Eleanor said with a note of suffering in her voice. She glanced at her watch, twisting the face up from where it had slipped to the inside of her wrist.

"Well, it'll have to do. At least it looks fine. Let's go," Mason said, ushering them both out the door.

Addy sat in the back seat of her father's car, feeling vaguely trapped, like a child. Eleanor twisted around to look at her one more time, her eyes assessing. "Just don't tell everyone you're buying used clothes now, please."

Addy gave her mother a syrupy smile. "Of course. This is Lacey's day."

"And when you graduate in December, I trust you'll be wearing academic regalia?" Mason asked.

"Of course," Addy said. Her chest tightened a little at the thought. The amount of writing she had to do between now and then felt insurmountable, and a little clock kept ticking in the back of her mind. "But let's focus on Lacey for today. I don't want to steal her thunder."

Eleanor gave her an impenetrable look, then turned back to the front to help Mason find a parking place. Addy closed her eyes, itching to just park the car herself and get it done, so she could get out of the back seat.

Addy trailed behind her parents as they made their way through the throng of people still milling about in the auditorium, Eleanor stopping every few feet to greet another mother. They looked like some sort of pink and green army, Addy thought, all wearing a variation on the theme of floral dresses and skirts with tasteful manicures and strappy sandals.

She was relieved when they finally found seats. She had gotten through a gauntlet of hugs, at least one of which had left her smelling of Chanel and hoping there wasn't frosted lipstick on her cheek. She settled into her seat with a smile plastered on her face and waited for the ceremony to begin.

When "Pomp and Circumstance" began to play, Addy stood with the rest of the audience, letting the nostalgia of the song wash over her. The graduates all looked so bright and shiny and optimistic, each face a unique portrait of hope even in the anonymity of their matching dark suits and white dresses. The succession of speakers, though, rubbed some of the shine from their faces.

The headmaster was new, she was relieved to see. Her face flamed at the memory of the humiliating moment when she'd been asked to leave the school, then she shoved it out of her mind. Today she was Lacey's sister, not a failed former student who had left in shame. There was no sense in dwelling on the past. She closed her eyes and let her mind wander as the speeches droned on.

She smiled to herself, amused by the irony of her own thought. *The past, indeed. It feels like this whole summer is flashing by in past tense.* She was spending her days looking backward, digging up stories that still clamored to be told. Next to her, Eleanor slipped a packet of tissues from her purse as the valedictorian finished speaking to a round of polite applause.

The graduates began to cross the stage.

When Lacey accepted her diploma, Addy put two fingers to her mouth and gave a loud wolf whistle. Onstage, Lacey bent low in a sweeping bow. Eleanor looked at Addy, furious, even as nostalgic tears were streaming down her cheeks. She turned back toward the stage, dabbing at her eyes. Addy could feel her thin shoulders trembling, but she could also see Lacey, still beaming and high-fiving friends as they filed back to their seats.

When it was finally over, the graduates tossed flowers in the air, and the parents and grandparents and brothers and sisters clapped as if their students, their sons and daughters, were the ones who really were going to change the world. Addy stood and turned, watching them file out of the theatre. As Lacey approached the door, a small figure stood, and Lacey leaned into the back row to receive Asia's hug. Addy felt, rather than heard, Eleanor's quiet strangled disapproval. She leaned forward.

"Mother!"

Eleanor looked over her shoulder at Addy, dabbing at her eyes again with a ragged tissue.

Addy paused, and shook her head. "Never mind."

At the sound of her name being called, Addy looked around to see Genevieve waving at her, picking her way through the crowd. She looked as if she were going to the same garden party as all the mothers, clad in a sleeveless floral dress that showed off her tan. Even her blonde perfection, though, couldn't hide the fact that she looked tired and a little stressed. When she caught up to Addy, she brushed each cheek with her own and linked her arm through Addy's.

"I've been trying to get hold of you for an age! We simply must have lunch."

Addy felt a sudden wave of sympathy for Genevieve. Here she was, at the graduation ceremony for the high school she'd attended a decade ago. Did she have nothing else to do on a beautiful Sunday afternoon? Was she still reliving those years, one of those sad women who had peaked at seventeen and was doomed to spend the rest of her life nostalgic for her youth?

"I'd love to, Genevieve, but I'm kind of swamped right now. Let me get through this next deadline, and then maybe I'll have a little breathing room." She only felt a little bad about putting Genevieve off; the thought of spending two hours hearing about wedding invitations and monogrammed towels made her twitch.

"Oh, I understand. Maybe later in the week, then? How about Thursday?" Her eagerness was disconcerting.

"This week is really not an option for me, but let me see about next week. Text me in a few days. But what are you doing here, Genevieve? Who are you here to send off into the world?" The words sounded abrupt, Addy knew, but she couldn't contain her curiosity. What in the world could keep someone living so far in the past?

"Oh, fundraising. For my Junior League project, you know—the parklets. I told you about them, didn't I?"

"Of course. At Mother's, right after I got to town. How's that going?" Addy tried to force a note of polite interest into her voice while her mind raced, trying to remember the parklets project. It was something about small urban parks, but she couldn't recall exactly what.

"Fine." Genevieve's perfect smile tightened just a bit. "That's what I wanted to talk to you about, actually—"

"Oh no, I have no money. Really. None at all." If that was the point of lunch, they might as well not bother. Behind her, she felt her mother's hand on her other elbow. She felt like she was trapped between a pair of bookends.

"Hello, Genevieve. How are you, dear?" Eleanor asked.

"I'm very well, Mrs. Quick. Addy and I were just planning to have lunch in a few days."

"That's wonderful. You should try the Tea Room—they have some lovely salads."

Addy felt as if her face was going to crack from smiling. Across the room, she could see Mason waving to them.

"Daddy is heading for the car. I think we should go."

"It's not about fundraising," Genevieve said in a low voice. "I just want to talk, that's all."

Addy looked at her more closely. Faint lines were beginning to track across her high forehead. The hand on Addy's arm, in spite of its winking diamond, was chapped and red. Her nails were bare. Addy nodded slowly. "Of course. Next week. It'll be fun," she said, and impulsively hugged Genevieve—a real hug this time—before threading her way toward the exit.

Chapter 21

The clock ticking in the back of Addy's mind woke her the next morning, a relentless reminder that losing a single day, even for her sister's graduation, was more than she could afford. She drove up to Biltmore early, hoping desperately that Cornelia Vanderbilt had left some kind of written record that would answer her questions. She also thought she might seek out Ford, the old gentleman she had met when she first went up there, and pick his brain before the house got crowded with visitors, now that tourist season was in full swing.

The curator who had offered to help her weeks earlier—the name Susan came back to her as soon as she entered the room—was at her desk in the cramped warren of cubicles. Susan was surprised to see her, but still as friendly and frazzled as she had been.

"Hey! We were starting to wonder what had happened to you."

Addy glanced guiltily toward the desk that had been reserved for her, still unoccupied, but now covered with stacks of files and papers. Apparently it had become someone's storage space; she was glad. She felt bad that she'd disappeared, when they'd been so nice to let her into the space. Susan saw her glance.

"I'm sorry. Just dump all that on the floor. We weren't sure…"

"It's fine. I don't want to get in anyone's way. I've kind of gone in a slightly different direction, so I've been doing a lot of background reading. Today I have a very specific question: did Cornelia Vanderbilt keep any sort of diary or journal?"

"I don't think so, but I can check." She tapped on her keyboard for a few moments, then sighed. "No, I'm sorry. If she did, we've never found it. There's nothing in the system."

Addy's heart sank, and she realized how much she'd been counting on Cornelia having left a simple written explanation that would confirm her hunch.

"That doesn't mean she didn't," Susan went on, "but honestly, it's doubtful. Cornelia was an artist, and most people don't realize how serious she was about her art. We have piles of sketches that she did whenever she was here, and eventually she moved to England to be a painter. I think she was probably more comfortable in a visual element, rather than in words."

"Thanks," Addy said with a sigh.

"Is there anything else I can help with? Maybe you'd like to look at some of her sketchbooks? There's one full of just noses! I can find it if you want. Some of them are surprisingly good, given that she was about twelve when she did them. I think she drew every nose she could find—must have convinced every staff person on the estate to sit for a drawing. I crack up every time I flip through it."

"Noses. How interesting," Addy said. She didn't want to be rude, but childhood sketches were not going to be helpful. "No, I think I'd better move on to the next thing on my list. Do you happen to know where that sweet old gentleman, Ford Collins, might be?"

Susan smiled, turning back to her desk. "I have no idea. Ford keeps his own schedule. You'll just have to look for him."

Frustrated by the first dead end, and unsure how or where Ford spent his days, Addy went downstairs to the guest information desk. The woman there suggested she check in the break room. Docents and security guards were still straggling in, but no one there had seen Ford. Someone told her to check at the conservatory, down at the bottom of the formal gardens.

She wound through the shade of the azalea garden now past its spring bloom. The wooded park surrounding the house had always felt like the Disney World of gardens to Addy—carefully planned wilderness. She inhaled the scent of pine needles and damp earth. Washington D.C. never smelled quite as lush.

Stepping out of the shade into the full sun that encouraged the riot of bloom in the formal garden, she shaded her eyes and took in the colors. Only a couple of guests had trailed down here this early, but a gardener in a wide-brimmed hat was already here, next to the wall, working around the base of an espaliered apple tree. She walked slowly under the wisteria-laden pergola, smiling to herself. She forgot, sometimes, how spectacular summer could be in the mountains.

Stepping through the glass doors of the huge hothouse, Addy stopped to catch her breath. She felt as if she'd stepped into an exotic jungle. The warm, moist air clung to her skin and filled her lungs. A dense, lush tangle of tropical vines and trees growing helter-skelter surrounded her. It looked like fecund chaos; Addy knew the effect was carefully calculated.

She stood under a tall banana tree, its leaves so broad she could've used one as an umbrella, and took in the room, trying to pick out any flash of non-vegetative color. A person wearing green could disappear in here. She plucked at the front of her blouse, trying to keep it from clinging. The path in here was a much finer gravel, and she stepped gingerly to keep it from spilling into her ballet flats. Passing into the next room, she saw Ford sitting on a bench, gazing into a small fountain. When she sat down on the far end of the bench, he looked up, but didn't appear at all surprised.

"Good morning, Mr. Collins."

"Mornin'. But call me Ford. What brings you out here today, young lady?"

"I was looking for you, Ford."

He nodded, still looking straight ahead at the water trickling over the edge of the stone basin. The steady, liquid patter was soothing.

"How long have you been sitting here?"

"A good long while. I come here every mornin'."

"How can you stand it? It's so hot."

"Feels good to my old bones. Loosens up m' rheumatism so I can get going."

"Sort of like a sauna," she said.

"Maybe so. Besides, it's peaceful before the guests get here. I like to jus' sit and think on things."

Addy looked at him, wiry and wizened. His leathery face was calm, but she had the feeling those sharp eyes didn't miss much.

He gave her a sideways glance. "But I don't suppose you came down here jus' for the quiet, did you?"

"Well, no. Like I said, I was looking for you."

He nodded.

"I'd like to pick your brain a little bit." She held her breath, hoping he'd be flattered.

"Thought you'd never ask," he said, squinting up at the glass roof.

This was going better than expected. "Well, that's excellent." She pulled out a notepad. "All right, first question. Did you know the old estate manager, Randolph Britton?"

"Of course I did. Everybody knew Judge Britton. He was the boss man after Mr. Vanderbilt died. But I didn't know Mr. Vanderbilt—I'm not that old," he said, grinning.

"No," Addy said wryly. "Obviously not. What was Judge Britton like?"

Ford gazed up at the clear glass panes of the roof.

Addy wondered if he'd lost his train of thought.

"He was a good one, Judge Britton," he finally said. "He was a right stickler; you had to be good to work for him. But he was fair, and always took up for us who was doing the work. He had his share of troubles, but that was always down in town. Mrs. Edith kept him on, even through the tough years, and I think that meant a lot to him."

"When you say troubles, you mean…?"

"The Great Depression," Ford said, in a hushed voice. "I don't remember it, mind you, I weren't but a boy, but I heard the talk the whole time I was coming along. It was hard on everybody, even people like the Judge. Shoot, it was tough on the Vanderbilts, although by then it was mostly Mr. John up here, and Mrs. Edith sometimes. Everybody had to make economies."

"So, you mean financial troubles?" she said, just to clarify.

"Course I do."

Addy pulled the firing letter from her purse and unfolded it. "This would have been before your time, but I'm curious what your take on it might be." She handed the letter to Ford and waited while he fumbled with a pair of reading glasses and skimmed the page.

He handed it back to her and shrugged. "Like I said, he was a stickler. Sometimes he had to let folks go if they weren't getting the job done."

She formulated her next sentence carefully. "Did he ever let folks go for, say, misbehaving?"

Ford looked at her.

She felt as if he could read her mind, and that he would certainly disapprove of the scenario she had imagined.

"What do you mean by misbehaving?"

"Things like relationships between staff members. What were the limits? Could, for instance, a lady's maid marry a footman?"

He laughed out loud. "I'm not that old. There weren't lady's maids and footmen up here when I was coming up. George Vanderbilt was long gone by the time I was born. I wasn't toting and carrying for rich folks. I had a skill. Most everyone up here did."

"I hadn't thought of it that way. That's fascinating—it fits with Edith's interest in supporting local fabric makers."

"You know about that? That's good. You should write that in your book. It's like I told you before, Mrs. Edith looked out for folks." He nodded some more, looking pleased.

Addy looked down at the letter in her hand, wondering how to steer him back to it. "Do you think a woman would've been fired for getting pregnant? Unmarried?" She hadn't meant to ask it so bluntly, but there it was.

He was quiet while looking up at the glass panes of the ceiling again. "I reckon so. It happened, sometimes. Folks make mistakes, and sometimes..." He shrugged. "It was a matter of station, I guess. Nobody seemed to pay much notice unless it was something folks down in town would see and talk about."

"So a woman was more likely to get fired than a man? A woman who worked in the public eye?"

"Why are you asking all these questions? Seems to me you're poking around in some kind of messy old business."

"I want to figure out why she was fired." Addy held out the letter again, but he didn't take it.

"Does it matter?"

"Maybe not. But maybe."

"Why? That was ninety years ago. Even I can't remember back that far."

"Exactly. Which is why I think it can't hurt to ask. She was my great-great-aunt."

"And what do you think you're going to find out that's going to make your life any better?" Again, she had that feeling that he was looking into her mind and finding it wanting.

"I think—" She uncrossed her legs, planting herself more firmly on the bench. "I think she had an affair with the Judge and got pregnant, and that's why he fired her."

Ford shrugged. "That doesn't answer my question. Why does that matter to you?"

"Do you think it's plausible?" She wasn't going to let him get her off track.

"Plausible, I reckon," he said.

She nodded. "That's what I thought."

"But you still didn't tell me why it matters."

It was Addy's turn to stare up at the ceiling, avoiding Ford's shrewd gaze. "I found something intriguing, another letter, which I don't really understand." She reached into her purse again and pulled out the envelope containing the letter and the short story, but held on to it, turning it over and over in her hands. It wasn't the piece of the puzzle that Ford was asking about, and on some level she knew it, but she wasn't ready to articulate the other pieces yet.

He waited.

"Obviously, my aunt Martha—the one Judge Britton let go, in that letter—had it, and brought it home from her job here. I'm beginning to think she was hiding it."

Ford sat up straighter. "Why would you think that?"

She opened the envelope and pulled out the letter, handing it to him.

He looked at the page for several long minutes. Addy listened to the quiet drip of water somewhere in a corner of the room. Tourists were beginning to wander through the space, but none had yet stumbled into their little alcove.

Ford handed the paper back to her without comment, and tucked his reading glasses into his shirt pocket.

"What do you think?" she asked.

"I think you're chasin' after your own tail, is what I think. What do you think?"

Addy refolded the page, running one finger along the crease. "I think," she said, choosing her words carefully, "that Judge Britton wanted my aunt Martha to throw this letter away without passing it on to Cornelia."

"Now you're just pullin' craziness out of thin air. Didn't you see that date? Miss Cornelia was off on her honeymoon then. She wasn't around here lookin' at the mail."

Addy nodded. She wasn't convinced that it was nothing, but it seemed unfair to get Ford riled up.

"Besides, that's all water under the bridge a long time ago, and it doesn't matter now," he said.

"Except that it's my dissertation," she said, the words slipping out before she could stop them. "And I disagree, anyway. I think it does matter now. I think it's an interesting insight into at least one, if not two, important figures in American history."

"I don't know what you're goin' on about," Ford said, but when Addy opened her mouth to lay it out in words, he put up a hand to stop her, then pushed himself up from the bench, leaning on his cane. "No, I'm done talking. Except for this: That letter you just showed me? I don't see how you have any claim on that, anyway, if it's like you say and it was meant for Miss Cornelia. By all rights, that ought to belong to the Cecils, seeing as Miss Cornelia was their grandmama."

"No, I don't think—" She started to protest, but he turned around and hobbled away before she could stop him.

Walking from the conservatory back to her car, Addy called Micah, ignoring the beauty that had so bewitched her just half an hour ago. She wasn't ready to talk to him about the birth certificates, but she was troubled by Ford's parting shot. What if he told the Cecils before she figured out what to do about it all, and they claimed ownership of the documents? The letter had clearly been meant for Cornelia, she was certain. Would that give them some kind of claim on it? Micah had mentioned some tricky copyright issues earlier, but she had put it out of her mind. It hadn't occurred to her that the Cecils might also have a claim on the documents. Her concern was accompanied by a twinge of something that felt uncomfortably like guilt.

"We've already had this conversation, but I'll double-check if it makes you feel better. She was born in 1900, right?" Micah was reassuring.

"Yes. The same year as Cornelia Vanderbilt."

"And when did she die again?"

"Zelda or Cornelia?" Addy said.

"Zelda. Cornelia is irrelevant to the short story."

"Even though it was written for her? A gift, so to speak?" She could hear his fingers clicking on the computer keyboard.

"That doesn't matter. There's a chart…oh, here it is. The story officially falls into the category of public domain. You're welcome to publish it. But understand anyone who wants to can reprint it. While you own the physical copy, you don't own any kind of copyright on the story itself."

"That's not what I was worried about. What about the letter? Do I own that?"

"Sure, if it was in your grandmother's house, but why are you worried about that? Who cares?"

She told him about the conversation with Ford, and explained her growing hunch about the letter—that Zelda's and Cornelia's relationship had been more than just friends, or at least had been perceived that way, and that Martha had been told to destroy the evidence. Choosing her words carefully, she skirted around the receipt books and the birth certificates. Some deep instinct told her to save that for an in-person conversation, but it was difficult. Addy was unaccustomed to censoring herself.

He was silent for a moment after she stopped talking. "It's a bit of a stretch," he finally said. "But I guess it's plausible."

"That was Ford's word too."

"I hate to think that of my grandfather, but I guess there was a lot I didn't know about him."

Welcome to the club, Addy thought. Out loud, she said as off-handedly as she could, "We can talk about it later. I just wanted to be sure I'm not violating some privacy law or something, if I submit that letter to a magazine, or even if I manage to write a book about it."

"No. It's definitely yours to publish. Whether it's worth it or not, that's a different issue."

"Well, you can't imagine how much I hate to admit this, but you were right when you told me to slow down before I got that editor in New York involved. Anyway, I have to go. We can get together later and talk about the rest of it."

Addy walked the rest of the way to her car with a knot slowly tightening in her stomach. Micah's last comment reverberated in her thoughts. Was it worth it? He meant publishing the story. She parsed out the end of their conversation—of course that's what he'd meant. But she was beginning to wonder about the entire endeavor, and that was a thought that wouldn't stand up to scrutiny. She was already walking on eggshells around her mother, stymied by Eleanor's volatility and mixed messages. Could she really do the kind of professional research that the dissertation required? Dr. McGregor had insisted the personal angle would strengthen her topic, but she was beginning to wonder if maybe that logic didn't apply to her. The notion of writing about the Zelda story and Martha's connection to it was feeling too personal, threatening to suck her in and nullify whatever scholarly objectivity she had maintained up to this point.

It occurred to her with a blunt force that took her breath away that she'd already found out things she didn't want to know. It shouldn't matter that her grandmother had two conflicting birth certificates. It certainly didn't matter that her salacious brain had jumped to the conclusion that she and Micah might be cousins. It didn't matter—and yet, somehow, it did. Could she write about that? Did she even want to?

Would he go digging in the files now, to find out more? Would logic lead him to the same place it had taken her? They really would have to sit down and talk about it, no matter how much the thought made her cringe.

Chapter 22

An email from Dr. McGregor asking why she had missed their weekly call on Monday awaited Addy in the morning. She groaned—she'd been so focused on getting up to Biltmore the morning before that their call had slipped her mind entirely. She wasn't ready now, so she slipped out early to go to the Biltmore archives downtown. If she could find some kind of evidence that Cornelia had known Zelda, perhaps Dr. McGregor would give her a little more breathing room. When she got there, she was disappointed but unsurprised to find that the collection contained no diaries or journals kept by Cornelia.

When the professor finally texted her, reminding her again, Addy knew she had no choice. She drove back to her parents' house and locked herself in her bedroom so she could make the call in private. The last thing she wanted was some friend of her mother's listening in while she tried to defend herself.

It didn't go well. Addy told her advisor that she had interviewed Ford, explaining that he had been on the estate his entire life and his recollections were giving her excellent insights into the people who lived on and ran Biltmore during its lean years. Dr. McGregor listened, then asked about Dr. Cavendish in her calm, focused way and reminded Addy of the ticking clock, their one-week agreement, the committee waiting to set a date for the defense, and the difficulty of coordinating schedules the closer it got to fall semester.

"I have a lead on a publisher, actually," Addy blurted, trying to get the focus off her lack of definitive progress on the dissertation.

"A publisher for what? The manuscripts? Or are you skipping the dissertation and going straight to a book?"

Addy bit her lip. That wasn't the impression she'd meant to give. "No, not at all. I'm still totally committed, I promise. I was just…exploring my options. Do you know Sequelae magazine?"

"I've heard of it."

"The editor specializes in digging up unpublished material and getting it into the public domain. He wants to come down here and take a look at the manuscript."

There was a moment of silence before Dr. McGregor said, "Isn't that a bit premature?"

"I'm just exploring my options, that's all. I've reached out to a couple of magazines and journals—I figure this will garner a lot of interest. I mean, a new Zelda Fitzgerald story will be huge."

"But in the meantime, all those people you've reached out to know the details about the manuscripts, while I've got your committee members sworn to secrecy so that all the publicity can be directed toward your dissertation?" Addy could almost hear air quotes in her advisor's words.

Addy hadn't thought about that. "I'm sorry. I just wanted to get a sense of how this all works. I didn't think—"

"Addy, I don't mean to be harsh, but I'm beginning to think perhaps you should come back to D.C. for the rest of the summer, after all. You seem to be on a bit of a boondoggle down there."

"No, I'm working, really…it's complicated."

"I can tell. But I would remind you that you don't have time for complications and distractions. Not right now with the clock ticking on your credit hours. You have a schedule, and you are falling behind. Questions of where and how to settle the manuscripts can be answered after you've written your dissertation."

Addy sighed. Dr. McGregor must have heard her, because she kept talking.

"Addy, I'm afraid it's the story itself that has thrown you off. I wish you had stuck with the topic you started with. I think the discovery of an unpublished manuscript is, of course, very exciting and full of potential, but honestly, I thought our idea about working women in 1920s Appalachia would've been a much better showcase for your analytical skills."

Our idea? The thought made Addy cringe. She couldn't go back to that topic—just the memory of writing that first prospectus filled her with mild desperation. "Dr. McGregor, honestly, there's no way I could write that now. I'll hang on to the idea, and maybe one day I'll get to it, but I can't even bear to think about it now that I'm confident about this Zelda story."

"That's what worries me. I'm concerned that the story has turned your head. You're more interested in publicity and money than you are in making a serious contribution to scholarship."

That stung. "No," she protested. "I just got a little distracted. It's not the story—it's personal stuff, really. My grandmother's house, and my sister's graduation." She waved a hand in the air as if she could wave it all away, as if Dr. McGregor could see her rubbing the slate clean and rededicating herself. "I'm focused, I promise."

"It's not to me that you need to be explaining, Addy," Dr. McGregor said gently. "You're only hurting yourself."

"Yes," Addy said, in a small, quiet voice. "I know."

There was a pause. "Well," Dr. McGregor finally said, "I've told you what I think, but ultimately it's your project. Write the dissertation that you want to write. But, Addy, remember that the clock is ticking."

After they hung up, Addy sat at her small desk and stared out the window, trying to motivate herself. It all seemed sort of hopeless—writing a two-hundred-page paper about a mediocre short story by a woman whose life had ended so long ago, in such a sad, tragic way. The old idea about working conditions for women nearly a century ago wasn't any better. It wasn't as if any paper of hers, no matter how good, how thorough, or how well-researched would make the workplace any better, fairer, or easier for women today. Her dissertation wasn't going to make the world a better place, and she was no longer sure how she felt about that. It had begun to feel like nothing more than a circus hoop she had to jump through.

She doodled a circle on the blotter and turned it into a flaming hoop while counting out the days she had left before the beginning of fall semester. If her dissertation really didn't matter in the grand scheme of things, then maybe all she had to do was crank out something moderately acceptable, just to fill the requirement. She pondered that for a moment, trying to reframe the dread hanging over her for so long now, and then opened up her laptop and got to work.

To her surprise, the conversation with Dr. McGregor galvanized Addy's determination to keep moving forward one step at a time, and get the dissertation written. Perhaps she'd finally hit on the secret—it didn't have to be her life's finest work. It was a requirement that she had to fulfill in order to get on with the things that did excite her. She shied away from thinking about what those things might be, and got to work. She even set a timer, telling herself she was going to stay at her desk, focused, for at least three hours.

When the rumblings in her stomach grew too loud to ignore, Addy sat back and listened, trying to figure out who else was home. Satisfied that all was quiet, she went down to the kitchen and made a sandwich. With no one to tell her to use a plate or a napkin, she took it upstairs in her hands and ate it while she stood in the middle of the room, assessing her progress. The prospectus was finally shaping up, as well as a very rough outline of the paper itself. She had also gotten a good start on a tentative bibliography, and come to the pleasing conclusion that even though she'd been beating herself up about not getting a handle on the research, she had actually done quite a lot, at least with regard to Zelda Fitzgerald. She printed out pages and pages of notes she'd taken on the books she'd read and perused, then stacked the books up to go back to the university library. But the Zelda research, as deep as it was, seemed terribly unbalanced. Now that Addy was more confident the letter's intended recipient was Cornelia Vanderbilt, she needed to flesh out her impressions of Cornelia if the dissertation was to present a plausible portrait of both women and how the short story came to be and disappeared.

She brushed a crumb from the front of her dress and carried all the books out to her car.

She started toward the university, but when she drove past Micah's office, she saw his car out front. On an impulse, she parked her car and headed for his door before she could lose her nerve. They needed to talk.

When she peered in at him, his desk was covered in files. He saw her and stood up. "Hey. I wasn't expecting you. Come see all this."

She glanced at the document in his hand, which looked like one of the thank-you notes from her Granny Isabella. "Yeah, I saw a lot of this on Saturday when I was here. Thank you, by the way. That's kind of why I'm here. I wanted to give back your key. And—"

"This is what you looked at? Excellent. Did it answer your questions?"

"More than I wanted to know, I'm afraid." She hesitated, suddenly reluctant to ask what she needed to know. Addy sat down on the edge of the chair, across the cluttered desk from him, and smoothed her dress. "How much of it have you read?"

He was still standing, holding the small notecard in his hand. "Barely any. I just had a few free minutes and thought I'd see what was here. The deed to your grandmother's house is here too."

"I saw it. I saw several peculiar things in that file, actually."

Micah dropped into his chair, the leather creaking as he leaned back into it. "What kind of things?"

Addy wondered for a fleeting second if she had broken some kind of legal rule by walking out with the two birth certificates, but it was too late to do anything about that now.

"There were two copies—different copies—of my grandmama's birth certificate."

"Different how?"

"One listed the parents as Granny and Granddaddy McLean. But the other only listed a mother—my great-great-aunt Martha. Granny Isabella's sister, who died two months after Grandmama was born."

Micah began flipping through the pile.

"Sorry, I took them with me when I left. I wanted to show Mother and Lacey. I'll bring them back, though."

"No worries," Micah shrugged. "They're yours, anyway. I just thought I'd take a look and see if I could make sense of them." He sat back in the chair, looking at the ceiling. "There's no father listed?"

Addy shook her head.

"I suspect," he said, "given the way you marched in here, that you have a theory."

Addy smoothed the soft cotton across her lap again, pressing out invisible wrinkles. "There are receipt books in that file too. Monthly payments of a hundred dollars to my great-grandmother, from the time Grandmama was born until she was twenty-one."

The corner of Micah's mouth turned up a little, as if he were enjoying the mystery. "So what do you think happened?"

"I think Martha got pregnant while she was working at Biltmore, unmarried, and got fired because of it. Then she died right after the baby was born, so Granny Isabella adopted her, and the father gave her a little monthly payment to help out."

"Very good. That kind of thing still happens today. Sounds totally plausible to me."

"And I think your grandfather was the one who got her pregnant," Addy said, watching him carefully.

Micah sat up straighter in the leather chair, frowning. "Why would you think that?"

"Well, he made the payments, for starters. His touch—his metaphorical fingerprint—is the thread that ties all these bits together. The firing, the payments, the house—look at the deed again. It has his signature, and my aunt Martha's. I even found a condolence note from him to Granny Isabella. And the Zelda documents—his initials are on the envelope, along with the word burn."

Micah was shaking his head. "I don't think that's enough evidence."

"I know it's disturbing. Believe me, I don't want to go there any more than you do. It makes us cousins."

His eyes widened, and Addy was gratified to see a faint flush creep up his throat. He seemed to struggle with something, then shook his head again. "There's that," he said, "but honestly, I just meant I don't think you have enough evidence. Legally speaking."

"Maybe not," Addy said, "although frankly, I can't see any other explanation that makes sense. Clearly someone was the father, and clearly those payments to Isabella were meant to support Grandmama."

"That doesn't mean it was Randolph."

"No, but who else would it have been? Who would've been involved in her life at the estate? Because I think clearly it was someone from up there. She was your grandfather's secretary. They were bound to have spent time together. And I can't fathom there was anyone else up there who had the means to make those payments for all those years."

"The Vanderbilts, obviously."

"I don't think so. George was long gone by then—he died in 1914. It was just Cornelia and Edith until John Cecil showed up to marry Cornelia."

"Maybe it was John," Micah said, but he looked doubtful.

Addy gave him a look. "Don't you think I've already done that math? It's not possible, within the dates. I just don't think there's another option. I keep going back to the deed. The names are right there. Plus, there's the perpetuity, which is just odd, don't you think? Maybe it was some kind of hush money."

Micah turned and looked out of the window behind him.

"It's a lot to absorb," Addy said. "That's why I've been texting you. I wanted to talk it through."

He looked back at her, his eyes dark. She couldn't tell if it was sorrow or regret or guilt.

"Sorry, my dad was out of sorts all weekend." He shook his head. "I wonder if he knew about any of this."

"Will you tell him?"

"There wouldn't be much point. Not now. I'll tell Mom, but she never liked my grandfather all that much. Families." He shrugged. "They're all a little quirky, right?"

Addy stood up. She'd been as blunt as she could. Apparently, he didn't want to talk about the fact that they'd slept together ten years ago, not realizing they were cousins. She couldn't quite bring herself to say the words out loud, but at least she'd given him the information to figure it out for himself. It might not even matter—water under the bridge and all—but she couldn't sit here any longer with this heavy weight of insinuation hanging over the room. She needed to get outside.

"Wait, though. I had a bit of news," Micah said.

Addy looked back at him. How could he possibly have any news that would rival the bombshell she'd just dropped on him?

"I think I know someone who might want to buy that manuscript from you."

She sat back down.

"I reached out to a former client in LA, since you seemed to be exploring the options. He's a Hollywood type, and would be willing to pay quite a bit to get his hands on it, I suspect."

"Oh God," Addy groaned, putting her head in her hands.

"What's wrong?"

"I just got a lecture from my dissertation advisor about academic integrity and documentation and all that stuff. I'm not supposed to tell anyone."

He stopped, running his hands through his hair. "You seemed interested last week in exploring your options. So I thought about it, and realized that I know a guy who would love to buy the story from you, if you're interested in selling it. But no pressure. I didn't give him any of your information, of course, and it was totally a preliminary inquiry. Just making the initial contact, that's all. No pressure."

"No pressure? You have no idea." She shook her head. "I have to go. I still have a deadline."

"Do you want me to—"

"No, don't." She turned back in the doorway and looked at him again for a long moment. At least he had the decency to look chagrined. "I'll have to talk to my advisor about it, as well as Mother and Lacey. I haven't really thought it through." Now that she'd gotten over her ten-year-old resentment of Micah, she was finding it difficult to be mad at him at all, whether they were cousins or not.

Chapter 23

On her way to the university library, Addy's mind kept drifting back to Micah's comment about all families being quirky. He'd never said this before that she could remember. In high school, it had always seemed as if his family was perfect. Or maybe that was just the impression she'd gotten from Eleanor. Addy was beginning to realize that it was difficult, from this distance, to know if memories were real or just burnished by nostalgia.

Had her mother known all along? Had she known even when they were in high school that they were related? It was a widely known but rarely mentioned fact that it had once been legal for first cousins to marry in North Carolina, in large part due to the scandalous marriage of a senator who had been born and raised right here in Asheville. Addy thought about the cousins on her father's side of the family and made a face. The thought of a romantic relationship with any of them kind of made her skin crawl. She and Micah weren't even first cousins—second, or once-removed, or something like that; the specifics of genealogical nomenclature had never stuck in her brain—but even that was a bit too close for comfort. Surely Eleanor wouldn't have let her date Micah if she'd had even a hint of all this history. Addy wasn't sure she had the stomach to ask.

Addy stayed at the university long enough to conclude that their holdings didn't include much of anything about Cornelia Vanderbilt's life. She'd have to go back to Biltmore's private archives. But even while she was methodically searching through the sparse records, her mind was replaying the conversation with Micah, and all the little tidbits that were beginning to line up in her mind.

Driving home, she decided it was time to talk to Eleanor. She had considered the problem of the perpetuity in every way she could think of, and kept coming back to the fact that if they told anyone about the story, they'd lose Nellie's house. It was inconceivable, but she couldn't see a way around it, and the conversation with her mother was likely to be rather unpleasant. Perhaps they could skirt around the topic of her relationship with Micah— that was an intimacy that she couldn't imagine sharing with her mother under any circumstances. There was also the matter of the historical marker Eleanor wanted her to draft. How was she going to document the house's history without noting how it came to be in their family? She sat in her car, staring at the house and half wishing someone else was home, but half glad no one was.

Eleanor was in the kitchen making a salad. "I wasn't expecting you, but you're welcome to join me. I didn't think any of us needed a big heavy meal. We've been eating too many sweets this week." She patted her trim stomach.

Addy rolled her eyes. She'd been thinking the same thing, especially given the wedge of pie she'd grabbed out of the fridge that morning in lieu of a more sensible breakfast. But hearing it from her mother's mouth rubbed her the wrong way. She opened the fridge and scanned the shelves, debating how to begin the conversation.

"What do you need?"

"A piece of cheese. Preferably something oozy. I can't live on salad."

Out of the corner of her eye, she saw Eleanor put her hands on her hips. There was a small, uncut Tomme on the top shelf, wrapped in paper.

"Can I cut this?"

"I suppose." Eleanor clipped the words, and began tossing the salad.

Addy put the round of cheese on a plate along with the remains of a crusty, grainy loaf of bread, then poured herself a glass of wine and took it all into the dining room. Eleanor came in a moment later with a small bowl of salad and a glass of water.

"That doesn't look like much of a dinner. Aren't you hungry?"

"Good heavens, Addison. You know better than to talk with food in your mouth. And be careful; you're scattering crumbs all over the table."

Addy looked up, surprised by the irritability in her mother's voice. When she managed to swallow down the large bite of cheese and bread, she cleared her throat.

"What's up? Why are you being snippy?"

"I'm not. I just wonder what's happened to your table manners. You're twenty-eight years old and making a mess like a toddler."

"Sorry. I'll clean up." Addy tried to sound contrite, knowing things were already going badly.

They ate in silence, Eleanor sitting rigid in her chair, stabbing at her salad, and chewing small bites. Addy felt her own frustration rising in response; she remembered this feeling, and it didn't sit well.

"Tell me about your day," she said, determined to hang onto some shred of rational behavior, even in the face of her mother's inexplicable crankiness.

"My day was fine, even if my entire family disappeared and no one had the decency to let me know of their whereabouts."

The crankiness made more sense. "I'm sorry. I went out to do some research, and then just got tied up with things. Where's Daddy?"

"He has Rotary on Tuesdays. You know that."

"Of course. I had forgotten."

"Where is your sister?"

"I don't know," Addy said, trying to figure out why Eleanor was so much more agitated than the evening seemed to warrant.

"She should be here. She has a graduation party to get ready for."

"The party will be fine, Mother. It's all about celebrating Lacey, right? She won't care if it's not perfect."

"She might not, but I will." Eleanor pushed her plate away.

Addy scooped some of the unctuous cheese onto her knife and held it toward her mother, handle first, as a sort of peace offering.

Eleanor wrinkled her nose and shook her head.

Addy sighed. There was no sense in stalling, and really no easy way into this. "Mother, I wanted to talk to you about Grandmama's house." *One explosion at a time.*

Eleanor's lips tightened into a thin line.

"I think we should put it on the market right now, as is." The words were out before she had a chance to process them, but maybe it was a good idea.

"Without cleaning it out and tidying up?"

"Yes. Today. Tomorrow, rather. Just hire an agent and be done with it. We'll get less for it, but it'll be done, and you won't have to think about it anymore. You get upset every time you go over there."

"No. Let people traipse in and out, seeing my mother's life laid out like that? Absolutely not."

"Mother, this is more than any of us needs right now." Now that the idea was percolating, it sounded almost genius, but maybe there was a tiny glitch, if she could only think what it was.

"Besides, why would I—you—want to rush it and take less than it's worth?"

Addy licked her finger and dabbed up the seeds and crumbs scattered on the tablecloth around her plate.

Eleanor made an exasperated noise in her throat.

"I think we're going to lose it," Addy said in a rush.

"Lose what?"

"Grandmama's house."

Eleanor blinked at Addy, then pushed back from the table and went into the kitchen.

Addy had no choice but to follow, calculating the best way to convince her mother, now that she'd started down this path.

Eleanor was standing in the corner, backed up to the sink. Her eyes darted around the room, refusing to meet Addy's. "That's our house—we own it. Mother never owed a cent on it. I don't know what you're talking about."

"You would if you'd let me explain. Remember the perpetuity that Micah told us about?"

Eleanor looked at her then, the rims of her eyes beginning to redden. She shook her head, denying.

"Yes, you do—Micah told us about it. Well, we figured it out. I still don't understand all the reasons, but it appears the house was a gift to Aunt Martha from Micah's grandfather, old Judge Britton. She signed a contract agreeing never to disclose anything she learned while working at Biltmore."

"None of which is relevant to us." Eleanor turned to the sink and began scrubbing the tile backsplash with a toothbrush.

"It is, Mother. I'm pretty certain the thing she wasn't meant to disclose was the letter from Zelda Fitzgerald to Cornelia Vanderbilt." *As well as the fact that he got her pregnant*, Addy thought.

She hadn't thought it was possible for Eleanor's shoulders to bunch up any tighter, but they did.

"The way I see it, if we sell the house now, before the story comes out, then the whole issue will be moot."

Eleanor turned around, shaking her head. "Addison, I know you're enjoying the drama of all this, but that is the most preposterous thing I've ever heard. That was almost a hundred years ago. My mother grew up in that house."

Addy was taken aback. She had expected disbelief or outrage or even stony silence, but not to be patted on the head like a misguided child. "No, it's real, Mother. Apparently a perpetuity really can last for exactly that—almost a hundred years. Ninety-nine, to be precise."

"I just don't believe you."

"Micah says he won't push it, so there's a chance, I guess, that we'd be able to keep the house, but why count on that if we don't have to? Besides, selling it is ultimately the goal anyway, right?"

"Micah says? Do the two of you really believe you're just going to hand over my mother's house?"

"Of course not. But it's a contract. I don't know that there's anything we can do about it. That's why I'm saying we should sell it and be done."

"Or throw that ridiculous letter and story in the garbage."

Addy looked at her mother, and the realization washed over her like a cold wave. That was the solution, and now that Eleanor had hit on it, she would never let it go. "No, Mother. I can't. You don't understand. That story is the academic lottery. People dream their whole lives of finding something like this. And Micah says he might've found a buyer—" Too late, she realized that was the wrong thing to say.

"Micah again. I would think Micah Britton would have a little more respect for his parents' situation right now, if not for mine. The two of you are colluding—again—to embarrass us all, and we all know who gets the short end of that stick."

"Oh, stop it. This is not high school. We both know what we're talking about."

"Well, you need to stop talking to each other. And to me. I'm finished with this absurd conversation." Eleanor turned and practically ran out of the kitchen.

Addy listened as her mother barely made a sound on the stairs, then her bedroom door slammed. Addy hadn't even gotten around to mentioning the historical marker, but it was too late now. She knew her mother wouldn't come back out again tonight.

Chapter 24

Addy tossed and turned before she could fall asleep, and then woke up with the sun. She sat staring out the window in a daze, unsure how to reconcile the conflicts warring in her mind. She reached for her phone on the impulse to talk to Micah again and get him to help her think things through, or maybe reassure her that she wasn't about to break her mother's heart. She was overwhelmed and in need of a sounding board. But she deleted the text without hitting send.

A long shower cleared away some of her confusion, and she realized that she wasn't ready to hear any more of Micah's advice. She needed to kick it around with her sister first, the other person who had something of a vested interest in the whole scenario. And Lacey was much better at staying calm in the face of Eleanor's agitation.

She found Lacey in her room, half awake, thumbs flying over the tiny screen of her phone. She tipped her chin toward the end of the bed, and Addy curled up on it, bunching a pillow up under her head.

"Who are you talking to?"

"Wait," Lacey said, concentrating. "There. Everybody." She dropped the phone on her chest and stretched out long, pushing against Addy through the puffy duvet. "So many graduation parties. I still haven't had a chance to really chill. Poor me."

Addy rolled her eyes, but was glad Lacey was so pleased. There was a poster on the ceiling above the bed of a young woman with spiky brown hair, wearing a jean jacket with nothing under it. "Who is that?"

"Shane McCutcheon. Only the most iconic lesbian in the world. Isn't she hot?" Lacey said. "What's up? I know you didn't come in here to check out my posters."

Addy sighed, a loud, dramatic sound. She wanted to wallow for a minute, here in the warm cocoon of Lacey's space, with her high school worries and pleasures. The still-closed window blinds let enough daylight sneak in around the edges to give the room a golden glow, but kept the world at bay. Maybe they could stay here all day, hiding from things like responsibility and sadness and narrow-minded, mean people.

"Addy? Talk to me."

Addy crawled up the bed and stretched out next to her sister. Lacey slept with her long hair in a thick braid, and by morning it lay loose and fuzzy across the pillow. Addy picked it up and examined the ends in the dim light. "You need a haircut."

"God, not you too. You sound just like Mom."

Addy dropped the braid in mock horror. "I do not."

Lacey turned her head on the pillow to give her a look, one eyebrow raised. "Fine. You don't want to talk about whatever it is."

"I talked to my dissertation advisor yesterday," Addy said, slowly, circling around the various things that had disrupted her sleep. "She's annoyed; thinks I'm slacking off."

"You are," Lacey said.

"I'm torn about what to do with the story and the letter," she said.

"Isn't that what you're writing about?" Lacey sounded mystified.

"Yes, but then what? They should go somewhere. I don't want to just stuff them in an envelope and lose track of them in the attic or something."

Next to her, Lacey shrugged. "Maybe you could frame them," she said. "That way they'd be protected. There's a frame shop downtown that has a sign in the window about archival protection. Isn't that what you need?"

"That would help," Addy said. "But how would I feel about hanging that on my wall? What if there's a fire? Or someone breaks in and steals them?"

"Do you think anyone would?" Lacey sounded doubtful.

"Well, they certainly need to be insured, and you only insure things that are valuable."

"How valuable?" Lacey asked.

"I don't know. I've seen a lot of different things on the internet. It would likely be an auction, so it just depends. But potentially very valuable."

"So I was right—we would get money. That's awesome."

"Wait, it's way more complicated than that," Addy said. "We're not going to get a wad of cash anytime soon. Plus, that's what I'm saying…I'm just not sure what the best thing is."

"How about a safe deposit box? They're fireproof, right? Or maybe you could get yourself a safe, one of those cool ones they have in the movies."

Addy made a frustrated noise. "I think that's one of the things—one of many, really—bothering me. I don't think I can feel good about hiding them away anywhere."

"Well, what would you rather do?"

She thought about it. This manuscript was a piece—albeit tiny—of cultural history, and for better or worse, it was now in her lap. Somewhere in the back of her mind, she'd been nurturing a fantasy about press releases, interviews, television appearances, and all that was slipping away, breaking apart and disappearing under a mountain of minutiae—sordid details of ordinary lives that had to be uncovered, rechecked, confirmed. The mundanity of it all made her want to weep.

"I think I'm feeling responsible for something that seems like a piece of literary history. American history, even. And I have an obligation to do the right thing. Not just preserve it, but make it available to anyone else who wants to read it. It's like a piece of heritage, you know?"

"So donate it to a museum."

Addy nodded, thinking. "Maybe that's the best idea. Especially if they'd put one of those little signs next to it: Donated by Addison Quick."

"Shouldn't it be: 'Donated by the Quick Family'?"

Addy smiled in the half-light. Lacey was right, but Addy was still the star of her own fantasy. She could see herself making the rounds of the morning shows. A rose-colored chiffon would do nicely—something simple but elegant, not too busy, maybe with a high neck, to bring out the color in her cheeks. The image was soothing, a pleasant distraction from the academic and familial challenges she was going to have to wade through to get there.

"Is that it?" Lacey asked. "All of what you were worried about?"

"Good Lord, no. I think maybe Micah's grandfather was our great-grandfather, and I want to put Grandmama's house on the market right now, and did you know first-cousins can still get married in North Carolina?"

Lacey's phone dinged a different chime than the muffled buzzes and whistles they had both been steadily ignoring. "Hold that thought, this is Asia." She pulled the phone out from under the pillow and looked at it. "She took the bus down to the village. Let's go meet her for breakfast." With the energy and resilience unique to teenagers, she threw the covers over Addy and bounced up.

"I thought her aunt and uncle had her phone."

Lacey's response was muffled by the t-shirt she was pulling over her head, but Addy thought she heard the words bought and lame. She wasn't interested enough to ask for a repeat.

"I'll stay here while you shower," Addy said. Had Lacey heard any of what she'd just told her?

"Dude. I'm hungry. Showers are overrated. Let's go."

Addy groaned, but she rolled out of the bed, straightened the lace collar on her blouse, and followed Lacey down the stairs.

Asia was in a booth in the back, eating pancakes as big as her face, with whipped cream and strawberries on top. They slid into the booth and Addy waved a server over while Lacey snagged Asia's fork and took a bite of pancake.

"Good morning," Asia said brightly.

"This is the best pancake in the world," Lacey said, around the mouthful.

The server set two more thick ceramic mugs of coffee on the table, along with more utensils.

Addy picked up a fork and joined Lacey in picking at Asia's plate.

"Y'all stop eating my food," Asia said. "I'm starving."

"I'll share mine," Lacey said.

Asia sighed loudly as Lacey took another big bite, then she looked at Addy. "How's the dissertation coming?"

"Slowly," Addy said. Something felt odd about that segue, but she couldn't put her finger on it. "It's fine. I'm just feeling less than inspired."

"She's distracted," Lacey said.

"Feel free to handle all the other things I've been doing. Like cleaning out Grandmama's house. And that historical marker for Mother. I've barely started on that, and already I know she's going to hate it." She closed her eyes for a second. "Anyway. Never mind about that. Speaking of Grandmama's, do you still have time to help us with the cleaning? I may want to get it done sooner rather than later, *if* we can get Mother on board."

"Of course. It's such a kind-feeling little house. As a matter of fact"— she glanced at Lacey—"I was thinking, maybe I could spend the night there sometimes, so I would have more time to help."

Addy took a sip from her coffee mug, trying to cover up the surprise that must have registered on her face at Asia's comment. What a bizarre suggestion. For a second, Addy felt a little off-kilter, as if her attention was being torn in so many directions she'd lost her hold on normalcy. The feeling was gone as quickly as it had appeared, in a flash, and she shook her head, as if to clear her vision. No, she wasn't crazy. Asia's idea was as absurd as it sounded.

She set the mug on the table with a thump and leaned forward, head in hands.

"What? What did I say?" Asia stage-whispered.

She felt Lacey's hand on her shoulder. "People are staring at you, Addy."

"I don't care." She raised her head and looked across the table at them. "Sorry. I'm feeling overwhelmed all of a sudden. I keep making lists and not crossing anything off."

The server stopped by the table to refill their coffee mugs. By the time she left, Addy had pulled herself together.

She tuned back in as Asia was speaking again, looking chagrined. "Never mind," she said. "It was just a thought."

A look passed between her and Lacey, but Addy couldn't interpret it.

"We can help you make a list," Lacey said. "You need to prioritize."

Addy thought for a long moment, all the loose threads a tangle in her mind. She closed her eyes, and finally one came into focus. "I guess the biggest question at this point is how Martha came to possess the letter and the short story."

"She got them from her job, right? I mean, that's sort of obvious," Lacey said.

"Yes, but I need to be able to document it. Or at least present a workable theory." As she began to think through the issues, Addy's mind settled back into the familiar litany of questions.

"She worked for the Vanderbilts, right?" Asia asked. "Don't you assume Cornelia gave them to her, since they were hers?"

"I guess. I'd give anything to see how she responded, if she wrote back. Did she give them to Martha because she didn't want them? I hate to admit this, but I've even wondered if Martha might have stolen them."

Lacey's eyes widened. "Good Lord. Mother will have a conniption."

"I know. She's already basically not speaking to me."

"Why?" Asia asked.

"That would definitely constitute rocking the boat, on Martha's part. No one is supposed to rock the boat, even dead relatives that we didn't know," Lacey said. She winked at Asia.

"I've figured that out," Asia said. "I meant, why is she not speaking to you?"

Addy ran her thumb up and down the handle of her coffee mug, thinking. She'd already said this much, so it didn't seem to matter if she kept going.

"Last night I suggested we go ahead and put the house on the market now, and not bother with cleaning it out. Just be done with it."

"I bet that went over like a lead balloon," Lacey said.

"Pretty much. Anyway. It's irrelevant, I guess. I need to put it out of my head and focus on figuring out how Zelda and Cornelia even knew each other." She drummed her fingers on the table, thinking and staring at the two girls.

Asia was looking down at her plate, blinking.

"When did the whole letter and story business happen, again?" Lacey asked.

"The letter is dated in June of 1924," Addy said, staring up at the pressed tin ceiling of the café as if the explanation she was looking for would be hidden in the pattern. Ford's words came back to her suddenly. *"Cornelia was on her honeymoon."* She looked from Lacey to Asia. Something had changed in Asia's posture—she looked smaller, as if she had drawn into herself—but the wheels were turning in Addy's mind, and she didn't stop to wonder what the problem was.

Certainty hit her like a brick. "I know what I need to find—the wedding records! They're bound to be up there somewhere. There's a whole display about the wedding, so you know they've found the guest list. The date is perfect, and there's that bit about the honeyed moon."

Lacey nodded. "You think Zelda was invited to the wedding, and that's how they met?"

"I don't know if it's how they met, but it would certainly establish that they knew each other, and that's what I need, I think. It's plausible, anyway." She could feel the flush of adrenalin creeping up her ears. She picked up her purse. "I have to go."

Chapter 25

As she drove toward Biltmore House, Addy formulated a plan. She'd seen an exhibit about the wedding in one of the outbuildings, and would check that first to see if there was any information that would be useful. If not—and she didn't have much hope for it—she'd go on up to the house and track down Susan, the nice curator who'd been so helpful last time. She thought about how to phrase her request with Dr. McGregor's admonition to keep the topic to herself still fresh in her mind. Keeping things to herself was difficult under the best of circumstances—how she was going to do that at Biltmore, nosing around asking more questions about Cornelia Vanderbilt, she had no idea.

As expected, the exhibit at the carriage house, while a beautiful insight into a spectacular high society wedding at the peak of the Jazz Age, didn't have the specific piece of information Addy needed. Cornelia had been a vision of lace and tulle, her smoky eyes nearly hidden under the elaborate, pearl-encrusted headband holding the yards-long veil in place. Addy gazed at the ensemble for a long while, memorizing the silhouette of the long, straight skirt, sheer lace up to the knee, where the under-slip began. She lightly traced the small strip of lace at her own collarbone, still mulling over the problem of how to get a look at the inside of the guest book. It was right there, in a glass cabinet, open to a page that listed a multitude of Honorables and Ladies, and several names she recognized, like Rockefeller and DuPont, but no Fitzgeralds.

Finally, aware that the morning was slipping away from her, she got back in her car and drove up to the house.

Susan was sitting at her desk, surrounded by piles of books and files. When Addy approached, she looked up and, like last time, looked guiltily at the desk that had been assigned to Addy.

"Oh dear. I'm so sorry about that mess. Just shove it over."

"It's okay, I just need to ask a question," Addy said. "I was wondering if I could take a look at some of the artifacts from the Cecil wedding?"

"Oh, good," Susan said. "That is an easy question. We've found boatloads of stuff, but it's not all documented yet. It was a huge society event. Have you seen the exhibit down in the carriage house?"

"I was just there. It's gorgeous. That dress! Y'all have done an amazing job of preserving it."

"Thanks. The textile department was particularly proud of it. Anyway, what did you want to see?"

"Well, in an ideal world, the guest register. But it's down there in the exhibit, I noticed. Is there any chance…" She held her breath, hesitant to ask outright, but not sure what she'd do if Susan said no.

"Oh, we have several copies. No worries. You'll just have to find one." She stood up, beckoning Addy to follow, and headed out into one of the cramped corridors. At the end of the hall, she opened a wooden door into a small room lined with wooden file cabinets and flipped a light switch. A lone bulb in the ceiling lit up as Addy watched, the shape of the filament visible even through the filmy, warped glass.

"It's kind of dusty, I'm afraid, but the window opens. That'll give you more light, anyway. This is where we keep copies of paper items that are either on exhibit or stored in the archives, for climate control. There's also a lot of provenance documentation in here. That stuff is on this side of the room." She waved toward her left. "The guest book is probably in this last cabinet here. I'll get out of the way and close the door so you can reach it. It should be fairly easy to find." She backed into the hall, hand on the doorknob.

"Thank you," Addy said hurriedly. Surprise must have shown on her face, because Susan looked apologetic.

"I'm sorry I can't stay and help you. I've got a meeting with Floral in a few minutes. Gearing up for Christmas, it starts early around here. I'll be back in a couple of hours, if you're still around."

"No, it's fine. Really, thank you so much."

Susan disappeared, closing the door behind her with a quiet click.

Addy gazed around the small room, trying to believe her luck. Dust prickled at the back of her throat, so she opened the casement window. She looked down at the small brick courtyard four stories below. This must have been a servant's room originally. She tried to imagine looking down at this view when it was a delivery yard. The produce and meat and household supplies needed to maintain a busy social calendar and full staff had passed through here, as well as guests' luggage and furniture deliveries and everything else. A short, wide pitch sloped down toward the far side wall, ending abruptly at a tall double-door. That had been the wagon entrance, where carts full of potatoes or milk cans or bolts of drapery fabric would offload their contents directly into the basement storerooms. A small pickup truck with the estate logo on the side pulled into the courtyard, bumping and rumbling over the uneven bricks. It was loud, even from this far up. This would not have been a peaceful room back when work began at the crack of dawn or earlier.

Addy smiled and turned back to the room, hugging herself a little. She hadn't expected to be left alone like this, but now that the opportunity had presented itself, she wanted to enjoy it. It might not happen again.

First, she went to the file cabinet Susan had indicated and pulled open the bottom drawer. Halfway back, she found the W tab. Everything behind it seemed to be wedding-related, and the files were packed in so tightly she could barely flip through to see what they were. Alphabetization appeared to have broken down past the first tier—there was no organizational logic that Addy could see beyond that W. She sank to the floor on her knees, with her feet wedged against the door so no one could open it and accidentally hit her, and began to read the tabs. Some were written in pencil, faded and difficult to read, while others were in ink, sharp and clear.

Finally, after wrapping a papercut in a tissue and tearing off a broken nail, she found a thick folder labelled Registry and wiggled it out of the drawer.

She stood up, stretched her back, and carried the folder over to the window so she could see better.

The pages were held together with a plastic coil binding. Inside, it looked like a typical wedding guest registration book, like the ones she'd seen and signed at every wedding she'd ever been to. Each page appeared to be a photocopy of the original; she thought about the pages in the glass case down the hill, and wished she could touch the original paper. She flipped the pages slowly, scanning the hundreds of signatures, each written in a distinctive hand. At this rate, it would take her hours to find the one she was looking for, if it was even there. She sat back against the closed door, cross-legged, thinking.

She put the guest book to one side and began pulling all the wedding folders from the drawer, so she could see them without getting a crick in her neck. There were files labelled Flowers, Food, Trains. What did trains have to do with the wedding? Her fingers hovered over the folder, but she stopped herself, dropping the Photography file over it. She finally found one labelled Guests, in the faded penciled script that seemed to indicate the folder had been compiled by an earlier curator.

Inside was exactly what she was looking for: a typed guest list. The letterhead indicated that it had been compiled, or at least typed up, by Mrs. Vanderbilt's secretary, a Mr. William Ashby. *How interesting*, Addy thought, *and surprising, that Mrs. Vanderbilt had a male secretary, while Judge Britton had a female secretary.* She made a mental note to find out who had succeeded Martha.

There were two separate lists, one for the ceremony and a much longer one for the reception. Both were alphabetized, until the last few pages of the reception list. The names on those pages appeared in what seemed no particular order, as if they'd been tacked on after the initial list was finished. That's where Addy found what she was looking for: Mr. and Mrs. Francis Scott Key Fitzgerald.

She sat on the floor of the small dusty room, grinning like a fool and feeling as if she'd just made the scoop of the century, simply by reading a list. She pulled out her phone and snapped a picture. She'd get copies before she left, but she couldn't resist the impulse to have her very own little piece of evidence, right there on her phone.

Glancing at the time, Addy decided she could treat herself by digging a little more, now that she had the most important thing she'd come for. She settled in, reaching first for the Trains folder, just out of curiosity.

The secretary, it turned out, had coordinated the arrivals and departures of all the wedding guests over a two-week period, each entry meticulously detailed right down to class of service. She put the folder aside and opened up the one labelled food, noting that she was starting to get a little hungry herself.

Half an hour later, as her stomach was really starting to growl, her phone rang. She'd been so engrossed in photographs of the grand society affair of ninety years ago that the electronic tune was incongruous in the silence. She tore her eyes away from the photos and glanced at the small screen.

The number was unfamiliar, so she considered it briefly, then let it ring and went back to the photos. A few minutes later, the phone rang again. Addy made a frustrated sound in her throat, but answered it this time. The fuzzy sound of her own hello told her that the signal up in this tiny room was weak.

"Addy?" It was Asia, breathless and crackly sounding. "Your mom. I heard the car, and I was—" Static.

Addy stood up quickly, moving to the open window. "Asia? I can barely hear you. Say that again?"

"She fell. I called 911—wait, I hear them now. I didn't want to—"

Faintly, through the crackles, Addy could make out the sound of a siren. The phone went dead. She dropped it into her purse, and began gathering up the folders she'd spread out and jamming them back into the file cabinet, setting aside the guest list. Hopefully, it would only take a minute or so to make a photocopy.

She walked out through the curatorial room, but there was no one around to care that she was leaving, or that she needed to use a copier. For a fleeting second, she wondered if she had the nerve to tuck the folder into her purse and bring it back later, but, for once, common sense overruled her impulsive nature. The photos she had already taken with her phone would be good enough. She dropped the file on Susan's desk, scrawled a hasty thank you on a sticky pad, and left.

Breathless, she got into her car and headed down Approach Road, frustrated by the slow-moving tourists gawking at every quaint stone bridge and sweeping vista. Her phone didn't pick up a decent signal until she got out onto the public road.

She called Lacey. "What's going on?" she demanded, without preamble.

"I'm not sure. I'm on my way to the hospital. Where are you?"

"I just left the estate. What happened?"

"It was so bizarre. Asia was hanging out at Grandmama's, and she heard a car pull up. She kind of freaked, because, you know…Mom. She grabbed her backpack and was about to sneak out the back door, but glanced out the kitchen window again and saw Mom sort of standing in the door of her car. Asia said she kind of rocked back and forth and crumpled to the ground."

"What's wrong with her? Is she okay?"

"I don't know. I told you, I'm on my way to the hospital."

"Did you call Daddy?"

"Yes. I told him Asia and I were both there and I ran out to get sodas, and Asia saw it happen. I'm going to be in so much trouble."

"Whatever. Back up. Why did she fall? She's not that old."

"How am I supposed to know? I'm just glad Asia had that stupid phone." Lacey gave a sharp, shaky laugh. "Asia was afraid she had knocked her head, so she called 911. I guess that counts as an emergency."

"Oh dear."

"She texted me that the ambulance came, and that the neighbor women started showing up, so she left through the back door. I'm pulling in at the hospital now."

"I'll be there in two minutes." Addy hung up, and accelerated around a slow car.

Chapter 26

She found her sister at the admissions desk of the emergency room. She walked up to hear the attendant telling Lacey to have a seat in the waiting area and the doctor would be out to talk to them in a while.

A few minutes later, Mason came in from the parking lot in a suit and tie, carrying his briefcase. He nodded an acknowledgement to his daughters and spoke to the man at the desk, who handed him a sticker and pointed toward the wide double doors leading into the rest of the hospital. He nodded again toward the girls, who had risen from the melamine chairs, and passed through the doors. They closed automatically behind him.

Treatment Area, the sign said. Security Tag Required. Turn off cell phones.

"Why can't we go?" Lacey asked.

"I'll be damned. I'm going to find out," Addy said. She was accustomed to academic bureaucracy, but this didn't seem like the right time to just sit quietly and wait.

"Only one visitor at a time," the desk attendant said.

"Just out of curiosity, why didn't you tell us that when we came in?"

"There are two of you."

Addy glared at him, but it had no effect. She stomped back to her seat.

They waited nearly half an hour. Addy googled heart attack symptoms, stroke symptoms, concussion, and sudden fainting. Something else was nudging at her thoughts, a question that wanted answering, but she couldn't remember what it was. She intermittently texted Mason, but he didn't respond. Lacey alternated between texting and chewing her fingernails, pausing once to take a photo of herself. When Mason finally came through the double doors and walked toward them, they both stood to meet him.

He had loosened his tie, but otherwise looked unperturbed.

"What's wrong?" they asked in unison.

"She's having a benign heart arrhythmia," he said. "She's dehydrated, and her electrolytes are out of balance. They aren't really sure what's going on, so she's going to have to stay until they've figured it out. But it's not a big deal."

"It sounds like a big deal," Lacey muttered.

"What kind of arrhythmia?"

"It's not dangerous, but they want to know why it started so suddenly. Obviously, fainting is a problem. Thus, the overnight."

Addy studied his face, trying to decide if he was telling them everything, then reached up to peel the sticker from his lapel. "Wait here, Lacey," she said, "and I'll bring this back out to you."

"Wait," Mason said, wrapping his fingers around Addy's. "You two head on home. Your mother is taking a nap, and there's nothing for you to do here."

"What are you going to do?" Lacey asked.

"I'll stay here. I brought some paperwork I can take care of."

Lacey shrugged and walked toward the door.

Addy reached for the sticker again. "I'll just peek, then we'll go."

He put his hand over the sticker. "No, really. We'll be fine. Y'all can go."

"Daddy, I'm not a child. I don't want to go. I want to at least lay eyes on my mother," Addy said, struggling to keep her voice down.

Mason looked somewhere over Addy's head. "No," he said firmly. "Go home now. I'll let you know when she's ready for visitors."

Addy studied him some more, and the truth dawned on her.

"She doesn't want to see us."

Mason still didn't meet her eyes. "Go on home." He turned back toward the double doors.

Addy and Lacey walked out together, not speaking. The sun had begun its afternoon slide, and they stepped in and out of shadows.

When they got to their cars, parked across from each other, Lacey said she was going to find Asia, to make sure she wasn't freaked out.

That was it—the odd little wrinkle that had been irritating her. "What was Asia doing at Grandmama's?"

Lacey shrugged. "Like I said. Just hanging out. She had some time before she had to go to work. She likes it there."

"How did she get in?"

Lacey was fumbling through her pockets, looking for her car keys. "I let her in. Don't worry about it."

Something was off, but she still couldn't put her finger on what it was. "Well, thank her for me," she said.

"Of course. Where are you going?"

"I think I'll go over there, to Grandmama's, and make sure everything got closed up properly."

Lacey nodded, and Addy wrapped her arms around her in a long hug.

"It's going to be fine," Lacey said, patting Addy's back.

Maybe she hadn't heard what Mason had—or hadn't—said. Maybe she hadn't understood, didn't realize. Addy felt a bubble of anger and hurt expanding in her chest, rising up, filling her throat. She swallowed and released her sister. "Yes. It's going to be fine."

It is going to be fine, she thought once alone in the quiet of her car. Eleanor's health would be fine, obviously, because to imagine anything otherwise was untenable. She was only in her fifties—not old enough to have a serious problem. Not wanting her own daughters to visit was the troubling part, but Addy managed to convince herself that was understandable. Eleanor wouldn't want them to see her looking ill or unkempt or vulnerable. That was just her mother's way—it wasn't at all surprising, really. Hovering in the back of her mind was a darker worry, a tiny flame of guilt about her own complicity. Had she pushed too hard last night, insisting that they needed to sell Nellie's house right away? She shied away from the thought, pulling into her grandmother's driveway and stopping behind Eleanor's car with a flash of mild surprise. She had half-forgotten that it would be there. She shook her head, appalled at her own distraction, and checked the doors; someone had locked it. She wondered vaguely where the keys were.

She wandered slowly through the rooms, checking the windows. She wondered what Eleanor had been planning to do. She might as well do something productive herself since she was there. She got a garbage bag and went into Nellie's bedroom, looking for something small she could clear out and throw away. Sorting and deciding and donating were all more effort than she could bring herself to do today.

She opened the top drawer of the highboy. It was full of underwear. Addy closed her eyes for a second, remembering her grandmother's decline: the month of addled discomfort after the fall that broke her hip, the pneumonia that weakened and finally killed her. She sniffled. An ambulance had taken her out of this little house, and she had never made it back. The last time Addy saw her alive, she'd been confused, rubbing at the cannula that wouldn't stay in her nostrils and turning her head away from the watery applesauce Eleanor was trying to feed her.

Addy sniffled, and began scooping the utilitarian white underthings into the garbage bag. The faint scent of lavender wafted up from a sachet. Grandmama had kept one in every drawer. Addy's fingers found the tiny lace bag, and pulled it out, and rolled it around, releasing more of the scent. She tucked it in the pocket of her dress.

When the top drawer was empty, she went to the next, which was full of bras and girdles and slips, then the next, full of pantyhose. All went into the garbage bag. She didn't have the heart to just pull out the drawer and dump them. Instead, she pulled out each sachet, saving it, and then pulled out the lingerie, letting the fabrics—silky, soft, cottony, worn—trail through her fingers.

The fourth drawer was nightgowns. Addy pulled them out one at a time and realized they all still had price tags. Grandmama had worn pajamas. Addy looked at the pink nightgowns with their lace trim and tiny flowers and pleats and ruffles. *So optimistic.* Eleanor must have bought them in anticipation of Grandmama coming home from the hospital and getting on with her life.

Addy shoved them back in the drawer without folding them, tied up the garbage bag, and left, closing and locking the front door. She put the bag in the trunk of her car, and was about to get in and drive away when she heard a shrill "yoo-hoo" that broke the evening quiet. She looked around.

A plump, white-haired woman was standing on the porch of the house across the street, waving to her. Addy waved back, then stepped across the street, trying to remember her name. It wouldn't come.

"You must be Addison. You probably don't remember me. I'm Betty Adcock."

"Of course, Mrs. Adcock. How are you?"

"I'm fine, dear, but I was terribly concerned about your mother this afternoon. Is she all right?"

Addy hesitated for a second, unsure how to answer. "She's fine," she said finally.

"I just happened to see it from my living room window. She kind of crumpled down to the ground. I was worried that she hit her head, but by the time I got my shoes on and found my stick so I could walk over here, the rescue squad showed up. I know I walk slow, but they sure did get here fast."

"Thank you for checking on her, Mrs. Adcock." She wasn't sure what else to say, so she reached up and patted the old woman's hand, resting on the porch rail.

"Oh, you're welcome, dear. She was always so good to your grandmother. Bless her heart. It does worry a body so, living alone at my age. But I'm surprised to see you over here. I guess they checked her out and sent her on home?"

"My father is with her at the hospital. I think she was dehydrated. I'm sure she'll be fine. She's probably on her way home now," she said, forcing a broad, brittle smile.

"You're sure it wasn't a stroke?" Mrs. Adcock squinted down at her, shading her eyes against the rose-gold evening light. "I do worry about a stroke. Oh, here comes Lorraine Wells. Lorraine got there before I did."

Lorraine was closer to Eleanor's age. They might even have known each other in high school, if Addy recalled correctly, but Addy hadn't seen her in years. She was struck now, uncomfortably, by the woman's graying hair and the small wrinkles around her mouth. She had on baggy knee-length shorts that showed off a network of purple veins, and a pair of those rubber scuffs with the holes in them, in a traffic-stopping shade of orange. Eleanor had never cared for her, Addy knew. Even if they had known each other forty years ago, they clearly had nothing in common now.

"Addison," the woman wheezed, shuffling up in her orange shoes.

"Hello, Mrs. Wells."

"Is your mother all right? She looked so thin and frail, like she might break. She doesn't have cancer, does she?" She dropped her voice theatrically on cancer, as if saying it out loud would make it true.

"No, no. She was just dehydrated. She'll be fine. Thanks for your help."

"I wanted to ride with her to the hospital, but they wouldn't let me."

Addy had to work to keep her face neutral. If her mother hadn't actually had a heart attack, waking up in an ambulance to see Lorraine Wells hovering over her might have given her one. Eleanor had, to Addy's knowledge, never been openly rude to her mother's neighbor, but they certainly weren't friends. When Addy was small, spending nights at Grandmama's, she'd wandered the neighborhood and often wound up at Lorraine's, drawn to the cheap sugary candy she kept in a bowl by the door, and the occasional appearance of a litter of kittens. Grandmama Nellie had warned her that the cats would give her ringworm; Eleanor had said Mrs. Wells was trashy, and forbidden Addy from going in her house.

"Louise Etheridge said they wouldn't let me go, but I thought it was worth a try. I didn't want your poor mama to come to all by herself in that ambulance and be scared half to death. What did they say was the matter with her?" There was something avid in her eyes that made Addy want to take a step backward.

This was probably the most exciting thing that had happened on the quiet street in ages. Out of the corner of her eye, Addy could see the aforementioned Louise Etheridge making her way down her front steps. Eleanor would be horrified to know this gaggle of gossips were all standing around talking about her public display of what was certainly nothing. Addy made herself a silent promise not to breathe a word of this to her mother.

"Addison Quick. What in the world is going on at your grandmother's house?" Mrs. Etheridge asked as she walked briskly through Mrs. Adcock's grass. "You young people coming and going at all hours, and now your poor mama laid out flat in the driveway like that. And I'm worried there are hoodlums sneaking around at night. Your grandmama must be rolling over in her grave. It's a travesty, the way you all have just left her house sitting empty like that."

"You just hush, Louise," Mrs. Adcock said. "The poor child's had enough of a scare today without you making a fuss."

"Nosy Parker," Mrs. Wells muttered, close to Addy's shoulder.

Addy bit the inside of her cheek. She'd begun to feel cornered, but suddenly a flash of hysteria shot through her chest and she knew she needed to extricate herself before she burst out laughing.

"I tried to tell Eleanor myself that I thought I saw a light in there in the middle of the night," Mrs. Etheridge went on, ignoring the other two women. "But she was out cold."

"Louise Etheridge, you did no such thing," Mrs. Wells said. "Go on back home and get back to scrubbing the life out of something. Leave Addy be."

Addy found herself liking the woman all over again, in spite of her unfortunate shoes.

"And furthermore," Mrs. Etheridge said, as if she was just getting warmed up, "I'd like to know how that ambulance got there before any of us had a chance to run back inside and call 911." She looked triumphantly at Mrs. Wells, hands on her hips, as if she'd trumped any contradiction.

"Well, good golly, Louise. Just be grateful someone had the sense to call instead of marching out and yelling at a poor unconscious woman about the state of the neighborhood," Mrs. Wells said.

Addy began to inch away from the group. "Thanks again, y'all. We really appreciate your help."

"Tell your mama to come say hey when she's feeling better," Mrs. Adcock said, leaning heavily on her cane.

"Of course," Addy said, and turned to cross the street, knowing she had no intention of telling Eleanor any such thing.

Addy and Lacey hung around the house the rest of the evening, waiting for Mason to come home from the hospital. When he finally did, he looked tired, but not particularly worried. Everything seemed fine, he told them. Their mother was staying for observation, but she'd had plenty of IV fluids and all the tests were coming back normal. Addy felt as if something was missing from the conversation, but when she pressed him, Mason just shrugged and said, clear-eyed and straight-faced, that Eleanor would be fine.

The next morning, though, when Addy went down to the kitchen and found Mason dressed down in khaki pants and a golf shirt, getting ready to go back to the hospital, she suggested he take the morning off. He looked tired, and she and Lacey could go sit with Eleanor to keep her company, she implored.

Her sister appeared just then, already dressed as well.

"Of course not. I'm fine."

"Really, Daddy. We don't mind. Right, Lacey?"

Mason fiddled with the top button of his shirt as if he felt lost without a tie.

"Sure," Lacey said. "I'm ready."

"Girls," Mason said finally. "Your mother doesn't want visitors. That's all. I will go stay with her, and then I will bring her home when she's released. You don't need to bother yourselves, she doesn't want that."

The silence stretched out until Mason turned and busied himself putting dishes in the sink and gathering up his newspaper.

"I'm going to take that at face value, then," Lacey said. "But text if you change your mind." She hovered by the door, waiting to see what would happen next.

Addy looked from one to the other, the words bubbling up in her chest, but when she opened her mouth, nothing came out. She thought about the meddling neighbors yesterday, all plying her for something salacious or at least gossip-worthy. She flushed again, remembering her stammering inability to answer any of their questions, and Mrs. Adcock's surprise that Addy was there instead of at her mother's bedside. She felt like she was banging her head against a locked door—even when she wanted to do the right thing, be the dutiful daughter, she couldn't get in.

Finally, she nodded once, unable to summon any words that wouldn't sound petulant and whiny.

Mason eyed them both again, and left.

Addy moved to the door that closed behind him and stood watching, out of sight, as he got into his car and backed out of the driveway.

"Let it go, Addy," Lacey said, coming up behind her.

"Really? Mother is in the hospital and doesn't want us to visit, and you want me to just let that go?"

Lacey shrugged. "It's how she is. You know that. She doesn't want to worry or bother us. She's used to being the mother, not the patient."

Again, Addy opened her mouth to retort, but stopped herself.

"Let it go," Lacey said gently, and slipped past her, out the door.

Addy watched as she too backed her car out of the driveway and left.

Alone in the house, Addy brooded. Was Lacey really that oblivious, or did she have some secret wisdom that Addy had somehow missed? How could she stay so calm when it was obvious their mother was just shutting them out?

Anger took her breath away. Anger at Eleanor, and at herself for her own fury, for her inability to be like Lacey. Was this what her relationship with Eleanor was doomed to be, forever? It was suffocating. She didn't want that, but didn't know how to make it stop. Every time she tried to get along with her mother, the doors slammed in her face again. It had been that way as long as she could remember, and she didn't know how to see it any differently. Nearly every time they interacted, her thoughts slipped into the familiar rutted tracks of hurt and resentment.

Too frustrated to settle into work and too caged to stay in the house, Addy finally stomped out for a walk, letting the door slam. Her feet turned automatically toward the gate that marked the boundary of the development— the large, quiet houses of her parents' friends and neighbors, set back from the street, felt like a judgement that she would never be the debutante, the bride, the Genevieve that her mother had wanted.

She walked for two hours, muttering to herself, occasionally wiping her eyes on her sleeve. She spoke to no one, and saw no one she knew. The road tilted up, and up, and she climbed, panting, heart pounding, forcing herself to keep up the pace. The sound of her breath filled her head and drove out everything else. Beads of sweat gathered at her hairline and dripped down her temples and the back of her neck. Her eyes stung.

By the time she made it back down the hill into Biltmore Village, the roiling storm of emotions had worn itself out. She sank onto the end one of the benches that were conveniently placed throughout the small historic district and closed her eyes, resting in the shade of an oak tree. Her mind was blessedly clear.

The bench creaked under the weight of another person sitting down, and Addy opened her eyes. Micah now sat at the other end of the bench, peering at her from under the brim of a straw hat.

"Good Lord, what are you wearing?" she asked, taking in his seersucker suit and white buckskin Oxfords.

"I just came from court," he said, sounding a little defensive.

"Well, good. That's exactly where that outfit belongs. I'm going to start calling you Atticus Finch."

He shrugged. "It gets the job done." He loosened his tie and leaned his head back, looking up into the branches above. "Why are you sitting here on this bench in the middle of the day?" he asked, a hint of curiosity tilting the question up at the end.

"I was walking it off."

A beat of silence passed. "How's your mom?" Micah finally asked.

"You heard?" Addy asked without looking over at him.

"Of course. Everyone hears everything. You know that."

"She's fine," Addy said. "She fainted getting out of her car. She was dehydrated, that's all."

"Well, that's good," Micah said. "That it's not worse. Is she home yet?"

"Nope."

"So what were you walking off?"

She waved a hand in a wide circle above her head, as if it could encompass the whole world. "Everything."

Micah cocked his head and remained still, listening.

He was always a very good listener, Addy thought.

"Everything," she said again, and smiled at him, a wide, calm smile that belied her morning's angst.

"And did it work?"

"It helped. Buy me lunch? I didn't bring my purse." She felt a twinge of guilt about the conversation they hadn't had, and that she had no intention of broaching today.

"Sure," Micah said, standing and holding out a hand to help her up.

Chapter 27

When Mason got home from the hospital in the early evening, Addy was in the kitchen waiting for him. She had made up her mind that if Eleanor wasn't with him, she was going to the hospital, and was not going to be talked out of it.

He tried to put her off again, saying Eleanor would be home in the morning.

"I feel guilty that I haven't been," Addy blurted, surprised to hear the sentence come out of her mouth.

Mason glanced up from the mail he was flipping through. "Fine," he said. "Go."

She hadn't expected that, and looked at him more closely. His chin was stubbly.

"Why did she change her mind?"

Mason set the mail down and looked up at her. "She didn't. I did. They're keeping her one more night to make sure her electrolytes are back in balance."

Addy thought it over. "Why is she having a problem with her electrolytes to begin with? And why would that prompt you to change your mind about my going over there?"

Mason rubbed his temples, palm splayed wide, hiding his eyes. "Your mother is stressed, that's all. The past couple of months have been difficult for her, and she hasn't been taking proper care of herself," he said stiffly. "And no, it's not anyone's fault."

"You mean she's having a nervous breakdown?" Addy gripped the back of a chair.

"No, that's not what I mean at all. She's just tired. She hasn't been eating enough, and has let herself get dehydrated. They'll have her back on track by tomorrow."

Addy let out a breath. Dehydration. That was manageable. She still didn't understand why Mason was telling her she could visit now when he wouldn't let them in yesterday, but she didn't want to stand around and wait for him to change his mind. She grabbed her purse and headed out the door.

When she found her mother's room, she tapped on the door.

"Come in," Eleanor called in what Addy thought of as her public voice—precise and slightly melodic, and pitched a little higher as if consciously making herself sound sweetly Southern.

Addy pushed the door open and peered around the edge.

Eleanor's small smile, the one she usually reserved for strangers and restaurant wait staff, faded. She looked almost like her usual self with her hair tidy and hands folded calmly in her lap, except for the tube taped to the back of one hand and the white quilted bed jacket exacerbating her pallor.

Addy left the door half open, unsure of hospital protocol, and sat down on the plastic chair next to the bed.

Eleanor looked out the window.

"How're you feeling, Mother?" she asked.

"Fine," Eleanor said, her head still turned away. "You didn't need to drive all the way over here. I told your father I didn't want any visitors."

Addy processed that. Her father had explicitly gone against Eleanor's instructions, which never happened. Her alarm sharpened. "I know. But I wanted to see you. It sounds like you're kind of worn out."

"I'm fine. I just said that."

Addy nodded and sat back in the chair, watching Eleanor's hands fold and refold the hem of the sheet. The veins stood out, blue under her pale skin, white surgical tape covering the intersection between medicine and flesh.

"You can head on home now," Eleanor said when the silence had stretched out longer than she could take.

Addy looked at those hands again. She wanted to feel sorry, or sympathetic, or even worried—something that would make her a decent person, a normal daughter. Instead, she felt like she was banging her head against a locked door as she usually did when interacting with her mother. Wasn't this the moment when families were supposed to come together and support each other, tears and hugs and proclamations of undying love and all that? Sitting in silence with a mother who wanted her to leave felt terribly wrong. She wanted to fix it somehow, or at least break through that shell and make her mother talk to her. Anything other than this cold silence.

"I saw Micah this morning," she said. "He says he hopes you feel better. And Mrs. Adcock, and all those crazy old neighbor women." So much for her resolve not to tell Eleanor about her encounter with the neighbors. Would she never learn when to keep her mouth shut?

Eleanor finally turned and looked at Addy. Her expression was inscrutable. "What did you tell them?"

"The truth. That you were dehydrated." She raised her chin, just a fraction. "You startled them. Mrs. Adcock saw you fall. She was worried you'd had a stroke."

Eleanor glared at her. "It's none of their business."

"Except for the part where you were lying on the driveway, unconscious."

A dark flush crept up Eleanor's throat, and Addy felt a tiny, shameful lick of satisfaction. Part of her wanted to twist the knife, but she didn't. Eleanor's cheeks were hollow beneath her sharp cheekbones and the circles under her eyes were dark. She really didn't look well. A realization began to dawn on Addy.

"My health is none of anyone's business. And that includes you."

Addy looked back at Eleanor's hands, still plucking at the sheet.

"Why were you dehydrated, Mother?" It was a point-blank question, and she doubted she'd get a response.

"It's all too much," Eleanor said. "You, and Lacey, and the house, and this ridiculous wild goose chase that you're on. And that girl, Asia." Her head nodded back and forth, rolling against the pillows.

"She hasn't been eating enough." Mason's words echoed in Addy's mind, prompting another direct question. "Are you eating?"

Eleanor's eyes popped open, inscrutable. "I find I don't have much appetite," she said in an acerbic voice. "You may head home now. And close that door. I don't need everyone and their cousin looking at me."

Addy reached over with one hand and pushed the door closed, but made no move to vacate her chair. She looked at Eleanor's hands and cheekbones, and the flat slope of her chest, falling away from the sharp ridge of her collarbones, and the truth clicked. "You're not eating. That's the problem. That explains it all."

The hectic flush was back in Eleanor's cheeks.

Addy felt sick. She had figured out what was wrong, and it was so… broken. So wrong. She had wormed her way into Eleanor's small, sad world, and found it was far lonelier than she ever realized. How could she have missed it? She was so absorbed in her own worries, so set against Eleanor even before she arrived in Asheville, that she hadn't even noticed.

"Mother, listen," she said, leaning forward and touching her mother's forearm. Eleanor flinched, but Addy didn't move her hand. "There was a girl on my hall when I was an undergrad who had an eating disorder. She got a ton of therapy and managed to graduate only a semester behind. And I had a student a couple of years ago, who didn't get behind at all. There are specialists nowadays who know how to help with this stuff."

Eleanor shrugged off Addy's hand, not looking at her.

"I do not have an eating disorder. I have simply been too stressed lately to eat very much. It caught up with me, that's all." She spat out the words 'eating' and 'disorder' as if they might leave a foul taste in her mouth. "As I have pointed out, my appetite is none of anyone's business. I'm fine," she said, but her voice was beginning to waver.

Addy swallowed down the lump in her throat. "You don't look fine."

The institutional clock on the wall ticked, each second that passed a louder reminder of her own uselessness. She was utterly unprepared for any of the situations she had stumbled into in the last few weeks. *All those classes,* she thought, shaking her head. All those lectures and books and exams and papers, and she didn't know how to settle an estate or help a homeless teenager or talk to her own mother. The realization made it hard to breathe.

She stood up abruptly and reached for the door, but with an effort, stopped herself. She paced around the tiny room, trying to find her center. After a few turns, she realized Eleanor was watching her. She wracked her brain for some way to dispel the suffocating atmosphere that blanketed them.

"Yesterday, before you fell, I was up at Biltmore. I found the wedding registry from Cornelia Vanderbilt's wedding. I can't believe I didn't think to look for it sooner."

Eleanor sighed. "Now, don't you know that wedding was something to see."

"It was." Addy nodded. Of course, this would be the way to get her mother talking, she thought. "You know, there's a new exhibit about the wedding at the carriage house. Have you seen it?"

"No, I haven't been up there in a while."

"We should go. Cornelia's dress is there. I've never seen so much tulle."

"That would be nice. Did you see anyone when you were there? Any of the Cecils?"

"No." She paused, choosing her words. "I guess they spend most of their time in an office, not in the exhibits."

"Well, I'm sure Mimi would be happy to help if you need anything. You should call her."

"No, I don't need to bother the Cecils. I was looking for the wedding registry, but it turns out they have photocopies up in the curatorial department. I found exactly what I needed. Scott and Zelda Fitzgerald were at the wedding."

Eleanor's face, which had begun to relax, snapped back to suspicion. "Are you back to that? Let it go, Addison."

"It's my dissertation, Mother. I need to get it done. I thought that was what you wanted?"

Eleanor seemed to struggle for a moment, confronted with the discrepancies in her own desires. "Not at the cost of my family's reputation."

"Mother, this has nothing to do with our family. Our reputation rests on our actions, not something that happened ninety years ago, whatever that was."

Eleanor closed her eyes and leaned back against the pillows. "One day, when you're older, maybe you'll understand."

"Help me understand now, Mother. I'm just trying to finish school. To do the thing you've been harping on my whole life."

Eleanor was unmoved.

Addy watched her face, looking for some sign that they were actually communicating instead of just sniping at each other. She wanted to weep with frustration. She'd never met anyone so stubborn.

"I don't harp," Eleanor finally said. Her face took on a hazy look for a minute. "That was Granny's job."

Addy frowned. "Granny Isabella? What do you mean?" She made a mental note not to point out the questions she still hadn't answered about Grandmama's birth in the hope that her mother would keep talking.

Eleanor sighed and opened her eyes. "It wasn't her fault. She didn't have an easy life."

"Tell me about that. I don't really know anything about her."

"She lived with us when I was small. She helped raise me. Mother went back to teaching, you know, after Daddy died."

Addy nodded. That was one of the only things she did know about her great-grandmother.

"She had high standards. High expectations. She spent her whole life working to make a better life for her family. She was born into nothing—a kind of poverty you girls can't imagine. Not much more than a shack in a hollow, up in the hills. They sent her out to work as a maid when she was just a teenager. She didn't even get to finish high school."

Addy sat back down in the chair, moving slowly so as not to break the spell. This was a piece of family history that Eleanor had never talked about. Grandmama had alluded to it, but Eleanor had always changed the subject.

"That was why she was such a stickler about education. She made sure your grandmother went to college, and she never let up on me. She meant well."

"How old was she when she died?" Addy asked. She'd always found the longevity in her family comforting. It was especially so now, with that tube taped to the back of her mother's hand.

"Eighty-five. She died while I was in graduate school. That was the only thing she ever wanted me to do."

Addy blinked, processing her mother's words. "What are you talking about? When were you in graduate school?"

Eleanor looked as if she had gotten lost in her memories during another long silence. Addy waited.

"A long time ago. After college. I never finished." There was a desolation in her voice that Addy had never heard before.

"Why didn't I know this?"

Eleanor's thin shoulders lifted and dropped. "It doesn't matter now."

"Where were you? What kind of degree was it? Why did you quit?"

"Oh, Addison. It was so long ago." She waved one hand vaguely in the air. "Never mind."

"Tell me, Mother." She took a breath. "Please."

"I was getting a Master's in Education. At Chapel Hill."

"But that's great. Why didn't you ever tell me that?"

"Because it doesn't matter."

"Yes, it does. You should be proud of it. Even starting is more than most people ever do. What made you stop?"

Eleanor looked directly at her. "I got pregnant."

"Oh." Addy realized in a flash what that meant. "Oh. You mean with me."

Her mother was looking toward the window again, with that inward expression. The color in her cheeks had faded, leaving her even more pale and drawn. Addy mulled over what she'd just said, wondering—but not, really—why she'd never heard any of this before. She was surprised that her grandmother, at the very least, had never mentioned it. The idea that her mother had once had a different plan for her life was discombobulating. She felt as if the world had tilted just enough to throw her balance off.

"You could've—"

"I came home. We got married. And that was that."

Addy felt a small surge of relief, tinged with shame at her own scandalous imaginings. Of course Mason was her father. Anyone could see that in the shape of her eyes and the set of her jaw. Of course she knew that. She'd always known her parents were high school sweethearts. She shook herself; Eleanor's melodrama was getting to her. Nothing had changed—nothing fundamental, anyway.

The unfinished graduate school, though—that was something to think about and process. Addy looked at her mother. Understanding her was almost like putting together a jigsaw puzzle, over many years. This was a new piece, and it connected some other bits that had never made sense. This was why Eleanor had been so hung up on Addy finishing her own degree. A straight line was coming clearer in Addy's mind, from Isabella, through Nellie, to Eleanor, leading right to Addy's own sleepless nights.

It was remarkable, really, like an invisible web that would never let her go. She looked at her mother, who had leaned back against the pillows and closed her eyes. Even at rest, the corners of her mouth turned down. Where Lacey might see worry or stress, Addy had always seen disapproval. She made herself sit with it now, studying her mother's face, trying to see beyond the criticism to the woman underneath who had given up her own dreams for Addy. Were they dreams? Had Eleanor dreamt of an academic life? Had she grown up with that vision of herself, or had that been Nellie's vision? Or even Granny Isabella's? The sticky thread binding their lives together pulled tighter. For a second, Addy felt as if she were falling down a rabbit hole, into a life that wasn't her own—as if she were unwittingly playing out a role that had been scripted and cast long before she came along.

Eleanor's breathing deepened. She had fallen asleep.

Addy thought about waking her up and demanding to know more. Why hadn't she finished? What had she wanted to do when she finished school? How had Daddy felt about her quitting? It wasn't all that long ago, really. It wasn't as if women were expected to stay home and raise babies in the eighties.

She realized, sitting there listening to Eleanor's soft, even breathing, that she wouldn't wake her up, and even if she did, the questions would just lodge in her throat. She was too afraid of the answers. Or maybe it was the asking that frightened her. Had she ever had a single genuine conversation with her mother? She'd kept her own soft emotional underbelly always hidden, behind a steady stream of identities—so many she'd lost track of which one was real. Addy the truth-teller, the honest one, was paralyzed by the fear of her own truth.

Why had Mason even sent her to the hospital? Maybe she already knew the answer. A hot wave of shame washed over her. Had things between her and Eleanor gotten so bad that even her unflappable father felt compelled to intervene?

Addy had been running away from conflict with her mother for as long as she could remember, and nothing had changed. Maybe one day she'd be able to face the conflict head-on, but today wasn't that day.

She stood up and tiptoed out of her mother's private hospital room.

Chapter 28

Addy didn't cry on the way home. She thought about it—a long, cathartic cry seemed like the appropriate response—but no tears came. She felt only tired and a little strung out. She went to bed and slept without dreaming.

When she finally got up the next morning, the house was quiet and there was a note on the kitchen counter. Eleanor was being discharged, and Mason had gone to pick her up. Addy felt as if she was still awash in the aftermath of an emotional storm, too vulnerable to face her mother head on. She headed back to the university library and stayed there all day.

Mother will want the peace and quiet.

By the time her phone pinged in the early afternoon, she had wrestled her most discomfiting feelings into the background and settled into the groove of writing. The new prospectus was almost ready to go. She just needed to clarify her thoughts about how the story had gotten from Biltmore House to the little bungalow on the other side of town. Dr. McGregor was probably apoplectic at how overdue it was, but Addy had begun to feel curiously confident in her progress. Her thoughts had lined up so clearly that she knew the writing would flow when she sat down to it.

The text was from Micah. *It's Friday. Drumming?*

Addy nodded to herself as she texted back. *Perfect.*

Micah would be a great sounding board. It was beginning to look as if he had as much of a stake in the story she was telling as she did. Besides, she needed a little bit of a mental health break. The last couple of days had been emotionally exhausting.

Micah stepped onto the front porch at six o'clock on the dot. Addy was waiting for him, already dressed in a lavender skirt and silvery jersey tank top. It was comfortable and perfect for dancing. The fact that it brought out the pink in her cheeks and made her feel as if she were floating was irrelevant. She stepped out from behind the screen door before he had a chance to knock.

In the car, they were both quiet. Something had shifted—this felt more like a date than their midweek taco lunch.

Micah broke the silence. "How's your mom?"

"Fine," Addy said. She wasn't ready to talk about it. "She was just dehydrated, so they pumped her full of fluids and now she's home. How's your dad?"

"Today was a pretty good day. You look great, by the way. I meant to say that."

"Thank you." Addy watched him out of the corner of her eye as he maneuvered the car into the heavy traffic headed for downtown. Dark blond curls tumbled loosely over his forehead. It was all Addy could do not to reach over and brush them back. Heavy stubble shadowed his jawline.

"You realize we're probably first cousins, right?" she said, unable to skirt the issue any longer.

Micah glanced over at her, then looked back at the traffic. "Second, but we don't have any proof," he said in a steady voice.

"We don't have any proof otherwise, either. Come on, Micah. It's too obvious."

He tapped his fingers on the steering wheel. "We could do a DNA test."

Addy gaped at him, opening and closing her mouth like a fish. That was a level of acknowledgement that she hadn't expected, hadn't even considered. It would be irrefutable.

Micah made a little throat-clearing sound. "I did some research. It's more specialized than just a paternity test, so it's kind of expensive. But we'd know for sure."

Addy nodded, processing. He had done some research. "So you think I'm right?"

He shrugged. "It seems…plausible."

"Okay. Let's do it."

"Slow down. It's expensive. It'll probably be a couple of thousand dollars. Plus, does it matter?"

Addy's mouth opened and closed again. She was flabbergasted. How could he even ask whether or not it mattered? "Whether or not your grandfather was my great-grandfather? Yes, I'd say it does."

"Think about it. Who is it going to impact? Not my parents. There wouldn't even be any point in telling my dad, and Mom really won't care. The manuscript belongs to y'all, free and clear, and frankly, I have no interest in your grandmother's house."

Addy watched the traffic, debating which parts of what he had just said were bothering her. She was beginning to feel a little trapped in the barely moving car.

"We could just park here."

Micah shot her a look. "Are you sure? We'd have to walk at least half a mile."

She waved him off. "Right there, behind that SUV. I like to walk."

He looked pointedly at her outfit, his blue eyes traveling the full length of her body, then coming back up to meet hers. "Tell me what you're upset about."

"There." She pointed. "Just park, already. Let's walk."

Micah shrugged and pulled off the road.

Addy got out and kicked her way through knee-high weeds, stifling the instinct to flail at imaginary bugs. She didn't slow down when she got to the sidewalk, but plunged into the stream of people walking toward the center of town.

Micah caught up with her and slipped a hand around her elbow. "Hey. Slow down. You nearly mowed down a toddler."

Addy allowed him to slow her down, matching her pace to his easy amble.

"Talk to me," he said.

She walked a few more paces, the rhythm distilling her thoughts. His hand slid down her arm and closed around her fingers.

"This," she said, raising their intertwined hands. "This is why we need to know."

Micah rubbed his thumb across the back of Addy's hand.

She glanced up at his blue eyes and noticed his jaw twitching as he seemed to be searching for words.

"It's…not a problem," he finally said.

Addy stepped off the sidewalk, into the grass, and dropped Micah's hand, turning to face him. "You mean it's legal for first cousins to date in North Carolina," she said.

A woman pushing a stroller glanced in their direction.

Micah nodded, but didn't quite meet her eyes.

At least he has the sense to look a little uncomfortable.

"I double-checked the statutes," he said.

"I did too. Also, for the record, even if it's true, we wouldn't quite be second cousins—we'd be off by half a step or so because I have an extra generation in there, but that's kind of splitting hairs, don't you think?" She didn't give him time to answer. "Because it's still cousins. It's still a little creepy."

"Addy." He stepped closer, his hands pulling her to him, then spanning the back of her waist.

Addy sighed, breathing in the smell of him. She refused to tip her head back and meet his eyes, instead looking closely at the hollow of his throat. She could see the pulse that beat there, slow and steady.

"Did it matter before?" he said.

"Obviously not. We didn't know."

"Exactly. So it doesn't matter now."

"Let me ask you something," she said, addressing his collar bone. "Remember that cousin Angie you told me about, at the beach that time, the one who was so hot? Would you date her?" Addy had never met Angie, but she'd heard about her years ago when Micah returned from his annual vacation with his mother's family.

He chuckled, the noise seeming to reverberate in his chest. "Of course not. But not because we're cousins. She's ten years older than I am, and I've known her my entire life. She used to babysit me, for Pete's sake. That would be weird. Come on, Addy. I've thought this through, top to bottom. There's nothing stopping us."

Addy shook her head and placed her palms flat on his chest, rubbing the pique knit with her thumb. "There's plenty stopping us," she said softly, and finally tipped her head back to look at him. "Are you here to stay? Because I'm not." Her voice sounded more convincing than she felt.

He looked at her for a long moment, his teasing smile slowly fading. "No, I don't suppose I am," he said.

Addy nodded and reached for his hand again, steering them back onto the sidewalk.

There isn't much else to say about our relationship, she thought with a pang of sadness. It hadn't ever really had a chance, and now it never would. They would be long-distance friends, maybe even cousins. It would have to be enough.

They strolled in silence for a couple of minutes, their hands linked more loosely now.

"Hang a right," Micah said at the end of the block. "We can cut through to Pack Square."

There were people everywhere, enjoying the warm evening.

Addy took it all in, trying to shake off the complicated emotions their conversation had evoked. She could hear the rumble of a crowd several blocks away. It was difficult to parse out the various sounds, but under it all was a deep, insistent rhythm. Addy was content to walk quietly and take in the scene. Her hometown had grown into its favorite bumper-sticker in the last few years: Keep Asheville Weird.

They passed a young man with a pushcart selling iced coffee and wearing a bowler hat. At the end of the block, a mime posed on a wooden crate in a tattered wedding dress and spray-painted entirely in silver, standing still as a statue, not even blinking. Micah wandered over to watch, but Addy wanted to keep moving, curious to see more. She was used to seeing buskers in Washington D.C., but rarely so many in one spot. Across the street, a crowd was gathered in the portico of an empty storefront, listening to a young woman singing "Amazing Grace" while a string quartet was setting up in the next block, all dressed in Depression-era newsboy knickers and caps.

Addy paused on the corner, stunned by the crowds and the energy.

Micah laughed at her. "We're not such a backwater after all."

This was not how she remembered the town of her childhood at all.

As they got closer to the park, which Addy remembered vaguely as an odd little brick pocket in the triangular center of a confusing intersection, the crowd thickened. The sound of drumming reverberated between the bank on the corner and the old Woolworth's across the street, too loud for them to talk over.

They darted across the street to the edge of the park and were absorbed into the crowd. Micah grabbed Addy's hand and pulled her forward, angling for a spot where they could see. The whole space was smaller than the Quicks' backyard, but hundreds of people were packed in. A motley group of people—maybe thirty or so—sat on the steps drumming. It looked to Addy as if anyone who felt like showing up with something percussive had been welcomed. People danced on the brick pavement, and many more packed around the perimeter watching and clapping and swaying to the rhythm.

For all the appearance of randomness, the drumming itself was insistent. Addy found herself rocking back and forth, feeling the beat thrumming through the earth and up through her feet. The distraction was working, pulling her out of her broodiness. It wasn't quite music since there was nothing melodic or tuneful about it, but pure percussion.

Micah was grinning down at her, their linked hands swinging together.

A tall bald man with a goatee beat out a rhythm on some kind of African-looking drum. Addy had no idea what it was called, but his hands were a blur and the rhythm infectious. She could feel it in her bones, traveling up through her feet, her legs, her hips, driving out her worries until her whole body was itching to move. She nodded toward the pulsating crowd, and Micah nodded agreement. They threaded their way through the crowd and down onto the bricks. Around them, the crowd seemed to be moving as one, a sinuous organism writhing to the persistent beat.

Addy pushed her way toward the front, toward the drummers, drawn toward the mysterious rhythm shifts. Micah followed. She wanted to see how it worked, such a big, disparate group with no apparent leader. Who was in charge? Who called the shots? She watched, shimmying in place, but couldn't pick out the signal. She watched the faces, intent, focused, each in its own world. She watched the shoulders, the arms, the hands, the bodies holding drums of every description, knees braced against paint buckets, bongos strapped across chests. She was mesmerized by the hands all moving in a blur.

Once again, the tempo shifted seamlessly, and she moved with it.

The new rhythm took over. The release was immediate and visceral. Her limbs loosened and swayed, the long lines of her skirt brushing against her bare legs. Micah moved with her; she had forgotten how well he could dance. He circled her, staying just outside of her space. Blond curls tumbled across his forehead as he swayed to the beat.

The noise grew louder, the thrumming in her body was stronger, her limbs were looser. She tipped her head back and twirled around, feeling the flare of her skirt and the air on her legs. When she bumped into Micah, he laughed and grabbed her by the hips, spinning her in front of him. She was aware of his hands, warm through the thin fabric of her skirt.

Addy put a hand to her hair automatically, suddenly conscious of the humidity that had flushed her skin and dampened her hair.

Micah leaned in and spoke in her ear. "Do you want some cotton candy?"

She smiled at the surprise of the question, and nodded.

Micah led her out of the crowd to a vendor on the corner. The young woman in a short, ruffled pink dress with a white apron looked like Little Bo Peep.

They shared a cone of pink sugary fluff, pinching off bites and licking sticky fingers. By the time it was gone, Addy was completely wired on sugar. While weaving their way through the crowds of people, she found herself repeatedly waving and cooing at people she'd known in the past. It seemed like all of Asheville had turned out for a beautiful evening downtown. She spoke to her parents' next-door neighbors, then a girl she remembered from her ninth-grade English class, now hugely pregnant with a husband who looked like he'd come straight from the golf course.

They turned a corner, laughing. Across the street was the strip of grass in front of a bank where the transient types hung out after hours—not quite homeless, but on the move, with big backpacks and not a lot of hygiene. It generally had a faint odor of urine, but most people just ignored it. Addy's eyes glided past like they always did, not really noticing, but then she did a double-take. There was a young woman standing in a lee of the building with her back to the wall. From across the street, she looked a lot like Asia.

Addy stopped and squinted in the twilight, tugging on Micah's hand. It was Asia, she was certain. She had a small backpack hanging over one shoulder. Addy raised one hand in a wave, and was about to call out to her, but the figure darted around the corner of the building and disappeared.

"What's wrong?" Micah asked, following her gaze.

"I'm not sure. I think I just saw my sister's girlfriend."

"Where?" He was looking around.

"Over by the bank," Addy said. "But she zipped around the corner."

"Come on. We'll go find her. She ought not to be hanging around with the hoboes."

"No," Addy said slowly. "I think she saw me and left on purpose. I think maybe she was avoiding me." Suddenly, the sugar turned her stomach and she felt a little nauseated.

Micah looked at her. "Why? Do you think she's getting into trouble?"

"I'm not sure. But I think maybe I should head home and talk to Lacey."

Lacey wasn't home yet, and Eleanor and Mason had already gone to bed, so Addy waited up after Micah left. To her great relief, he had made no move to kiss her good night. She knew she ought to feel something stronger— squeamishness, or revulsion, even, but mostly she just felt hollow. It would take her a while to process this new reality between them, she knew, but this evening held more pressing concerns.

When she finally heard Lacey's car, Addy went quietly downstairs to meet her sister in the kitchen.

"Hey," Addy said.

"Hey. Why're you still up?"

"Waiting for you."

"You're as bad as Mother. How is she, anyway?"

"In bed, I assume. Their door is closed. But Lacey, I'm up because I was worried. I saw Asia downtown. What is she up to?"

Lacey's face was perfectly neutral. "What do you mean, 'up to'?"

"She was…skulking. In front of that bank on Patton Avenue. It looked suspicious, to be quite honest."

Lacey went to the sink and turned on the tap, filling a glass. She took a long drink, then refilled it. Addy waited, recognizing her own delaying tactic.

"She doesn't skulk," Lacey finally said, stiffly. "Her parents"—Lacey made air-quotes around 'parents'—"kicked her out."

"You're kidding. That's horrible." Lacey looked miserable, and the penny dropped in Addy's mind. "Oh, my God. Because of you two?"

Lacey nodded. "Don't say anything to Mother and Daddy, okay?"

"Lacey, we need to help her. She can stay here until her parents calm down."

Lacey shook her head. "Seriously? There's no way Mother is going to let that happen. She already thinks Asia's a bad influence. This'll just confirm her worst fears. Promise me you won't mention it."

Addy stared at her sister, weighing her words. It was a hopelessly tangled situation, but the heart of the matter was a teenager sleeping on the street. Surely that was the important part. She shook her head. "I can't feel good about that. Her safety has to come first. She needs to come and stay here, and we'll help her sort it out with her folks."

"No. No way. Mother won't even let her sleep over. She won't let anyone, not since I came out. It's the only way she even acknowledges I'm gay. I think it's how she's getting back at me for embarrassing her. And Asia's parents are magnitudes worse, believe me. You don't want to get involved with them." Lacey had tucked her chin in until it looked like she was glaring up at Addy, even though she was an inch taller.

"This is ridiculous, Lacey. And dangerous. Seriously, you didn't see her hanging out around that bank where all the homeless men are."

"I did see her, trust me. Don't worry, I made sure she's safe."

Addy threw her hands up in frustration. "I have half a mind to just drive downtown and get her. Y'all are being stupid."

"Leave it alone, Addy." Lacey's voice was low but sharp. "Really. I appreciate your concern, but honestly, you're leaving soon. This is the life I'm in, and it'll work out. Don't rock the boat, okay?"

Something clicked again in Addy's mind. "Lacey, she's not living at Grandmama's, is she?"

Lacey looked down at her feet. "I let her stay there the first couple of nights. But she's not there now. She's at a friend's house."

"She can't stay at Grandmama's, you know that. Mother will find out, and her head will explode. And I still think she should go talk to her parents. They're bound to be calmer now. I'll go with her."

Lacey pressed her hands against the sides of her head. "They're not going to be calmer. They're religious freaks."

"What is she going to do tomorrow? And the next day? What about school?"

"Long term? I have no idea."

Chapter 29

This is all too much, Addy thought. She couldn't carry the weight of anyone else's emotional crisis. It was probably only teenaged melodrama, anyway. After all, she'd had raging battles with her own parents when she was that age. She just had never realized how exhausting it was for everyone else. For the first time since she drove out of Washington D.C., the dissertation felt like a welcome escape rather than a dreaded burden.

She couldn't get anything done at home. The air of martyrdom surrounding Eleanor was impossible to ignore. Meals were strained events. Addy was torn between surreptitiously watching every bite that went into her mother's mouth and ignoring her beleaguered sighs. She felt as if they should be talking about it more, working together to make sure Eleanor was eating or getting family therapy, or at the very least acknowledging that something was off-kilter, but that wasn't the Quick way. There had been a time when Addy would have forced the issue, bringing it up at dinner and refusing to let the topic go while everyone ignored her, but that didn't feel right somehow, with Eleanor sitting next to her, picking at a salad. So she followed the rules, keeping the conversation light and inoffensive.

Lacey wasn't around much, presumably hanging out with Asia, who seemed to be keeping her distance from the Quick home. Addy checked in with Lacey enough to know the girl was floating between friends' couches, and Lacey was still adamant that Addy stay out of it. She felt as if she was waiting for something else to happen, to catalyze something, but she didn't know what or which problem it would be, so she tried to focus on the one thing she could control.

It didn't take her long, once she put her mind to it, to finish the revised version of her prospectus. She emailed it to Dr. McGregor, and the terse response came quickly—she had lost a lot of time, but it would do. Flooded with relief and knowing the outline had already practically written itself, she set out to meet her parents and sister for a command performance dinner. She had no hope that dinner would be fun, exactly, but perhaps it would be tolerable.

It was, at first. It was Mason's birthday, and they met at his favorite restaurant downtown. The glow of attention and family woke up his wicked dry sense of humor, and Addy had decided not to worry about Eleanor for as long as she could, so some of the tension of the last weeks began to dissipate. Eleanor's smile looked as if it might shatter, but she was quiet as long as the conversation was innocuous. Any time it veered toward Asia, or Addy's dissertation, or the state of Nellie's house, they all moved seamlessly on to a different topic. At least it wasn't open warfare, and Addy didn't want to be the one to ruin it. But at the same time, she was antsy. There was nothing safe to talk about except neighborhood gossip and country club politics. She hid her hands in her lap to keep from drumming on the table.

A furtive-looking young man with two-inch gauges in his ears and a cobweb tattooed around his throat began to clear the table next to them, and Lacey jumped up from her seat to give him a hug. They were classmates. That was the moment things began to go off the rails. Addy saw her mother's eyes dart around the room, taking stock of who else was watching until Lacey sat back down after a brief but animated chat with the young man.

Eleanor watched until he carried his dish bin back to the kitchen, then asked in a strained voice, "Is that really necessary, Lacey? In the middle of dinner?"

Lacey rolled her eyes. "He's a friend of mine, Mom."

"He's clearing tables. And he looks like a hoodlum."

"He's also ranked sixth in my class. Stop judging."

"People judge, Lacey," Eleanor said. "It's a fact of life. Guilt by association."

"Oh, for Pete's sake," she said, and stood up, throwing her napkin on the table. She stomped toward the bathroom.

Addy frowned, watching her go. Lacey was usually more sanguine about Eleanor's needling.

"Leave her alone, Mother. She's stressed. It's a weird time between high school and college—it's scary and emotional."

At that moment, the waitress approached the table. She put a beautiful salad in front of Eleanor, glistening baby leaves so fresh they looked as if they'd come straight from the garden, with shaved, striped radishes and strips of grilled salmon, blush-colored, crispy around the edges. Perfect wedges of blood orange encircled the plate. Addy was impressed.

"Your entrees will be out in a few minutes," the waitress said, refilling their wine glasses.

The three of them sat in silence, waiting for Lacey to return. Eleanor picked up her fork and poked at the salad, then put her fork down on the side of the plate.

"What's wrong?" Addy asked.

"I asked for the dressing on the side."

Addy plucked a leaf from her mother's plate and popped it in her mouth. "It's delicious. Citrusy. You'll like it."

"Well, I don't need all that. It's too much." She reached for her water glass.

Addy tried to catch Mason's eye, but he was watching Eleanor.

Addy shrugged. "If it's not what you ordered, send it back. But I think you'd like it."

"It's fine. I don't want to make a fuss. I'm not that hungry, anyway."

Addy caught the waitress's attention.

"What are you doing?"

"You can send it back. They'll remake it for you."

"Addison. I just said I didn't want to make a fuss."

"Mother, it's not making a fuss. You should get what you ordered."

Color crept up in Eleanor's cheeks as the waitress returned to the table with a concerned look on her face. "Is there a problem?"

"No, everything is fine, thank you," Eleanor said.

"No, it's not," Addy closed her eyes for a second in exasperation, then turned her sweetest smile on the waitress. "I'm so sorry to be a nuisance, but my mother ordered her salad with the dressing on the side. Would it be possible to switch it out?"

"Of course. It's not a problem at all." She smiled at Eleanor and patted her on the arm. "I'm glad you told me. I should've noticed before I brought it. I'll have a new one out in a few minutes." She whisked the plate off the table and was gone before anyone else could speak.

Lacey dropped into her seat. "What did I miss?"

"Just your sister running interference with the staff," Mason said drily.

"What is that supposed to mean?" Addy asked. "Did you expect her to eat a salad she didn't want?"

"I can manage for myself, Addison," Eleanor said. "I simply prefer not to make a scene in public."

"That was hardly a scene."

At that moment, a tall man in a suit approached the table and rested one hand on the back of Eleanor's chair. "Good evening, folks. I'm Ryan Short, the manager. I'm so sorry about the mix-up with your salad, ma'am. We'll have it straight in just a minute, and it's on the house."

Eleanor's blush deepened, but she smiled tightly and thanked him.

"The rest of your meals will be out momentarily—ah, here they are." Two servers appeared, each carrying two plates, and the manager took them and began distributing. Addy looked happily at her quivering, eggy custard studded with bits of corn and zucchini. She took a bite and closed her eyes, savoring the sweet, sharp bite of the balsamic drizzle, when she heard her mother's public voice again.

"Oh, hello, Anne. How are you?" Eleanor said.

Addy looked up to see Genevieve Ingram and her parents. She mustered an appropriate smile, hoping they would keep moving toward their table, but the two mothers exchanged air kisses. Genevieve bent to give Addy an awkward hug.

"It's wonderful to see you, Eleanor. We're just talking through the final details of the wedding," Anne Ingram said.

"You remember our daughters, Lacey and Addison, don't you?" Mason said.

"Of course," Anne said. "Good to see you both. Genevieve told us Addison was visiting. I didn't realize you were still here."

"We still haven't had that lunch, Addy," Genevieve said. "I want to catch up."

"I'm sorry, Genevieve, it totally slipped my mind. I'm working on my dissertation, Mrs. Ingram. I still have quite a bit of work to do. Deadlines and all, you know how it goes."

"How interesting," Anne said. "I'm afraid I can't quite remember what you're studying, though."

"She's getting a PhD in American Studies," Eleanor said, turning her biggest smile on the Ingrams. Her voice was brittle and precise, setting Addy's teeth on edge.

"Well, that is terribly interesting. Are you home for good, then? Can we expect to be seeing more of you?"

"No, I'm afraid I'm headed back to Washington D.C. before fall semester begins," she said. She felt like charm was oozing out of her and if she smiled any more broadly, her face might crack.

"Oh, that's too bad. You'll have to come back for the wedding. Eleanor, you can't imagine what a lot of work it's been." She put up one hand to cover her mouth, as if to let Eleanor in on some scandalous secret. "Brides think it's all about them, but really, I think the bulk of the work falls on us mothers."

Genevieve slipped an arm around her mother's shoulder. "You've been perfect. It's going to be divine." She nodded toward her father, who had gone on to their table. "I'll text you about that lunch, Addy. We're on for this week, right? Plus, I do want to talk to you about that parklet project, after all. Remember, I told you about it at the board meeting?"

That board meeting on Addy's first morning back in town seemed like ages ago, even though it had been less than a month. She nodded, still smiling like a fool. Genevieve waggled her fingers at them all, and followed her father.

There was an awkward pause, and Addy saw something wistful flash across Eleanor's face before she managed to paste her smile back on. "I'm sure you'll rise to the occasion, Anne. You always entertain so beautifully."

"Oh, you're so sweet." She beamed around the table at them.

When the silence stretched out a second past the edge of comfortable, Anne took her leave and followed her husband and daughter to their table. Addy turned her attention back to her food, but an idea was beginning to take root in her mind. Maybe she should have that lunch with Genevieve, after all. Perhaps they could help each other out.

They ate mostly in silence, only commenting occasionally on the food. When the waitress came back to clear their plates, Addy started to hope that they were finished, but then Mason called the young woman back.

"Don't y'all want dessert? They have the most sinful bread pudding."

"Really, dear," her mother said. "Don't you think we've all had quite enough?"

"Second stomach," Mason said. "There's always room for dessert. Especially on a birthday. We'll have four, please."

"Make that three. Dessert is the last thing I need." Eleanor interrupted, patting her stomach.

Addy looked at the remains of the salad that had been her mother's whole dinner, but kept her mouth shut. On her other side, Lacey was peering under the edge of the tablecloth at her phone. Addy heard her gasp, then felt her reach over and put the phone in Addy's lap.

She glanced down. It was a message from Asia.

I'm at the police station downtown. They said I was loitering. They're threatening to call my parents. Come get me.

Addy leaned over to whisper in Lacey's ear. "Do you want me to come too?"

Lacey nodded mutely, her eyes round and worried. Addy tipped her head toward their parents, questioning, and Lacey grimaced. Addy bent to pick up her purse and took a breath. This was not going to be easy.

They pushed their chairs back at the same moment, amplifying the sound. Eleanor bridled.

"What are you two doing?"

"We need to go," Addy said, glancing at Lacey again.

Eleanor's voice rose, even as she whispered so no one else could hear her. "Don't be rude. We're not finished."

Addy ignored her. "Happy birthday, Daddy." She leaned over to kiss his cheek and patted her mother on the shoulder.

She and Lacey walked quickly away from the table.

Addy woke up remembering the evening before in bits and pieces. Lacey, pale and tearful as they waited at the police station for Asia to be brought out. The smudges of ink on Asia's thumbs where she'd been fingerprinted. The brusque, harried officer who had finally given them her backpack and told her to be sensible and go home to her parents. Asia's shaken silence in the backseat of Addy's car as they sat in the parking deck, debating what to do next.

Ultimately, they had taken Asia to Nellie's house and let her in. Addy didn't know what else to do. She couldn't live with the thought of a vulnerable teenager on the street at night, and clearly the holding cell at the police station was not an option. They agreed to keep track of Eleanor's whereabouts between them, and call if she appeared to be headed over there, so Asia could slip out.

They had stayed out late enough that their parents were in bed when they got home. Addy opened her eyes wide and stretched. That imperceptible moment had passed, when edges coalesced into the solid reality of daytime. Dark was lightening to gray. Addy had planned to work on her outline today, probably at the Biltmore archives where she'd have access to Cornelia Vanderbilt's papers if she needed them. It felt odd to carry on with work as if she hadn't just bailed a kid out of jail. But she wasn't sure what else she could do to help, other than hang out with Asia, which didn't seem useful at all. Besides, she had gone up against the system, hadn't she? Asia had been released without any charges, thanks to Addy agreeing to take responsibility for her. That was something; she chose to see it as a victory.

Lacey would be at loose ends today, anyway; she could make sure Asia slipped out of Nellie's house if necessary. Addy couldn't afford to take the day off from research, so she got dressed and headed downtown to the archives.

Chapter 30

When she had outlined and written and read until her eyes were beginning to cross, Addy drove toward her grandmother's house. In the last couple of weeks, it had begun to seem like the best place for clearing her head. She put her key in the lock on the front door, but it swung open before she turned it. Her heart skipped a beat—had she forgotten to lock it? Then all of the previous evening's drama at the police station came rushing back to her again, and Asia was standing in the parlor, just behind the door.

Addy stepped inside. "You startled me. For a second, I had forgotten you were here."

"I didn't know you were coming. When I heard the car pull up, I was afraid it was Mrs. Q, so I came in here to peek out behind the sheers, so no one could see me."

"Good thinking. Did you get some sleep?"

"Like a log. I love this little house so much. It's the perfect size, and it's so homey. Sorry, I know that sounds sappy." The circles under her eyes had faded to faint blue smudges, and her hair was still damp from the shower.

Addy sniffed. "Is something burning?"

Asia's shoulders slumped. "I'm so sorry. That's my fault. I thought you wouldn't mind if I had some of that canned soup, but I kind of nodded off a little, and I guess there was dust or something on the burner. I opened some windows in the back to air it out, but I was scared someone would notice and think I was a burglar or something."

"Oh no. Did it catch on fire?" Addy asked, going into the kitchen to see what had happened.

"No, nothing like that. The pan got a little scorched, though. I scrubbed it as much as I could, but—" She pulled a saucepan out of her backpack, abashed. "I wasn't sure what to do with it, but I didn't want Mrs. Q. to find it."

Addy shook her head. "Don't worry about a pot. Eventually, we're going to have to clear them all out, anyway. I'm just glad there wasn't a fire—that would've been much harder to ignore." She sat down on the kitchen couch, chewing on her lip.

Asia sat down in a chair she had pulled over to the window for keeping watch on the driveway. "This isn't going to work, is it?" she asked.

"Well, not long term, no," Addy said. "For starters, the whole point is that we're trying to sell the house. I mean, it's not like we can advertise a house for sale that includes a teenager," she said.

Asia smiled a little, but didn't laugh.

"I know I keep saying this, Asia, but I really think you need to talk to your parents," Addy said. "I'd be happy to go with you. Surely they've calmed down by now."

Asia's eyes filled with tears. She shook her head mutely. "No. But I'll get out of here. I won't be in the way."

The sound of a car pulling in the driveway caused her to look out the window. "Lacey's here," she said, wiping her eyes on her sleeve. "Do I look like I was crying?"

Addy shook her head, a little aghast that the child would care, but Asia took it as assurance. *Such an innocent question*, Addy thought as Lacey pushed the screen door open. She remembered worrying that much about her hair, her makeup, having just the right clothes, but here and now? Under these circumstances? It seemed like Asia should have much bigger concerns than puffy eyes. Maybe it was instinctive at that age—so automatic they didn't even realize they were doing it.

She got up and went into her grandmother's bedroom, leaving the two girls wrapped around each other on the couch, patting and murmuring, reestablishing their togetherness like litter mates reunited. She sat down on the stool at the dressing table to check her email.

Dr. McGregor wrote to say that the other members of Addy's committee had signed off on her prospectus, and she had approval to keep moving forward. Dr. McGregor would look forward to seeing an outline next week. In the meantime, the committee had agreed to her request that they not leak any information about the discovery. Addy tried to ignore a small twinge of guilt.

She could hear the girls moving around in the kitchen now, Lacey laughing and a quiet hollow thump. Asia must have shown her the scorched pot. Addy put her head in her hands. She felt responsible for this situation, simply because there didn't appear to be any other adults involved. For a second, she had trouble catching a breath; too many things were clamoring for her attention.

She looked at the clutter on the dressing table, tiny pots of desiccated rouge and a cardboard box of loose powder, and idly twisted the lid off a jar of cold cream. The smell dragged her instantly back to her childhood when she would sleep over at Grandmama's and sit on this very stool, dressed in old prom dresses and making up her face like a tiny clown. She wasn't allowed to plunder through her mother's things, but Grandmama never minded. Addy sighed. She didn't have time to hang out here, tripping down memory lane and hiding from her grown-up life.

Back in the kitchen, she picked up the scorched pot.

"I'm going now, y'all. I'll take this with me and toss it somewhere. Asia, be really careful, okay? I don't want to think what would happen if there was a fire."

Asia blushed and nodded.

Lacey jumped in. "Hey, I went by school today to return some books, and I told my English teacher about the story you found. He was super-interested. Could I take it in and show it to him?"

"Whoa, no. Hold on. I only just now got an email from my advisor talking about how my committee says we need to keep it quiet for now."

"Why?"

Addy shrugged. "Well, I hadn't really thought about it. Academic credibility, I guess. Not giving up all my information before I'm ready. If I leak my theories, then I guess I'm leaving myself vulnerable to other people stealing my ideas. Plus, there are still issues I need to nail down, like the authentication and maybe copyright. Micah says it's in the public domain, but I'm still a little nervous about that."

"What are your theories?" Asia asked. "Lacey's only told me a little bit. I haven't heard all this."

"I did too tell you," Lacey said. "Secret births and star-crossed lovers—the whole bit."

"Stop being melodramatic," Addy said. "It's not that romantic. Basically, I think the manager at Biltmore—Judge Britton, who was this seriously loyal protector of the family reputation—started to be concerned that Cornelia and Zelda might be more than friends, and in the 1920s that would have been scandalous. So when Cornelia got this lovey-dovey letter from Zelda, he gave it to his secretary. Enter our great-great-aunt Martha, with whom I suspect he was having his own little fling. Anyway, he told her to get rid of it, but she took it home and saved it. Later, when she was pregnant, he gave her this house, sort of to buy her off, but they signed a contract in which she agreed never to tell what she knew about Cornelia and Zelda. Then she died having the baby, and it all passed on to our great-grandmother Isabella, including the baby and the house."

"There are still some holes, you know," Lacey said.

"I know. Which is why I need to get back to it."

"Ninety years ago," Asia said quietly. They both looked at her. "Here we are, ninety years later, and—" She gripped her elbows, trying to stop herself from shaking.

Lacey wrapped her arms around her girlfriend.

Addy took advantage of the moment to slip out, closing the screen door quietly. She felt bad leaving them, but she couldn't solve anything by standing there patting everyone on the back.

Addy stayed out for the rest of the afternoon, thinking about the holes Lacey had mentioned in the scenario she'd worked out in her mind. She went back downtown to the Biltmore archives, trying to find any further evidence of a relationship between Zelda Fitzgerald and Cornelia Vanderbilt, but Judge Britton's meticulous records were mind-numbing. Even the bits and pieces of correspondence that were initialed MRC, indicating they'd been typed by Great-Aunt Martha, failed to spark any feeling of recognition or kinship. As far as Addy could tell, Martha had worked at Biltmore for about a year, during which time she had taken dictation and run errands and filed an endless stream of letters and invoices, but there was no noticeable imprint of her personality in the records.

When Addy headed home at dinner time, her head ached from poring over faded, unfamiliar handwriting. Exhausted, she went in through the kitchen, uncomfortably aware that she was reflexively bracing herself against her mother. *Be normal,* she thought, catching the screen door before it could slap closed behind her.

The kitchen was empty. A roasted chicken was resting on a cutting board; the familiar savory smell made her mouth water. A rainbow of red and pink and orange and yellow tomatoes had been sliced onto a platter and sprinkled with shreds of dark green basil. It was the first proper meal her mother had cooked since the hospital, she realized, lifting the lid on a pot of butterbeans. Maybe there was one small worry she could let go of for a while.

The small breakfast table was littered with cards and envelopes, and she picked one up to see what was going on. It was an invitation to Lacey's graduation party. A few had been addressed in Eleanor's handwriting. It looked as if there were a lot still to be done.

Addy poked her head into the dining room to see if the table needed to be set, and heard voices drifting down from upstairs. She stepped back, and busied herself washing her hands and getting out plates and glasses. By the time she had poured the tea, Lacey appeared.

"Hey! We didn't hear you come in."

"It sounded like yelling, so I stayed down here. Is everything okay?"

"Oh, sure. Mom's in a snit about my graduation party, but it's not really even my party anymore. She's all wound up about following the etiquette rules. So whatever. Her friends will come, she'll make me write thank-you notes, and then it'll all be over. I'm not worried about it."

Addy nodded sympathetically. Their mother still had the same Emily

Post book that she'd used to plan her wedding almost thirty years earlier, and she wielded it like a bible. She would work herself to the bone making sure everything was perfect, and do her best to badger everyone else into compliance. Lacey had always had a knack for avoiding the guilt train.

"It'll be fine." It was the best she could offer. The age difference suddenly stretched out between them, and Addy felt older than she ever had.

"I'm not worried about it." Lacey began to straighten the mess on the breakfast table.

Addy watched her sister. Had she been that blasé as a teenager? Or even yesterday? Seeing Asia at the police station and then again at Nellie's house, so obviously frightened and vulnerable, had shaken Addy.

"Where's Asia?" she asked in a low voice.

"I left her at Grandmama's. It seemed safe enough, for now. I think Dad doesn't want Mom going over there, since the hospital. It's a little weird, to see him hovering over her."

"That's an understatement," Addy muttered. "Is she okay?"

"Mom or Asia?"

Addy stared at Lacey for a second, watching the absurdity of the situation hit her. Their mother, whose life had always looked perfect from the outside, was on some kind of hunger strike because she was freaked out about being embarrassed, while Asia, barely sixteen, was basically homeless because she refused to be embarrassed. She felt as if the ground had tipped under her feet, throwing off her balance. She shrugged, confounded.

Lacey gave her a small, wry smile. "The only people who aren't crazy are the ones you don't know very well. We'll all be fine. I have confidence," she said, and took the plates into the dining room.

Addy could hear her through the door, singing to herself. She had never understood how her sister could be so upbeat even when things seemed to be falling apart and everyone around her was ill as a snake. She could use some of that optimism right now. Her stomach was tied up in anxious knots. She focused on the sound of Lacey's quiet singing while she poured glasses of tea.

When they all finally sat down at the table, Eleanor joining them last and without a word, Lacey was practically vibrating with excitement. She produced a flyer and dropped it in the center of the table with a flourish.

"This is going to be my big break."

Addy picked it up first.

"What is it?" Mason asked.

Lacey jumped in before Addy could respond. "They're going to make a documentary at Biltmore House. They need some actors. I'm going to audition."

"When?" Mason asked.

"Oh, no. I don't think you should do that. Not at all," Eleanor said. "You don't have time. You have a graduation party, and you have to get ready for college. Didn't you get that acting silliness out of your system?"

"Oh, stop stressing, Mom. It'll be fine," Lacey said.

"It will not, if you don't spend some time helping me get things done."

Lacey rolled her eyes. "Like what? Addressing the envelopes? You said my handwriting wasn't good enough."

Addy had a sudden flash of memory. Eleanor had said the same thing ten years earlier, about Addy's handwriting.

"What's the documentary about?" Addy asked, trying to steer the conversation back into safer waters.

"It's part of a series about what happened to famous Gilded Age mansions during the Depression. I talked to a casting person on the phone. I think Biltmore is kind of going to be the centerpiece."

"What kind of documentary has a casting call? I thought documentaries were supposed to be nonfiction," Mason said.

"It's a style. Nonfiction, but with actors playing out snippets of the story," Lacey said.

"It doesn't matter. You still don't have time," Eleanor said.

Addy picked up the flyer and looked at it. "It's really soon. They're filming next week. Can you be ready that quickly?"

"Of course. I do stuff for drama class on a week turn-around. This is no big deal."

"Well, in that case, it sounds perfect."

"No. I'm sorry, but that is just not how you need to be spending this time before you go off to college. You do not have permission," Eleanor said. She got up from the table, taking her still-full plate into the kitchen. The rest of them sat in silence for a moment, then Mason got up and followed his wife.

"That went well, I thought," Lacey said. Her eyes were twinkling.

"Are you okay?" Addy asked. "I'm sorry…"

Lacey waved her off. "Don't worry about it. I'm not. She's just uncomfortable. It freaks her out seeing me on stage."

"That would've made me psychotic when I was your age."

Lacey grinned at her. "No kidding. But I'm not you. Mom worrying about an audition is the least of my concerns." She looked past Addy, listening to the sound of two sets of footsteps going out to the front porch. "Besides, it's not the audition she's worried about."

Addy nodded, wondering again how her kid sister had gotten to be so insightful. "I know. I feel like it's my fault—that my being here is forcing everything to a head and making her crazy."

Lacey stared at her for a second. "Addy, dude. It's not you. Trust me, it was like this before you showed up. It's just as much me. Or rather, it's me and Asia."

Addy thought about that, about the image of both of them, each in her own orbit, feeling responsible for their mother's tailspin. Suddenly the bigger picture of their mother's life snapped into focus, and the missing pieces neither of them had ever been aware of, had never asked about—life with Grandmama Nellie and Granny Isabella, the pressure to conform and be perfect in a small Southern town, the abandoned education.

"Maybe it's not either of us," she said slowly. "Maybe it's just her way of dealing with change."

"I don't know. She's been pretty freaked out ever since Asia and I started dating. But whatever. Just don't mention the audition again, okay? She'll forget about it."

It was good to know Lacey was a perfectly normal, self-absorbed teenager, Addy realized. It was all she could do not to pat her sister on the head like some kind of patronizing grown-up. Instead, she stood up and helped her clear the table.

Chapter 31

When Genevieve texted the next morning, Addy didn't have the heart to put her off any longer. She was feeling too guilty, too worried about all the other people in her life. Besides, she had to eat. She'd stayed up late writing, and it was as if the entire dissertation had dropped, fully formed, into her mind, in spite of all her worries—or was it because of them? She could afford to take an hour off. Lunch with Genevieve was one small thing she could do easily, and hopefully get right. Perhaps Genevieve, with all of her enthusiasm for the Junior League and their service projects, would have some insights into what Addy could do to help Asia. It might be good to have someone neutral to help her think it through.

She began to have second thoughts on the way to the restaurant, though. An hour of gossip was more than she could bear, especially if it was about her own mother's health. She didn't want to talk about her dissertation either. She found herself feeling curiously reluctant to share the details of her recent discoveries—the perpetuity on Grandmama's house, the conflicting birth certificates, the question of whether she and Micah were cousins. She wasn't sure yet how she felt about any of it, and the thought of Genevieve blowing it all up into some kind of juicy historical scandal made her want to keep it all to herself. It had the potential to be a difficult hour, dodging topics.

Genevieve stepped into the tiny restaurant with the air of someone who expected heads to turn. Addy, already seated, watched her scan the room, a beaming smile seeming to hover at the corners of her mouth, ready to bless the first familiar face she saw.

When Genevieve got to the table, Addy submitted to her hug and was surprised to find herself feeling a bit nostalgic. They had, after all, been friends once upon a time, even if that time had been buried under years and miles.

Apparently Genevieve's mind had been running along the same track. "Do you remember," she said as she sat down, "the giant crush you had on Billy Mack in the sixth grade, and how you tried to kiss him in the library?"

Addy laughed. There was something here after all, a shared prehistory from those luminescent days before the angst of adolescence turned them against each other. She began to relax a little as they chatted and ordered salads with poached salmon and pickled blueberries. Genevieve's chatter was easy and inoffensive, mostly reminiscing about childhood scrapes Addy had almost forgotten about, slowly drawing her into Genevieve's rose-tinted view of their hometown. Mercifully, she steered well clear of Addy's research and what it had uncovered.

The arrival of the salads slowed her a little, until the waitress had refilled their glasses and stepped away from the table. Genevieve picked up her fork and broke her salmon into pieces, but didn't take a bite.

Aware of the stillness that had come over her, Addy deliberately took a bite and chewed. The blueberries were sweet and tart while the salmon was almost buttery against the crunch of vibrantly fresh lettuce. "What's wrong?" she asked between bites.

"Nothing, it's fine," Genevieve said, spearing a berry.

"No, Genevieve, I mean what's bothering you?" She hesitated, not wanting to sound too blunt. "Why the lunch? I don't think you just wanted to reminisce about elementary school."

"Not specifically," Genevieve shrugged. "I just wanted to chat, that's all. You've been away so long…" She frowned a little, tiny lines wrinkling the bridge of her nose, then took a breath. "I've been feeling like I need some perspective, and I thought you'd be a good person to talk to."

Addy nodded, feeling suddenly as if she was in her office waiting for a student to feel comfortable enough to spit out a worry, something bigger and more distressing than an illogical thesis sentence. Some take longer than others, she reminded herself, thinking of Dr. McGregor's peaceful stillness.

She waited.

"I'm blissfully happy about the wedding, of course," Genevieve said, twisting the diamond on her ring finger. "Emory and I are just meant to be together." She looked around as if someone might be listening.

"And I love all my volunteer work. I want to make a difference. I love this town, and I want to help make it a better place, and I'm lucky to be in a position to be able to do that."

Addy nodded again, mystified. If this was leading to some kind of confession, she couldn't imagine what it would be.

"I thought, since you've lived in Washington, that you might be able to help me—"

"Genevieve, I'm a starving graduate student, and so are all my friends. We don't have any money, I'm afraid."

"Oh no. It's not money." Genevieve gave her a wry smile. "That's the part I'm good at. It's the ick factor."

Addy blinked. Now she really was stumped. "What do you mean?"

Genevieve glanced around again. "I'm kind of embarrassed to admit this. You know I've been working on this parklet project, trying to set up small urban green spaces?"

"I don't know much about it, but yes. You mentioned it."

Genevieve waved a hand in the air, that diamond winking. "The details don't matter. The problem is that I have to deal with a lot of people that I've never really talked to before. Like—" She was clearly struggling with her conscience, and cleared her throat before continuing in a lower voice. "Homeless people. Hoboes. And extremely poor people, from the projects. And people who've been arrested, drug addicts, and I haven't really talked to anyone about it because I don't know anyone who would understand. And I kind of hate myself for it, but I'm incredibly uncomfortable. I'm worried I'm going to offend someone, or say the wrong thing, or make matters worse."

The words had tumbled out, picking up speed toward the end, and now she was still, intently focused on her glass of iced tea.

Addy made a sympathetic noise, unsure what she could say. She wasn't a therapist, for Pete's sake, but "maybe you need a shrink" didn't seem helpful. She finally decided to go with noncommittal.

"I'm sorry. That sounds terribly upsetting."

"It is! I so wanted to make this project work, and the fundraising is going great. But the implementation—dealing with all these people—is turning out to be more than I know how to handle. I just come home shaking after these meetings, and I don't know how to communicate effectively." She blinked, looking a little surprised at the accuracy of her own assessment.

Addy nodded again. "That's great that the fundraising is going well, though."

"It is. I met the target in the first month, and am twenty-five percent over as of last week." She sat up a little straighter.

"That's amazing. I know plenty of professors who would give anything to be able to raise funds like that."

"Yes, but how do you cope with all the people in a city like Washington D.C.? I mean, isn't it a really mixed population, with a lot of people from… sort of, all walks of life?"

Addy kept her face carefully neutral. It was a difficult question, and she didn't want to dwell on what the broader implications might be of whatever Genevieve thought Addy's life in Washington must look like.

"I guess I just assume that people are people, and I try to treat everyone the same."

"Even if they frighten you?"

"Genevieve, is there some kind of specific situation that feels dangerous?"

"No, of course not." She couldn't meet Addy's gaze. "Well, I don't think so. I'm just so uncomfortable, and it makes me feel so guilty." She blinked rapidly, looking up at the ceiling.

Addy cast around in her mind for the right response. Something told her there wasn't one, though. She took a breath and reached over the table to rub the back of Genevieve's hand.

"I'm sorry," she said.

Genevieve turned her hand over and gripped Addy's with an unexpected strength.

"Thank you," she said. "Thank you so much for understanding. You were always good at seeing right through to what really matters."

Addy opened her mouth in surprise but caught herself before she spoke. If Genevieve felt better because Addy had sat there helplessly, then that was all that mattered. She smiled weakly and gave Genevieve's hand a little squeeze.

"You know," she said, "I was actually wondering if I could ask you for some advice, given all of your excellent connections in the advocacy world—"

Genevieve's hands flew to cover the flush spreading over her cheeks. "Do you really think that? Advocacy, it's such a powerful word. I hadn't even thought of it that way. In my head, I'm just doing charity work to fill up my days…"

"Of course. You should be proud of yourself for trying to make people's lives better."

Something lightened in Genevieve's expression. "Tell me what you're concerned about. I'm an excellent listener. It's the least I can do, given how much you've helped me this morning."

Addy told her about Lacey and Asia, and Asia's aunt and uncle having apparently turned her out onto the street. She left Eleanor out of the story since her discomfort seemed irrelevant, anyway. Genevieve listened, true to her word, shock and sadness and sympathy playing across her face in quick succession.

"The poor child. And poor Lacey. How awful to be faced with such meanness at her tender age."

Addy was beginning to realize that Genevieve's melodramatic pronouncements were simply the only means of expression she knew. Underneath the sentimentality, she really did seem to care about making a difference. She nodded, hoping she looked appropriately emotional.

"I was wondering if you knew of a shelter or an organization that would take her in and keep her safe, or maybe convince her aunt and uncle to take her back."

Genevieve tapped a finger on the rim of her iced tea glass, as if she were accustomed to using her nails, now short and bare, as a metronome. "I'm afraid I don't know," she finally said. "There are only three shelters that I know of, and off the top of my head, I don't know what their rules are regarding children, but I would imagine there are rules of some kind. I certainly don't remember seeing teenagers in any of them, and I've visited all three." She shuddered delicately. "But why don't you just talk to the parents, or fosters, or whatever they are?"

"I've thought of that," Addy said. "Lacey doesn't want me to. She says they won't listen to any kind of reason, but I'm beginning to think I should give it a try."

Genevieve's tapping finger slowed, then stopped, signaling that she'd made some internal decision. She sat up straighter and said, "I can go with you if you want."

Addy looked at Genevieve, at her perfect hair and her thin, tanned arms and her glittering diamond. There was a relief in the sharing of this worry, like the release of a burden, but really this wasn't Genevieve's problem, and Addy was uncomfortable dragging her into it.

"Thank you. That's very supportive." She patted Genevieve's hand. "But I think I need to do this one by myself."

Chapter 32

Addy sat on the porch waiting for Lacey to come home, but her sister was focused on learning the lines for her audition, so Addy was left to brood as night fell. In the warm darkness, her thoughts swirled around the edge of a whirlpool that threatened to suck her in. She tossed and turned for hours that night after giving up her vigil to talk with Lacey.

By morning, she had made up her mind to tackle at least one problem, even if it meant taking a whole day off from writing. Armed with the address that popped up immediately on the internet, she headed into the country to talk some sense into Asia's aunt and uncle.

As soon as she left the outskirts of Asheville, the road began to climb and twist. A blinking yellow light warned her to slow through a crossroad; a country gas station and a single-engine firehouse marked the town that the internet had told her was Asia's home. The road changed to gravel and climbed up some more. Trees arched over the road. Light and shadow flickered until the treetops converged in full canopy and she had to take off her sunglasses. A small hand-lettered sign pointed to a white frame church up a dirt road. Twenty minutes out of town and she felt as if she'd slipped backward half a century. She wondered if she might have felt more confident with Genevieve along, but dismissed the idea just as quickly. Genevieve had admitted these were the very interactions that freaked her out—trying to figure out how to diplomatically interact with people whose lives looked radically different from her own.

As far as Addy could tell, she was the only adult in the world who was seriously concerned about Asia's safety; she was the only logical person to try to get to the root of the problem.

The GPS told her to turn right, so she did, and promptly lost the signal. The road changed from gravel to dirt and curved up and around the side of a mountain. It was steep and narrow, broken only by the occasional driveway cut through trees and dense undergrowth. Fences, where there were any, were of the broken-post-sagging-wire variety. Around the next curve, she startled a small herd of goats munching on the grass growing on the near-vertical embankment.

Finally, the dirt road became a rutted track and simply ended. In front of Addy's car was a dense growth of trees; to the right, a breath-taking view of the peaks of the Blue Ridge, stretching away in every shade of blue. She guessed her passenger side door was maybe five feet from a drop-off that she had no desire to assess. When she looked to her left, she realized that a man— Asia's uncle, she assumed—had stepped out onto the porch of a frame house with a tin roof. Addy watched him for a second, suddenly nervous. Perhaps she had driven up here too hastily, assuming her education and powers of persuasion would steer these strangers right around to her way of seeing the world. What if he pulled out a shotgun, or loosed a pack of pit bulls to tear her limb from limb? She glanced at her phone—still no signal.

The man made no move toward her—she could still drive away. Although, glancing back over her shoulder, she realized it would be awkward to get the car turned around without some help. Would he buy that she'd gotten lost and wound up here on accident? *Courage to the sticking point*, she thought, and stepped out of the car. That was when she saw the beat-up old Volkswagen that she'd seen Asia driving weeks ago. Her heart sank; she was in the right place.

"Mr. Ledford?" She moved warily toward the tidy house.

"Yes. And you are?"

"My name is Addison Quick. I was hoping I could talk to you for a minute," she replied, drawing herself up as tall as she could, but it did no good. She felt like a child standing at the bottom of the steps, looking up at him.

His face was a careful blank. "What do you need, Miss Quick?"

He knew who she was. She stalled. She needed him to hear her out. "I just wanted to chat, that's all. Asia doesn't know I'm here."

Behind him, in the dim interior of the house, Addy could see movement. A small face appeared at the screen; it looked like a boy of nine or ten. A hand pulled him away, and a woman's face appeared.

"I'm sorry you came all this way," Mr. Ledford said in a low voice, "but I don't think—"

The screen door opened and the woman stepped out, pulling the proper door closed behind her. She was dressed in jeans and a pink t-shirt—one of the ones with the funny little graphic saying "Life is Good." She looked like any other slightly harried mom. A look passed between the couple; Addy couldn't read it, but they clearly weren't whoever she had expected them to be. They didn't look like some backwoods cult of doomsday preppers or members of an off-the-grid religious cult. Glancing around the property, she realized there was a minivan parked alongside the house. If they weren't practically hanging off the side of a mountain, they could be standing in any suburban driveway in the country.

"Please, have a seat." The woman pointed to a rocker, padded with a cushion in a bright red and yellow geometric pattern. It looked incongruous out here in the woods. Everything about this scenario was incongruous, keeping Addy off balance.

"Be careful," the woman said. "The steps are a little uneven."

Addy hesitated, but there was no graceful way to turn around now. The stone steps were indeed uneven, and very steep, increasing the vertiginous feeling of the place.

She sat down on the edge of the proffered chair, and they sat as well, one on either side. "I'm sorry to bother you so early," Addy said, "but I'm a little concerned about Asia."

Mr. Ledford folded his arms across his chest, but his wife nodded encouragingly, so Addy went on.

"Lacey and I told her she could stay at my grandmother's house for a few nights, but she can't stay there indefinitely." She hesitated, embarrassed about Eleanor's discomfort with Lacey's sexuality, about her own unwillingness to confront her mother, about the fact that she was even thinking these things while she sat here with these people who seemed so normal, but couldn't possibly be.

"To be quite honest, I don't want our mother to find out she's staying there—it's complicated, but I really think it might be better for everyone if Asia came home."

"Well, yes. It is complicated," the woman said. "I'm Theresa Ledford, by the way. I assume you're Addy?"

"Yes, ma'am."

"Well, you've wasted a gallon of gas," Mr. Ledford said, standing up. He stomped down the steps and disappeared around the side of the house. Addy could feel the empty chair rocking slightly next to her, but she didn't take her eyes off Mrs. Ledford, who was looking down at her hands and blushing furiously.

"He's not a bad person, actually," she said.

Addy waited, grateful, once again, for Dr. McGregor's patient example. She knew how to do this, she realized. She knew how to sit and listen, and wait for the story to unfold, then help a student look at solutions. Mrs. Ledford was no student, but Addy could wait. She had done it just yesterday with Genevieve. She would do it again with Mrs. Ledford. She could solve this problem.

After a moment, they heard a gate rattle behind the house, and Mrs. Ledford nodded, as if she'd been listening for it.

"It's difficult. He's terribly uncomfortable. Asia is our niece. I assume you know?"

Addy nodded.

"We've raised her as a daughter ever since her parents died, but we have three children of our own, all younger than Asia. He's worried about the influence on them, and about the neighbors, honestly. It's a pretty homophobic community out here."

Addy had to work to keep her face neutral. How could the woman sound this intelligent and articulate, and be so narrow-minded?

"Asia has chosen—and you know this, of course, given that your sister is the same way—a lifestyle that is fraught with hardships. That is her choice. But we've chosen not to have that in our home. It sounds as if your mother might feel the same way?"

Addy opened her mouth, then closed it. That wasn't what she meant, not at all. She could hear muted footsteps in the house, the sound of small feet running and small voices laughing. A hummingbird darted toward the bird feeder dangling from the overhang, then darted away again. Down the road, a dog barked.

"My mother is uncomfortable, but she wouldn't kick her own daughter out of the house. Never. There's no way." Suddenly, Addy was blinking rapidly. It almost would have been easier if they hadn't looked so normal.

Mrs. Ledford looked off into the distance toward the mountain tops. "She's welcome to come back. I want her back, very much. We've found a therapist who will be more than happy to help her. I can give your mother his name if she wants."

"Help her what?" Addy asked. She knew the answer, but she was going to make this woman—this mother—say it out loud.

"Help her solve this…problem." Her chin was set.

Addy's stomach lurched a little at the echo of her own internal words, but she forced herself to remember the sight of Asia, unkempt, exhausted, anxious. "You understand that she's been living on the street, right? Trying to sleep in, I don't know, empty parking decks and under bushes in the middle of downtown Asheville. It's terribly unhealthy, not to mention dangerous. She needs to be in a safe place so she can, at least, finish high school."

Mrs. Ledford's eyes glittered, but her chin didn't so much as wobble. "I am well aware of the risks, on both sides of the equation. We are confident that Asia will come home when she sees the error of her ways."

"But you can't mean that!" Addy said, more loudly than she meant to.

The footsteps pattered in the house again, and Mrs. Ledford stood up. "I think maybe you should go. Do tell Asia we love her and want her home." She looked toward the distant mountains. "Back down to the bottom of the driveway to turn around." She went into the house, leaving Addy alone on the porch.

Rattled, Addy drove down the mountain, picking up speed without realizing it until the ruts and gullies in the dirt road bounced her so hard she hit the headrest on the back of her seat. She braked, the car fishtailing a little in the dirt, spewing rocks and gravel. She kept her foot hovering over the brake after that. It was beautiful up here, but remote, and she didn't want to have a problem and need to go back to the Ledfords for help.

When she got back into range for a cell signal, she breathed a sigh of relief and loosened her grip on the steering wheel. Some of the tension began to ease from her shoulders, but she didn't feel any better. Asia's situation was untenable—Addy could see that. She didn't know how to help, other than making sure Asia had a safe place to sleep, and that was getting increasingly difficult. They were going to sell Nellie's house—clearly she needed somewhere to go. Addy turned the problem around and around in her head, unable to see a way to unravel what appeared to be a knot of yarn that had no loose end to pull.

She had to tell Asia the truth, though—that much she knew. Addy didn't think she could hide the fact that she had met the Ledfords. The child was already distressed that she couldn't stay in Grandmama's bungalow indefinitely; this was only going to upset her even more. Or that the house was going away, one way or another. She wasn't sure which point was going to be more upsetting.

When she got to Nellie's house, Asia was sitting in the chair by the kitchen window, keeping an eye on the street. Her backpack was by the door in case she needed to slip out in a hurry. The photocopies Addy had given her were on the kitchen table; she had been rereading the story, she said.

"It's kind of a dumb story," she observed.

"Yes, but it's academically interesting. Things like this—unpublished early works by authors who later got famous, or even only moderately famous—always are. And Zelda Fitzgerald is sort of unique, in that she was a writer herself and was married to Scott, who was obviously much more talented. But she was also his subject—his muse—and that was another whole level of fame. Or notoriety." She shrugged. "There are a ton of reasons that this is a big deal."

Asia looked out the window again. Anxiety and fatigue were stamped on her face, in her posture. "She was in love with Cornelia, you know. You can see it in that letter." Her voice was soft.

"Maybe," Addy said. "It was almost a hundred years ago. Things were different, and not just for gay people. Relationships were different, even plain old platonic friendships. Sometimes young women were just more affectionate, more willing to express that affection, than they are now."

"People say that now too, you know." Asia continued to look out the window, gripping her elbows. "That teenage girls are more affectionate, more physical, more dramatic. Whatever. Like we don't know our own minds."

Her words were quiet but unwavering. She didn't sound like a histrionic teenager, Addy realized.

"You're right," she said. "I didn't mean to…" She flailed, inarticulate.

"You didn't mean to discount everything about my identity, you mean?" Asia asked, turning around to look at Addy, her chin held high.

"No. I didn't. I'm sorry. I shouldn't have said that. But speaking of things I shouldn't have done." She cringed, but made herself spit it out. "I should probably tell you I went to see your aunt and uncle this morning."

Asia had turned back to the window.

Addy watched her still back. In the silence, she could hear birds twittering in the branches of the dogwood in the front yard.

"Did you hear me?"

"Of course I heard you."

Addy chewed her lip. This was going badly. She didn't know what else to say, how much to tell. "Do you want to know what they said?"

Asia turned around again and met Addy's gaze directly. "Have they changed their minds about anything?" she asked, her tone a challenge, daring Addy to soft-pedal anything the Ledfords had said.

"It doesn't sound like it, no. I'm sorry."

"Why would you even go out there?"

"I thought maybe I could help. I'm sorry."

"You can't." Her eyes dropped, unable to hold the defiance. "Stop saying you're sorry. None of this is your fault, and you're letting me stay here."

Addy's heart sank. She was worried about how much longer she and Lacey could hide Asia's presence from their mother. She couldn't fathom how furious Eleanor would be if she found out, but she couldn't bring herself to tell Asia that she'd need to clear out. For the first time that she could remember in her whole life, the truth failed her. "Of course," she said weakly.

"It feels safe," Asia went on. "I didn't know your grandmother—I met Lacey right after she died—but I like her house. It's cozy, and feels like… welcome, or kind. Like a good person lived here."

Addy nodded, unable to speak, choked by a sudden wave of grief for her grandmother and for this vulnerable child, and her own shame that she was only making things worse.

She was saved by Lacey's appearance. She'd come to bundle Asia into her car and get her out of the house for the rest of the day. Addy watched as they drove down the street, then closed and locked the door. She couldn't stay there in the bungalow. It might be a safe haven for Asia, but it was beginning to feel like the source of Addy's problems.

She drove to Micah's office. If he was in, she could ask him what to do about Asia. They hadn't talked since Friday night, but she had a feeling they hit some kind of reset button on their relationship, such as it was, and if she showed up now with a legal question, they'd be back on a safe, platonic footing.

He was there. Addy told him the whole story about Asia having been kicked out of her home, and her own unfortunate conversation with the Ledfords. She left out the fact that Asia was currently at Nellie's house.

"Poor kid," he said.

"Is there a reason she can't go to a shelter?"

He looked grim. "Again—I feel like I keep saying this to you—you must think I don't know anything about practicing law, but I swear I do. I'd have to look it up to be sure, but I suspect shelters won't take minors."

"Then where are they supposed to go?"

"Home."

"But what if home won't take them?"

"Then I guess they go into foster care."

"You're kidding," Addy said. That wasn't at all what she had expected. She knew Asia had technically grown up in the system, but she'd always been with her aunt and uncle. It wasn't the same thing, really. What Micah was saying sounded so…irrevocable. "What about kids like this, who just need a place to be safe until she can figure out what she's going to do?"

"She needs to be home with her parents, or, from what you're saying, her aunt and uncle."

"I keep telling her that, but then I remember what it was like to be sixteen and fighting with my folks. I may not have gotten along with them very well, but at least I never worried that they didn't want me at all. They put her out on the street, Micah. If they'd do that, how is she ever going to feel safe in their house?"

"I agree, it's terrible. But I'd be surprised if a shelter was willing to take a kid. What if the aunt and uncle change their minds, and she refuses to go back? What kind of position would that put the shelter in? Like I said, it all goes back to Child Protective Services."

"What would they do with her?" Images of Dickensian orphanages ran through her mind.

His fingers clicked on the keyboard. "Well, I suspect they'd start by contacting the aunt and uncle to clarify the circumstances. Probably put her in a temporary foster home. Then either charge the aunt and uncle, or counsel them to take her back, or both. Probably both, actually, now that I think about it."

"That's awful."

"Well, that's what they're meant to do. They intervene in cases where the kids are endangered, but that's the last resort. This one is a little more complicated because her biological parents are deceased, but she's been with these folks for so long. They're mandated to keep families together as much as possible, and from what you're telling me, this is the only family she's ever known."

"They think they can pray it out of her." She pressed her hands on top of her head. "What if they won't take her back?"

"Then I guess she stays in a different foster home."

"But what happens to the Ledfords?"

"I guess they'll be charged with something—neglect, or endangerment, or something. I'm not sure what the standards are, since they're technically foster parents."

"Could you help me get her into a shelter?"

"Addy, I just explained, no, I don't think any shelter will take her. They just can't do that. The only legal place she can go is another foster home—another family who was willing to take guardianship."

Addy's phone pinged. Out of habit, she glanced down to see who was texting her. Dr. McGregor. It was all she could do not to throw the phone across the room. Instead, she dropped it back into her purse, leaving the message unread.

As if he could feel the agitation rolling off her, Micah suggested in a soothing voice that she could turn off the ringer.

"I can't. There are too many people…" She stood up. "I have to go."

"Addy, slow down. Running in circles won't solve anything."

"I have to do something," she snapped. "I can't just sit here twiddling my thumbs and being distracted by everyone else's craziness. I don't have time. It's been one crisis after another, and I'm not getting my own work done."

"Call if I can help," she heard him say, as she pushed open the front door.

Even driving failed to calm her like it usually did. The jarring, rutted trek up that isolated mountain was too fresh in her mind. Before she had time to formulate a plan, she was home, the screen door slapping behind her as she entered the kitchen.

Eleanor was sitting at the breakfast table with a notepad and a glass of iced tea.

"Good," she said. "Have a seat and help me finalize the catering menu for Lacey's party. She's off gallivanting somewhere, and this has to get done."

"She's not gallivanting. She's—" Addy caught herself. It wasn't her story to tell, and Lacey had specifically asked her not to. She turned to the sink, filled a glass with water, and drank it down in one go.

"She's what?" Eleanor asked.

Addy refilled the glass but set it down without drinking. "She's taking care of Asia."

Eleanor had a way of pursing her lips and simultaneously turning them down at the corners. It made her look as if she'd caught a whiff of sour milk.

"She has important things to do at home, family obligations. She doesn't have time to be running around with those friends. I do wish you'd stop encouraging her."

Addy took a breath, deliberately ignoring the criticism. "Mother, Asia's aunt and uncle have kicked her out of the house. She's basically living on the street. Lacey is trying to help."

Eleanor stared at Addy, blinking, as if she couldn't process the words. "I don't know what you're talking about," she finally said, and looked back down at the invitations scattered across the table.

"Asia. Lacey's girlfriend."

"I know who Asia is," she snapped.

"Her aunt and uncle—the people who raised her—told her to leave. They say she can only come home if she submits to conversion therapy."

Eleanor gave her a skeptical look. "Teenagers are terribly prone to exaggeration, Addison. You'd do well to remember that if you're going to keep teaching."

Again, Addy let it slide, focusing on the real issue. "I went out to Madison County this morning to talk to them. They're totally serious."

"You did not."

Addy made a little noise in her throat and sat down in the chair opposite her mother. "I did. I met them both. They're sort of alarming, just because they seem so normal, but they're so dead-set on 'curing' Asia. And Lacey, for the record."

That got Eleanor's attention.

"What is that supposed to mean?"

"It means they want to put Asia in a 'conversion therapy' program. To turn her straight. And they'd be happy to share the name of the 'therapist' with you if you want." She made air-quotes with her fingers, unable to disguise her disgust.

Eleanor was quiet, shuffling the thick, creamy envelopes.

"Mother. You can't be taking that seriously. It's abusive! It ought to be illegal, for Pete's sake!"

Eleanor's face was a careful blank. "I'm in no position to judge what goes on in other families. It's none of my business."

"But you couldn't possibly think about doing that to Lacey, right? You have to see how horrible that is."

"I love you both just like you are, although less outlandish clothing and a little more decorum wouldn't be amiss. But no, of course not. I've read about those programs—they're ridiculous."

"Good. So what are we going to do about Asia?"

"What do you mean?"

"She's sixteen years old and homeless. We need to do something to help her."

"Oh no. You need to respect their privacy, Addison. Mind your own business." Eleanor stood and began to gather up the envelopes and invitations. They looked pretentious, Addy thought, in stark contrast to the exigency of Asia's fractured life.

"You can't just ignore it," she said.

Eleanor pressed her lips together in that familiar thin line, but there was sadness in her eyes. She shook her head, mute, and left the room, leaving Addy alone and troubled.

Chapter 33

The next day, reassured by Lacey that Asia was safely ensconced in Grandmama's bungalow, Addy got back to work. For some reason, which probably wouldn't bear close examination, the writing was pouring out of her. It must be some kind of denial or avoidance, she thought. Her mind's way of coping with frustration. She sighed, even as her fingers flew over the keyboard, still half-wondering if she should hop in the car and head back to Washington. The dissertation was practically writing itself at this point. The outline was almost done, and she'd gotten a good start on the first chapter. Did she really need to keep subjecting herself to the emotional stress here in Asheville?

But something kept her from packing up her clothes and leaving, a feeling that she still had things to take care of. The historical marker that she'd promised her mother, the clearing out of Grandmama's house—even as she told herself these were the things hanging over her, the memory of Mrs. Ledford's cheery pink t-shirt and stony face hovered in her memory. She put her head down and kept writing.

As Lacey had predicted, everyone seemed to have forgotten about her audition that afternoon. Eleanor headed off to a committee meeting at the country club, so Addy offered to go with her sister. Asia had said she felt too out of place up at Biltmore, and promised to hang out downtown, away from the bungalow, in case Eleanor showed up. Addy drove to Biltmore House, chattering the whole way about nothing in particular. Lacey was pale and quiet. As Addy pulled the car into a space in the visitor parking lot, Lacey took a breath.

"Thank you for driving," she said in a grave tone.

"You're welcome, silly. Are you really that nervous?"

"I am, actually. It's kind of weird. Auditions don't usually bother me."

"How can I help?"

Lacey cracked her knuckles. "Don't take this the wrong way, but I think I need to walk on by myself. Get into a calmer head space, you know?"

"Of course. Shall I…" She wanted to support Lacey, but didn't want to be pushy. Plus, she had an agenda of her own.

"I kind of don't want you to watch. And don't tell her I said so, but I'm glad Asia didn't come. Is that bad?"

Addy laughed. "No. I don't blame you. Hold on." She jumped out and ran around to open Lacey's door, and gave her a hug. "Text me when you're done. And break a leg!"

Addy watched as Lacey squared her shoulders and strode away by herself. Dawdling a little, giving her sister time to get away, she got her purse and checked to be sure she had her annual pass. She wanted to wander through the house like a tourist, and see if it would stimulate her creative thinking. The pass was a Christmas gift from her mother, renewed every year even though Addy had yet to use it; a sign of Eleanor's unflagging expectation that Addy would eventually follow her into the ranks of the ladies who lunch. The house had been a fixture in her childhood too, so it was only to be expected, Addy supposed. Technically, she still had a visiting researcher ID, but she felt kind of guilty about using that if she wasn't really working.

The walk from the upper parking lot down to the house wound through deep woods. Birds twittered and the smell of earth and pine needles rose up from beneath her shoes, a welcome relief from the intensity of staring at her computer screen. When she reached the bottom of the path, sunlight dazzled her eyes for a moment. She paused to blink and let them adjust, then stepped out onto the gray stone of the formal approach ramp. Turning, she gazed down the full length of the esplanade, taking in the wide, elegant front of Biltmore House. It looked more like a painting—a landscape—than a home. The perfect green lawn flanked by two rows of birch trees was broken by a round stone pool with a fountain rising up in the middle. The hazy peaks of the Blue Ridge Mountains rose in the distance, making her feel as if she were standing at the top of the world.

Looking up at it now, she was struck, as she had been every time she came here as a child, by the sheer scale of the place. It had been one of the greatest of the Gilded Age mansions, and now it was one of the only ones still standing. Asheville had been a backwater when George Vanderbilt fell in love with the surrounding mountains, and the city had grown up virtually in the shadow of his great estate. She had always felt a little more elegant, more romantic, when she was here. She strolled along the edge of the emerald lawn, her pleats swinging in rhythm with each step.

She slowed as she stepped onto the paved forecourt, trying to imagine an elegant phaeton with high-stepping horses pulling up to the portico, graceful young women, a house party perhaps, chattering and laughing as footmen lifted them down. A delicate slipper, layers of lace and silk, a flash of slender white ankle. Addy lingered, indulging herself. Her wild romantic streak had been born in the shadow of this glamorous past, and being back always set her imagination running at full tilt.

She made her way slowly toward the entrance, where she showed her pass to the security guard at the door, then filed into the soaring front hall. Pausing to let her eyes adjust, she deliberated. She didn't particularly want to run into anyone she'd met from the museum staff. It would be too hard to explain why she kept showing up and disappearing. She didn't want to seem wishy-washy, even if that was the feeling that woke her up in the middle of the night.

The whole thing seemed a little worrisome in the broad light of day, standing in the middle of the Great Hall. Addy thought about it for a second, counting the generations. If she was calculating correctly, the current owners of Biltmore would be the grandchildren of Cornelia. How would they feel about her, technically the great-granddaughter of a former housemaid, turning up with their grandmother's correspondence? Perhaps she should just fall in with the tourists and get some culture.

She skirted the edge of the tour group and slipped into the throngs beginning their stroll around the first floor of the mansion. She followed the flow—it was impossible not to; ropes and docents kept everyone moving in the same direction. The Tapestry Room, the Banquet Hall, the Breakfast Room: she moved through the rooms leisurely, torn between trying to see it all through the eyes of a visitor and remembering how often she'd come here as a child. For a second, that feeling of destiny came back with a vertiginous tilt, as if her life was folding in on itself, all paths leading her inevitably back here. She'd only meant to have a look around and absorb the vibe, not trip down memory lane.

When she was a child, the staff scattered around the rooms had seemed so stern, unapproachable. So much about this house had intrigued her for so long. How had it gone from such glamour, such excess, to just another tourist attraction in a city built on tourism? She fingered the thick velvet rope keeping visitors from touching the elaborate dining table, remembering how she'd tried to swing on one of those ropes once, and knocked over the brass pole, bringing the whole rigging—and her mother's profound embarrassment— right down on her head. It had all been so untouchable.

Walking along the vaguely gothic Tapestry Gallery, she caught sight of a familiar stooped figure out on the vast balcony, staring out at Mt. Pisgah in the distance. She turned around and pushed her way through the throngs of tourists to get to the door that would allow her to step outside. By the time she caught sight of him again, he was shuffling along, leaning on his cane. When he saw her, he stopped and leaned back on the stone balustrade.

"Mr. Collins! I hoped I'd bump into you today." Addy scrutinized his face for any sign that he had forgiven whatever made him go off in a huff after their last conversation, in the conservatory.

"Well, look who it is. And didn't I tell you to call me Ford?" It wasn't necessarily forgiveness, but at least he wasn't ignoring her.

"You're right, you did. How've you been, Ford?"

"Oh, I get along. Better than the alternative, I reckon. I've been wondering where you'd gotten to, though. You haven't been back by to see me."

"No, I'm so sorry. I haven't had a chance."

"You getting that big paper of yours done?"

"Yes, actually. It's moving right along."

"Well, that's just great. You keep at it. Schooling's important."

The irony of the comment struck Addy. Her 'schooling' at this point felt so very unimportant in the grand scheme of things, but that was a conversation she didn't want to have, with Ford or anyone else. Perhaps she was even avoiding having it with herself.

"I don't think it'll be too long now," she said. "What's keeping you busy on this beautiful day?"

He scowled at her. "I've been keeping an eye on that ruckus upstairs."

Addy was confused for a second, wondering if maybe he'd suddenly remembered to be angry with her after all, before she realized what he meant. "Oh, the casting call? My sister's there. Auditioning."

Ford made a disapproving noise. "They need to stop letting those movie folks traipse around in here. They make trouble every time they come around."

"How do you mean?"

"Just disrespectful. Wanting to move the furniture and shining all those big lights and not having a bit of care about the folks who take care of this place. It's not easy, you know. Keeping all this up."

"How about if we sit down and you can tell me about it?"

"Oh, go on. You've got better things to do than listen to an old fellow like me."

"No, really. There's a nice soft bench inside. Let's go sit for a while."

He gave her a look. "I know where all the benches are. And I know you're just humoring me. But I reckon I'll let you, this time."

When they were settled, she asked him again why he was bothered by the audition going on upstairs. He looked around at the crowd of tourists milling about the Great Hall.

"They've made a lot of movies up here, ever since I was a boy. I don't like having those folks around, never have. They don't always behave like they ought to, and often as not they act like they own the place."

"Really? That surprises me."

"Folks get too excited about it, all star-struck, and they don't think about the consequences."

"I assume the estate gets paid when a film crew comes in?"

"A whole lot of money. But I don't reckon it's worth it."

"Maybe this one will be different. It's a documentary, you know, not a big feature film. As a matter of fact, it's about the house itself. Perhaps that kind of crew is inherently more respectful."

He gave her a dour look and leaned back against the stone wall, seemingly determined to expect the worst.

Addy felt bad, watching him. It must be difficult to feel responsible for the fate of the place, but to be essentially powerless. He'd been here since the day he was born, and so didn't know anything else. She couldn't imagine feeling roots that ran that deep. Ever since she could remember, she'd been looking outward, away from Asheville, beyond the mountains. Here was a man for whom Asheville was the outer periphery. The thought blew her mind a little. She was still curious what memories he might have hidden away behind those sharp eyes, but she didn't want to push until he clammed up.

"Ford? How much time did you spend in town, growing up?"

He looked at her from the corner of his eye. "You don't want to hear about that."

"Yes, I do. I've never met anyone who lived in one place for eighty-seven years. I'd love to hear about it, if you have time."

"What are you talking about, time? I got nothing but time, or not much time at all. No time like right now."

"Then tell me, what was it like growing up here?"

"Well. My daddy laid brick, you know. His daddy did too. He worked on the house from the beginning, then my daddy came along, and he worked on the dairy and the truck farm, and a whole lot of other buildings. They're not all standing now. It's a shame. Anyway, my mama worked in the house, cooking in the big kitchen when they was a separate one for the staff. Then when they had to start making economies, all the cooks just worked together in one. She stayed on after she and Daddy married, but not when the babies started coming."

"Do you have siblings?" Addy was surprised, and intrigued by the thought that there might be more Fords wandering around, keeping tabs on the estate.

"I do, but they all moved down into town as soon as they could. My brother died a while back, so now I just got two sisters. They both got families, though, so I see them some."

"What about you? Do you have children?"

"No, girl. You're getting me all out of order. Like I was saying, my daddy laid brick. I was born right before the Great Depression, and times got hard all over, but Miss Edith did her best to take care of her own. It weren't easy on the estate, but folks was better off up here than in a lot of places. So, my daddy taught me how to lay brick as soon as I was old enough so I could stay on and work here. But I had to go to school too. My mama and daddy made sure of that. I was the first person in my family to graduate from high school."

"That's fantastic. Was there a school up here on the estate?"

"Not a high school. There was a primary school for the young 'uns, but they closed that down in the fifties. Us big kids went to school down in the village. Bus picked us up after we did the chores. But that was the only time I spent down there."

A far-away look washed over his face. "Weren't many of us left when the Depression took hold, but we were family. Miss Edith and Miss Cornelia and Mr. John, they did right by us. Family, yes, ma'am."

Addy sat silently, watching the old man dip back into a lifetime of memories. He seemed very far away.

"Can I ask you something?" she finally said, drawing him back to the present.

"You can ask."

"It sounds like your life pretty much revolved around the estate, but I'm curious. Did you ever know anything about Zelda Fitzgerald? She was a famous flapper, and was married to Scott Fitzgerald. You know, he wrote the novel *The Great Gatsby*? She spent some time at Highland Hospital, down in town. It would've been when you were a kid, I guess."

He looked at her for a long moment with an intensity that was startling.

Addy wondered if he was connecting the dots with their earlier conversation, when she had shown him Zelda's letter.

"I know who you're talking about, but I don't know much of anything about her. I remember hearing tales, though. Died in a fire, right?"

Addy nodded again.

"Seems like she weren't quite right in the head, if folks were telling it straight. It was a sad story about that fire. A whole bunch of women died that night. Mighty bad."

"Do you know if she ever visited up here, at the house?"

Ford tipped his head back. "Not that I recall, but I was a young 'un when she died, so I don't reckon I would. But why would someone like that be up here? Like I told you, she was a little off in the head. That's why she was in that hospital where she died."

"I know. I was just curious. I was wondering if she might've been friends with Cornelia. They were the same age, and Zelda and her husband were very famous. I think they spent time in Asheville before Zelda got sick, but that would've been before you were born, so I guess it doesn't matter."

He gave her that sharp look again. "I don't rightly know what matters anymore. I've got all these memories that I don't know what to do with, and here I set, worrying about what foolishness those movie folks are getting into upstairs. Getting old is a mystery, I'll tell you that, young lady. You don't know what to hang on to and what to turn loose."

Something in those words reverberated in Addy's head. "Isn't that the truth," she mumbled to herself, but Ford heard her.

"This is about that letter you showed me, isn't it?"

Addy chewed her lip for a second, then admitted it was. She told him about the short story, about her hunch, and the confirmation from Dr. Cavendish in Alabama.

When she paused for a breath, he made a grumbling sound in his throat. "That sounds to me like one of those things that might not matter, when it gets right down to it."

"Why do you think that?" she asked. She should never have said anything.

"Well, I didn't know Miss Cornelia real well—she left when I was a boy and never came back. But I don't think that Fitzgerald woman was the kind of person she would've taken up with. I don't mean to be speaking ill of the dead, but she wasn't right in the head. And Miss Cornelia, she was a Vanderbilt. I think you and your professor are just wrong about that letter."

Addy sighed. Getting through this publication without making enemies was going to be difficult, but no scholar worth her salt would walk away from this.

"I know it's surprising, but Dr. Cavendish wrote the definitive biography of Zelda Fitzgerald."

He sniffed. "I don't reckon any of us can judge what another person's life meant, especially after they're long gone."

At that moment, Addy's phone pinged, alerting her to a text message. Her hand reached for it in her pocket, but she stopped herself. She didn't want to offend Ford any more than she already had.

He had noticed. "Don't mind me. Y'all nowadays have got those phones making all kinds of noises at you, seems like you can't ever get away from them. I'm just glad I never had to contend with that, always at the beck and call of some gadget."

"I'm sorry, I hate to be rude." She slipped it out and looked at the text. It was Lacey saying she'd finished her audition and wondered if Addy wanted to see behind the scenes at a casting call.

"I'm sorry, Ford. That was rude of me. But my sister's finished upstairs."

"Go on and go, then."

She hesitated, trying to decide if he seemed annoyed with her. "Can I walk you somewhere, on my way out?"

"No. I'm just going to set here for a while and rest my voice. Talking does wear me out."

"Thank you," she said.

"For what?"

"For trusting me with your stories."

His eyes were closed, his head leaning back against the stone wall, but he nodded once.

Addy patted his hand and stood up. "If my sister gets the part, I'll be back up here in a few days," she said. "Hopefully, I'll see you then."

He shrugged, eyes still closed.

Addy turned and made her way through the throngs of tourists, out into the sunshine.

Chapter 34

Lacey got the part as Addy had assumed she would, and broke the news at dinner that night, with the request that they all come Monday to watch the filming, "for moral support." Addy instinctively glanced at Eleanor to gauge her reaction—she seemed unimpressed, but also curiously unsurprised. Addy wondered if she'd known all along that Lacey would audition in spite of her earlier disapproval.

As always, Eleanor brushed it all aside, saying she had a meeting on Monday, and besides, she couldn't imagine the Cecils wanted all the neighbors hanging around, ogling. "It sounds like a spectacle," she said, sniffing.

"It is. The whole estate is a spectacle. It's a tourist attraction. That's the point," Addy said.

"That doesn't mean I need to participate."

"Think of it as supporting me," Lacey said.

Eleanor poked at her salad with her fork, but didn't respond.

After dinner, Eleanor and Mason went for a walk instead of sitting on the front porch. It was just unusual enough to get Addy's attention, like a nagging twitch. Quiet settled over the house, and suddenly she was alone with her dissertation and her worries. She proofread her outline one last time, then attached the file to an email and hit send, hoping to preempt Dr. McGregor's Monday morning query. All that was left was the writing of the thing. She put in her earbuds and cued up a swing playlist, trying to drown out the silence. She wrote a paragraph and deleted it, then went down to the kitchen and poured herself a glass of wine, hoping it would help her settle.

It didn't.

The filming was set to begin on Monday, so Lacey's attention was consumed for the rest of the weekend. Asia was with her on Sunday, quietly helping her learn lines and stay calm. Addy was surprised by the younger girl's ability to ignore her own precarious situation, even if just for a few hours. She prowled around, listening to them run lines, but Lacey said she was hovering and making her nervous. She went for a walk, until she saw thunderheads mushrooming behind the mountains, pent-up energy flashing gold and white and pink inside the ominous clouds.

Lacey left early Monday morning, driving up to Biltmore alone, having quietly extracted Addy's promise to pick Asia up at Nellie's and bring her to watch. By the time Addy got in her car, Mason had long since gone to his office, having gently told Lacey he couldn't watch her filming in the middle of a work day. Eleanor was nowhere to be found. She found Asia trudging down the busy street a few blocks from the bungalow, hugging close to the hedge next to the sidewalk and lugging her backpack.

Asia got in the car and dropped her backpack into the back seat, slumping down in the seat next to Addy, clutching her phone in one hand.

"Is everything okay?" Addy asked. It seemed like a stupid question, but it was the only way she knew to open up a conversation.

Asia was noticeably more agitated than she had been the afternoon before. Hunched over, she looked almost hollow-chested, gripping her elbows tight to her body. "Fine."

Addy hesitated for a second, thinking she ought to give the child time and space to open up, but she felt as if she'd been doing that all summer. Surely they'd established some level of trust by now.

"Forgive me if I don't believe you," she said, giving Asia a sidelong look. "Talk to me."

Asia shrugged. "I'm just stressed for Lacey, that's all. She really wants this gig to lead to something." Her phone made a quiet buzz, and she glanced down at it.

"She's ready, isn't she?"

"She knows her lines. I mean, she's really smart. And she's good at acting. So yeah, I hope so."

There was a touch of admiration in her voice, but Addy couldn't help thinking there was more that she wasn't saying.

The phone buzzed again.

"Are you in the theatre program at your school?"

"Oh no. I'm sure I'd have terrible stage fright. I'd feel…naked. Exposed. I don't think I'd mind the acting—pretending to be someone else, I'm pretty damn good at that—but I couldn't bear for people to stare at me."

She looked truly horrified at the thought, so Addy let it go, but an image came to her, unbidden, of the Asia who had greeted her when she arrived in Asheville not two months earlier. How had she not noticed it sooner? It was as if all the verve had been leached out of Asia, leaving her pale and subdued. Addy glanced over at Asia, who was looking surreptitiously at her phone.

"Speaking of school," Addy said. "When does it start?"

Asia looked out the window. They were on the Biltmore Estate now, twisting steadily upward toward the house, flicking in and out of the deep summer green of the forest.

"Sometime in August," she said. "I'm not really sure of the date." She looked back down at her phone, and this time her thumbs flew over the keypad, texting.

Addy remembered her own mother, circling the date in red on the wall calendar that had always hung in the kitchen, taking Addy to buy a new outfit for the first day, complete with shoes and socks and usually a hair ribbon or purse or belt. There was always a new backpack and a lunchbox—one of those large, soft-sided ones, big enough to hold a multi-course meal. Eleanor had made Addy's lunches all through elementary school. At her expensive private school, buying lunch was a sign that your mother didn't have time to make your lunch. Addy still remembered cafeteria lunches as a rare treat.

She wondered now who would get Asia ready for the first day of school, not that a high school senior would need quite as much hand-holding as an elementary-aged child. For that matter, where would she sleep the night before? Once again, the sheer impossibility of Asia's situation struck Addy like a blow, leaving her breathless and impotent and seething.

She parked the car in the graveled visitor's lot, and they made their way up to the house. Addy asked at the front desk where the filming was going on, and they were checked off on a guest list and given visitor passes.

They followed the docent's directions down to a servants' room in the basement. The hall had been blocked off and tourists were being routed in a different direction. Lights and reflection screens were set up in the doorway, and Addy could hear Lacey's voice, but couldn't make out her words. As they approached, a young woman saw them and, noting their passes, waved them to the doorway, miming caution on the tangle of cords snaking across the floor.

Lacey stood in a pool of light in the middle of the room, dressed in a plain, tidy lavender dress that showed only her ankles and old-fashioned looking Mary-Janes. Her hair was pulled back in a bun at the nape of her neck.

A youngish man with a short, pointed beard and suspenders was talking to Lacey, pointing out tiny pieces of tape on the floor. As her eyes adjusted to the bright light, Addy realized that there were people in a corner of the room, perched on stools—Ford and Eleanor. Asia, who had slipped into the doorway beside her, must have seen Eleanor at the same moment, because she stepped back out into the hall.

"Hi." The suspendered man took two steps in Addy's direction and shook her hand. "I'm Sven. I'm the director, producer, and jack-of-all-trades. You must be the sister. Thanks for coming. Lacey's told me about your research. I hoped you might be here to give us some extra historical background."

Even though she was still standing in the doorway, Addy suddenly felt as if the lights were trained directly in her eyes. She glanced toward Lacey, wondering what she had told him. Lacey fiddled with her buttoned cuffs, paying careful attention to a loose thread at the hem. Addy could feel both Ford and Eleanor watching her, waiting for her response.

"I'm Addy, but I imagine your research has been much broader than mine. You know how academics are—the narrower the focus, the better."

"We've done our best." He beamed at her and waved an arm, encompassing the small room. "It's a series, you know. We've filmed on some other properties in South Carolina and Virginia and up in the Hudson Valley. It's kind of a big project, but we're in the homestretch now, and Biltmore is really going to be the centerpiece."

It looked to Addy like a tangle of cords and wobbly poles crammed into a tiny, warm room, but she thought she understood the pride of creation. She felt a little pang of envy, thinking of her own project moving at a snail's pace.

"Congratulations. I can't wait to see the final product." She took a step backward to move out of the way, but Sven touched her elbow.

"I'd love it if you'd stay and watch. I've got more folding chairs."

He dug two more lightweight camp stools out of a bag. Eleanor pulled one into the corner next to hers, and motioned for Asia to sit. She perched tensely on the edge of the stool while Addy settled in next to Ford. She reached over and rubbed his arm, glad to see him again. He gave her a gruff nod, and pointed toward Lacey, as if saying "hush and pay attention."

Sven had Lacey going through a series of small, silent actions in the room, tying on a starched white apron and making up her small, iron bed. They'd add the narrator's voice-over later, he explained. It looked to Addy as if filming was as much about computers as anything else. He looked up from a laptop at one point, and asked the room at large, "Do you folks have anything to add, about how bad things got for the servants after old man Vanderbilt died?"

Addy felt Ford stiffen beside her.

Sven was beaming around at them, oblivious to the threads of disapproval that his question pulled taut between them.

For a second, the room was so silent Addy could hear the floodlights humming.

"Why would we know anything about the servants?" Eleanor asked. She sounded as if she was accusing Sven of a personal slur.

"Now, you see here," Ford said. "Mrs. Edith always did her best by her people."

Addy sighed. Poor Sven had no idea what a mess he was making of things. She put a hand on Ford's arm—he looked as if his head was about to explode. Lacey had magically produced another folding stool and sat down next to

Asia. Suddenly Addy felt sorry for the director. They were all staring at him, waiting for him to explain himself, to defend his project. She knew all too well what that felt like.

She stood up, facing Ford and her mother.

"I think what Sven wants to know is whether we, as locals, have any insight that might make the film more authentic, right, Sven?"

He nodded enthusiastically. "Exactly. You had an aunt who was a maid, right? And if I understand correctly, you worked on the estate, right?" He looked at Ford.

"I told you that, didn't I?" Ford still sounded peevish.

Addy touched him on the shoulder. "Have you told Sven any of your stories, about Mrs. Edith, and learning to lay bricks, and going to school down in the village?"

Ford looked flustered. "I don't reckon he wants to hear all those old stories," he mumbled.

"Are you kidding? That's what I'm here for—that's exactly what I want to hear," Sven said. He was like a child in a toy store. "I want to document real life on these fairy-tale estates. Dude, you are the story I'm trying to tell."

Addy said to Sven, in a quiet voice, "Take him to lunch."

Sven blinked at her. "Of course! Why didn't I think of that? Can I buy you lunch?" He trailed off hopefully.

Addy cringed. "Call him Mr. Collins," she whispered.

"And you too, Mom," Sven said, looking at Eleanor. "We'll all go. You can tell me about your aunt, too."

"Maybe it would be better if it was just you and Mr. Collins," Addy said quickly. "Primary sources are better than secondary, right?"

"That's true," Sven said. A thoughtful look crossed his face, but it was gone as quickly as it had appeared. The man's enthusiasm was irrepressible.

Eleanor stood up. "I can't fathom what you think I might know about how servants lived nearly a hundred years ago." She looked down at Asia. "Aren't you ready for lunch, dear?"

Asia looked shocked, but she got up and followed Eleanor to the door. Flabbergasted, Addy turned to follow.

"What the hell?" Lacey mouthed.

Addy shrugged.

"We'll be filming down at Biltmore Dairy tomorrow," Sven said. "You'll come, won't you?"

"Of course," Addy said as she scurried to keep up with her mother, whose heels were already tapping down the long hall.

"And bring that story," he called after her. "I'd love to see it!"

Addy grimaced. Now she knew exactly what Lacey had told him.

Chapter 35

They followed the same routine the next morning, all pretending to be coming from places they weren't.

"I bumped into Asia on my way here," Addy lied as they met Eleanor in the parking lot of the Biltmore Dairy, which was really just an ice cream parlor that wouldn't open until later in the day.

"I had an early committee meeting," Eleanor said, rummaging for something in her purse and not finding it.

Ford was already there. Addy got the impression that Sven had driven up to his home on the estate grounds and given him a ride. She was surprised, and touched, and curious about where Ford lived. He'd told her that the Cecils let him stay in his cottage for life, but she hadn't figured out how to wrangle an invitation to see it. She looked at Sven more appreciatively—he seemed to have impressed Ford.

They all watched as Lacey did the morning's marketing with a wicker basket over one arm, chatting with the rotund actor behind the counter. He wore a pristine white uniform, complete with a long apron and a soda-jerk style cap. His handlebar mustache curled up at the ends in two perfect spirals. Addy wondered who had advised Sven on costuming. The actor looked an odd mash-up between a turn-of-the-century butcher and a mid-century high schooler.

During a break, Sven pulled his stool over to sit next to Addy, asking if she'd brought the Zelda story so he could see it. She hesitated. She had tried to leave it at home, tucked away safely in her desk, but an odd pride had compelled her to bring it along. She'd kept it to herself for weeks now, as much as she could, although admittedly not as much as Dr. McGregor wanted her to. Sven seemed genuinely curious. Besides, he was here—physically present, not a faceless email address or theoretical authority. He seemed kind and authentic, and legitimately passionate about his work. She'd told herself all these things when she put the file of papers in her bag that morning. Now, though, in this white-tiled room full of bright lights, she felt protective, as if she were exposing not just her own work and the document that could jumpstart her career, but someone else's truth.

She wasn't even sure whose truth it was—whose secret—Zelda's? Great-Aunt Martha's? The Cecils'? Would any of them have felt as responsible for it as she did? Or perhaps it was her mother's secret to tell. She was no longer sure. Maybe it didn't matter. She held the manila envelope in her hand, paralyzed by her own doubts, until Sven gently slid it from between her fingers.

His face was thoughtful as he read the letter, then amused. Addy kept her eyes on his face. She could feel Ford watching, but couldn't bring herself to look in his direction, unwilling to risk seeing disapproval or disappointment in his sharp eyes. She could tell Sven was skimming the story itself.

"It's not exactly brilliant stuff," he said.

Addy didn't bother responding. She'd come to terms with the story—its significance was historical, not literary. Zelda herself would probably have been horrified to think of it being seen in public.

He handed it back to her. "It's interesting, but it doesn't really support the notion that she was the force behind Scott's writing, does it?"

"No, and I won't ever claim that it does. But I do think it's an interesting peek at a side of her we don't usually see. She's always portrayed as such an appendage of Scott."

"Why do you suppose that is? Or more importantly, why are we Americans so fascinated with them?"

Before Addy could try to formulate an answer, the door from the parking lot opened, and Asia's aunt and uncle walked in. Suddenly, it felt as if all the air had left the room, leaving them all exposed in the bright white light.

Addy stood up without thinking and stepped in front of Asia, who seemed to be shrinking, trying to disappear into the crease of the folding chair she was sitting on.

"There you are, Asia. I couldn't tell from your text which ice cream place you meant, so we checked at two others first," Mrs. Ledford said, breaking the silence.

Sven seemed to remember that he was the authority in the room. "Can I help you?" he asked pleasantly, stepping forward and extending a hand.

"We don't want to get in your way, we've just come for our daughter," Mr. Ledford said, ignoring the proffered hand.

Sven looked confused, and Addy could see his assistant, over in the corner, surreptitiously pull out her phone.

Next to Addy, Eleanor stood up slowly, almost regally.

"I'm Eleanor Quick, Lacey's mother. What do you mean you've come for Asia?"

Addy had never heard such ice in her mother's voice.

"I'm Theresa Ledford. It's so nice to finally meet you. I met Addy a few days ago," she said, then nodded at Lacey. "And you must be Lacey." She turned back to Eleanor and lowered her voice as if they were old friends. "Teenagers are a handful, aren't they?"

Eleanor looked her in the eye. "Not these two. These two are good kids."

Mrs. Ledford pressed her lips together in a thin line. It was a look Addy would have expected from her mother, but instead, Eleanor had drawn herself up tall.

Mr. Ledford stepped forward. "Well, we're finished with this nonsense. We're here to take Asia home. I don't want people talking about how we let her run wild on the streets."

"Are you kidding me?" Lacey blurted.

"Hush, Lacey. I'll handle this," Addy said, putting a hand on Mrs. Ledford's back to turn her toward the door.

"Maybe you should handle your sister, since your mother isn't going to,"

Mr. Ledford said, stubbornly holding his ground directly under one of Sven's lights. A sheen of sweat had broken out on his face.

"Hold on, folks," Sven said. "I'm not sure what's going on, but we've got a show to film here."

It was the dig at Eleanor that propelled Addy into action. She took both Ledfords by the elbows and propelled them toward the door, pulling a little to get Mr. Ledford moving. She looked back at her mother and Asia and mouthed "Stay here."

In the parking lot, Mr. Ledford pulled his arm free and stepped away from Addy, as if her touch might contaminate him.

Mrs. Ledford had pulled out a brochure and was waving it around. "These folks do amazing work. They'll straighten Lacey right out. Here, you can keep this. I can give your mother another copy."

Addy glared at her, hands on her hips. "I did some research on this place, and frankly, I don't even know how it's legal. I've consulted my attorney. Asia is old enough to make a case that your guardianship is detrimental to her health, and I'm prepared to back her up." She looked from one to the other, determined not to let them know how much she was bluffing.

"I don't intend to sit back and watch our child go to hell in a hand basket," Mr. Ledford said.

"Asia is not your child," Addy said, surprised at how steady she felt.

"She might as well be," Theresa Ledford said in a thick voice. "She's been with us for twelve years. That's most of her life!"

"Nonetheless, she's not," Addy said, forcing a calm she didn't feel. She fumbled in her purse for a scrap of paper and jotted down Micah's number. "This is my attorney," she said, holding it toward Mrs. Ledford. "Feel free to give him a call. In the meantime, don't worry. Asia is safe and taken care of."

Mrs. Ledford turned away. Her husband stared at the paper but didn't take it. In a flash, Addy realized she had won. She'd seen that modest little house on the top of the mountain. They wouldn't be able to afford the kind of lawyer who would be willing to go up against Micah. Even if they could, it wouldn't be worth it to them. Asia would be eighteen in less than two years, and that would be the end of the Social Security payments that were probably the only reason they'd stayed interested this long anyway.

Addy held her breath. They all did, something elemental hanging in the balance, but the moment passed. She blinked, and Mr. Ledford's bluster was gone. He was a tired-looking, weather-beaten man with thinning, colorless hair. He met her gaze and held up his hands in defeat.

"Fine. It's all on you. But don't come running to me when you realize what a trouble-maker you've got on your hands." He turned and followed his wife to the minivan parked on the far side of the lot.

"Now what are you going to do?" Eleanor's voice was quiet.

Addy turned around. "Did you hear all that?"

"Of course. I wasn't going to let you face them by yourself again."

Addy pressed her hands together, trying to stop them from shaking. "I didn't realize you were there. You didn't say anything."

"I didn't need to. You had it under control."

"Did I? I'm afraid that's all going to come back and bite me in the butt."

"You were very impressive. We'll figure out a way to make it work."

Addy stared at her mother, feeling as if the ground had shifted under her feet. All the words had drained out of her. Together, they watched the minivan pull out into traffic.

Chapter 36

"Is everything okay out there?" Sven's head poked around the edge of the door.

"They're gone," Addy said, more to Asia than to Sven, as she and Eleanor stepped back into the shop.

Asia closed her eyes for a second. "What did they say?" she asked when she opened them again.

Addy hesitated, then squatted down next to Asia. "Are you okay?"

The last bit of color had drained from her face except for the red rims of her eyes. She shook her head. "I'm so sorry. I thought they were beginning to thaw a little bit when they texted. My M—Aunt Theresa—was being all chatty. I shouldn't have told them we were going to be here. I'm so sorry. I've ruined everything."

"Don't be sorry, it's not your fault. But I don't want to make things worse for you."

Asia made a bleak noise. "The only thing worse would be going to that camp they want to send me to." She looked directly at Addy. "I won't go. I just won't."

Something clicked then, as if Addy had turned a puzzle piece just a few degrees and suddenly knew exactly where it belonged. She could almost feel it slip into place, somewhere deep in her gut, or maybe in her mind.

"You can stay with us," she said, glancing at her mother.

Eleanor looked a little wobbly.

Addy pulled over a folding chair and her mother sank into it.

She looked at Eleanor, still stunned by her presence in the parking lot, but this didn't seem like the right time to ask what she'd been thinking. They'd have to talk about it later, when the kids weren't listening, Addy thought, and felt another little piece of her identity click into place. She wanted to know where her mother had found that strength, so she would ask. It was a question, and she would ask, and they would talk.

In the meantime, everyone in the room was looking at her, waiting for her to tell them what to do. Even Sven looked rattled.

"I hate to say it, but I think your filming might be over for today," she said.

Sven nodded vigorously. "I need a cigarette," he said, patting his pockets. "Does anyone have a cigarette?"

"You quit," his assistant said.

"That doesn't mean I don't need one now," he muttered, and began unplugging lights, yanking the sockets out of the wall. "That's it, folks. Thanks for everything. I'll email you about the release date."

Ford stood up, leaning on his cane. "Are you quitting just because you ran into some rude folks? Because I'll tell you what, son. You got to learn to ignore the rude folks, and tell the stories you think are important. Isn't that right, young lady?" He tipped his chin in Addy's direction.

She looked between them, then between Asia and Lacey and Eleanor.

"Yes," she said. "Of course." She picked up the manila envelope that Sven had left next to his laptop. "And that's exactly what I'm going to do."

When they all pitched in and helped Sven load his car, he calmed down enough to stop talking about cigarettes. He said he'd email Lacey about where and when he'd want to film some B-roll, but Addy wondered if that would really happen. With an air of emptiness like the end of summer camp, they all got back into their respective vehicles, except Asia, who rode with Lacey this time. Addy suspected it would be a few hours before either of them would be ready to talk about what had transpired.

She was exhausted herself, and wanted nothing more than solitude, but she followed her mother's car home. They needed to talk.

In the kitchen, Addy opened a bottle of wine.

"I know it's not dinnertime, but I don't care," she said, handing her mother a glass.

"Neither do I," Eleanor said, and swallowed half the glass in one go.

"I don't know where to start," Addy said.

Eleanor shrugged. "I don't know what you mean."

"Yes, you do, and we're going to talk about it." She took a breath, trying to formulate sentences that would order her jumbled thoughts. "Tell me what changed your mind about Asia."

"I didn't—" she began.

Addy looked at her, but didn't speak, summoning all her patience.

"I read about that therapy they wanted to send her to. And I thought about how alone she must feel, being raised by people who would try to do that to her. It broke my heart, that's all."

"Mine too."

"I know," Eleanor said quietly. "And you and Lacey did the right thing, letting her stay at Mother's. I'm sorry you didn't feel like you could tell me, and that I didn't react so well when you tried the other day, but I'm glad you did it anyway."

Addy opened her mouth, then closed it again, with a little pop sound. They'd been so careful.

"I didn't realize you knew. Sorry," she said.

"I put two and two together when I went over there after you told me about her 'parents.'" She made air quotes around the word. "And if I hadn't figured it out myself, Lorraine Wells made sure I knew. She doesn't miss a beat."

Addy looked at her mother, remembering the histrionics in the hospital. What had changed in Eleanor's mind? Her blue eyes held Addy's without wavering, and Addy saw in them nothing of accusation or judgment, just a resignation that seemed to mirror her own.

It didn't matter how far she went or how much she tried to distance herself—she would always find herself looking back, thinking of home. She could almost see a thin gold thread binding her to this family, this place, these people.

"I don't think I'm going to finish my dissertation," she said.

"Isn't it almost done?"

"Well, the hard part is done. I sent the outline in yesterday. All that's left is the writing, but I don't think I can bear to waste even another month on it."

Eleanor seemed to catch herself before she spoke, as if she were thinking better of one sentence and choosing another. "You've invested a lot of time already, but if your heart's not in it, I understand."

Something loosened in Addy's chest that she hadn't realized was constricting her. Suddenly, she could breathe a little more deeply.

"Asia's not the only one. Genevieve was telling me—"

"When did you run into Genevieve?" Eleanor interrupted, striving for casual but not quite making it.

"We had lunch last week. Anyway, we were talking about the homeless population around here, and she was saying that the number of homeless teenagers is shocking. I keep thinking about that, and the idea of hiding away in the academic ivory tower makes me feel like a useless human."

Eleanor nodded. "I understand," she said, a wry smile lifting one corner of her mouth. "It's the opposite of what I felt when I left graduate school, but I realize that you're the only person who has to live with your decision. Believe me, it will stay with you forever." She took another sip of her wine. "I didn't realize you and Genevieve had gotten together. What else did you chat about?" she asked, as if the subject of her graduate career might not bear much more examination.

Addy gave her a look. Now that they were in this tentative new territory, she didn't want to go back to the rocky ground they'd always trod together. She took a breath and shoved down the instinct that made her want to clam up and turn away from her mother, or shock her with something that would knock Genevieve off the pedestal she occupied in Eleanor's mind.

It doesn't mean anything, she told herself. *We're just chatting.*

"School, and her Junior League project, mostly. It turns out she's really good at fundraising, but the rest of the project—dealing with the community, I guess—is not for her."

"You didn't talk about the wedding?"

"No, actually, it barely came up." They were both tiptoeing around the subject of the manuscript, and Addy thought they both knew it, but it seemed less important now than it had just this morning. Wheels were turning in her mind as she thought back to Genevieve's excitement about how much money she'd raised.

"I'm surprised. Her mother is so excited."

Addy ignored the comment, and the landmines that lurked beneath it. Old habits were hard to change, and Eleanor's conversational wheels had been stuck in the same gossipy rut for Addy's entire life. It would take time. "You've given me a good idea. Maybe what I need to do is get Genevieve to do some fundraising for me. She's so good at it."

"For what? What are you going to do?"

The idea had dropped into Addy's head fully-formed, and excitement bubbled up in her like it hadn't in longer than she could remember.

"I'm going to start a shelter for homeless gay teenagers," she said, standing up to dump her wine down the sink. "And I won't be home for dinner tonight. There's work to be done."

Chapter 37

By the next evening, Addy had turned her life—and a few others—upside down. Micah had agreed to advise her, *pro bono*, on setting up a foundation to help homeless gay youth.

"The first thing you have to do is establish a board of directors, with yourself at the helm, of course."

"Okay. Welcome to the board."

"Attorneys aren't required on boards."

"No, but old friends are. Especially old friends whose grandfathers helped start the whole mess to begin with." She watched him carefully, worried she might be pushing a sensitive button, but he looked amused.

"I don't believe he knew a single homeless gay teenager."

"You know what I mean. If it hadn't been for him firing Martha, I would never have come back to Asheville, and this whole summer wouldn't have happened. Besides, I really will need your advice. Academia hasn't exactly been good training for dealing with the real world."

Micah gave her a long, assessing look. "I don't know," he finally said. "I think you've always been an activist; it just took you awhile to remember."

She held out a hand. "Like I said, welcome to the board, cousin."

He shook, and she knew his reluctance was feigned.

"What's next?" she asked, pulling out a notepad, ready to jump in with both feet.

"More board members. Fundraising. A mission statement. A plan. Non-profit status. Grant applications."

Addy heard fundraising and stood up again, snapping her fingers.

"Genevieve Ingram. It turns out she's really good at fundraising."

Micah gave her a stern look. "Can you two get along?"

"Actually, I think so. Don't look at me like that. If you and I can work together, anything is possible."

"True. And you're right, Genevieve is perfect. Her entire life has been about cultivating relationships."

Addy thought about that for a second. "Maybe that's what it's supposed to be," she said, mostly to herself.

She met Genevieve for coffee a little while later and explained her idea—a foundation, a board of directors, a shelter for homeless gay youth. Every time she articulated it, the plan sounded more legitimate, more obvious, more possible.

She watched Genevieve while she was talking, and saw the moment the spark caught.

"This isn't some kind of vague, maybe-it'll-help-but-we-won't-really-know proposition. It will literally get kids off the street. And the fundraising is the most important part."

"I'd love to help. When do we start?"

Addy beamed at her old friend. "We just did."

When she got home, Lacey and Asia were sitting in the porch swing with glasses of iced tea, but no one else was home. Addy collapsed into a rocking chair.

"You look tired," Lacey said. "Where did you work today?"

Addy looked over at them. Asia looked better already, she thought—the circles under her eyes were beginning to fade, and she looked less likely to bolt up out of the swing and run.

She leaned her head against the back of the rocking chair and closed her eyes, listening to the familiar creak of the porch swing. "I met with Micah, and then Genevieve. And then I made lists. Lots of lists."

"No, I meant your research."

Addy heard a note of confusion in her sister's voice, and her eyes popped open. She looked over at the two girls, both of whom were frowning slightly.

"Mother didn't tell y'all?"

"Tell us what?"

"I'm quitting school."

Lacey's frown deepened, her eyebrows bunching together, worry darkening her eyes. "What are you talking about? What happened?"

"I had a better idea."

"So why do you have to quit? Can't you just switch topics again?"

"No, I had a better idea than school. I spent today setting up a non-profit organization. I'm going to open a shelter for homeless gay teenagers."

The porch swing stopped creaking with a metallic clank.

"Mom and Daddy know this, and their heads didn't explode?"

"No. As a matter of fact, I think Mother gets it. I think she understands that I have to do what's right for me, because she didn't do what was right for her. Or maybe she did—she wound up with us. I don't know. I think maybe it's complicated, and there aren't any clear right or wrong answers. Anyway, my gut is telling me—screaming at me—to do this, so I am."

"Do you have any idea how to run a non-profit or a shelter?"

"No. But I can find people who do, and I can learn."

Asia was listening to the two of them, chewing on the inside of her mouth.

"Asia? You look worried. Tell me what you're thinking," Addy said.

"Nothing much." She shrugged. "I guess it's a good idea."

Addy settled back against the column, prepared to wait as long as necessary to hear Asia out, but it only took a moment.

"I don't mean to sound selfish, but what does it mean for me?" Asia said, the words coming out in a rush.

Addy was surprised, then it clicked. "Oh, nothing, honey. Unless you want it to, of course. But Mother still wants you to stay here. We talked about it."

Asia leaned against Lacey's shoulder. "Good," she said in a muffled voice.

Lacey patted her knee and whispered something to her.

Addy looked beyond the edge of the yard, toward the rolling tops of the Blue Ridge in the near distance. Twilight had cast them in indigo shadow against a lavender sky shot through with rose and gold. As much as she had railed against being back in the mountains, their beauty still filled her with peace.

Genevieve emailed the next morning with a list of prospective donors. Addy requested that she hold off on contacting one—the Cecils. She needed to sort out one other piece of business before they tapped that particular family for a donation.

It turned out to be much simpler than she had expected. She called and made an appointment to meet with the brother and sister who, between them, were responsible for the Vanderbilt family legacy. They met her in a simple office at the company headquarters in downtown Asheville.

She handed Bill the envelope, but couldn't think of a graceful preamble, so she jumped right in. "I found this in my great-great-aunt Martha's papers. It's what I've been working on this summer, but I think ultimately it should belong to the two of you. I have a publisher lined up for it—a magazine editor who specializes in unpublished manuscripts. And I'm working on writing the accompanying article, but I wanted you to see it, and be thinking about what you want to do with it after the article comes out."

Looking mystified, Bill unsealed the flap and tipped the thin sheets of paper out into his hand. He and his sister both peered at them. Dini looked up at Addy, frowning.

"I can't read this. What is it?"

"We're pretty certain it's a letter from Zelda Fitzgerald to Cornelia Vanderbilt, your grandmother. And a short story that Zelda wrote in her honor. Or something like that."

Bill scanned the story. "Why do you think it belongs to us?"

"I guess that's debatable. It could just as well belong to the Fitzgerald family."

"You misunderstand me. Isn't it yours?"

They were legally correct, of course, but Addy wanted them to understand her motives. Bill and Dini were both looking at her, expectant, but infinitely kind.

"Technically, yes, but I think you're in a better position to take care of it and do it justice." She turned her hands over, palms up. "Plus, it's your grandmother. I think it only makes sense for the letter, at least, to live at the house."

They looked at each other, brother and sister, and Addy realized for the first time that there really was an ironclad family bond that held the whole endeavor together. She couldn't read the look that passed between them. Bill slid the papers back into the envelope and handed them to her.

"Thanks for showing them to us, Addy. We'll look forward to reading your article about them. I'm sure there will be some publicity, and we appreciate you giving us advance notice. In the meantime, we'll be thinking about how best to display them."

Addy left the office satisfied. She had their blessing to write the article. No one was going to be blindsided, and she was going to maintain her academic integrity. It was only for her own benefit at this point, but years of thinking of herself as a scholar had etched themselves onto her identity.

Chapter 38

When the tent was set up in the backyard, Lacey and Asia strung it with rainbow-striped streamers and primary-colored balloons. There were no twinkling fairy lights in the trees, no delicate pink sweetheart roses or airy baby's breath. Eleanor had compromised on the party—the decor suited Lacey, the guest list suited Eleanor. Those were the things that mattered to them. The rest—the food, the music, the general atmosphere of friends and family coming together to mark rites of passage—would take care of itself.

It was, as Asia kept pointing out, the spirit of the party that mattered, not the trappings. Addy saw Eleanor roll her eyes the third time they heard the earnest platitude, but by the time Genevieve showed up, the first guest to arrive, even Eleanor had relaxed and embraced the spirit of the thing. She was even, Addy noted with relief, attacking a plate of chicken wings with gusto.

Micah arrived shortly thereafter, trudging up the driveway behind a large group of gangly teenagers still euphoric over their summer freedom, with an envelope tucked in his back pocket full of documents for Addy, Eleanor, and Lacey to sign. Eleanor had finally decided she was ready to move ahead with selling her mother's house, and Micah was helping her arrange for an auction of the remaining contents. Addy was reasonably sure there were no more surprises tucked away in any of Grandmama's old papers, or Martha's.

She had sorted through the last of the papers in record time, searching for just enough information to help her flesh out the text of the historical marker. Eleanor had surprised her by insisting that she wanted to go ahead with it. She wanted her family's century in the bungalow to be noted for perpetuity, she said, laughing at her own use of the word that had caused them such consternation. The paperwork had been sent off to the state historical preservation department, and the marker would be installed with a small ceremony in about a month.

Addy kept a copy of the text on her phone, and glanced at it every now and again when the loose ends threatened to undo her: Built in 1910 by renowned architect Richard Sharp Smith, Cameron House is a pure example of the Arts and Crafts Movement as it was uniquely expressed in Asheville. A gift from Judge Randolph Britton (manager of Biltmore Estate) to his secretary, Martha Cameron, in 1925, it remained in the family for 90 years.

During a lull in the hubbub, Mason offered up a toast to Lacey's future as an actor. One of his golf buddies offered up another toast to Mason's and Eleanor's impending empty nest.

Eleanor stepped forward and raised her own glass.

"I have to correct you on that one, Rob," she said. "This is Asia Dalston. She's going to be living with us for her senior year of high school." She tucked an arm through Asia's elbow and pulled her forward. "I know y'all will make her feel welcome here in the neighborhood."

Addy beamed and raised her glass. Micah nudged her from behind.

"Shall I make a toast to you staying?"

Addy thought about it for a second—it would be the easiest way to make the announcement, after she'd spent the last two months declaring that she couldn't wait to leave.

"No," she whispered. "It's Lacey's day. Besides, it doesn't matter."

It was true, she thought later while helping the caterer gather up glasses. It didn't matter to her parents' neighbors. It mattered to her, and to the kids she wanted to help, and possibly to Dr. McGregor, whom she hadn't yet told.

When the tent had been taken down and the kitchen set to rights, she went up to her room and called Dr. McGregor. It was like ripping off a bandage—best to do it all at once without thinking about it too much.

"Addy. I wasn't expecting to hear from you until Monday."

Addy jumped in with both feet and told her advisor that, after all this time, she'd decided not to finish her degree.

There was a long silence, followed by an uncomfortable conversation in which Dr. McGregor tried, but only half-heartedly, to convince her to finish, if only to avoid being an ABD statistic.

Addy demurred. For once, she knew beyond any shadow of a doubt that she was making the right decision.

"Is it the money? Do you need more teaching sections? Or maybe some research money? The fall budget is looking better. I could talk to Dr. Torrisi for you. I know he won't want you to give up at this point."

"I'm not giving up. I'm going in a different direction. It's more important to me to help people, that's all."

"And don't you think that what we do helps people? Documenting who the American people are, and how we got here—you know how important that is, Addy." Defensiveness had crept into Dr. McGregor's voice.

"No, that's not what I mean. I just know that I need to do this. I've seen these kids, and if no one steps up and helps them, they're going to slip through the cracks and be lost. I can make a difference right now, right here."

"You help your students every day."

"I know. I'm really sorry, Dr. McGregor. I'm truly grateful for everything you've done for me. I've learned a tremendous amount from you. But my mind is made up."

Dr. McGregor's sigh was long and martyred, as if Addy's defection was a personal affront. Perhaps it was, Addy thought after she had ended the call, but she knew in her soul this was the right thing to do. Besides, it was a *fait accompli*. She'd promised the Cecils they could have the story after her article came out. Her notes had come together quickly once she stepped away from the pressure of writing a whole book. She had sent the article off to the magazine editor immediately after her meeting with the Cecils. It focused on the short story, and the concrete evidence she'd compiled—the accompanying letter, the wedding registry. She refrained from speculating about the nature of the relationship between Zelda and Cornelia. Looking down the long lens of time, it didn't really seem to matter, and besides, that part of the story wasn't hers to tell. After feeling like she was treading water for so long, taking definitive action was exhilarating.

Addy found herself bounding out of bed in the mornings, drawing up plans for an emergency shelter, a school support program to keep high schoolers in class, on-site counseling for traumatized youth, work-study outreach to give kids a chance to earn some money, and the lists went on. She'd seen a giant, gaping hole of need in her hometown, and somehow, she found herself in a position to fill it.

Chapter 39

A cool breeze sprang up as the sun slid down behind the slumped shoulders of the mountains. Eleanor and Mason came out onto the front porch where Addy, Lacey, and Asia were waiting for them.

"Let's go," Lacey said, bouncing a little on her toes. "I don't want to be late."

Mason glanced at his watch. "Barring floods or conflagration, we'll be twenty minutes early."

"No one will care," Eleanor said, leading the way to the car.

"Hell, no one will even notice," Addy mumbled. She hadn't really meant to say it out loud.

"Language, dear," Eleanor said mildly.

Addy smiled. Some things hadn't changed, after all.

Sven, the director, was back in town to show off his Biltmore film. *He had proven to be a bit of a marketing genius,* Addy thought as they joined the crowd, mostly locals, making their way up to the terrace where Biltmore's summer concert series was held. A huge movie screen had been set up at one end of the flagstone space, fronted by rows of folding chairs. Under the pergola, tables draped with white linens were set with hors d'oeuvres and vases of sweet-scented lilies. Tuxedo-clad waiters circulated with wine and champagne. Addy took a glass, and saw Eleanor give Lacey and Asia a stern look. She smiled again, and scanned the quietly buzzing crowd.

The large double doors that led from George Vanderbilt's famous library opened, and Ford stepped onto the terrace, followed closely by Sven. Addy hadn't seen Ford in a couple of weeks. He leaned heavily on his cane, more heavily than she remembered, but his eyes were bright and lively, taking in the crowd with pleasure. He made his way to a seat in the first row, and Addy found a spot in the second row where she could see his profile.

Sven said a few words about the role of the Vanderbilts and their peers in American cultural heritage, and the importance of documenting the history of the great Gilded Age mansions. He thanked Ford specifically for sharing his memories, and the film began with a credit, thanking Ford again.

As the film played, Addy was torn between watching the beautiful scenery on the screen, the moon rising in the sky above it, and the emotions playing across the faces of the people around her—Lacey, Eleanor, Asia, and there in the front row, Ford. Lacey had played her role perfectly. Addy found herself swept up in the story of faded glamour and straitened circumstances, the dwindling staff who were lucky enough to be kept on through the lean years of the Great Depression.

A montage of photos showed Micah's grandfather in his office, at the helm of the operation when there was no one else available to manage the daily minutiae. Addy hadn't taken the time to study his face, looking for a resemblance. She couldn't see it now, but that didn't mean much. Micah was right—a DNA test would tell them for sure. She wasn't sure if she wanted to know, but the story was there, in her cells, and would still be there when she was ready to know.

There was very little mention of Cornelia. She had left the country in 1934 and never returned. And no mention at all of Zelda Fitzgerald. Sven could've taken the idea and run with it, she knew, but he had stayed true to his vision and to the memories Ford shared. The stories of those troubled women—and that of Great-Great-Aunt Martha—were lost to history.

She kept sneaking glances at Ford, who nodded his head throughout the film as if blessing the story. Even during the difficult parts—George's death, the selling off of Mt. Pisgah, floods and epidemics, losing staff and status and wealth—he beamed with pride. The Biltmore story was being told, and that was all he had ever wanted.

Author's Note

This book began with a season pass to historic Biltmore House in Asheville, North Carolina. I've spent many blissful afternoons wandering around the grounds, spinning fantasies in my head while my children were at summer camp. Biltmore is a special place—if you enjoyed *Downton Abbey*, you'll love Biltmore.

All that time in Asheville prompted a question that I've wondered about for years: did Cornelia Vanderbilt and Zelda Fitzgerald ever cross paths, and if so, what did they think of each other? Surely there would've been fireworks of some kind between two such interesting women born in the same year.

But my story, while it contains the names of some real people, both historical and contemporary, is purely a story running off in directions that have nothing to do with anyone I've ever met or heard of, living or not.

The most significant of those directions is my personal interest in the welfare of gay and lesbian youths. Statistics show that gay and lesbian teenagers make up a disproportionate percentage of the homeless youth population—the cause is most often family rejection.

I've known some of these kids personally, and my heart breaks a little more every time I hear about another teen who had to leave their home because their parents freaked out. Homeless teenagers, no matter their orientation, are at horrifyingly high risk for rape, suicide, drug abuse, and a whole host of other problems that can derail a life permanently in a heartbeat.

If you or someone you know is a homeless gay teenager, or at risk of becoming homeless, please see nationalhomeless.org/issues/lgbt/ for more information on how to help.

If you or someone you know is a gay teenager contemplating suicide, please contact www.thetrevorproject.org/, or dial 866-488-7386.

Acknowledgements

It takes a special kind of courage to tell a writer that the book she has written is not fit for public consumption. I worked on *A Thin Gold Thread* for nearly four years, and in the end, what you hold in your hands is not the story I set out to write. I have to thank the brave souls who told me that original book didn't work. My writing group warned me—Barb Davis, Matt King, Doug Simpson, and Mitch Richmond. Y'all were right—I know how hard it must have been to tell me I'd written a hot mess. Thank you.

When developmental editor Howard Mittelmark told me to start over, again, I wasn't even all that surprised. He was right, too. And when it was line editor Debra L Hartmann's turn to give it her special polish, she too insisted it could be better.

Thanks to all of you, from the bottom of my heart, for pushing me to keep at it.

It goes without saying, of course, that I'm eternally grateful to my husband and children for listening, offering feedback, and even occasionally signing off on whole chapters. The three of you are my heart.

More than a thank you, though, goes to the kids who inspire me—the kids who insist on living honestly, no matter what anyone else thinks. Your courage and compassion are making the world a better place for all of us.

About the Author

Lisa Rosen is an empty nester with a bad case of wanderlust. A former resident of North Carolina, where she earned a PhD in literature at the University of North Carolina, Chapel Hill, she now travels the world with a laptop and a carry-on, and an equally peripatetic husband.

A Thin Gold Thread is her second novel. Her first, *Motherline*, published in 2013, is available on Amazon.

For more information about the author, or upcoming books,
please visit lisarosen.me

Connect with me on social media at:
facebook.com/lisacameronrosen
instagram.com/bookwomanlcr
twitter.com/LisaRosen